FLOWERS ON
MY GRAVE

FLOWERS ON MY GRAVE

*How an Ojibwa Boy's Death
Helped Break the Silence
on Child Abuse*

RUTH TEICHROEB

A Phyllis Bruce Book
HarperPerennial
HarperCollins*PublishersLtd*

http://www.harpercollins.com/canada

HarperCollins books may be purchased for educational, business, or sales promotional use. For information please write: Special Markets Department, HarperCollins Canada, 55 Avenue Road, Suite 2900, Toronto, Ontario M5R 3L2.

First edition

Canadian Cataloguing in Publication Data

Teichroeb, Ruth, 1956–
    Flowers on my grave : how an Ojibwa boy's death helped break the silence on child abuse

1st HarperPerennial ed.
"A Phyllis Bruce book".

Includes bibliographical references.
ISBN 0-00-638636-9

1. Desjarlais, Lester, 1974-1988. 2. Indian children - Abuse of - Manitoba - Sandy Bay Indian Reserve. 3. Child welfare - Manitoba - Sandy Bay Indian Reserve. I. Title

E99.C6D386 1998   362.76′089′973   C97-932313-4

---

98 99 00 ❖ HC 10 9 8 7 6 5 4 3 2 1

Printed and bound in the United States

For my mother,
Phyllis Irene Plummer Teichroeb,
1931–1975

CONTENTS

ACKNOWLEDGEMENTS

I am grateful to the *Winnipeg Free Press* for the opportunity to report extensively on the inquest into Lester's death and for supporting my ongoing coverage of child-abuse issues. Also, I appreciate the newspaper's willingness to grant me time off while writing this book.

Thanks to my friends and co-workers at the *Free Press*, especially Lindor, Catherine, and Alex, who offered encouragement when the going got rough.

Thanks are also due to my publisher, Phyllis Bruce, who provided expert guidance and showed great patience despite numerous unexpected delays.

I am indebted to all those who shared their insights and entrusted me with the gift of their personal stories during the writing of this book, especially David and Lester's sisters Sherry, Nancy, and Annette.

I also relied on long-time friends Jeanette, Beth, Betsy, and Adelia, whose interest in this project never wavered.

Most of all, I want to thank my husband, Dwight, who first believed in the vision of this book and supported me every step of the way. Without his steadfast love, this book would never have come to fruition.

LIST OF FAMILY MEMBERS

Joyce (McIvor) Desjarlais: Lester Desjarlais' mother
Norman Anderson: Lester's father
Cecil Desjarlais: Lester's stepfather
Joe Desjarlais: Cecil Desjarlais' brother, Lester's step-uncle
Adele McIvor: Lester's maternal grandmother
Alex McIvor: Lester's maternal step-grandfather

Lester's half-siblings (in order of birth):
Cecil McIvor: Lester's oldest brother
Sherry McIvor: Lester's oldest sister
Nancy McIvor: Lester's second sister
Annette Desjarlais: Lester's third sister
Lester's fourth sister (name withheld because of young age)
Lester's youngest brother (name withheld because of young age)

INTRODUCTION

I first heard of Lester Desjarlais in October 1991 while scanning a brief news item from Brandon, Manitoba, about an inquest into the thirteen-year-old Ojibwa boy's suicide. At the time, I was covering social affairs for the *Winnipeg Free Press*, and had a special interest in child welfare. I remember wondering what deep sorrows had driven such a young boy to take his own life—and why the Aboriginal child-welfare agency responsible for his care had failed to keep him safe. But I was already immersed in other projects and didn't have time to pursue my questions. Besides, the inquest appeared to be winding down.

Soon after that, controversies arose about how several of Manitoba's Native-run child-welfare agencies had handled child-abuse cases. When I heard that the inquest into Lester's death was resuming in Brandon in the winter of 1992, I asked to cover the hearings, which promised to provide an unusual glimpse into the inner workings of one such agency. The inquest was expected to last, at most, three or four weeks. Instead, the hearings took on a life of their own, stretching out over almost three months. I packed my bags and moved into a Brandon motel room, writing and filing my stories every evening, and returning home only on weekends. During those gruelling months, I was consumed by how the child-welfare system, both Aboriginal and mainstream, had failed to protect Lester and other children from physical and sexual abuse. Yet at the end of the inquest—the longest to date in Manitoba history—I was still troubled by questions about Lester's death. I was finding it hard to simply walk away from this story, as reporters so often must do. I wanted to know more about Lester, his family and community. Over the next year, the idea of writing a book began to take root.

From the beginning, this project has been daunting. I agonized over whether a college-educated, childless, white woman from a middle-class background could do justice to Lester's story. But deciding not to write this book on that basis alone didn't seem right. For a year, I tested the waters, unsure whether I should proceed. Those whom I consulted, both Aboriginal and white, reminded me that no one else was ready to delve into what they believed was an important story. They urged me to recognize my limitations and write from the only perspective I have—my own. As each potential roadblock disappeared, from finding a publisher to being granted a leave of absence from my job to work on the book, I felt more sure about pursuing this project. But the deciding factor was when Lester's older sisters agreed to share their memories of him, and their own stories, as part of the book. If they had the courage to open up their lives, who was I to baulk at a few obstacles? I set my fears aside and took the plunge, feeling all the while as if this story had chosen me, rather than the other way around. That in itself has been humbling.

Poverty, alcoholism, and intergenerational physical and sexual abuse are devastating the lives of children throughout society. Many Native communities struggle with the added burdens of cultural and social breakdown fostered by more than a century of mistreatment by mainstream society. The heartache Lester suffered was no different from that of any abused child. When I share his story with others, I'm surprised how often it triggers disclosures of childhood trauma, even from those who have hidden their pain well. Yet the reasons for Lester's anguish were more complex, indelibly linked to the historic losses and dislocation of his Ojibwa community. One need only look at

the epidemic of suicide among Aboriginal youth in this country to realize that the reasons for their desperation go beyond any one individual
or community.

Children depend on adults for love, nurturance, and protection.
When this trust is violated, young lives are ravaged, sometimes irrev-
ocably. Not long ago, no one questioned why bruised and battered
children were regularly brought to hospital emergency rooms after
mysterious "falls" and "accidents." Some tiny victims were too young
to explain what had really happened to them; others were too frightened and confused. Then came studies in the late 1960s and early
1970s revealing that many of these cases were not accidents—children were suffering terrible physical abuse at the hands of parents
and other caretakers. Their stories stirred public concern and broke
through the widespread denial that had allowed us to ignore the unthinkable. By the early 1980s, a second wave of disclosures began
about another insidious threat—the sexual abuse of children.
Canadians were shocked at the extent of such abuse when the federal
government's 1984 Badgley Report, based on a survey of 10,000
cases, estimated that one in four girls and one in seven boys were sexually abused during childhood. Today, those are considered to be
conservative estimates, as increasing numbers of boys report sexual
violations by trusted adults, from parents to scout-troop leaders.
These statistics add up to a staggering toll on young lives. The abuse
of children is a major underlying cause of many social problems, from
prostitution to youth suicide, to juvenile crime. And as more and
more victims speak out, it is obvious that neither wealth nor privilege
nor race guarantees safety: abuse cuts across all social and economic
lines. High-profile cases have made that clear, like the Anglican choir-
master at St. George's Cathedral in Kingston who pleaded guilty in
1990 to twenty counts of sexually abusing thirteen boys. The offenders are priests and politicians, businessmen and unemployed labour-
ers, parents and babysitters. Their victims are sons and daughters of
the élite, and children of the working class.

The Native community is no exception. As in most societies, physical and sexual abuse were taboo in traditional Aboriginal cultures.
Children were valued members of the community—even spanking was

frowned upon. Instead, children had free rein to learn by trial and error as they participated in the life of the community. When band members violated cultural norms by mistreating the vulnerable, they were socially ostracized, or even banished. But, after more than a century of cultural breakdown, many of the traditional safeguards which helped protect children have been eroded. Families have been torn apart by residential schools, the child-welfare system, and alcohol introduced originally by European fur traders. Generations of children were physically and sexually abused in residential schools and foster homes. When those children grew up, the cycle of abuse and neglect repeated itself.

To understand the story of Lester and his family, and that of so many others, is to understand the cost of marginalizing a people. I believe that the retelling of these stories, however painful, is part of the healing process for both individuals and society. Not everyone would agree. There are those who did not want this book to be written. Some were men in positions of power with an image to protect or secrets to hide. But confronting a topic as disturbing as child abuse inevitably triggers a certain amount of resistance and anger. Others feared that recounting Lester's story would further tarnish the image of his home community. It is certainly not my wish to do that. I've gained a deep respect for the strength of spirit of many people of Sandy Bay First Nation. I am also awed by the vision of reconciliation which inspires Aboriginal communities as they develop creative ways to work with both victims and perpetrators of child abuse. Our violence-torn society has much to learn about true healing from the First Nations.

What kept me going during the discouraging times were the many people who shared their stories, despite the threat of backlash in some instances. Mostly they were women who knew of other potential Lesters. Lester's three oldest sisters courageously chose to have their real names used, despite the horrific abuse they suffered as children, though I knew that in cases of abuse it is customary to protect those victimized as much as possible. All of them came forward because they, too, believe truth-telling is the first step towards healing. They did so because they want a better future for children, both Aboriginal and non-Aboriginal. They did so because they believe that we must not forget. A quote from an anonymous abuse survivor, interviewed for an Assembly of First Nations study on residential schools entitled *Breaking the Silence*, sums up what those I met told me in different ways: "My story is a gift. If I give you a gift and you accept that gift, then you don't go and throw that gift in the waste basket. You do something with it."

Over the course of writing this book, my personal circumstances changed dramatically. For almost a decade, my husband and I had longed for a child of our own. When that did not happen, I channelled my energies into my career with the hope that my writing could better the lot of children in some small way. Then, to our amazement, I became pregnant in the autumn of 1994 and gave birth to a son in June 1995. I believe it is no coincidence that my son was born the day before what would have been Lester's twenty-first birthday, and two days before the birthday of one of Lester's half-sisters. When our lives become entwined with others', a kind of synchronicity develops that is one of the mysteries of being human.

Becoming a mother has both deepened my commitment to telling Lester's story and made it vastly more difficult. Now that I am familiar with the demands of motherhood, I have greater empathy for the tremendous struggles Lester's mother faced. And when I look into the bright eyes of my own son, I cannot imagine the pain she must have felt at losing a child. At the same time, as I re-experience the total vulnerability of childhood through my own son, I grieve for the torment Lester suffered, and that other children still endure at the hands of those they trust. Children deserve better than that. We owe it to them to speak out on their behalf, to protect their innocence and fight for a society in which all of our little ones come first.

CHAPTER ONE

GOING HOME

"... no one ever wanted us but our mom."

—Cecil McIvor

Lester jumped to answer the phone when his mom called that Sunday in early March. He'd been brooding about her since his custody hearing was delayed the previous week, dashing his hopes of being able to head home to Sandy Bay with her. But to make sure she knew how he felt, Lester had scrawled "I love you mom forever" in big letters on a sheet of white paper and sent it to her.

No one overheard their conversation that morning. The slight, thirteen-year-old boy chatted softly in Saulteaux, cradling the phone, his straight, glossy black hair brushing his collar. After the call, he mentioned something to his foster mother, Lillian Starr, about his gun being pawned. Then Lester hopped on a bike and pedalled off with his foster brother to hunt birds near the Starr family's bungalow just south of Brandon, Manitoba. When Lillian and her husband, Angus, left for an out-of-town hockey game at noon, Lester seemed fine—maybe a bit agitated, Angus later recalled, but nothing out of the ordinary.

Although the boy had lived with them for less than a month, they came from the same Ojibwa community and had known his family for years.

Sometime that afternoon, Lester made a flurry of phone calls to family and friends. He called his child-welfare worker, Marion Glover; left a message on her machine; and tried to track her down by phoning three of her friends. He also phoned his oldest sister, Sherry McIvor, one of his six half-siblings, who lived at Sandy Bay. The nineteen-year-old mother happened to be in the midst of bathing her baby boy and couldn't come to the phone, so Lester spoke with Sherry's common-law husband, Norbert Sutherland. Other than Lester's usual talk about wanting to come home, there was no indication that he was upset. But Lester did tell Norbert he'd tried to persuade his mother, Joyce, to rescue his cherished pellet gun from the pawnshop. The gun had been a gift from Joyce. But he'd been forced to leave it behind when he went into foster care. Someone in the family had pawned the gun for cash, and Lester now wanted his mom to reclaim it. Norbert tried to keep Lester on the line until Sherry was free, but her brother grew impatient and hung up. A little while later, when Sherry tried to call Lester back, there was no answer. She tried several more times, and then gave up when visitors dropped in. He'd call again. He always did.

It was just after 5:00 P.M. when the Starrs' twenty-three-year-old daughter, Darlene Spence, who had come over to babysit, began cooking supper for the household. She helped Lester get potatoes from the furnace room and, as she worked in the kitchen, noticed his slight figure pacing back and forth to his room. When she ran out of potatoes, she yelled for Lester to fetch some more. When he didn't respond, she got them herself.

By the time supper was ready, there was still no sign of the boy. Darlene sent her sixteen-year-old sister, Maxine, after him. The girl checked in his room and searched the house. Finally, Maxine glanced out the west-facing dining-room window and thought she saw something in the fading afternoon light. She stepped outside to get a better look and rushed back to summon Darlene's boyfriend, Linus Woods. Linus crossed the yard, where a mild spell had melted much of the snow, and saw Lester hanging from a wooden structure. For a moment, he thought the teenager was pulling a prank. Everyone knew

7

Lester loved to joke around. But as Linus got closer, he saw a thin line of blood trickling from the boy's mouth.

He raced back inside, shouting for Darlene to get help. It was about 6:30 when neighbour Paul Roy got the panic-stricken call from Darlene and drove over with his son. As Paul approached the wooden structure, made of four eight-foot posts joined with crosspieces, used to store the Starrs' camper shell, he remembered noticing that Lester's toes were touching the ground. It was a detail that would later haunt the boy's family. The Roys cut Lester down from the makeshift gallows and laid him on the frozen earth. The noose, fashioned out of bright yellow nylon rope, reminded Paul of something he'd seen in the movies.

During the next two hours, Brandon RCMP and the medical examiner arrived to investigate. Dr. Nicholas Petrinack pronounced Lester Norman Desjarlais dead at 9:00 P.M. on March 6, 1988, after estimating the boy had died about 6:15 P.M. Petrinack quickly ruled out foul play and ordered that an autopsy be done the next day. Meanwhile, police took statements from stunned members of the Starr household while a child-welfare worker from Dakota Ojibway Child and Family Services (DOCFS), the agency which had placed Lester with the Starrs, tried to locate other officials. A short time later, Angus and Lillian walked in on the bleak scene. Marion, the DOCFS worker whom Lester had tried to reach a few hours earlier, got word and arrived as well. Ironically, Marion, one of the agency's few non-Aboriginal staff members, had just returned from a day-long seminar in Winnipeg about teen suicide.

In the hours after Lester's death, Marion sat with Angus and Lillian, trying to piece together what had happened. It was then that Lillian revealed a disturbing detail. A few days after Lester had moved in with them, Lillian had discovered a noose made of yellow nylon rope underneath some towels in the hall closet. Rather than alert anybody to her strange find, she'd hidden the rope behind the hot-water tank in the furnace room—the room in which the potatoes were stored. When Lester's death came under official scrutiny at an inquest more than four years later, Lillian would testify she had no idea that the boy had threatened suicide in the past. DOCFS workers had shared only sketchy information about the teenager's history, she said.

Meanwhile, Dakota Ojibway Tribal Council (DOTC) police at Sandy Bay tried to locate Lester's mother. Lester's sister Sherry, a young woman with long, luxuriant black hair, and her partner, Norbert, were playing cards in their house trailer with friends when they heard the first calls on the police scanner. Eavesdropping on the scanner was a handy way of keeping track of what was going on in the community. But this time, they heard police putting out calls for Joyce. Curious, but not wanting to be nosy, Sherry ignored the scanner and eventually told Norbert to turn it off. Then the phone rang. When she answered, Sherry heard the strained voice of her mother's aunt Audrey. Then Audrey's husband, Harry, came on the line. "She didn't have the courage to tell me what went wrong," Sherry says. "Harry told me, 'Do you hear someone crying in the background? Everybody's just crying.' I said, 'What's wrong?' I knew right away, the way you know— you just feel it inside of you that something has gone wrong. It goes through your mind right away. Everything runs through your head." Stunned, Sherry insisted that her mother's uncle must be lying to her. How could it be true? Then she dropped the phone and rushed over to her relatives' home to be with her mother, who had collapsed upon hearing about Lester. "She was crying like crazy," Sherry says. "There was nothing we could do to calm her." Just two days earlier, Lester had called Joyce and begged to come home.

Later that evening, a cousin broke the tragic news to another of Lester's sisters, Nancy McIvor, who was exactly three years and one day older than Lester. Like her sister, the gregarious, rosy-cheeked teenager could not believe what she was hearing: "I said, don't lie," Nancy says. "That's what I said to him. Don't lie ... It just felt so empty inside." That night, the family gathered in a huddle of grief in the empty white bungalow across from the home of Joyce's parents, Alex and Adele McIvor. When morning arrived, Joyce, exhausted from the night of tears, made the dreaded two-hour trip to Brandon to claim her son's body.

Suicides had been rare at Sandy Bay, an Ojibwa community of about 3,000 residents hugging ten kilometres of shoreline on the southwest shore of Lake Manitoba. Then, suddenly, in the year or two preceding Lester's death, several young people killed themselves. According to Ojibwa teachings, to die by one's own hand is unnatural, and therefore wrong. It is believed that the spirit of such a person wanders restlessly until reaching the age at which he or she was meant to die. This taboo against suicide was further reinforced by the Roman Catholic Church's long history in the community. As well, Sandy Bay had fostered a strong cultural identity, despite its proximity to large urban centres. But now residents feared they were being hit by the same epidemic that had claimed so many young lives in other Aboriginal communities. And they had reason to be anxious. The suicide rate for Native youth under age twenty-four in Manitoba was ten times higher than that of the general population at the time when Lester died.

As Lester's family gathered for a three-day wake at the home of Joyce's parents, the boy's never-ending pleas to come home echoed in their minds. His six half-siblings all remembered times when he'd phoned in tears over the previous year. Two weeks before his death, Lester called Nancy from the Starrs'. He was crying as he talked about how much he missed everyone. Nancy warned Lester that their mom was drinking again, but he didn't seem to hear her: "He said, someday I'm going to come home. I don't care, like, how I come home, he said ... I really, really want to come home." It was Nancy's last conversation with him.

Lester had phoned his oldest brother, Cecil McIvor, with a similiar message about three days before his death. This time, Lester gave little hint of his inner turmoil and joined in their usual brotherly banter. As they joked around, Lester, who was seven years younger than Cecil, and much smaller, vowed to fight his brother and win when he turned eighteen. That made Cecil, a reserved young man of medium height, chuckle. Before the call ended, Cecil promised to pick Lester up when he finally got permission to come home. During another call to Sherry, Lester had seemed fine. He'd asked about his baby nephew, Norbert Jr., and made her laugh by calling himself "Uncle Strong."

Around the same time, Annette Desjarlais, who was a year older than Lester, saw her brother for the last time at the custody hearing in Portage la Prairie. Joyce had filed legal documents to regain custody of both Lester and Annette from DOCFS. When the hearing was delayed, Lester, bitterly disappointed, suggested to Annette he might kill himself. But she hadn't really taken him seriously—he'd talked that way before.

During the wake for Lester, time seemed to stretch in all directions.

Nancy, almost nine months pregnant with her second child, felt as if she was lost in a dream. Usually outgoing, the dark-eyed young woman could barely eat or sleep. Neither could Joyce, as a steady stream of family and friends came to pay their respects. In one room of her parents' modest house, family and friends gathered around the table, playing cards, drinking coffee and tea, and smoking cigarettes. Out of respect for the family, guests brought traditional gifts of tobacco, believing that the smoke would carry prayers for Lester to the Great Spirit. In the next room, the boy's body lay in a blue velvet casket. Marion, uncomfortable because she'd never been to a wake before, stopped in briefly. As representative of the agency, she'd insisted that DOCFS pay for something nicer than the usual plain pine box. But Marion's visit upset Joyce, who blamed her for Lester's death. She was about to tell Marion to leave, when Sherry intervened, convincing her mom to overlook the unwanted guest.

Joyce leaned heavily on Sherry during the wake and funeral, unable to cope alone with the burden of practical arrangements. Sherry and Norbert went to the credit union to borrow $500 to help pay for the funeral, while neighbours took up a collection for them. Although it seemed like a bad dream, Sherry took her mother shopping for Lester's burial clothes, a stone-washed denim jacket and jeans, a sweater, and blue-and-white high-topped running shoes. She helped pick a burial spot in the Sandy Bay cemetery and arranged for pallbearers for the funeral. Stoically, she put her own grief aside in order to be strong for her mother. But inside she was churning with anger, frustration, fear. How could Lester have done this to them? Didn't he love them? Maybe she hadn't loved him enough?

As Lester's family sat with his body during the long days and nights leading up to the funeral, two inexplicable things happened. At one point, Sherry and others in the room gazed into Lester's casket and were amazed to see a few tears trickle from beneath the boy's pale eyelids. "People were saying, he wanted to come home, but not like that. That's why his tears came out," Sherry explains matter-of-factly. A little while later, following tradition, she snapped a few pictures of Lester in the coffin. But weeks later, when the film was developed, Sherry was startled to find that these final photos of Lester had come back blank.

Fresh snow blanketed the ground on the chilly afternoon of Thursday, March 10, when friends and family gathered for Lester's funeral at Our Lady of Guadalupe Roman Catholic Church, a cramped, faded-yellow building in the heart of the community. As mourners entered the church, they joined the line waiting to file past Lester's open coffin, where each person paused to kiss the boy on his forehead. Ushers handed out small, white bulletins with "In Remembrance" written beneath a yellow cross and rose. Inside, a black-and-white school picture of a younger Lester smiled back above a few lines of a poem chosen by Sherry and her mother: "Just when your life was brightest,/ Just when your years were best,/ You were called from this world of sorrow,/ To a home of eternal rest."

As one of the few outsiders at the service, Marion wasn't sure what to expect. The tall, slender brunette had never been to a funeral on a reserve. Tormented by guilt and grief over Lester's death, the child-welfare worker waited in line, her stomach knotting up at the prospect of gazing into the casket. But when she approached the coffin, she glanced up and saw a respected medicine man from the reserve standing next to her. He had appeared out of nowhere, radiating a reassuring presence. Marion leaned down and kissed Lester's forehead. When she looked up, the man was gone.

Six friends and relatives served as pallbearers, carrying Lester's coffin past his family seated in the front row. Father Maurice Comeault officiated at the brief service, as incense wafted through the crowded sanctuary. Sherry wept throughout the ceremony, remembering Lester as a chubby-cheeked baby, smiling up at her from his crib. Nearby, her brother Cecil was unable to shed a tear. But the familiar hymns, from "Amazing Grace" to "The Lord's My Shepherd," deeply affected Nancy and set off waves of grief. For weeks afterward, she found herself humming fragments of songs from the funeral and other tunes Lester loved. Music was in the family's blood, and Lester, like his mother, had liked nothing better than to pluck away at a guitar.

In a booklet titled *Ode to Lester*, handed out at the service, some of his classmates from the Sandy Bay school shared their goodbyes. A girl named Lisa wrote:

Lester
Nice, kind,
Funny, sad, lonesome,
I miss Lester alot,
Boy.

After the service, everyone gathered for a short ceremony at the community's graveyard, within sight of the glistening ice of Lake Manitoba on the eastern horizon. As Lester's casket was lowered into the grave, Joyce began to keen and other women joined in. At the same time, Marion, hovering at the edge of the mourners, looked across the crowd and into the eyes of Lester's uncle Joe Desjarlais. Joe, a large, bear-like man with rounded shoulders, had once tried to intimidate her by bragging that he was the community's gravedigger. He was also the man Lester had accused of raping him during the last year of his life. Overwhelmed, Marion fled before the ceremony was finished.

During the funeral supper of sandwiches and coffee at the school auditorium, Marion approached Joyce. She wanted to say how sorry she was about Lester's death, to acknowledge how he'd loved his mother. But an anguished Joyce brushed her aside. As Marion retreated, Nancy and her sisters watched helplessly as their mother dissolved into tears.

Lester's death had been a blow to Marion, who had grown fond of the boy during the six months she'd worked with him. Hired by the agency on a short-term contract about four months earlier, she'd first met Lester in September 1987, when she was assigned to supervise the agency's four child-welfare workers at Sandy Bay. Marion did not even have a high-school diploma. After a short stint at a Brandon child-welfare agency five years earlier, she'd been fired when officials discovered she'd lied about having a university degree. Since then, the resourceful, extroverted single parent had found ways to keep her hand in social-service work, setting up a support group in southwestern Manitoba for survivors of sexual abuse. When she was hired by DOCFS to set up a child-abuse program, she had never worked for an Aboriginal organization.

Something about Lester pulled at Marion's heart from the moment she met him, and she found herself becoming more and more involved with the forlorn, confused boy. She took him on numerous weekend visits to her home, a practice frowned upon by agency officials, who believed it undermined professional objectivity. A couple of months before his death, Lester had begged to come live with Marion and her four children. Although tempted, she realized she had her hands full with her own family. Besides, such an unorthodox arrangement would never have been approved by agency or reserve officials. Instead, although Lester was no longer officially part of her caseload, she'd helped place him at the Starrs' home after the teenager was released from his third stay at the Brandon Mental Health Centre. She believed the foster family's ties to Sandy Bay would help Lester settle in quickly and provide the stability he needed.

Lester called her constantly during his last few weeks, often asking when he could go home. The week before he died, he begged for permission to visit Sandy Bay. But Marion overruled his request, deciding Lester just wasn't ready to see his mother. Besides, she'd noticed he usually returned from such visits in worse shape than when he went. While Marion recognized the intense bond between the boy and his mom, Joyce's lifestyle was often chaotic, and she was struggling with a drinking problem and could not always cope with her son. Yet none of that ever seemed to matter to Lester. When Marion first met him, she'd noticed he had a habit of inking up his arms with his mother's name, sometimes etching it right into his skin. "L.D. loves Joyce," he'd write inside a heart pierced with a cupid's arrow. Before she knew better, Marion had wondered if the "Joyce" in question was Lester's girlfriend.

When the medical examiner's report suggested Lester had had an argument with Joyce about reclaiming his gun from the pawnshop, Marion was convinced that incident had triggered the boy's suicide. After all, the gun was one of his few personal belongings, other than the clothes on his back. Marion believed the gun in question was an old rifle given to Lester by his grandfather Desjarlais. At the inquest, Angus Starr would also testify that his wife had said Lester was upset about the rifle being sold. But family members now say the weapon was a pellet gun and that Lester never owned a rifle. Marion also seized on another reference in the medical examiner's report which said that Joyce had supposedly "pawned the gun for booze." She believed that

14

was the last straw for Lester, whose hopes of coming home were contingent upon his mother's remaining sober. But at the inquest, no one, including the investigating RCMP officer, would be able to verify who had provided that version of events. To this day, family members say Joyce was not the one who pawned the gun.

The child-welfare agency paid approximately $750 towards the cost of Lester's wake and funeral and filed a brief report about his suicide with the province in April 1988. The two-page letter from DOCFS referred to the agency's long involvement with Lester and his family, claimed to have offered a broad range of services to them, and said the boy had been "successfully" treated for addictions to solvents and alcohol. Lester's case was closed and the pressing needs of other children demanded attention.

After Lester's funeral, Joyce had called the boy's father, Norman Anderson, who lived in Winnipeg, to tell him of the tragedy. Although Norman rarely visited Lester, Joyce believed he'd want to know about his son's death. No one knows how Norman reacted to the news, or whether it was a factor in what happened next. For by July 1988, Norman's life was disintegrating before his eyes.

Norman and his young wife had been battling child-welfare authorities since the birth of their triplets in May 1984. Awasis Agency of Northern Manitoba, a Native-run child-welfare agency based in Thompson, had apprehended the newborn girls at birth and placed them in foster care on a northern reserve. Norman's long history of alcoholism, drug addiction, and frequent jail terms for property offences and assault, had convinced agency officials that he was an unfit parent. The authorities also had little faith in his wife's ability to care for three infants, especially after Norman was jailed for eight months shortly after the triplets' birth. The couple's oldest child, a boy born the year before the triplets, had already been neglected on several occasions when both Norman and his wife went on drinking binges.

The shaken couple, both from the remote northern Cree reserve of Shamattawa, hired a lawyer and began proceedings to regain custody of the triplets from Awasis. Between 1984 and 1988, they were in and out of court repeatedly, fighting to get their babies back. At one point they even sought help from the Winnipeg media. But things went from bad to worse when they also lost custody of their oldest son and their youngest daughter, born in July 1986. Although a provincial court judge ordered all five children returned to the couple in late 1986, the couple's chaotic lifestyle soon prompted a higher court to reverse that decision. During one court hearing, the lawyer from Awasis accused Norman of using his son's hyperactivity to obtain prescription drugs to feed his own addiction. In the end, the same judge who had ordered the children's return a year and a half earlier, ruled in the spring of 1988 that the couple had failed miserably as parents and should forfeit all rights to their children. The couple appealed one last time, desperate to get their kids back.

In early July, a letter arrived telling the couple they'd lost their final court battle. A judge had given permission for the triplets to be adopted by their foster parents and had granted the agency permanent custody of the other two children. Norman, a man plagued by volatile moods, spun into a deep depression, his behaviour becoming more and more erratic. On the afternoon of July 9, 1988, his wife tried to stop him as he popped a combination of Tylenol and tranquillizers. But every ten minutes he'd swallow a few more. About 5:30 P.M., he lay down for a nap. When his wife tried unsuccessfully to rouse him late that evening, she became alarmed and called an ambulance. On the way to the hospital, thirty-eight-year-old Norman died of the overdose. Later, during the autopsy, the pathologist noticed that the word "Love" was tattooed on Norman's chest, and other markings, including a "happy face," were scattered across his left arm and hand. He died four months and three days after his son Lester.

Manitoba's chief medical examiner ruled Norman's death a suicide. But Norman's wife, eight months pregnant with their sixth child, told a family friend she did not believe Norman had wanted to die. She blamed his death on a curse placed by those who had taken their children away. After claiming her husband's body, she flew back home to bury him at Shamattawa.

In the months after Lester's suicide, his mother and siblings wrestled with their grief. Less than two weeks after the funeral, Lester's spirit visited Nancy for the first time. The young mother was in hospital in

Portage la Prairie, about to give birth to her second child, when she saw her brother. It was the middle of the night and she had just inhaled what she thought was oxygen to help ease her labour. She was weary, almost sick, and another painful contraction was building. When she opened her eyes, there was Lester at the end of her bed, watching. She looked, looked again. It was him. And he would come to her in visions and dreams many more times in the months and years to come.

Although Joyce was usually a gentle, fun-loving woman, her son's death seemed to extinguish her spirit. Her heartache grew worse until she could not even bear to have Lester's picture on her wall. Night after night, the sound of her muffled sobs through the thin walls tore at Sherry's heart. Unsettling images of Lester and Joyce, standing side by side, haunted Nancy's dreams. Troubled, she tried to persuade her mother to quit drinking: "I told my mom: Mom, don't drink no more. But I couldn't stop her. But I should have tried harder, that's how I feel."

Joyce did make an effort to curb her drinking the summer after Lester's death. At Marion's urging, Joyce and her partner reluctantly agreed to attend a Native-run alcohol treatment program at Alkali Lake, near Williams Lake, B.C. Later, Joyce would say she went only because Marion made it a condition for regaining custody of her daughter Annette, who was in foster care on another reserve at the time.

DOCFS workers had been especially worried about Annette since Lester's death. The teenager, a heavy-set girl with a round face and ivory complexion set off by her black hair, talked frequently about suicide and sniffed gasoline at every opportunity. She also dreamed often about Lester. When Annette was admitted to the Brandon Mental Health Centre in June 1988, a social worker bluntly wrote in her notes that she considered the girl at great risk for following in her brother Lester's footsteps.

As the chilly autumn nights turned the poplar trees golden at Sandy Bay, Joyce and her family had a scare. After she suddenly experienced symptoms of what was suspected to be a minor stroke, Joyce was rushed to hospital in Portage la Prairie. Sherry was at her mother's side during the anxious, hour-long ride to hospital. "All the way to the hospital, she held my hand," Sherry says. "Sometimes I can still feel it."

But within a few days, Joyce checked herself out of the hospital, insisting she was fine. Sherry wasn't particularly concerned about her mom's health at the time. Only later would she recall some worrisome symptoms: Joyce once put her clothes on backwards and her eyes occasionally crossed in an odd way. Sherry sought reassurance by telling herself that her mother was only thirty-six and would surely recover.

Friends noticed Joyce seemed to be sliding into a deeper depression. Sometimes she'd knock on her friend Violet Roulette's door in the middle of the night and dissolve into tears as they smoked and talked into the early hours of the morning. In the past, Violet had seen Joyce bravely pick herself up and go on when faced with daunting hardships. She had been a survivor. But this time seemed different. About five days before she collapsed again, Joyce hinted at what was to come. "I'm dying, she told me," Violet says. "She let herself go because of what happened to Lester. She just gave up."

A few weeks later, Joyce didn't return from a trip to the outhouse. Her youngest daughter, ten years old at the time, got worried and went to look for her. She found her mother unconscious, lying in the doorway of the outhouse. Once again, Joyce was rushed to hospital in Portage. Three hours later, on October 25, 1988, Joyce Linda Desjarlais died of a cerebral hemorrhage without regaining consciousness. A pathologist later suggested her death could have been linked to not taking her medication for high blood pressure.

For the second time in eight months, the family gathered to mourn a loved one. Joyce's sudden passing left her children shattered, their one source of security ripped away. At one point, Sherry's father, Cecil Desjarlais, in a rare show of affection, put his arms around her. But instead of feeling comforted, all she could think was that she wanted her mom more. After all, as Cecil Jr. would say later, Joyce had been "number one" to all her kids, despite her shortcomings. "My mom did the best she could with what she had," Cecil Jr. said. "It wasn't much but it was home ... Like, no one ever wanted us but our mom."

A few months later, troubled by dreams about her mother, Annette would write a note to a former counsellor insisting "bad medicine" played a part in Joyce's death. Always a strong believer in the supernatural, Annette believed someone had killed her mother with a curse.

Looking back, Sherry realized her mother had started slipping away from them soon after Lester's death. Joyce was tormented by her son's suicide and dreamt constantly about him. A few days before she died, Joyce dreamt about being back in one of her previous homes. In the dream, Lester was in a rambunctious mood, bouncing up and down on the bed. When she asked him to stop, he hopped off and dashed out the front door. Joyce ran after him, but when she got outside, Lester was nowhere in sight. In another dream at around the same time, Lester came running towards her. His face glowed with happiness as he said: "Mom, it's time. Come with me."

Other dreams fuelled her suspicions that Lester might have died at someone else's hands. After all, she wondered over and over, how could he have suffocated if his toes were touching the ground? Why would Lester kill himself? He didn't want to die. He was just a boy. Why had it happened now? Had her little boy suffered in his last moments? People tried to ease Joyce's distress by offering to go to a medicine man to seek the truth. But an anguished Joyce told her children she hoped officials would call an inquest into Lester's death to answer the questions that haunted her.

After Joyce's death, disturbing images of Lester once again filled the dreams of his sisters. Nancy was especially troubled by one dream in which two men, one short-haired and the other with two braids, were beating Lester. Her brother fell, hitting his head near the base of a huge tree with a big branch. Then the two men tied a rope around Lester's neck and hanged him on the wooden structure. Nancy awoke screaming, frantic at being unable to save him.

CHAPTER TWO

BETRAYAL

"If that isn't hell, I don't know what is."

—former student of the Sandy Bay residential school

The community of Sandy Bay First Nation is a mere two-hour drive from the outskirts of Winnipeg, on paved provincial highways. Yet, despite its proximity to a major urban centre, Sandy Bay has remained outside the mainstream, buffeted over the last century by forces that have fostered social and economic, if not geographical, isolation.

To reach Sandy Bay, you drive west from Winnipeg past Portage la Prairie on the four-lane Trans-Canada, then turn at the Yellowhead Highway, which slices straight north through tabletop-flat grain fields before bending westward. About thirty minutes later, a glistening steel Manitoba Pool grain elevator rises on the right. Just past the elevator, you turn right onto Highway 50, cross the railway tracks, and drive north on the two-lane paved road.

It's the sweep of the sky which dominates this landscape, in good weather and bad. During the last fifty kilometres to Amaranth on a September day, the sky seems to droop almost to the highway in misty banks of purple and grey. When the clouds split open, a streak of sun lights yellow buttercups, black-eyed susans, and purple thistles overflowing the ditches at the side of the highway. Red-winged blackbirds pick at seeds along the gravel shoulders. On either side of the highway, boulders are heaped in the midst of cultivated fields, a testament to the region's rocky soil. In one field, a herd of dirty-white cows grazes around bales of freshly cut hay scattered like plump golden raisins. Midway to Amaranth, the speed limit drops to fifty kilometres per hour through the village of Langruth, marked by an Esso station, general and grocery store, hotel, and community hall.

Between Langruth and Amaranth, construction crews are trying to finish widening the road before winter sets in. Beyond the raw dirt shoulders, clumps of scruffy poplars line the road, and horses—white, black, brown, and dappled grey—romp in a field. Soon, a white canvas teepee pitched behind a brown bungalow appears on the horizon, heralding the southern border of Sandy Bay. Just a little farther on, the standard white-letters-on-green highway sign for "Sandy Bay Indian Reserve" points east onto a gravel road. The turn-off is also marked by a hand-painted sign for the Sandy Bay Badgers Community School— the Badgers being the community's square-dance group. A couple of kilometres beyond the turn-off is the village of Amaranth, with the regional RCMP detachment, as well as another Esso station, grocery store, school, hotel with a coffee shop, and community hall. Across from the hotel is the junction of the highway and a gravel road marking the northern border of Sandy Bay.

Having turned east onto the main road into Sandy Bay, the car bumps along the deeply rutted, two-lane gravel thoroughfare. The speed limit of seventy kliks seems like a bad joke until first one pick-up truck, and then another, races by, kicking up choking clouds of dust. A glimpse of one truck's cracked windshield says it all: welcome to the infamous roads of Sandy Bay, renowned for chewing up vehicles and spitting them out in record time.

Bushes grow close to the road at first, and then open up to reveal cracker-box bungalows scattered here and there. Most houses have big, black satellite dishes in the yards, the cheapest form of entertainment in rural areas not endowed with cable television. Outside some homes are signs of an entrepreneurial spirit: "Harry's Arcade" says one sign; "Shirley's Chip Shop," says another. Rusting vehicles and appliances are strewn like bones in some yards, while others boast manicured lawns and red-potted geraniums. The size and condition of housing vary widely, from the occasional sprawling, ranch-style house to the more common wood-frame bungalow or two-storey with raised basement. As is the case on most cash-strapped reserves, residents here spend years on band waiting-lists to get out of drafty, crowded, thirty-year-old houses into decent but cheaply constructed new homes. The housing backlog—which had reached 275 families in 1993—was caused by inadequate housing budgets allotted by the Department of Indian Affairs. Just under $30,000 was set aside to build each new house, while band leaders say it costs closer to $50,000. But the statistic which is the most surprising—and revealing—is that about one-third of the homes at Sandy Bay still do not have running water.

If you drive east on the main road—which ends just short of Lake Manitoba—a cluster of buildings, including a hockey arena, band office, and school, signals the centre of the community. What has been dubbed the "local civil service" is based in these buildings, providing what little stable employment exists at Sandy Bay. The band employs about 120 residents, everyone from band councillors to welfare and family-services workers and school staff. Jobs are doled out by those in elected positions, from the chief and council to the school board, fuelling heated elections every three years. Representatives of major family groups vie for positions of power to better not only their own economic lot but that of their relatives. With an unemployment rate of at least 50 per cent in the community, there are few other opportunities to earn an income beyond seasonal farm work.

As elected officials, the chief and council assume overall responsibility for local services, from road maintenance to housing and some social services. The exceptions include medical services, run by Health and Welfare Canada; policing; and child-welfare services. Until recently, the RCMP investigated major crimes, such as murder and sexual assault, while the Dakota Ojibway Tribal Police responded to minor incidents, such as speeding or break-ins. But under a three-year agreement struck in 1995 between the province, Ottawa, and the Dakota

Ojibway Tribal Council, the tribal police force is gradually taking over complete control of all policing. The tribal police are run by the Dakota Ojibway Tribal Council, of which Sandy Bay is one of eight members. The tribal council also has responsibility for Dakota Ojibway Child and Family Services, which provides mandated child-protection and other child-welfare services. Of Manitoba's sixty-one Indian bands, all but three belong to one of seven tribal councils. The councils, made up of the chiefs of affiliate bands, oversee regional services and cooperate on political issues.

Perhaps the true heart of the community is the Sandy Bay school, a decade-old brick building which is bulging at the seams with more than 1,000 students and offers programs extending from Kindergarten to Grade 12. Children are everywhere, even crammed into basement rooms once set aside for science labs and art studies. Nearby buildings also house makeshift classrooms for the burgeoning student body. The reserve's baby boom has been caused not only by high birth rates, but also by an influx of new residents under Bill C-31, the federal legislation that restored status in the mid-1980s to many Native people disenfranchised through marriage to outsiders or other unfair legal technicalities. Despite the school's cramped quarters, the community is proud of its history as one of the first to be Native-run in Canada in the 1970s. In the school's lobby, the ceiling panels are painted with brightly coloured eagles, moose, geese, and other Aboriginal symbols. Under this roof, the children of Sandy Bay learn not only the three R's—reading, writing, and arithmetic—but how to speak Saulteaux, respect their elders, and reclaim their history.

Until the federal government forced them onto reserves a century ago, the Ojibwa of this region did not live at Sandy Bay. Known as the Whitemud River band, they spent their winters in a village about seventy kilometres south of Sandy Bay, where the Whitemud River empties into Lake Manitoba. They named the community Totogan, which means "soft earth" in Saulteaux, their language. In the summers, the band lived in tents, following the hunt, collecting berries, and visiting other tribes. Furs were traded at the Hudson's Bay post, also located at Totogan. By the mid-1800s, some families also began to farm the land at Totogan. Another extended family which was part of the band, the

Desjarlais clan, settled about thirty kilometres west, where the town of Gladstone is now located.

The Whitemud band were part of the Saulteaux people—Plains Ojibwa whose ancestors had moved west in the 1700s from what would become Ontario, displaced by the increasing population of white settlers. They likely adopted the name "Saulteaux" while trading with settlers near Sault Ste. Marie during that era. Upon their arrival on the prairies in the 1700s, the Saulteaux joined in the buffalo hunt, an activity that shaped the values and culture of all Plains people. The hunt required a group effort and fostered a strong tribal identity. Individual survival depended on everyone working together. But over the next century, the disastrous impact of diseases brought by European settlers, combined with famine caused by declining buffalo herds, began to undermine the traditional way of life. The first smallpox epidemic, in about 1780, is estimated to have killed a staggering 50 per cent of Prairie and Woodlands Indians. In 1837, a second devastating smallpox epidemic claimed more victims. At the same time, the decline of the buffalo by the mid-1800s, as well as decreasing numbers of other big game such as caribou and moose, prompted some Plains people, including the Saulteaux, to turn to agriculture. By the 1860s, some hunters also relied on part-time jobs in the fur trade to survive.

To the Ojibwa, the concept of "owning" land was unthinkable. Land was a gift to be used by everyone, a sacred trust. When the white government officials began offering them compensation for the "sale" of their land, the Whitemud people were no doubt amused at such strange behaviour. As one Sandy Bay elder, Angela Eastman, says of her ancestors: "They figured they really had these guys, you know! They're giving us all these gifts and they want land and nobody can own land. Everybody knows that. The land is here for all the people." Like other Aboriginal peoples, they believed the treaties were meant to be agreements about how to share the land with the European newcomers.

The families which made up the Whitemud band were part of a larger network called the Portage bands. When the newly formed government of Canada negotiated Treaty One with the Portage bands in the summer of 1871, Chief Yellowquill, accompanied by leaders from each band, led the lengthy negotiations at Lower Fort Garry, also known as the Stone Fort. As documented by Alexander Morris in *The Treaties of Canada with the Indians of Manitoba and the North-West Territories*, Manitoba's Lieutenant-Governor Archibald opened the proceedings with a speech that, from today's vantage point, was not only patronizing, but blatantly misleading:

> Your Great Mother [the Queen] wishes the good of all races under her sway. She wishes her red children to be happy and contented. She wishes them to live in comfort. She would like them to adopt the habits of the whites, to till land and raise food, and store it up against a time of want. She thinks this would be the best thing for her red children to do, that it would make them safer from famine and distress, and make their homes more comfortable.
>
> But the Queen, though she may think it good for you to adopt civilized habits, has no idea of compelling you to do so. This she leaves to your choice, and you need not live like the white man unless you can be persuaded to do so of your own free will.

Chief Yellowquill and the other leaders responded by asking that two-thirds of Manitoba be set aside as a reserve. This was clearly not what government officials, bent on obtaining land for settlers, had in mind. As the lieutenant-governor wrote in a letter to Ottawa:

> We heard them out, and then told them it was quite clear that they had entirely misunderstood the meaning and intention of reserves. We explained the object of these in something like the language of the memorandum enclosed, and then told them it was of no use for them to entertain any such ideas, which were entirely out of the question. We told them that whether they wished it or not, immigrants would come in and fill up the country ... and that now was the time for them to come to an arrangement that would secure homes and annuities for themselves and their children.

By the time Treaty One was concluded, southern Manitoba tribes ended up with a fraction of what they had originally wanted, and substantially less than what was granted to Plains people farther west. Treaty One bands were given written guarantees that they'd receive a tract of land equalling 160 acres per family of five and an annuity of three dollars per head. By contrast, Indians who signed Treaties Three, Four, Six, Nine, and Ten over the next few years were eventually promised one square mile (640 acres) per family of five.

Treaty One also included the promise that the government would maintain schools on every reserve, and the understanding that the sale of alcohol would be banned. In addition, oral promises were made that each family would receive a plough and harrow for farming; chiefs would be given a cow and other farm animals; each reserve would have a bull; and chiefs and councillors would receive special clothes and buggies. When the government did not follow through on these terms, Indian leaders let officials know they felt betrayed and angry. Four years later, Treaty One had to be revised to include everything they'd been promised.

Disputes also arose during the process of determining where the reserves would be located. Chief Yellowquill was lobbying for one large reserve, even though the band was actually made up of three separate groups—Yellowquill's followers, those led by Short Bear, and the Whitemud band—living in different areas. In the end, the band was divided into three, each with a separate reserve. The Whitemud River band, which numbered about 130 people by the 1870s, chose He-Who-Stands-in-the-Centre-of-the-Earth (Nanakagabo) as their head man and made it clear they wanted to be recognized as a separate band and be given land at Big Point, west of Langruth. The government refused, saying settlers had already laid claim to that land. Instead, officials tried again to persuade the Whitemud River Indians to merge with one of the other Portage bands, a proposition they rejected. Eventually, the government agreed to choose a property for them, setting aside a marshy strip of shoreline at Sandy Bay, about ten kilometres north of Big Point. Officials then began forcing reluctant band members to move to their new home. As an extra incentive, the RCMP would sometimes pull down a family's log house, promising to provide materials to build a new one at Sandy Bay. In other cases, widows at Totogan lost their land because of unpaid land taxes—another concept foreign to the Ojibwa. By the time the population of Sandy Bay had swelled to 460 people a few years later, band members were already complaining to the government about their land. Cultivating productive crops, as they'd done at Totogan, was impossible because the land was too wet. Sandy Bay, like many other reservations across Canada, would never provide a decent economic base for the rapidly growing community.

Once the reserve system was established, the federal government used an even more insidious tool in its attempt to assimilate Native peoples into white society. Its treaty promise to maintain schools on reserves quickly became an avenue to force change on reluctant communities. Ottawa appointed Nicholas F. Davin to examine the Americans' approach of sending Indian children away to large industrial schools. In 1879, Davin submitted a report to Parliament praising the Americans' "aggressive civilization policy," which he believed had been so successful because it cut children off from the negative influences of their families. As Davin said, "If anything is to be done with the Indian, we must catch him very young." But Davin recommended that the residential schools in Canada be run by Christian missionaries, rather than by the government.

With the government's blessing, two types of residential schools were set up across the country by Protestant and Catholic missionaries. Older children, from about fourteen to eighteen years of age, were sent far from home to industrial schools where they were supposed to learn practical skills as well as get an education. In reality, only half-days were spent in the classroom, where the emphasis was on religious instruction and rudimentary reading and arithmetic. Children spent the rest of the day doing hard manual labour, with boys required to work at blacksmithing, shoemaking, ranching, and farming, while girls cooked and sewed and cleaned. Missionaries, horrified at the relaxed approach to parenting adopted by Natives, set about correcting the children's "uncivilized" manners with rigid schedules and harsh physical discipline. By 1896, twenty-four industrial schools had been set up across Canada, four in Ontario and the rest in Manitoba, British Columbia, and the Northwest Territories.

Younger children were sent to boarding-schools located in or near their home communities, where they endured a similar mix of rigid instruction and hard work, aimed at obliterating their "pagan" roots. Parents who refused to send their children to the schools were threatened by Indian agents, who forced compliance by imposing such measures as withdrawing food rations. By the turn of the century, thirty-nine boarding-schools existed in Canada. One-sixth of all Status Indian children—or 3,285 of 20,000—were attending a boarding- or industrial school by the early 1900s. After the act was amended in 1920 to make school attendance mandatory, residential-school populations increased, until in the 1940s about 50 per cent of Indian students, or 8,000, were enrolled in seventy-six schools across Canada.

At Sandy Bay, a residential school was established in 1905 by the Roman Catholic Church. The Sandy Bay boarding-school was administered by the Oblate Fathers, under the authority of the Archdiocese of Winnipeg, for most of its sixty-five-year history. At its peak, the school had 154 residential students and 107 day students. By the 1950s students were given the option to live at home while attending classes. But already several generations of children had endured traumatic separations from their families during every academic year. One Sandy Bay elder, Isaac Beaulieu, who lived at the school as a child, recalled how lonely and confused he felt during those years. He remembers standing at the window on the third floor of the brick building. From that vantage point, he could gaze across the reserve and see the roof of his family's home just a few kilometres away. As he eyed his home longingly, he wondered all over again why his parents weren't allowed to visit and why he went home only at Christmas and for summer vacation.

As part of the missionaries' attempts to turn their small charges into "good Christians," children who slipped into Saulteaux rather than speaking English were punished by the priests and nuns who operated the Sandy Bay school. Children had their heads shaved, were slapped while their peers watched, and had wooden clothespins clamped to their tongues. The same brutal tactics were used at other residential schools in many parts of Canada. But literally being silenced had a devastating effect on children at Sandy Bay and elsewhere. A special study released in 1994 by the Assembly of First Nations, entitled

Breaking the Silence: An Interpretive Study of Residential School Impact and Healing as Illustrated by the Stories of First Nations Individuals, documents the long-term consequences. Outlawing Aboriginal languages effectively cut children off from their roots. As one former residential-school student told the study's authors:

> I didn't speak any English; neither did my parents. But I had to learn it in a hurry because that's all we were allowed to speak. I remember other kids getting hit for talking their language.
>
> Today I understand quite a few words in my language. But every time I try and talk it my tongue hurts. I didn't know why. I ran into another woman who went to residential school with me and we were talking about it. She asked me if I remembered how they would stick a needle in our tongue if we got caught talking our language. I don't remember that … But maybe what she said is true: Maybe that's why my tongue hurts whenever I try and talk my language.

After several generations of children endured such treatment in residential schools, it is no surprise that fifty of fifty-three Aboriginal languages in Canada today are on the verge of being lost forever.

But being forced to speak English was not the only way children were alienated from their families and culture. Often, they were forbidden to talk about home or relate to siblings who attended the same school. They heard themselves described as "pagans," as "dirty" or "dumb," or as "savages." Aboriginal ceremonies—like sweat lodges or the sundance at Sandy Bay—were labelled "works of the Devil." Missionaries instilled the "fear of God" in children with their teachings about Heaven and Hell. As a former residential-school student recalled: "I dabbed my finger in a bowl of brown-sugar sauce one day when I was working in the kitchen. I got caught. The nun wiped it off my finger and drew a picture of the Devil on my finger to remind me that stealing was wrong … I thought the Devil had me for sure then." Needless to say, many children grew ashamed of their families and blamed their parents for their unhappiness. With few chances to renew family bonds, the estrangement between children and parents only worsened over the years. As the authors of *Breaking the Silence* observed: "Children hold a community together. By removing children from their families and community, residential schools seriously undermined the capacity of First Nations people to act communally."

Emotional abuse of children was common, including being forced to wear soiled underwear over their heads for failing to wipe themselves properly. One former resident of the Sandy Bay school remembered watching the nuns force a young girl—who they'd branded a "devil child"—to eat her own vomit after she couldn't keep her meal down. Isaac Beaulieu recalled that he and other students were made to earn their keep by milking the school's four dozen cows and collecting as many as 200 eggs each day. Yet fresh dairy products were rarely a part of their diets. Sandy Bay elder Angela Eastman remembered her father telling stories about how he and other boys at the school would carry little medicine bottles with them. At milking time, they'd fill their bottles when the supervisor wasn't looking and secretly hoard the precious liquid for their evening tea. At meals, her father said, the priest often ate at a table laden with sumptuous food while the students watched, sitting with their bowls of boiled wheat.

But punishment didn't stop at ridicule or deprivation. Many children suffered severe physical and sexual abuse in church-run residential schools. School officials relied on forms of corporal punishment which would today be considered child abuse. Children of all ages were beaten, often in front of their peers, for everything from minor infractions, like failing to finish their supper, to running away. As an indication of how widespread this abuse was, every one of the adults interviewed for the *Breaking the Silence* study had been beaten at school or had watched other students being hit. The physical abuse left children feeling powerless and enraged, but with no way to express their emotions. While many students sought solace from each other, older children sometimes took out their frustration by bullying younger students.

Even worse was the sexual violation endured by many residential-school students at the hands of both school officials and older children. Reports have surfaced across the country in the last decade from adults who were sexually abused as children while attending boarding-schools, including Sandy Bay's. The incidents have included everything from ritualistic washing of genitals and fondling, to rape, impregnation, and forced abortions. One former eight-year resident of the Sandy Bay school said he was just one of many boys who were sexually abused by a supervisor. He was also raped by an older student, and molested once by a priest. His abusers kept him quiet by threatening that if he told anyone what was going on, he'd be kicked out of the school, and his parents would end up going to jail because of his truancy. "If that isn't hell, I don't know what is," the now middle-aged man said. He even heard stories of nuns demanding sex from boys at the school, and was once approached by a nun himself. Finally, he ran away from the school at age sixteen, hoping to put that nightmare behind him. But more than thirty years later, he's still coming to terms with the abuse he suffered.

Residential schools provided the perfect setting for taking advantage of vulnerable children. Some who were abused at the hands of school officials went on to become abusers themselves, continuing the cycle of violence. Other victims turned to the justice system, resulting in the convictions of a growing list of former priests and other school officials. For example, Derek Clarke, a former dormitory supervisor at the Anglican-run St. George's School in Lytton, B.C., pleaded guilty in 1987 to eleven counts of buggery and six counts of indecent assault involving seventeen boys between 1964 and 1974. He was sentenced to twelve years in prison for his involvement in as many as 700 incidents of sexual abuse. Still, most abuse survivors have not turned to the legal system. Some have blocked out the terrible memories for fear of not being believed, or struggle with the shame of feeling that they were somehow to blame. Many more are just beginning to seek healing for the violations of body, mind, and spirit they suffered.

Children coped with this multitude of assaults on their well-being in a variety of ways. While having no choice but to adapt to many aspects of residential-school life, they also found ways to survive and even resist the oppressive atmosphere. Some sought comfort from other students, developing a subculture of cliques that offered a semblance of belonging. The theft of food was common, to assuage both hunger and the sense of powerlessness. Some students openly rebelled, defying the rules and running away at every opportunity. Others tried

31

to avoid punishment by seeking approval from their caretakers and hiding their misery behind a smile. But regardless of how they handled the stresses of daily life, children were traumatized by the residential school experience, which crushed their spirits and erased their identities. When they finally reached an age at which they could escape, a whole new set of problems awaited them.

Once out on their own, many former residential-school students discovered they lacked the skills to fit in to either Aboriginal or white society. The loss of their first language and their alienation from their culture limited communication with parents and other relatives back home. The psychic scars of physical, sexual, and emotional abuse made healthy marital relationships difficult, if not impossible. With no role models for raising their children—except the authoritarian example of school officials—parenting became overwhelming. At the same time, the poor quality of their education left them unable to pursue further schooling or find stable employment off the reserve. In 1930, only 3 per cent of Aboriginal students went beyond Grade 6. By 1950, only 10 per cent went beyond that level, one-third the success rate of white children in provincial schools. Norma Sluman and Jean Goodwill's book *John Tootoosis* quotes one former residential-school survivor:

> When an Indian comes out of these places it is like being put betweeen two walls in a room and left hanging in the middle. On one side are all the things he learned from his people and their way of life that was being wiped out, and on the other are the white man's way which he could never fully understand since he never had the right amount of education and could not be part of it. There he is, hanging in the middle of the two cultures and he is not a white man and he is not an Indian. They washed away practically everything an Indian needed to help himself, to think the way a human person should in order to survive.

It is no wonder that many former residential-school students turned to alcohol and drugs to ease their anger and pain at lost childhoods and disintegrating adult lives.

Yet not everyone who attended residential schools, at Sandy Bay and elsewhere, found them oppressive. There are those who have fond memories of those years, remembering the residential school as a welcome escape from alcoholic parents, a turbulent family life, and the deprivation of poverty. Some developed special relationships with priests or nuns who shielded them from the harsh school routine. Others look back upon those years as an opportunity to learn self-discipline and get an education. But many, like Isaac Beaulieu, believe the demoralizing messages school officials drummed into several generations of children were a form of "cultural assassination" and are at the root of many of the social ills still troubling communities like Sandy Bay.

By the 1950s, the federal government realized that residential schools had failed to assimilate Indian children. Once again, it amended the Indian Act, recommending that children be integrated into the public-school system rather than going to boarding-schools. During the transition, some residential schools, like the one at Sandy Bay, gave children the option of living at home and attending as day students. In other communities, children were bussed to schools in nearby towns, where they faced discrimination and ostracization in the white education system. When failure rates and drop-out rates of more than 90 per cent for Aboriginal children didn't diminish over the next two decades, it again became clear that the government's plan had failed. In 1973, Ottawa finally acquiesced to Native leaders and allowed bands to run their own reserve-based schools. In the mid-1970s, the community of Sandy Bay was among the first reserves in Canada to set up its own school board. By 1990, about 28 per cent of Canada's 82,000 Indian elementary- and high-school students attended one of the 240 band-controlled schools.

But even as the residential-school system lost its grip on Aboriginal communities, another threat took its place. In 1951, the Indian Act was amended to allow provinces to provide child-welfare services on reserve. Since no additional funding was granted by Ottawa, few services were offered at first, and children were rarely apprehended. In 1955, for example, less than 1 per cent of the children in care in British Columbia were of Indian ancestry. Yet as child-welfare services expanded onto reserves in B.C. and elsewhere over the next decade, that statistic jumped dramatically. By 1964, 34.2 per cent of the children in care in B.C. were Aboriginal. When the federal government agreed in 1966 to help the provinces foot the bill for providing social services on reserves under the Canada Assistance Plan, the stage was set for another widespread intrusion into the lives of Aboriginal families.

This time the agents of the state were white social workers. Shocked by the alcoholism, poverty, and family disintegration they encountered on reserves, and with little understanding of the factors behind the social breakdown, child-welfare officials saw only one solution: rescue the children from their negligent parents and miserable surroundings. What ensued became known as the "Sixties Scoop," during which thousands of Aboriginal children across Canada, especially in the western provinces, were removed from their parents and communities. A survey by the Canadian Council on Social Development found that, by 1983, Aboriginal children were vastly overrepresented in the child-welfare system. In Manitoba, about 60 per cent of the children in care were Aboriginal, while in Alberta they made up about 50 per cent of the caseload, and up to 70 per cent in Saskatchewan.

Once put in foster care or adopted out, few would ever return home. Most were sent to live with non-Aboriginal families, often in other provinces, the United States, or other countries. Raised by middle-class, white parents, they grew up with little or no awareness of their roots. Yet they were often discriminated against because of the colour of their skin. Some were also physically and sexually abused by foster or adoptive parents. By the time they reached adolescence, many were in crisis, running away repeatedly and turning to alcohol, drugs, and crime to ease their torment.

In Manitoba, the federal government and the province signed an agreement in 1966 which resulted in three Children's Aid societies extending their services to fourteen bands in southern Manitoba, including Sandy Bay. The other 75 per cent of bands in the province relied on sporadic services from Indian Affairs, with provincial social workers intervening only in "life and death" situations. But it soon became obvious that more child-welfare services meant only one thing: the removal of large numbers of children. Sometimes social workers apprehended children for legitimate reasons, like severe abuse or neglect. But too often they seized children because of crowded living conditions, or even because children required medical care. Between 1971 and 1981, more than 3,400 Native children were sent out of the province for adoption, including many from Sandy Bay. About one-third of them ended up in the United States, where laws limiting cross-cultural adoptions of Indian and black children had reduced the number of babies available. South of the border, private adoption agencies had waiting-lists of childless couples who were willing to pay thousands of dollars for healthy infants. But when those babies grew up, in many cases there was a much higher price to pay for all involved. As one former adoptee told the Aboriginal Justice Inquiry:

> You adopt a Metis child into a white community and you expect it to work? You take his total culture away from him, his heritage and you expect it to work? When I was going to school, an all white school, and this was a time that Indians didn't have respect in the States, and that is what they considered me, I really had a tough time in school. They expected us all to work out, to come out beautiful. I was supposed to come out with a scholarship and become a lawyer or a doctor. This is what they thought. Well, I sure fooled them. I came back and I didn't have nothing to show for it. I have nothing but hate. Hate for the system, the welfare system, the child and family services system that has put me in this situation as well as other people.

By 1982, Manitoba was the only province still allowing out-of-country adoptions. Distraught about the ongoing loss of their children, Native leaders accused the province of "selling babies." In response to public pressure, the provincial government banned out-of-province adoptions of Native children and appointed Associate Chief Judge Edwin Kimelman, of the provincial family court, to preside over an inquiry into the child-welfare system. Kimelman held hearings across Manitoba and reviewed the files of ninety-three Aboriginal children who had been adopted out-of-province in 1981 alone. Letters were sent to hundreds of children who had been adopted into non-

Aboriginal homes, seeking information about how the placements had worked out.

The final Kimelman report in 1985, entitled *No Quiet Place*, concluded that the concerns raised by the Native community were well founded. To the surprise of child-welfare officials, the report agreed that the export of children from their home communities was "cultural genocide." It criticized social workers for applying white standards—like a bedroom for each child and running water—when considering whether to apprehend children and where to place them. Child-welfare workers were culturally biased, the report said, lacking the knowledge about or sensitivity towards Aboriginal culture to make decisions in the best interests of children. Parents whose children were apprehended were often denied information about their whereabouts and weren't given the opportunity to regain custody. Every aspect of the system was stacked against those it was supposed to help. As Kimelman said, "It would be reassuring if blame could be laid to any single part of the system. The appalling reality is that everyone involved believed they were doing their best and stood firm in their belief that the system was working well ... The road to hell was paved with good intentions and the child welfare system was the paving contractor."

The report pointed out that the child-welfare system had taken over where residential schools left off: "At least under that system [residential schools], the children knew who their parents were and they returned home for the summer months. With the closing of the residential schools, rather than providing the resources on reserves to build economic security and providing the services to support responsible parenting, society found it easier and cheaper to remove the children from their homes and apparently fill the market demand for children in Eastern Canada and the United States." Like the generations of children forced to attend residential schools, many adoptees discovered as adults that they did not fit into the white world of their childhood or the Aboriginal community of their ancestry.

In the end, the Kimelman report recommended sweeping changes to Manitoba's child-welfare system, aimed at incorporating cultural considerations into all decisions made on behalf of children. The goal of child welfare should be to strengthen family ties, not sever them.

Kimelman urged the province to make efforts to contact Aboriginal children who had been sent out of the province and offer them help reconciling with their birth families and home communities. By the time Kimelman released his report, the first Native-run child-welfare agencies had been established in Manitoba. Many of the report's recommendations were directed towards strengthening the fledgling agencies, including notifying them when Aboriginal children came into care, hiring more Aboriginal staff, and developing more Aboriginal foster homes on reserves. Placement in non-Native homes should be used only as a last resort, the report said. But it pointed out that, to accomplish these goals, the federal and provincial governments would have to increase funding to Native agencies.

The Kimelman report confirmed what Aboriginal leaders had been telling both levels of government for years: that child welfare, like education and other services, belonged under the jurisdiction of bands. With the dawn of Native-run child-welfare agencies in Manitoba, communities like Sandy Bay had taken another step towards reclaiming control of their lives. But trying to undo more than a century of colonization would be a daunting task.

The driving force behind the establishment of Dakota Ojibway Child and Family Services was the desire to halt their communities' loss of children to the white child-welfare system. Between 1966 and 1980, an estimated 335 children had been removed from the eight Dakota Ojibway Tribal Council communities, including Sandy Bay, and sent out of the province for adoption. As the adoptees grew up, stories began to filter back about their struggles. Many placements had broken down, and some adoptees had suffered abuse. The chiefs vowed that the primary goal of their new agency would be putting a stop to this.

By the early 1980s, DOTC communities, like other reserves across Manitoba, were tired of receiving only minimal services from provincial Children's Aid societies, even though about 50 per cent of the children in care were of Native descent. In 1979, DOTC chiefs passed a resolution outlining their intent to set up their own child-welfare agency. The next year, they began negotiating with the federal and provincial governments to win approval for their initiative. A June 1980 proposal outlining the agency's structure, mandate, governance, and funding included this vision statement: "It is only when people experience a sense of freedom that they can learn responsiblity; it is only when people participate in the decision-making which shapes their lives that alienation is discouraged; it is only when people are helped to see alternatives in their lives that changes take place; and it is only in an atmosphere of flexibility that any of this can happen." Under the tripartite agreement hammered out between the DOTC and the provincial and federal governments, Ottawa agreed to provide the bulk of the funding for the new agency, which would operate within provincial child-welfare guidelines. On July 1, 1981, Dakota Ojibway Child and Family Services received its legal mandate and took over care of 49 children who had been apprehended by Children's Aid societies. Within three years, the number of children in the care of DOCFS had more than doubled, to 115, reflecting the tremendous demand for services the new agency faced from the moment it opened its doors.

DOCFS, with its goal of providing a full range of culturally sensitive child-welfare services, soon became a model for Aboriginal communities across the country and a source of great pride. By the time the agency was less than a year old, agency officials and DOTC chiefs had convinced provincial politicians to declare a moratorium on the out-of-country adoptions of Indian and Metis children, and been instrumental in the launch of the Kimelman inquiry. DOCFS officials kept the pressure on by publicizing the tragic results of the adoption policy and intervening on behalf of young people like Cameron Kerley. Cameron had been removed from his home at Sioux Valley and sent for adoption by a single man in Wichita, Kansas. There, the boy was beaten and sexually abused for years. Finally, he killed his adoptive father with a baseball bat in 1983 and was sentenced to eighteen years to life in prison. When DOCFS officials heard about his fate, they sent a delegation to a sentence-review hearing and convinced the judge to reduce his sentence slightly. Further lobbying resulted in Cameron being transferred to Stony Mountain Penitentiary north of Winnipeg in 1985.

From the beginning, DOCFS had hoped to focus on providing preventative services that would promote healthy families. But the agency was quickly inundated with requests to meet the immediate needs of poverty-stricken communities in which more than half the population was under twenty years old. Despite constant battles with government officials, adequate funding to train staff and foster parents, as well as to set up reserve-based treatment facilities, was not provided. As federal funding lagged behind the demands for service, the pressures on workers increased, resulting in burn-out and high turnover rates.

Meanwhile, in the mainstream child-welfare system, stricter child-abuse reporting guidelines and investigation procedures had produced a growing number of such cases, especially related to sexual abuse. But this trend was not apparent in the early years of DOCFS. An internal review of the agency done in 1983 noted that only nine cases of child abuse had been reported from DOTC reserves. Although the agency had received more than these nine complaints, preliminary investigations "did not show sufficient cause for official registration of these complaints." The review team raised concerns about the inconsistent follow-up and reporting of abuse cases, then issued this warning:

> Of particular concern to provincial officials are recent reports of sexual abuse on some reserves, and their concern that this reflects a much more widespread problem involving young, adolescent girls and older men. Within the relatively close network of relationships in a small community there can be a tendency to undervalue the seriousness of these incidents and protect those responsible for such abuse. This may result in a failure to respond appropriately both to the abusers and to the victims of this abuse. The review team was unable to determine whether such a pattern was apparent in DOTC communities, but this is an issue that requires continued monitoring by the agency.

It was an admonition that would become more significant than anyone imagined.

Chapter Three

LITTLE CREE

"... a normal life, that's all I ever wanted."

—Nancy McIvor

Born the fifth of Joyce's children, Lester arrived in a family frayed by poverty and strife. His young mother was on the verge of being abandoned by her husband, Cecil Desjarlais, when she gave birth to Lester on June 7, 1974, in a Portage la Prairie hospital. She'd started living with Cecil seven years earlier, when she was fourteen years old and pregnant. Joyce would eventually tell her daughter Sherry that she'd been "given away" to Cecil by her stepfather, Alex McIvor, when he was drunk. But Alex and his wife, Adele McIvor, insist they were furious with Cecil for getting their young daughter pregnant and considered legal action because of Joyce's age. They relented when Cecil, who was eight years Joyce's senior, agreed to set things right by becoming her partner.

Joyce had been happy at first, content to be a full-time mother to Cecil Jr., born in 1967; Sherry, born the following year; and Nancy, born in 1971. The family lived near the community's town site, in an orange bungalow Joyce had purchased for $150. In the early years, Joyce kept the house spotless and the refrigerator stocked with food. But as her marriage faltered under the weight of alcohol and marital disputes, she had trouble coping.

Even as a young child, Sherry knew all was not well between her parents. Sometimes when her father drank, he put Sherry and her older brother in a bedroom and closed the door. As they huddled together, they'd hear their mother's cries as their parents fought. The children would scream through the door for him to stop. Eventually Cecil would respond and try to comfort the frantic children.

It didn't help matters when Cecil moved away from Sandy Bay to attend university in Brandon, leaving Joyce alone with their three young children. While at school, Cecil became involved with another woman. Along with the widening educational gap between himself and his wife, the affair seemed to clinch their break-up. Ironically, not long before that, after years of living common law, Joyce and Cecil had legally married before the birth of their fourth child, Annette. Left with no means to support her children, Joyce felt she had no choice but to place Annette, born in April 1973, in private foster care with a couple who were related to Cecil. Joyce also left her second daughter, Nancy, with the couple for a while. Her two oldest children, Sherry and Cecil Jr., were sent to live with Cecil's parents. On the day Sherry was dropped off to live with her grandparents, she thought she was just going for a visit. As the five-year-old girl and her older brother walked to the home of Ida and Andrew Desjarlais with their father, the children lagged behind and played along the way. After they arrived, Sherry curled up and fell asleep while Cecil chatted with his mother. When Sherry awoke, her father had vanished from her life. "It seems like I never saw him after that," she says. "Like, we were just dumped there."

With her marriage disintegrating, Joyce became enamoured with a well-built young man named Norman Anderson, whom she met during a trip to Winnipeg sometime in 1973. Details about their relationship are sketchy. But, late that year, Norman took Joyce back to his home at Shamattawa, a Cree community about 750 kilometres north of Winnipeg and accessible only by plane. Joyce didn't tell her family about her move, leaving her parents, Alex and Adele McIvor, wondering what had happened to her. Worried, Adele went to Winnipeg a few times to ask around about her. Then, out of the blue, an urgent letter arrived from Joyce, begging for money. She didn't like Shamattawa, where she felt isolated and lonely because she couldn't speak Cree, she wrote. Norman was mistreating her, and the only way to escape was by plane. Alex went to the band council for help and arranged for payment of the plane fare. They also radioed a message to Shamattawa, asking for Joyce to come home. One day, while Norman, a lumberjack, was at work, Joyce sneaked out of the house and onto the plane. By the end of January 1974, she had arrived back at Sandy Bay, almost five months pregnant with Lester.

After Lester was born, Norman returned from Shamattawa and moved in with Joyce, who was now living with her parents at Sandy Bay. Then Norman persuaded Joyce that she and their newborn son should move to Winnipeg with him. From Lester's earliest days, he had a tough fight on his hands. When he was two months old, Joyce took her infant to a Winnipeg hospital, where he was treated for a bowel infection. Six months later, she showed up with him again. This time Lester not only had another bowel infection, but was seriously dehydrated and had to be admitted to hospital. A doctor noted that Joyce appeared bruised and battered when she arrived with her baby.

Eventually, Joyce reclaimed Cecil Jr., Sherry, and Nancy, who by then were living with her parents. She brought them to Winnipeg, where the family drifted from one apartment to another. When Norman drank, which was often, he became mean and abusive and picked fights with Joyce. One day Sherry saw her mother despondently packing Lester's baby clothes into a box and asked why. Joyce explained that Norman was taking them back to Shamattawa. Later, she heard her mother and Norman arguing. Furious at Joyce's opposition to his plan, Norman lost his temper and hurled a boot through the window of their apartment on Aberdeen Avenue in Winnipeg's north end. When the family arrived at the Winnipeg airport to fly to Shamattawa, Norman again angered Joyce by throwing some money at Cecil Jr. after he begged for some candy. That was the last straw. Joyce took her four children and moved back to Sandy Bay. Norman would never again be more than a peripheral part of Lester's life.

Joyce loved all her children fiercely. She carried infant Lester everywhere and did her best to care for him. But coping alone with four lively kids under the age of eight strained her financial and emotional resources to the breaking-point. On top of that, she got little or no financial help from her ex-husband, Cecil, who had remarried. Although Joyce was known for always having a smile on her face, friends knew she brooded over the breakdown of her marriage. More and more often, Joyce turned to alcohol to ease her pain, as she had watched her father and other relatives do. Growing up in cramped quarters, where there was never enough of anything—money or privacy or attention—had taught Joyce the value of escaping any way she could. As the eldest surviving child of ten, she had learned that lesson well.

As in any community, subtle class differences delineated life at Sandy Bay. There were the leaders—who were usually better off financially and otherwise—and the followers. Joyce's stepfather, Alex, was in the latter category. He occasionally brought in money through seasonal labour, such as working on another band member's cattle ranch, and winter fishing for Winnipeg goldeye on the lake. But with high unemployment—from 50 to 80 per cent at Sandy Bay—there were few other opportunities for work. Some band members grazed small herds of cattle or horses in the flat, rocky fields of the reserve, and others relied on commercial fishing, but neither activity provided enough jobs for the rapidly growing population. By the time Lester was born, the community had grown to more than 1,200 people and would more than double in size over the next two decades. The only chance for an education for both Joyce and her parents had been at Sandy Bay's residential school, run by the Roman Catholic Church. By the time Joyce attended in the 1950s, she'd gone to the day school rather than being forced to live in residence, as her parents had been.

During Lester's early years, Joyce drifted back and forth from Sandy Bay to Portage la Prairie to Winnipeg, setting up one temporary household after another. But despite the family's hardships, life wasn't all doom and gloom. A spirited, playful woman, Joyce loved to joke and tease with her friends and her kids. There was always something to laugh at. She took pleasure in simple diversions, whether that was playing cards with her friends for an evening, or singing or listening to music. Although she was shy about singing at community events, she loved nothing better than to croon country tunes for friends or perform in local bars. Even when she was drinking, her lively sense of humour was apparent. A favourite pastime was teasing her cousin Arlene Levasseur, who was six years younger. But Arlene soon learned to dish it right back. Once, when they were drinking together, Joyce passed out in the living-room. As a joke, Arlene put a Smurf doll in her arms and snapped a picture of her sprawled in a pose that was anything but ladylike. The photo was a source of great hilarity, and Joyce vowed to get back at Arlene.

As the baby in the family, Lester was doted on by his older sisters, who changed his diapers, and fed and played with him. Sherry became a "little mother," even though she was only six or seven years old. She'd sleep beside Lester's crib, waking to give him a bottle in the night. His good looks appeared early, as did his sense of humour, and he charmed everyone with his baby antics. As a toddler, Lester was always busy, always into something. Sherry nicknamed him "Bunny Rabbit" because of his two big front teeth, which seemed all the more conspicuous because of his small size. One day, Lester anxiously came to Sherry, pointed to his teeth, and asked: "Are these always going to be so big?" Trying not to laugh, Sherry replied: "Don't worry—when you get older, you'll grow into them!" Although she was unaware of it at the time, Sherry's baby name for Lester alluded to the creature known in Ojibwa legends as the powerful trickster–transformer—the "big rabbit" or "great hare." Lester soon acquired another nickname as well. Because of his father, Norman's, heritage, he was called "Mashkgiigo," which means "Cree" in Saulteaux. The nickname stuck, even though Norman's greatest impact on his son's life was his almost complete absence.

While living at Sandy Bay during Lester's early years, Joyce and her four children stayed with relatives—sometimes her former husband's parents and sometimes her own. Welcoming five extra mouths to an already overcrowded household couldn't have been easy for her family. The noise and chaos caused tempers to flare at times. And Joyce's ragtag brood often felt they bore the brunt of their relatives' frustration. Lester's sister Nancy was scared much of the time. Sometimes her grandfather McIvor got drunk and chased them out of the house. He seemed unaware of their fright and unconcerned when they ended up wandering barefoot outside in sub-zero winter temperatures.

Food was often scarce as well. And when Joyce wasn't around, her children were on their own. Often, the only way Nancy could ease the gnawing in her stomach was to go outside and eat mudpies and weeds from the field. Or she and her siblings would steal frozen french fries from the freezer and eat them raw. Nancy had learned there was no point begging for food from relatives. On too many occasions she'd watched wide-eyed as adults opened cans of food for their own children while she went hungry. "We were tortured in a way," Nancy says. "That's why I'm so fat now. I ate to fill up my stomach."

Sometimes Joyce's male companions lashed out at her children. Beatings with pussy-willow branches, belt buckles, and broom handles left angry purple bruises on their bodies. As a child, Nancy would squeeze her small bottom tightly as her older sister Sherry had taught her, trying to dull the pain of the blows. She and her siblings would be kept home from school for days until the welts disappeared. Other times, they'd sit at the kitchen table with bowls of soup, peering hungrily at one of Joyce's boyfriends as he enjoyed a substantial dinner of meat and potatoes. When a piece of apple pie went missing, Nancy was accused of taking it. As punishment, she was forced to sit down and eat the entire pie, until she felt sick to her stomach. Then there were the all-night drinking parties, when the children lay awake, hoping their mom would be okay. Once, one of her boyfriends smashed a beer bottle over Joyce's head, leaving a deep gash. On other occasions, he pounded her with his fists, leaving her bruised and battered. Or he tried to choke her when he was drunk. Once he threatened her with a gun. His beatings may also have caused a miscarriage and stillbirth Joyce suffered. A few years later, another partner terrorized Joyce by dragging her into the bushes and thrashing her with his belt. Joyce told Sherry that she'd been afraid he was going to kill her. She'd escaped by convincing her boyfriend that he'd be charged if she disappeared, because she'd last been seen with him. For Sherry, it wasn't hard to understand where her mother had learned to endure such abuse. Although Joyce rarely talked about her childhood, Sherry knew her mother had suffered as a result of her stepfather's alcoholic rages. Sherry suspected her mother had become a target because she was not Alex's natural child.

The soul-destroying tentacles of sexual abuse had also gripped several generations of Joyce's extended clan by that time. Among Joyce's kin, as well as those she married into, intergenerational abuse had secretly warped intimate relationships, turning family life inside out and upside down. The abnormal became normal. What should have been a place of refuge became an emotional minefield. It's not clear exactly what happened to Joyce. She rarely spoke about the deep sorrows she harboured. Friends say she confided she'd been molested as a girl by a male relative. When she tried to tell her parents, they apparently refused to listen. Joyce's daughters also suspected their mother had been molested as a child. But the abuse did not stop with Joyce's generation. Eventually, most of her children were also to suffer deeply at the hands of abusers, both within and outside the family circle. It would be years before the truth began to emerge, and by then the damage had wreaked havoc on their lives. Through it all, her children never stopped longing for one thing: "I wanted a normal life," Nancy says. "That's all I ever wanted, a normal life."

However bleak life could be, Lester and his siblings were blessed with the remarkable resilience of children, romping and teasing and tussling their way through their early years. When Lester was a preschooler, his mother bought him a little red-and-white tricycle, which he loved to pedal at breakneck speeds around the house. Nancy would hop on the back, pushing with her foot until they were flying out of control and laughing uproariously. Inevitably, they'd crash and Lester would burst into tears. But he recovered quickly and they'd soon be at it again.

As Lester grew into boyhood, Joyce settled into a relationship with a new partner, and had two more children: a daughter, born in 1978, and a son two years later. Before their arrival, the family lived in what seemed to the children to be an enormous, two-storey brown house in the nearby town of Amaranth. It was so big that the children could play lengthy games of hide-and-seek, which had been impossible in the crowded houses they'd previously inhabited.

Lester admired his older brother, Cecil, who made him his first slingshot and taught him how to hit targets. Despite the seven-year gap in their ages, they enjoyed shooting cans together, or bird hunting or playing catch. But as he got older, Cecil was also drawn into some more risky ventures. He began doing drugs and joining other boys in break-ins on the reserve. Many years later, he'd look back and feel bad about the poor example he set for Lester. But as a teenager, what mattered most was the sense of belonging he discovered with his friends.

From an early age, Lester had a special affinity for the numerous stray dogs who roamed the reserve. One low whistle from Lester, and dogs would come running from all directions. A pack of six or seven dogs would usually trail him wherever he went. To ensure their loyalty, he'd sneak pork chops from the refrigerator and feed the luscious raw meat to them on the sly. It didn't seem to matter that he'd catch hell later for wasting the costly food on animals.

He also developed a reputation as a prankster, always dreaming up a new trick to play on friends and family. One day his oldest sister, Sherry, made bannock, a type of fried bread which is a staple among the Ojibwa people. She burnt the entire batch, and threw it in the garbage in frustration. But Lester was waiting in the wings. When her back was turned, he fished the blackened mess from the trash and nailed it to the wall, just before Sherry's boyfriend dropped in. Mortified, she ripped it down and tossed it back in the garbage, as Lester howled in delight.

By the fall of 1982, the family was embroiled in another crisis. Joyce's partner had been convicted of criminal negligence causing bodily harm and had been sentenced to four years in jail the previous year. Left alone again, Joyce sold her house and all her furniture in March 1982, leaving her children once more to depend on the goodwill of relatives for a roof over their heads. Adrift and drinking heavily, Joyce often seemed oblivious to her children's needs. They routinely missed school, and often had no possessions but the clothes on their back, the rest of their belongings having been lost in transit.

Meanwhile, child-welfare workers at the Sandy Bay branch of the newly established Dakota Ojibway Child and Family Services (DOCFS) were about to have their first official contact with Joyce's family. The referral came from the nursing station in mid-September 1982. A community health worker reported that eleven-year-old Nancy had run away from the home of her McIvor grandparents. Scared and confused, Nancy said she was being molested by three teenage boys. That same day, a DOCFS worker took Nancy to the Amaranth RCMP to give a statement, and then placed the girl in foster care with an aunt. But by evening, the RCMP had already closed the investigation. The police had decided there was insufficient evidence, although they noted her allegations had not been disproved.

Two days later, Joyce flagged down a DOCFS worker on the road and begged her to take the rest of her children into care. Her stepfather, furious about Nancy's allegations, had thrown the rest of her children out of the house. DOCFS immediately apprehended Sherry, Lester, and the two youngest children and put them in foster homes on the reserve. Eight-year-old Lester was sent to live with his great-uncle Arthur Roulette and great-aunt Virginia. But soon, Joyce, at loose ends with her partner in jail, moved in with one of the foster families, disrupting their efforts to care for her children. She also began to baulk at the agency's plan to seek a one-year guardianship order on her children. Although she seemed to realize her drinking was creating chaos in their lives, she told a child-welfare worker she feared her kids would be too lonely in foster care. Instead, Joyce tried to devise a plan to keep her family together, promising to rent a house in Portage la Prairie, attend Alcoholics Anonymous, and get job training. No sooner had she vowed to turn over a new leaf than she went on an all-night drinking binge.

By the time Nancy reached out for help, she was an extremely anxious, dishevelled child. A medical doctor who examined her observed that the little girl spoke in a monotone when describing the abuse, drinking, and sniffing that was tearing her family apart. She told the doctor she didn't know how to protect herself from the three teenagers, who had threatened to hurt her if she reported them. The doctor wrote a letter to DOCFS, saying he couldn't be certain whether or not Nancy had been sexually abused. But he pointed out that she was very depressed and no doubt living in an abusive environment. After investigating Nancy's allegations, DOCFS workers filed a report with the province's child-abuse registry, saying their probe had been inconclusive. For Nancy, the whole experience deepened her feelings of betrayal: she had shared her secret with adults and they had not believed her.

While in foster care, fourteen-year-old Sherry spent a lot of time worrying about what was to become of herself and her siblings. By necessity, the teenager had become a surrogate parent to her younger sisters and brothers, and even looked after Joyce at times. At home, she did endless laundry, cooked meals, swept floors, washed dishes, made beds, and looked after the younger children. She often felt like the scapegoat, the one everyone dumped on. Still, she felt responsible for her family and dreaded ending up back in care if their mother resumed drinking when they were sent back to live with her in Portage la Prairie. Even worse, she feared they would be separated and sent to different foster homes, she told a DOCFS worker. Still, Sherry also longed to have a teenager's life and resented being saddled with raising her younger siblings. Displaying a remarkable maturity for her age, she laid down the following poignant conditions for their return to Joyce: to be well fed, well clothed and cared for as they were in foster care; to have a permanent residence; to go to school; and to have their mother at home instead of carousing with boyfriends. Sherry even wrote to a judge, pleading that her mother be sent to an alcohol treatment centre.

Just before Christmas 1982, four months after being apprehended, the children were returned to Joyce, who, along with her boyfriend, had moved into a furnished house forty kilometres south of Sandy Bay. Although DOCFS had been granted a six-month order of guardianship on the children, workers had agreed to send them back if Joyce found a place to live. In desperation, Joyce rented the only place she could find, a cramped two-bedroom bungalow on the edge of a farmer's field beside the highway. Between band welfare payments and family allowances, Joyce had a meagre $1,000 a month to feed, clothe, and house herself and her six children. But the isolation of living so far from Sandy Bay was too much for them, and they soon moved back to the reserve.

No sooner had child-welfare officials reunited Joyce with her children than a crisis erupted with her fourth child, nine-year-old Annette, who had been raised since infancy by her guardians. During a visit, Annette told her mother she had been sexually abused on several occasions by two teenage boys while her foster parents were away at bingo. Annette also complained that her guardians had used harsh physical discipline on her. Alarmed, Joyce took her daughter to the nearest hospital in the town of Gladstone on a Friday evening in late January 1983. The doctor on duty performed a cursory physical exam, forgoing an internal because he decided it wasn't necessary for such a young girl. Then the doctor informed the RCMP he could find no evidence of sexual abuse. Unsure of what to do next, Joyce took Annette home for the weekend.

By Sunday, Annette's irate foster father had come to retrieve the girl. As soon as he left with Annette, Joyce called the Amaranth RCMP, pleading for help. The police responded by removing Annette from her guardians and taking her back to Joyce. Furious, the child's foster father contacted DOCFS and demanded her return. He accused Joyce of helping Annette fabricate the abuse allegations and threatened legal action. When DOCFS workers talked to Annette after the chaotic weekend, she was subdued, insisting that she remain with her mother. She said she liked her guardians but not some of the other people who frequented their home. Child-welfare workers agreed to let Annette live with Joyce temporarily and filed a report on her alleged abusers with the province's abuse registry. A few months later, Annette's guardians filed legal documents in an effort to adopt her and, by the end of the year, had regained custody.

Despite high hopes for a more stable family life, Nancy continued to have problems after she returned home. By spring, Nancy was once again placed in foster care with an aunt after the girl became so despondent that she talked about suicide. Nancy told a DOCFS worker that she felt scapegoated by all the demands at home, from babysitting her younger siblings to household chores. On a more hopeful note, the worker observed that Joyce was making progress and attending a local AA program. Mother–daughter counselling sessions were set up to try to sort out their conflicts and, within a few weeks, Nancy moved home again.

Meanwhile, nine-year-old Lester escaped his turbulent home life by hanging out with a group of older boys who sniffed and drank and did break-ins on the reserve. Small and lithe, Lester had a talent for wriggling through half-open windows and other tight spaces that his older friends could not manage. By October 1983, the Amaranth RCMP had received several complaints about vandalism and thefts at Sandy Bay. On two separate occasions, trailers belonging to construction workers building the new school had been ransacked, and liquor and food stolen. Police began questioning a number of youths, and eventually ended up at Lester's door. Under duress, he confessed to doing the break-ins along with two other boys, aged fifteen and sixteen. Joyce couldn't be located, so police promised to return to take a statement from Lester the next day.

Within a week, three more break-ins in the community were reported to police. The thieves had lifted a long list of items, from jackets to tools, to liquor. Once again, police questioned Lester, who admitted to two of the three break-ins. But his partners-in-crime blamed Lester for being the ringleader and led police to a cache of some of the stolen loot near the boy's home. The RCMP officers went back and confronted Lester, who gave them several more versions of events. It wasn't until Sherry gently intervened that he admitted to the thefts. Exasperated, RCMP officers wrote in their report that the mischievous youngster had obviously enjoyed toying with them. Lester's two teenaged friends were charged, but he was too young to face any legal consequences.

The next month, DOCFS workers were asked to investigate rumours that Nancy, now twelve, was being sexually abused. This time the agency sent Nancy and two of her sisters, Sherry, fifteen, and Annette, ten, to specialists at the Child Protection Centre, a branch of the Children's Hospital in Winnipeg, for a thorough assessment in December 1983. Doctors who examined the girls found that all three had been sexually active, although the children were reluctant to reveal many details. However, a few days later, all three sisters gave detailed statements to the Amaranth RCMP. Nancy graphically described a litany of abuse by several teenage boys, including being jumped in the bushes and raped at knife-point in her own home. She told police she'd be willing to testify in court about the incidents. Nancy also admitted she'd accepted money from one youth who molested her. After enduring his fondling, she'd used the cash to buy candy.

Sherry told the RCMP she'd been raped by two older teenagers on the reserve, although she insisted she'd be too afraid to testify. One boy had attacked her in her bedroom while her unsuspecting younger sisters sat in the next room. Instead of screaming for help, she'd stifled her panic to avoid scaring her sisters. Meanwhile, Annette told police she'd been raped by an older boy. Unsure of how to handle the disturbing information, DOCFS officials notified members of the local child-welfare committee at Sandy Bay, as well as other band officials, and asked to meet with them in late December to discuss the matter. There's no indication in DOCFS records that the meeting ever took place.

The next summer, while the family was living in Winnipeg, another child-welfare agency removed Nancy from her mother for a short time. The Winnipeg agency intervened after Nancy again complained of being sexually and physically abused. It's not clear what, if anything, was done to investigate her allegations. During the same month, her sister Annette ran away from her guardians' home at Sandy Bay, and also complained of sexual abuse. Annette was sent to a foster home on the reserve, and her accusations were investigated by Amaranth RCMP. But when questioned by police, Annette recanted, saying she'd made up the incidents because she was unhappy at home. Police closed her file in August 1984. But an RCMP report to DOCFS contained this disturbing warning:

> A point that did turn up during the investigation and which was confirmed by several witnesses is the fact that several young children on the reserve are freely engaging in sexual activity on a voluntary basis. The problem is widespread and many children are involved; neither the motive nor the reason could be discovered. Observations indicate that this has been occurring for many years with no signs of recession.
>
> Because it is not apparent that the adults are aware of this, a suggestion is being made that your department implement some sort of public awareness/education program in order to alert the people on the reserve of the possible complication of "free sexual activity." It is quite possible the intensity of this problem is not known to the parents and adults; therefore, it might be well [worth] the time and effort to try and curb the situation before serious problems arise.

It would be four years before a concerted, but unsuccessful, effort was made by a DOCFS worker to address the rampant sexual abuse at Sandy Bay, and an additional four years before the full extent of the problem became public.

Suspicions that both Nancy and Annette were still being sexually abused on the reserve led a DOCFS worker to reapprehend both of them in early October 1984. The two girls were furious about being snatched from school and sent to a Brandon foster home without even a chance to say goodbye to their families or pack any belongings. Two weeks later, child-welfare workers removed the bewildered, anxious girls from that home after marital problems erupted between their foster parents. This time, the girls were sent to an emergency receiving home in Virden. But by the end of the month, they were transferred again, to another foster home in Brandon. Worried almost to the point of being physically ill, thirteen-year-old Nancy insisted she be sent home to look after her mother and younger sister and her brothers. Annette seemed more detached and sought attention, especially physical reassurance, from any adult who would respond. While the sisters didn't appear to be close, one DOCFS worker noticed during a visit to their foster home that they giggled, and joked constantly in Saulteaux.

But the girls' boisterous spirits soon annoyed their foster parents, who weren't used to older children and who couldn't cope with the children's refusal to speak English. The girls were barely keeping up in school, with Nancy functioning at an academic level four years below that of a normal Grade 7 student. At first, Nancy didn't mind living in Brandon, because their foster parents let them smoke cigarettes and do just about anything. However, the novelty soon wore off, and she and Annette decided to pack their bags and head back to Sandy Bay. But before they even slipped out the front door, the would-be runaways were caught. After only three weeks in that foster home, the agency decided to move them again.

DOCFS was under pressure from the girls' relatives to send them to separate foster homes. Both sets of guardians feared the girls were a bad influence on each other. Annette, who had been expelled from school in Brandon, was shuttled among three more foster homes over the next month. Nancy was moved twice, and eventually ended up in the same foster home as Annette at the Long Plain reserve. But as outsiders in the community, both girls complained bitterly about being teased and harassed at school by other students.

By February 1985, Nancy had been sent back home to live with Joyce, although that arrangement didn't last long. When Nancy complained again about being molested, she was sent from an emergency foster home on the reserve to a locked-care facility in Winnipeg, Seven Oaks Centre for Youth. Most teenagers who ended up at the institution, a kind of jail for troubled kids, chafed at the centre's restrictive setting. Strangely enough, Nancy remembered it as a haven of security: "I felt safe," she says. "I liked it there. That's where I'd rather be than anywhere else because you feel safe. All these people are protecting you. You have to do your chores, but that was okay."

After three peaceful weeks, she was sent to a foster home on yet another reserve, and then back to Joyce. Following a round of meetings among DOCFS workers, the Sandy Bay chief and council, and Nancy's relatives, the agency decided to close her case in May 1985. The Crown attorney had decided not to charge anyone on the basis of the girl's sexual-abuse allegations. A memo in her child-welfare file declared she was no longer in need of protection. Just over a year later, in September 1986, Nancy, who had just turned fifteen years old, gave birth to her first child, a son.

Meanwhile, Sherry had begun to rebel against all the demands at home. She began to drink and stay out late at parties. Soon she met a man who was interested in her. Although the seventeen-year-old Sherry had hoped to finish school and "make something of herself," her mother had other ideas. Joyce pressured the reluctant Sherry into living with her boyfriend. As an adult, Sherry would look back and resent being forced into a common-law relationship she wasn't ready for.

There's little evidence of what was happening to Lester during Nancy and Annette's dizzying array of placements in 1984 and 1985. But the turmoil in the boy's life was no doubt taking its toll. His grandmother Adele McIvor recalled one troubling incident when the boy was about ten years old. Lester came to her one day, angry and upset, and announced he was going to kill himself. Upon questioning her grandson, she discovered he was carrying two bullets, which she quickly confiscated.

Complaints from the Sandy Bay school about Lester's absenteeism and disruptive behaviour became more pointed during the winter and spring of 1986. Teachers told child-welfare workers that the boy was often high on sniff or alcohol, fell asleep during class, and pushed and shoved other students. At home, Joyce was also having more trouble coping with him. When Lester was caught breaking windows at the school in late April, she suggested the agency send him away for a month to teach him a lesson. On another day he showed up drunk, and looking for a fight, at the DOTC police office, where he spat in the face of an officer. The officer decided to take him to his grandfather McIvor's home. But when the officer tried to drop Lester off, Alex refused to let the boy come in, saying he couldn't control him. Instead, the officer had no choice but to take Lester back to the Amaranth RCMP station and lock him up until he was sober. Yet although Lester was outwardly belligerent, his sister Sherry knew there was a frightened little boy inside. Once, after the police questioned Lester at their home, she had to rock him in her arms to calm his anguished sobs.

Late one summer evening, Lester, now twelve, came stumbling home from the neighbours'. When his mother questioned him about where he'd been, an argument broke out. He admitted he'd been drinking beer and popping little white pills. Frightened, Joyce insisted on taking him to the emergency room in Portage la Prairie, a ninety-minute drive south. She arrived at 2:00 A.M., a hostile Lester in tow. The boy smelled of booze and could barely string a sentence together. But by morning he'd sobered up and was sent home with his mother.

Lester's problems at school worsened that fall. He skipped half his classes and was caught sniffing cleaning fluid in the school. After a series of break-ins at the school, Lester was once more a prime suspect. Worried school officials sent frequent memos to child-welfare workers, urging them to get the boy help. One day he mentioned to the principal that no one was looking after him and he stayed at different places on the reserve. The principal promptly reported the conversation to

DOCFS. Lester was in desperate need of treatment not available at Sandy Bay.

By November, Lester's grandfather Alex had also contacted child-welfare workers, complaining that his grandson was out of control. Early that morning, Lester had played an annoying prank on him. At 1:00 A.M., Alex had been awakened by a Sandy Bay taxi driver pounding on his door. The taxi driver had received an emergency call, saying Alex was very ill and needed to be driven to hospital. Alex told a child-welfare worker he suspected Lester was trying to get even for Alex's having chased his grandson away the previous day. When Lester had come to his door begging for bannock to eat, Alex had ordered him to go home to Joyce.

When the child-welfare worker went to talk to Joyce after the incident, Lester's mother again admitted she couldn't handle her son and said she'd be relieved if he was taken off her hands for a while. If the worker offered her any specific options, there's no record of it. Four months later, in March 1987, an increasingly desperate Joyce called the agency, again demanding help. Lester had been panhandling to buy gasoline to sniff. He'd also been expelled from school after turning in a stolen master key to the building. Still, nothing was done until later that month, when Lester wandered home at 4:00 A.M., drunk and reeking of gasoline. Joyce scolded Lester, who threatened to burn the house down by heating up a grease-filled pan on the stove. Joyce called the police, and DOCFS finally stepped in. An agency worker apprehended the boy and sent him to the Seven Oaks Centre for Youth in Winnipeg, the locked-care facility where Nancy had stayed two years earlier. But for Lester, the institution turned out to be anything but a safe haven. Instead, the downward spiral of Lester's last year had begun.

CHAPTER FOUR

BROKEN PROMISES

"Dogs are forgiving. Like, they could be trusted not to turn
their backs on you."

—Lester to Angela Eastman

Subdued and close to tears, Lester forced himself to answer the routine
but embarrassing questions when he arrived at the Seven Oaks Centre
for Youth in Winnipeg. Clad in jeans, a t-shirt, and black-and-silver
runners, twelve-year-old Lester hesitated often and rarely looked up
during the admission interview. Sexually active? No. Drink alcohol or
sniff solvents? Occasionally. Weight? Ninety-eight pounds. Height? Five
feet. Lester didn't like the look of the place. After he had roamed at
will, the centre's locked doors and faint smell of disinfectant reminded
him of a cage.

Lester lay low for the first couple of days, sizing up the place. But
he soon became restless. Bored with playing volleyball, cards, or pool
all day, Lester teamed up with another boy he'd known on the outside
to stir up some excitement. On his third morning at the centre, he
caused an uproar by yanking the shower curtain open on a group of

boys. Then he tried to intimidate another teenager who refused him a drag on his cigarette. The following day, suspicious staff accused Lester of plotting an escape, along with another resident. As punishment for his insolence, staff insisted that Lester change into sweat pants for a few hours and remain in his room for a "time-out." Although Lester was publicly nonchalant about the penalty, a worker later found him sobbing in his room. Lester refused to talk about what was wrong.

The environment at Seven Oaks had little to do with providing treatment for troubled kids. The centre was used as a holding facility for children from around the province who were out of control and deemed a danger to themselves or others—a kind of unofficial jail for kids who couldn't be charged with criminal offences. Some child-care workers had the training and experience needed to cope with the residents, who were some of the most disturbed youth in the child-welfare system, but others did not. Chronic burn-out plagued workers as they tried to maintain around-the-clock control of several dozen restless teenagers at close quarters.

Daily records kept by staff during Lester's first admission in April 1987 revealed an alarming lack of understanding about disturbed children. Descriptions of Lester's behaviour—"likeable but sneaky" or "minding his p's and q's"—showed little insight into the boy. A couple of days after he arrived, an entry written by a male worker reflected the outright callousness of some staff:

> April 5: Lester has had a fair day although he likes to test limits. Was out for fresh air and tryed [sic] climbing the fence. Didn't know that it wasn't allowed. Nice try kid. Was informed that if he should try it again I would break both his little legs.

An entry two days later by the same staff member reads:

> April 7: Lester a lot better around the bathroom. But is starting to flap his gums more and more. A lot of comments under his breath. But I couldn't make out what he was saying so I couldn't nail him.

A week later, it was obvious that the power struggle was escalating:

> April 14: Lester pushing his luck to the limit. Lots of dirty looks and remarks. Was T.O.ed [given time out] from 12:15 P.M. to 1:15 P.M. for wandering the halls. Then on our way down for last class I was only three feet behind him and he tryed [sic] hiding around the dining room. Tomorrow he cannot leave this cottage unless he has a staff by the hand. Also, he eats up in his room tonight because he was throwing food during lunch. I'm sure that we are now just seeing the real Lester and he's going to give us a run for our money. Any more garbage from him today and it is eight hours R.C. [room confinement]. No more warnings. He knowes [sic] this."

After two weeks, Lester was granted a weekend pass to Sandy Bay. He could hardly wait to go home after phoning his mother almost every night from Seven Oaks. But when he returned from the visit three days later, he was dishevelled and exhausted, and workers noticed his right hand was swollen. Lester's only explanation was that he'd been injured during a fight at home. Meanwhile, tensions continued to build between Lester and some staff and residents. A fight broke out in the gymnasium's equipment room when another boy teased Lester about his fascination with girls. In a flash, Lester jumped the resident and slugged him. As one staff member observed, Lester loved to rib others but had a short fuse if the tables were turned. After being confined to his room for eight hours, Lester was allowed out, and promptly got into an argument with another boy. Staff once again sent Lester, seething with indignation, back to his room. But when a female child-care worker checked on him later, he was in tears. Spurred on by her sympathetic questions, he shared some of his family woes, including several embellishments of the truth. He told the unsuspecting worker that his mother was dying and that he'd lost several brothers and sisters as a young boy. The one part of his story he didn't exaggerate had to do with Norman Anderson: Lester told her his natural father drank and took drugs all the time, and that he "hated him."

His last major clash with staff happened a few days before his re-lease. After an argument with another resident, Lester was ordered to his room. When he refused to go, a male worker grabbed the boy and forcibly dragged him there, with Lester fighting, spitting, and scream-ing. As Lester continued to hurl insults at staff, they took his clothes away, stripped his room of anything he could use as a weapon, and left him to fume. After the heated confrontation, a worker naïvely sug-gested in the staff logbook that the following punishment might be ef-fective: "Maybe Lester could write lines 'I must not threaten people or fight' for something to do and think about."

After Lester had spent a month at Seven Oaks, his DOCFS worker abruptly decided to send him home, despite earlier plans to refer him to a group home. Excited about being released, Lester packed his few belongings on the morning of May 1 and waited for his mother to pick him up. When Joyce hadn't arrived by late afternoon, he tried his best to rationalize the delay. But by evening, he could no longer mask his disappointment and hid in his room. Just before midnight, Joyce sud-denly appeared and signed her son out.

As was increasingly the pattern for Joyce's children, Lester's home-coming was short-lived. He no sooner arrived back at Sandy Bay when he began sniffing gasoline, plastic cement, and anything else he and his friends could find. One night, two weeks after his return, he sniffed up and wandered aimlessly into the bush. When Joyce realized he was gone, she went after him and found her son passed out in a crumpled heap. She roused him and somehow got him back to the house, where Lester cried uncontrollably and talked of killing himself. Once again, realizing she couldn't handle her son, she turned to DOCFS for help. This time, the agency sent the boy to the Brandon Mental Health Centre (BMHC) for an assessment. A social worker at the BMHC wrote in Lester's file that she believed it was no coincidence Joyce had "fallen off the wagon" about the time her son began acting up.

Joyce went along when DOTC police escorted Lester to the BMHC. Still hung over from the sniffing episode, Lester was hostile when he arrived, his speech slurred. He tried to convince them this was the first time he'd abused solvents. In the next breath, he boasted he could down a dozen beers in a row. After telling a psychologist he wouldn't answer her "stupid" questions, Lester demanded to be released. But when staff made it clear that wasn't going to happen, his defiance fizzled and he burst into tears. Over the next week at the BMHC, his moods evened out, but he continued to tell anyone who'd listen that he wasn't "crazy" and had no reason to be there. Lester no doubt felt humiliated about being sent to the institution locals had nicknamed "The Mental." He phoned Joyce every day, pressuring her to rescue him.

As he had done at Seven Oaks, Lester delighted in testing the rules. But BMHC staff seemed to have more insight into his attention-seeking. A treatment team made up of a psychiatrist, social worker, and nurses concluded the obvious: this was a lonely, angry child from a chaotic family who escaped his unhappiness by abusing solvents and alcohol. Blood tests taken when Lester was admitted revealed elevated lead levels, leaving no doubt he had been sniffing heavily. Once he was treated for substance abuse, the staff recommended he be placed in a stable foster home while counsellors worked with the boy and his family. Without intensive therapy, they predicted, Lester would inevitably deteriorate. He'd also tested positive for exposure to tuberculosis and needed follow-up medical care. But the next day, May 22, Joyce and the DOCFS worker from Sandy Bay arrived at the institution and signed Lester out against medical advice.

This time Lester lasted less than two weeks at home before being picked up by DOTC police, along with another boy, for sniffing and vandalism. Two days before his thirteenth birthday, Lester was back in Seven Oaks, along with his partner in crime. Familiar now with the routine, he settled in quickly, spending most of his time with his friend. Every night he called Joyce, begging to come home, until, in frustration, she refused to talk to him. A few days later, his mother failed to show up for a meeting at the centre to discuss plans for his discharge. The DOCFS worker who was supposed to give her a ride to Winnipeg had not appeared. But staff felt that Joyce was avoiding them, because she'd told Lester he was welcome at home, while giving the opposite message to DOCFS workers.

When Lester discovered that plans were in the works to place him in a group home on the Sioux Valley reserve west of Brandon, he was furious. He vowed to run away at the first opportunity. Then he phoned his mother and threatened to kill himself if he was sent there. If Joyce didn't want him, he begged her to ask his great-aunt Virginia Roulette—who had fostered him at a younger age—to take him in. Joyce relented in the face of his frantic pleas, and eventually promised he could come home. But this time she would have to go to court to regain custody, because DOCFS had filed for temporary guardianship.

Increasingly despondent, Lester approached a Seven Oaks staff member one evening to talk. Although he rarely volunteered anything about himself, this time was different. He told her he was haunted by the suicide of his friend Harry Roulette Jr. about six months earlier at Sandy Bay. Just seventeen, Harry had put a gun to his chin and pulled the trigger. Now Harry came to Lester in dreams, urging his friend to join him. What scared Lester was that there were times when he couldn't think of any reason not to. He felt his life was going "nowhere," just like Harry's had. Concerned, the worker alerted other staff and told them to keep a closer eye on the boy.

Meanwhile, Seven Oaks staff became increasingly suspicious that Lester and several other boys were masterminding an escape. Lester's initial compliance had worn thin. He'd twice been caught half-heartedly trying to scale the fence in the yard. Staff also noticed he was more and more edgy. Then, just before bedtime one evening, Lester and his three co-conspirators saw their chance. They kicked open a door while a staff member was distracted, and ran into the darkness. But within twenty-four hours, Lester and another boy phoned to say they wanted to return. They'd spent all their money at the Red River Exhibition and were tired and hungry. The next day, a worker noticed the two boys taunting each other with sexually explicit comments. She pulled Lester aside and soon discovered their adventure had had a darker side. While staying at a friend's place in Winnipeg, Lester had wandered outside and seen one of his friends raping another boy. Frightened, he'd convinced the boy who had been assaulted to return to Seven Oaks with him rather than risking another night on the streets. He also told the worker he was worried his friend might have AIDS. But when the worker tried to talk with the victim of the attack, the boy denied anything had happened. Later, standing outside the bathroom door, she overheard him angrily chastising Lester.

"You told," the boy said, as they brushed their teeth. "Why did you? You've got a big mouth."

"I was scared," Lester replied.

"Fuck you," the other boy said.

The next morning, after almost three weeks at Seven Oaks, Lester was picked up by a DOCFS worker and driven three hours west of Winnipeg to the Sioux Valley group home.

How long Lester lasted before he bolted from Sioux Valley isn't clear. But his escape became the stuff of family legends. Sometime in July 1987, Alex McIvor was driving along a rural highway near Gladstone when he spotted a familiar figure pedalling along the side of the road. He slowed down and, to his astonishment, discovered it was his grandson Lester. Sweating in the summer heat, Lester explained that he and the boy he was with had sneaked out of the Sioux Valley group home, stolen bicycles, and set out on the more than 200-kilometre ride back to Sandy Bay. Alex picked up the exhausted boys, loaded their bikes in the back of his vehicle, and drove them the rest of the way home.

For the next few weeks, Lester roamed the reserve, wandering between the homes of his maternal grandparents and his mother. Joyce was drinking and in no shape to offer her son any guidance. Lester's grandfather Alex went out a few times late at night searching for the boy, who had slipped back into sniffing and drinking with his old gang. But he had little success. He also complained to DOCFS, Lester's legal guardian. But little was done, even when Lester was caught breaking into the school again. Although DOCFS staff discussed the boy's behaviour, no plans were made to reapprehend him. Workers seemed to have given up in light of the way Lester had sabotaged previous placements.

By the time Marion Glover took over as supervisor of DOCFS at Sandy Bay that September, Lester's reputation had preceded him. Although she'd never met the boy, who was still on the loose, she'd heard about him at staff meetings. A few days after she began her new job, the special-education teacher at Sandy Bay school called to report that Lester had burned himself with cigarettes and inflicted a superficial cut on one of his wrists. The teacher was worried because Lester seemed depressed. He offered to keep the boy in his office while

Marion sent someone over to pick him up. But while they talked on the phone, Lester darted out of the school. Concerned, Marion immediately asked DOTC police to find Lester and take him to the Brandon Mental Health Centre, where she'd meet them. Expecting an unruly, hard-bitten teenager—a "monster," according to stories she'd heard—Marion couldn't believe her eyes when she met Lester. The boy who greeted her was an unkempt but handsome child, small for his age, and obviously very scared. To Marion, he looked like a stray cat who had been dragged in off the street.

During his second admission at the Brandon Mental Health Centre, Lester again insisted he was just fine and had no reason to be there. He tried to convince them he hadn't sniffed for over a year and denied feeling suicidal. He claimed he'd slashed his wrist to win a five-dollar bet with two friends about who was the toughest. He explained that the cigarette burn had likely been inflicted after he passed out from drinking one night.

Lester adjusted quickly this time to the institutional routine, and was friendly and complacent for the first couple of weeks. But as his stay dragged on, he became bored and began stirring up trouble on the ward. When he'd arrived at the centre, Marion had hinted to staff that Lester might have been sexually abused. But she'd offered no specifics, and Lester denied it. The teenager did tell his psychiatrist that he was angry at his mother for ignoring him that summer. For the first time, he admitted he wasn't sure he wanted to return home. He said his mother had made things worse for him by letting kids who abused solvents hang around the house over the summer. When he showed his psychiatrist a collection of his drawings, the doctor could see the boy's frustration and obvious alienation reflected in the images. His psychiatrist also noted that Lester had promising artistic talent.

After almost a month, Marion suddenly announced to Lester's psychiatrist that she was signing the teenager out and placing him back at Sandy Bay in a foster home. His psychiatrist objected, saying the teenager wasn't ready to be released and would be better off in another community, where there'd be fewer temptations. The doctor was clearly annoyed at what she and other staff interpreted as Marion's attempts to undermine their treatment plans. On the other hand, Marion felt staff often ignored her suggestions. Besides, Lester had already agreed to move in with his relatives Arthur and Virginia Roulette. Since Joyce had recently moved to Winnipeg, Marion believed there'd be less chance of interference from her.

What didn't become clear until much later was that band officials, especially Cecil Desjarlais, who had the child-welfare portfolio, were pressuring Marion to return the teenager to the community. They told Marion that putting a child in a mental institution undermined the community's goal of keeping children close to home. Feeling caught in the middle and unsure of how to resolve the conflict, Marion resigned herself to finding the best possible foster home on the reserve. She arranged to have Arthur and Virginia's home licensed for foster care. As well, Lester agreed to abide by the rules by attending school and avoiding his old friends. On October 14, Marion signed the boy out of the BMHC against medical advice and drove him back to Sandy Bay.

For a few weeks, Lester seemed to be making progress. He was attending school and adjusting to his foster home. Lester admired his foster father, Arthur, and talked about following in his footsteps when he grew up. After school each day, he helped his foster mother, Virginia, vacuum the building to fulfil his court-ordered restitution for previous break-ins. But in the classroom, Lester was struggling to keep up with other Grade 7 students after missing so much school. A bright child with plenty of potential, he was still classified as "special needs" after testing several grades behind in most subjects. Lester compensated by attention-seeking antics, which regularly landed him in the vice-principal's office. However, Lester discovered he enjoyed his trips to visit Vice-principal Angela Eastman, a sensitive, warm woman who listened attentively to him. She suspected the boy sometimes deliberately stirred up trouble in order to visit her. "He was just an ordinary little kid," Angela says. "He used to get into mischief and he'd be sent to the office for his little shenanigans, more so than other children. But he wasn't bad. He was a very likeable little boy."

It was during one of these visits that Lester hesitantly revealed something that had happened over the summer. Sitting in a bright yellow chair, cosily wedged between Angela's desk and the filing cabinet, Lester casually asked how a person caught venereal disease. He had an itch in his crotch and was worried. She explained that VD came from having sex with someone who was infected but said Lester was too young to have that problem. That didn't seem to ease Lester's anxiety. Finally, he swore her to secrecy before revealing what was troubling him: he said Joe Desjarlais had tied him up with a belt and raped him. Shocked, Angela urged the boy to tell his social worker. She had no doubt he was telling the truth. Parents in the community regularly warned their children to stay away from Joe, whom they called the "bogeyman."

On another occasion, a teacher sent Lester to Angela's office after he pricked his hand repeatedly with a pin until he drew blood. Angela sat down with the boy and gently asked why he was hurting himself. But Lester was evasive, and instead began talking about the funeral of his seventeen-year-old friend Harry Roulette Jr., who had recently committed suicide. Then he startled her with a question she would never forget.

"Would you cry if I died?" Lester asked suddenly.

Unnerved, Angela told him not to talk like that, but he persisted.

"When I die, will you buy me flowers?" he wondered.

"Don't be silly, Lester—you're too young to die," Angela replied, and quickly changed the subject.

While Lester was in foster care with Arthur and Virginia, Marion visited regularly, usually eating lunch with them on Tuesdays and Thursdays. By now, she'd spent a lot of time with the teenager, who was beginning to open up. Although, as a supervisor, she didn't usually work directly with children, she'd made an exception in Lester's case. Her heart went out to the boy, who seemed so desperate for a normal family life. Marion invited him home with her occasionally on weekend visits. In the company of her three teenage sons, Lester seemed to thrive. He loved ice-skating with them on the pond or going to movies. As he began to trust her more, he also revealed his inner turmoil. After warning her to beware of Joe Desjarlais, Lester disclosed that Joe had tied him up with a belt and tried to rape him. But, contrary to what he'd told Angela, he insisted he'd gotten away. Suspecting otherwise, Marion took Lester to the Amaranth RCMP to give a statement. But when they got there, he clammed up and offered only vague information.

Looking back, others at Sandy Bay also suspected Joe was abusing Lester. One woman remembered seeing Joe grab Lester by the hair and try to drag him towards Joe's house. Fortunately, her older brother and Cecil Jr. were nearby. They chased Joe, knocked him down, and rescued Lester, who hid at her mother's house until he felt safe enough to leave.

Lester also complained to Marion about being molested by a male teacher at the school. The teacher had kept Lester after school one day. To the boy's surprise, the teacher then pulled pornographic magazines from his desk drawer and began showing them to the boy. When the man tried to stroke Lester's thigh, the boy fled in a panic. Alarmed at Lester's story, Marion made some calls and discovered that the teacher had had his professional certification revoked in British Columbia after being accused of sexually abusing children. She gave this information to school officials, who eventually fired him.

It isn't clear what shattered Lester's fragile equilibrium in late November 1987. Some say he was upset about a phone call from his mother, who was drinking again and had called to cancel a visit. Others say it was the death of his beloved dog, Sport, who was shot by a neighbour. The dog's killing was a wrenching loss for Lester, who counted on the steady companionship of his canine friends. "He'd always say, 'Like, even if I'm mad at my dogs, even if I kick them, they're always my friends,' Angela remembers. "'I'll call them and they'll come right away. They're not mad at me. It's just like, dogs are forgiving. Like, they could be trusted not to turn their backs on you.'"

Whether prompted by grief over Sport's death, an argument with his mother, or both, Lester flew off the handle one day, grabbed a rifle at his grandparents' home, and vanished into the bush. High on booze and sniff, he began firing shots to keep people away. Eventually, he wore himself out and returned the rifle to his grandfather. But a day later, he ran away from his foster home and appeared at his mother's door in Winnipeg. That annoyed Marion, who realized that her plans for the boy were unravelling. She ordered the DOCFS worker to retrieve the boy from his mother, and then decided it would be faster to do it herself. Marion drove directly to Winnipeg and knocked on Joyce's door. After exchanging some angry words with her, Marion drove Lester back to Sandy Bay.

To add to the confusion, members of the local child-welfare committee at Sandy Bay, primarily Cecil Desjarlais and Isaac Beaulieu, decided it was time to intervene. The committee, set up by DOCFS to advise child-welfare workers, believed that Marion was mishandling Lester's case. Behind the scenes, they'd had complaints from local child-welfare workers, who were increasingly resentful of Marion. The workers, who were all from Sandy Bay, said Marion often ordered them around, talked to them "like five-year-olds," and second-guessed their decisions. The local child-welfare committee decided to overrule Marion and send Lester back to live with his mother in Winnipeg. Marion objected, pointing out that DOCFS—as Lester's temporary guardian—not the local committee, had the final say on what happened. Marion also predicted Lester wouldn't last long with Joyce. Within less than a week, Joyce called Winnipeg police and asked them to pick up her son, who was drunk and out of control. The police took Lester to the Manitoba Youth Centre, and then to Seven Oaks.

During the same period, Marion was also embroiled in conflicts with the off-reserve DOCFS worker in Winnipeg, Danta Kunzman, over plans for Lester's sister Annette. Annette, now fourteen, had run away from her guardians' home and gone to see Joyce, who was visiting at Sandy Bay. The teenager told her mother that she'd been physically and sexually abused over the previous few months. Concerned, Joyce left for Winnipeg with her daughter and took her to a doctor. The doctor then notified Marion of the girl's allegations. As a result, Marion asked a Winnipeg child-welfare agency to apprehend Annette, convinced that Joyce wasn't any more capable of providing a safe environment. When Annette was placed in a Winnipeg emergency foster home, Danta Kunzman, who supervised DOCFS placements in the city, also got involved with the family. Danta met several times with Joyce and Annette. The girl was angrily insisting she be allowed to live with her mother. Without consulting Marion or reviewing the family's files, Danta promised to help Joyce regain custody of both Annette and Lester. Despite the family's turbulent history, Danta believed Joyce deserved another chance.

But back at Sandy Bay, Marion was under pressure to return Annette to her guardians' care. They had solicited help from their relative Harry

Desjarlais, who was chief of Sandy Bay at the time. At the very least, Annette's guardians demanded that she be moved out of Winnipeg. Marion agreed to explore the possibility of sending her to the Sioux Valley group home. But when Danta discovered what Marion was doing, she complained angrily in writing to the director of DOCFS. In her letter, she said Marion had interfered in her case, discredited Joyce, and tried to exclude the mother from being involved in plans for her children. Danta accused Marion of having a "callous" attitude towards the entire matter.

Over the next month, several staff meetings were called to resolve the tensions. The agency's lawyer complained that on one day alone he had received phone calls from two different DOCFS staff, giving him opposite instructions on the case. In the end, their only point of agreement was that Annette—and Lester—were caught in what Danta later described as a "tug of war" over control of the children. However, by late December, Danta's efforts to reunite Joyce with her children were irrelevant. Joyce had changed her mind again about pursuing custody of the two teenagers, saying she couldn't handle them. Annette, having recanted the abuse allegations by then, went back to live with her guardians at Sandy Bay.

Meanwhile, Lester's third stay at Seven Oaks was a mirror image of previous admissions, as he fluctuated between compliance and rebellion. A few days after his arrival in early December, Lester escaped out the gymnasium door and ran to a neighbouring house. There he phoned his mother, hoping she'd aid in his flight. But to his chagrin, Joyce told the neighbour to return him to Seven Oaks. When Lester got back, he was tearful and angry. A week later, staff intercepted Lester and two other boys as they attempted a late-night break from the centre. Going AWOL (absent without leave) had become a game to the bored teenagers. Soon Lester was spending plenty of time in his room as punishment for mouthing off at staff or pranks like using his toes to turn on the ward's shiny new television. When he wasn't confined to his room, Lester attended classes, strummed his guitar for hours, and plotted his next escape. About two weeks into his stay, he took off again, this time accompanied by another resident, and ran to his mother's home in Winnipeg's north end. It was three days before a Seven Oaks worker showed up to reclaim him.

On one of his break-outs that month, Lester appeared at the group home in Winnipeg where Annette was now living. The two of them decided to try their hand at shoplifting, and managed to steal clothes for their mother. Their first attempt was so successful that they made several more excursions to supply the unsuspecting Joyce with her favourite brand of tobacco. They explained their windfall by telling Joyce that Annette had earned extra cash at a part-time job. "We never stole for each other," Annette says. "Just for our mom."

At Christmas, Lester received a pass to spend a week with his mother in Winnipeg. After the visit, he returned to Seven Oaks with a black eye, swollen nose, and gash on his hand. At first, the only explanation the despondent teenager gave for the injuries was that he'd fallen on the stairs while fooling around. But during a conversation with a worker a few days later, he admitted the visit had been miserable. He'd been kept awake by late-night drinking parties at his mother's house. He insisted Joyce had not been drinking, but admitted that some of her guests frightened him. He'd also been beaten up several times but refused to say who'd hurt him. More depressed than ever, Lester conceded for the first time that living with his mother might not work. Then, on New Year's Day, Joyce called to say her ex–father-in-law Andrew Desjarlais had died. Staff gave Lester a pass to attend the wake at Sandy Bay. They never saw him again.

Early in January 1988, Joyce appeared at a custody hearing for Lester and Annette with a badly bruised eye. In court, the DOCFS lawyer noticed her shiner and wondered to himself whether she was being abused. But the hearing no sooner began than it was adjourned for a month. Joyce's lawyer told the judge his client was having second thoughts about pursuing custody.

Meanwhile, Lester, who had been placed in yet another foster home at Sandy Bay, began to disintegrate. His latest foster mother soon reached her wits' end as the teenager stayed out night after night, and returned smelling of booze and sniff. On January 21, DOTC police were called to pick up Lester, who was drunk and out of control. When they tried to put him in the cruiser, he fought like a wildcat, displaying remarkable strength, despite his small build. The police notified Marion, who asked them to drive the teenager to a doctor in Gladstone to authorize a compulsory admission to the Brandon Mental Health Centre. Without immediate treatment, Marion feared, Lester would end up at Seven Oaks again, a place she knew he hated. But while at the hospital in Gladstone, Lester dashed out a back door and disappeared into the bitterly cold, stormy winter afternoon. Afraid that Lester would freeze to death in the brutal weather, DOTC police asked the Portage la Prairie RCMP to bring their tracking dogs to help find the child. Just before dark, police located the frightened boy, huddled in an abandoned building. This time he offered no resistance when they put him in a police cruiser and drove him to the Brandon Mental Health Centre.

During the admission interview, Lester, reeking of alcohol, his speech slurred, fell asleep after telling a nurse he didn't know what the fuss was about. Eventually, he said he'd tried to escape from police because he was on probation and afraid that his behaviour would get him in trouble at an upcoming court appearance. During his first few days at the BMHC, staff insisted Lester wear pyjamas twenty-four hours a day to prevent another escape. He paced the ward like a nervous cat and phoned everyone, from Marion to his mother, demanding to be let out. Marion visited and tried to ease his anxiety. But on the first day that staff returned his clothes, Lester sneaked off the ward and dashed out into the sub-zero temperatures wearing only jeans, a t-shirt, and runners. A staff member gave chase, grabbed Lester as he sprinted across an icy field, and hauled the furious teenager back to the ward. Once inside, Lester burst into tears, saying another patient had reneged on a promise to throw his coat out the window as he fled. When his plan went awry, he realized he was in trouble but decided he had nothing to lose. All he wanted was to go home, he repeated over and over. He also wrote a poignant note to his mother around this time:

> Dear Mom, How are you? I was hooping [sic] if you could come and visit me for a while please. I'm sorry what I said to you on the telephone. I really love you very much. I love you guys more than any thing in the world mom, I really do mom. Marion Glover told me I have to stay in a foster home for six months and ... that I'll be going back with you. I

would really love to go back with you mom. Please phone
me. I love you all.

Over the next week, Lester gradually realized he wasn't going back
to Sandy Bay for a while and seemed resigned about moving into yet
another foster home. In early February, Marion arranged for him to
visit Angus and Lillian Starr, who lived just south of Brandon. The
couple, who were also from Sandy Bay, had agreed to take Lester into
their home as a foster child. The Starrs knew his family and seemed like
a good match for the boy. Angus, a former chief of the reserve, now
owned a motel in Brandon, and was active in sports leagues. When
Lester returned to the BMHC from the weekend visit, he told everyone he was excited about living with the Starr family. He'd had a great
time with them, tobogganing and cross-country skiing on their
acreage. Marion decided to go ahead with the placement and promised
to hire a tutor for Lester until he could be admitted to a special program for troubled teenagers in Brandon. On February 11, Lester was
released from the BMHC and moved into his new foster home, his
tenth official placement in less than a year. After so many rocky
months, Lester's life seemed to be levelling out. Now that he had a stable foster home and plenty of support, the future appeared brighter.
But despite Lester's outward acceptance of his new living situation, his
distraught phone calls to family members continued in the three weeks
before his death. Lester was obsessed with going home and vowed to
them that he'd find a way.

CHAPTER FIVE

BREAKING THE SILENCE

"... when I see something wrong, I persist in trying to correct
that problem, and sometimes that gets me into a lot of trouble."

—Joyce Wasicuna

The suicide of Lester Norman Desjarlais on March 6, 1988, went un-
noticed beyond his circle of family and friends and a few officials. The
sad reality was that the suicide rate among young people of Aboriginal
descent was ten times that of youth in the general population. The year
Lester died, twenty-six other Aboriginal youth under the age of
twenty-five killed themselves in Manitoba. The death of one more desperate teenager, even one in the care of a child-welfare agency, did not
warrant as much as a press release.

Yet three days after Lester's death, the fatal shooting of Aboriginal
leader J.J. Harper during a struggle with a Winnipeg policeman
grabbed headlines across the country. The death of Harper, director of
the Island Lake Tribal Council, sparked an outcry in the Native community. Public outrage grew when Winnipeg's police chief exonerated
the officer involved within a day. Harper's shooting rekindled demands

for a public inquiry into racism in Manitoba's justice system, coming as it did just months after the high-profile November 1987 trial of two men charged with the murder of Helen Betty Osborne in The Pas. Four white youths had been linked to the 1971 murder of Osborne, a Cree teenager. But it took sixteen years to bring two of the suspects to trial, and only one was convicted. Under increasing public pressure, Manitoba's NDP government ordered a judicial inquiry into the deaths of both Osborne and Harper in April 1988. Known as the Aboriginal Justice Inquiry (AJI), it was also charged with probing complaints of widespread, systemic discrimination against Aboriginals in the legal system. Over the next two years, the inquiry would travel to more than thirty-six Aboriginal communities and hear more than 1,200 presentations. Across the province, Native people came forward to tell their stories, fuelling a deep desire for change that would re-emerge during the inquest into Lester's death.

The final report of the AJI, authored by Associate Chief Justice Alvin Hamilton and Associate Chief Judge Murray Sinclair, identified a host of problems, ranging from the need for a separate Aboriginal justice system to the disproportionate number of Native youth who ended up in jail. Their report, released in August 1991, also warned that an epidemic of physical and sexual abuse was devastating the lives of Aboriginal women and children. Using surprisingly strong language, they chastised chiefs and band councils for ignoring the problem of domestic violence, calling their inaction "unconscionable." The commissioners had listened to abused women tell heartbreaking stories of being turned away when they sought help from band officials. Male-dominated Aboriginal governments had to examine their tendency to side with abusers in domestic disputes and start helping the real victims, the commissioners wrote. While most media coverage of the AJI report focused on its sweeping recommendations for reform of the justice system, the document also lent support to Aboriginal women's increasing demands for accountability from their leaders. Urban women had become especially vocal about what they called "double discrimination"—unfair treatment by both society at large and men within the Native community.

Women's second-class status in Native communities had been fostered by the sexual discrimination built into white laws over a century earlier. As far back as 1868, federal legislation revoked an Aboriginal woman's Indian status—and that of her children—if she married a white man. Yet a white woman could gain status by marrying an Aboriginal man. Under the Indian Act, Aboriginal women were also stripped of their right to vote in band elections, marginalizing their participation in political decisions. Yet, as the AJI report noted, Aboriginal women had traditionally held respected roles in the family, government, and spiritual ceremonies:

> In Aboriginal teachings, passed on through the oral histories of the Aboriginal people of this province from generation to generation, Aboriginal men and women were equal in power and each had autonomy within their personal lives.
>
> Women figured centrally in almost all Aboriginal creation legends. In Ojibway and Cree legends, it was a woman who came to earth through a hole in the sky to care for the earth. It was a woman, Nokomis (grandmother) who taught Original Man (Anishinabe, an Ojibway word meaning "human being") about the medicines of the earth and about technology. When a traditional Ojibway person prays, thanks is given and the pipe is raised in each of the four directions, then to Mother Earth as well as to grandfather, Mishomis, in the sky.

In 1951, the Indian Act was finally revised to give Aboriginal women the right to vote in band-council elections. By 1985, lobbying from Aboriginal women's groups had also forced the federal government to pass Bill C-31, reinstating their right to retain status, regardless of whom they married. But Bill C-31 became law only after Aboriginal women took their complaint of discrimination to the United Nations Human Rights Committee. To Canada's embarrassment, that committee declared it to be in violation of the International Covenant on Civil and Political Rights.

The month after the release of the AJI report—and a few weeks before the inquest into Lester's death was to begin—a Winnipeg-based group, the Aboriginal Women's Unity Coalition, grabbed the public spotlight. The coalition had rallied behind a mother's public battle to win custody of her children from her ex-husband, the chief of a southern Manitoba reserve. In desperation, the mother pitched a tent on the grounds of the Manitoba legislature and began a ten-day fast, alleging that the chief had used his political influence to prevent an Aboriginal child-welfare agency from investigating complaints that he'd physically abused their children. For several weeks, the dispute made headlines in Winnipeg, as the coalition of women's groups tried to convince the powerful Assembly of Manitoba Chiefs (AMC) to acknowledge the mother's concerns. Instead, AMC leader Phil Fontaine defended the chief and the agency embroiled in the controversy, insisting that the case had been properly handled. Fontaine's response only reinforced the coalition's complaint that he was biased in favour of protecting the male power structure rather than abuse victims. A series of court hearings eventually settled the custody dispute in favour of the father. But the entire episode was a public-relations disaster for Fontaine and the AMC.

When a series of articles in the *Winnipeg Free Press* in January 1992 raised concerns about political interference by band leaders in several suspicious child-death investigations, Fontaine again went to bat for the chiefs. He maintained that the claims amounted to a personal attack on all chiefs, as well as an ill-disguised effort by then Justice Minister Jim McCrae to undermine the push for Aboriginal self-government. Chief Louis Stevenson, an influential leader from the Peguis First Nation, went so far as to file a lawsuit against a member of one outspoken women's group. Stevenson claimed Kathy Mallett, spokeswoman of the Original Women's Network, had tarnished the reputations of all Manitoba chiefs by publicly suggesting that some leaders wielded their power like dictators. Although the Aboriginal Women's Unity Coalition denounced the lawsuit as an intimidation tactic, they were forced to raise money to hire a lawyer for Mallett, a single parent with few financial resources. A few months later, Stevenson quietly dropped the lawsuit. At the same time, Mallett and other members of the coalition were targeted with anonymous hate mail and vicious rumours because of their criticism of the chiefs' silence on domestic violence. Some of the backlash came from other Aboriginal women. During a late-March rally organized in support of the chiefs, women from a dozen Manitoba reserves denounced the coalition, saying the urban group didn't speak for them. They accused the coalition of fostering disunity and undermining public support for self-government. The demonstration had been organized by women from Stevenson's reserve and a lobby group allied with the AMC called the Indigenous Women's Collective.

It was against this tumultuous backdrop that several Aboriginal women would step forward at the inquest into Lester's suicide and challenge the status quo. Any minority community, especially one struggling to overcome burdens of poverty and racism, has an aversion to airing its "dirty laundry" in public. Only when efforts to resolve problems internally fail do those seeking change go public. Five women—Ellen Cook, Joyce Wasicuna, Ella McKay, Bev Flett, and Angela Eastman—would risk being shunned by their communities for speaking out at the inquest on behalf of Lester and other abused children. To get to know them is to understand why.

Making headlines was nothing new to Ellen Cook when she took the stand at Lester's inquest. Three years earlier, Cook, an elementary-school teacher, had attracted media attention while testifying at the AJI hearings at Chemawawin First Nation. There, Cook had risked speaking publicly about the backlash she'd suffered while trying to report a suspected child abuser.

On a frigid winter evening in 1994, the gregarious forty-eight-year-old mother of four sipped tea at the white kitchen table in her Winnipeg townhouse and reflected on her propensity for taking unpopular stands. The fact that she had no regrets was rooted in her convictions. Growing up as one of thirteen children in a close-knit Cree family, she learned a deep respect for traditional values, including children's right to be protected and loved. Her parents managed to mesh the teachings of the Anglican church they attended in their home community of Grand Rapids with traditional Indian cultural and spiritual beliefs. Although her parents had only eight years of education between them, they instilled in all their children a love of learning that would lead to successful, satisfying careers. Even more significantly, her parents nurtured a strong sense of identity in their children to shield them against the debilitating effects of racism.

As Ellen reminisced about her childhood, singer Leonard Cohen crooned on the stereo in the background and her teenage daughter Karen worked on homework across the table. A few streaks of grey peppered Ellen's long, thick, black hair as she leaned over a photograph of her first grandchild. She proudly pointed out the two-year-old child's strong resemblance to her. A comparison with another photo, of her own grandmother, showed that the likeness between generations was unmistakable.

Memories of her family are permeated by the same warmth now apparent between Ellen and her own children. Every summer, her family travelled from the mouth of the Saskatchewan River on the northwestern tip of Lake Winnipeg up through the sparkling rapids which gave her home community its name. The long, hot days were spent digging seneca root for sale to pharmaceutical companies, which used the herb in cold remedies and other medicines. The family gathered strawberries, high-bush cranberries, and other wild fruits, which their mother used to make jams and jellies for the winter months. Her father hunted moose, or fished, and dried the meat. Evenings, they camped with other families and sat around the fire as the elders told stories. Then Manitoba Hydro flooded the entire area to build a hydro-electric dam in the 1960s, destroying the cherished land of her ancestors. "It was heartbreaking for all of us to see," Ellen says. "But the memories are still with us."

During the rest of the year, Ellen was fortunate to attend a little log schoolhouse near her home instead of being sent away to residential school like the Status Indian children on the reserve. Ellen's great-grandfather, Edward Cook, had refused to sign the treaty when the reserve was established, freeing his descendants from the trauma of church-run boarding-schools. When the Indian agent arrived each autumn to herd the Status children onto the plane for residential school, Ellen watched neighbour children scream and cry and hide in the bush. Upon their return each summer, Ellen heard horror stories about their experiences. "The spirituality was vacuumed out of them at residential school," she says. "My own spiritual strength is what carries me through."

Her family regained their treaty status when Bill C-31 was introduced in 1985. Despite having had what some might have considered to be an inferior education at the local school, most of Ellen's brothers and sisters went on to university. Among her siblings, there are now three teachers, a restaurant owner, a nurse, an electrician, and a pilot. Ellen herself has a Bachelor of Education, with a German major, and speaks at least five other languages: French, Cree, Ojibwa, Arabic, and English.

With a limited income, Ellen's parents expected their children to pull their weight around the house. Children worked hard alongside adults, cutting firewood, hauling water, cooking, and cleaning. At supper, everyone sat down together to share a meal and talk about their day. Then her father often pulled out his guitar and sang his children to sleep. When Ellen eventually became a mother, she did the same with her children.

At age eighteen, Ellen left the protective fold of her family to get married. By the time her marriage broke up a few years later, she had four children to support and only a high-school education. Determined to earn a decent living for her young family, Ellen moved more than 400 kilometres south to Winnipeg, where she trained as a welder and worked shifts at a bus-manufacturing company. When she heard about a community-college training program up north, she decided to move again. Over the next few years she studied to become a nutritional adviser and then worked at the local school.

She also became enmeshed in an abusive relationship with a man that soon shattered her self-confidence and left her feeling trapped. When she arrived at work more than once with black eyes, her worried principal would pull her aside. "You can make more of yourself," he'd tell her. "Go to university, become a teacher." One night, her partner came home drunk at 3:00 A.M., demanding that she fry up some bacon and eggs. Sensing he was on the verge of exploding, she made an unsuccessful attempt to appease him. He responded by hurling the hot food at her. She finally fled to her sister's home in Brandon, taking her four kids and her ex-partner's little girl as well.

Soon after that, Ellen decided to take her former boss's advice. In 1981, she enrolled at the University of Manitoba. For the next four years, she juggled the almost overwhelming tasks of mothering five children, being a full-time student, and holding down a part-time job to supplement her meagre income of about $760 a month. But no matter how tight her budget, she always put aside enough money for their family ritual of stopping for milk and donuts on the way to church each Sunday. Finding time for her children was a priority, even if it often meant doing homework in the wee hours of the morning. To her credit, her grown son often says that, despite her hectic days as a university student, he doesn't remember her ever not being there.

What did cast a shadow over those years was her marriage to a student whom she met at university. Their initially close, loving relationship turned ugly soon after they married, and she suffered through three turbulent years. Once her husband obtained his landed-immigrant status, he walked out on the family in 1986. Ellen vowed not to marry again and, although she jokes about her bad luck with men, it was obviously a painful time: "I just felt that marriage wasn't a thing for me. I wanted to be independent ... You either end up with a white man, which is a cross-cultural marriage ... or a Native man who has a good possibility of being an alcoholic."

When she graduated from university in the spring of 1985, she was hired to teach elementary school at Garden Hill, a fly-in reserve in northeastern Manitoba. But she missed her family, and the next year she decided to accept a teaching job at the band-run school in Chemawawin First Nation, a Cree community also known as Easterville. Chemawawin was close to Grand Rapids and would allow more frequent visits to her ageing parents. Then, Ellen's daughter came home from school and announced that her fourteen-year-old classmate was having sex with a teacher's aide in the supply room of the gymnasium. Ellen's instinct was to report the man immediately. But she also knew it would be a touchy situation. Whoever reported the incident to officials would be putting his or her job in jeopardy.

Determined not to ignore the abuse, Ellen organized secret meetings with other teachers to discuss the dilemma. The man was already known to have a drinking problem and was rumoured to have preyed sexually on another student a few months earlier. Everyone agreed something had to be done to protect other children. But no one was eager to face the personal consequences. In the end, Ellen volunteered to take their suspicions to the principal. She knew she was well liked in the community. She'd organized a drop-in centre for kids and played the organ in the local church on Sundays. While she had no illusions about the price she might pay, she hoped justice would prevail.

Instead of investigating her allegations, the principal called her in and warned Ellen he'd fire her if she didn't retract her complaints and apologize. A short, solidly built woman with a penetrating gaze, Ellen looked him in the eye and refused to comply on both counts. Although the other teachers involved in the complaint offered to come forward, she decided that one "scapegoat" was enough. Who'd watch out for the kids if they all got fired? Besides, Ellen, who was a single parent, no longer wanted her daughters attending the school. To her, it was a clear case of band officials using their power to cover up child abuse. After the abuse came to light, residents circulated a petition demanding that the school board chairman be removed because he was in a conflict-of-interest position. But no action was taken at the time. Ellen was fired in May 1987 and by September had been offered a job at the Sandy Bay elementary school.

One of the hundreds of children who came through her music classes that year at Sandy Bay was Lester Desjarlais. Ellen's first impression of Lester was that he was a kid with "an attitude"—an angry shell that seemed to say "Nothing is going to hurt me, no matter what." Since then, she's taught a long line of kids like Lester, students who are aching for someone to see beyond their tough exterior. But in the months before Lester died, Ellen didn't get to know him very well because he was rarely in class. Rather, it was her involvement with a six-year-old girl whom she and other teachers suspected was being abused that would eventually lead to her being subpoenaed to testify at the inquest into Lester's death. At those hearings, Ellen would once again find herself speaking out about the controversial issue of how family and political pressures squelched teachers' attempts to report child abuse on reserves. By the time she was called to testify at the inquest, Ellen had left Sandy Bay after two years and was teaching in the eastern Manitoba town of Birch River. A year later, in September 1993, she joined the staff of the new Aboriginal elementary school in Winnipeg's north end called Niji Mahkwa.

In Ellen's Grade 6 classroom, on an early spring morning in 1994, the scent of sweetgrass hung in the air. Her classroom walls were bright with students' paintings and stories. One student's poem, written on a red Valentine's heart, defined love as someone who "stops when a mother duck and her ducklings are crossing the street." On a table by the wall, sacred Indian objects, from braids of sweetgrass to sage and an eagle feather, waited. A protective sprig of cedar was pinned over the doorway. By the window, a prayer was written on a large sheet of paper:

O Great Spirit, whose voice I hear in the winds and whose breath gives life to all the world

Hear me! I am small and weak. I need your strength and wisdom.

Let me walk in beauty and make my eyes ever see the red and purple sunset.

Make my hands respect the things you have made and my ears sharp to hear your voice and to hear only good things.

Make me wise so that I may understand the ways of my people.

Help me to learn the lessons you have hidden in every leaf and rock.

Let my hands do only good deeds and my body work in harmony with all of creation.

After gently coaching her ten students through a gruelling hour of math, she began their regular sharing circle. Plastic chairs were pulled close together; Ellen lit the dry sage in a brass bowl and fanned it with an eagle feather. Then she handed the objects to Darcel, a slight twelve-year-old boy from Pukatawagan, who fanned the bowl of sweet smoke as each member of the circle swept it over his or her body. The cleansing ritual completed, Ellen held a smooth black talking stone between her palms and shared a story about the death of her friend's mother. As the stone was passed from student to student, the group greeted each recipient by name, then waited for his or her words, or listened to the silence. Speaking softly, the children talked of haircuts, visits to a relative in jail, and fathers who had to be taken to court to force them to pay child support. They shared the anticipation of new clothes and Easter toys, and frustration at a brother who'd received only ten months in jail after cracking his sister's head open with a beer bottle. Listening intently, Ellen offered encouragement or probed gently, reminding one restless trio of boys to respect their peers. The talking circle had been much bigger, with twenty-four students, early in the school year. But the class had dwindled in size as the children's chaotic lives set them adrift. Many lived in foster homes or moved constantly with transient parents.

Teaching at Niji Mahkwa has been a welcome change from Ellen's years in reserve schools, where she had baulked at political pressures that sometimes interfered with doing the best for children. She no longer worries about losing her job for reporting her suspicions about an abused child. "You feel almost like a prisoner when you work on a reserve, because you don't have a leg to stand on. Sandy Bay was a little better because it [the school] was affiliated with the Manitoba Teachers' Society ... But not much better because they [band officials] could still do darned well anything they pleased with you. If they didn't want to renew your contract, the onus was on them. You can't do anything or say anything that might offend someone. The truth might hurt."

Truth-telling had also landed Joyce Wasicuna in hot water by the time she testified at the inquest of a boy she'd never even met. An intense, dark-eyed woman, Joyce has long been blessed—or burdened—with a passion for doing the right thing. That was obvious as the forty-five-year-old former child-welfare worker told her story over coffee at a Brandon motel one bitterly cold February evening in the winter of 1994. A few days after the interview, she called to apologize for evading one particularly uncomfortable question. She said she couldn't live with herself unless she set the record straight. That same integrity became a source of both strength and heartache when Joyce landed a job doing child protection for Dakota Ojibway Child and Family Services in 1988.

Born on the Sioux Valley reserve in July 1948, the youngest of six children, Joyce was raised by loving parents who cherished traditional values such as respect for oneself and others, honesty, and compassion. The Dakota Sioux village is located about forty-five kilometres west of Brandon and is bounded on the south by the Assiniboine River. The community of her childhood was close-knit and cohesive, a place where people had few material possessions but looked after each other. If a family lost everything in a house fire, her parents and others went door to door, collecting bedding and furniture and food for them. Children who lost their parents were taken in by the extended family. Women looked after their children, planned community events, and cared for the elders. It was unheard of in the 1950s for women to drink alcohol. On the rare occasions when a man came home drunk, his wife would simply pack up the children and stay with family or friends until he sobered up. If a man beat his wife, he was ostracized by the community. Although many residents attended the Anglican and Roman Catholic churches on the reserve, people also clung to the old ways, integrating traditional spirituality and Christianity. It wasn't until the late 1960s and 1970s that other Christian denominations, as well as Indian medicine people, began to infiltrate the community. At the same time, a divisiveness took root that she believes has never healed. "The community was healthy when I was growing up," Joyce says. "I saw the good life. I experienced the good life."

A serious childhood illness meant that Joyce, unlike her siblings, was not sent away to residential school until she was a teenager. Struck by polio at age four, she lay paralysed in a hospital for more than a year, yearning for the day when she could get out of bed. Doctors told her family she would never walk again. But during those anxious months, her family kept a vigil at her side. Back home, people often gathered in the evenings at her parents' house to pray for her recovery. "I've always felt that's what gave me the will to fight, the will to get better. Through prayer, through faith and all the support from the family, the community, I got better. And I've always felt I owe the community something."

When Joyce was finally released from hospital, she endured a long recuperation at home. But, while unable to join others her age at school, she whiled away many happy hours at the side of her maternal grandmother, who told stories about their ancestors and shared teachings about the old ways. Her grandmother reaffirmed her parents' values and nurtured in Joyce a deep pride in her identity as a Dakota Sioux woman. "Thank goodness, with all these teachings from my parents and my grandmother, I knew who I was and I was able to survive," she says. "I had my culture. I had my language and I was able to survive out here because I knew who I was."

At the age of nine, she finally started school on the reserve. Luckily, she'd picked up English during her lengthy hospital stay, which eased what could have been a difficult transition to the English-only school. Learning came easily for her, and she caught up quickly with her classmates. But her academic prowess also made her vulnerable to being labelled "teacher's pet." As well, her physical limitations prevented her from joining in playground games, making it even tougher to fit in. Still, what was most painful to the bright, sensitive girl was being picked on because her father was a "halfbreed" with such light skin he could pass for white. Other kids would taunt her, whack her with metal-edged rulers to see if she'd cry, or dip her long hair into the inkwells. They would pick on her because she had hairy arms, whereas most full-blooded Indians were hairless. So Joyce wore long-sleeved sweaters to hide the hair. Afraid to tell her parents, she suffered in silence until her mother finally questioned her about why she covered her arms. After that, Joyce's mother used fine sandpaper to get rid of the fuzz that was causing her daughter so much grief. While Joyce loved the academic side of school, the emotional torment soon filled her with longing for the day when she could escape.

Consequently, she was eager to sign up for a new integration program in which students from Sioux Valley were bussed to a white school in the nearby town of Kenton. To thirteen-year-old Joyce, it was a ticket to something better. The only other period during which she'd spent substantial time off-reserve had been at the hospital, where people had been friendly and kind. But when she and the other Sioux Valley children arrived in Kenton, they encountered a barrage of racist taunts from white classmates. To survive the verbal abuse, the Sioux Valley kids stuck together at school. But once they were back on the bus headed home, it was a different story. Joyce and several other girls of mixed blood endured merciless harassment from their peers. More and more miserable, Joyce had no sooner turned sixteen when she announced to her parents she was quitting school. "I was experiencing reverse discrimination ... on the bus going [to school]. And then when we arrived at the school, all of a sudden, I was a 'brown cow.' I was labelled a 'brown cow' along with all the other kids ... Kids can be the cruellest, cruellest people."

Her parents convinced her to try the residential school in Portage la Prairie instead of dropping out of school. But when she arrived, Joyce was dismayed to find that students attended classes only half-days. The rest of the time, they were expected to toil at hard, manual labour in the fields. With her health still fragile, Joyce rebelled at the unreasonable demands. School officials reacted to her protests by locking her in the principal's office for hours on end. But what likely alarmed them even more were her complaints about one of the school officials. Often at night, the man prowled the girls' makeshift dorm, temporarily located in the school's gymnasium while the main building was under construction. Joyce often saw him stop at the bunk-bed next to hers where two young girls from a northern reserve slept. Having lived in a tent back home, the girls had a habit of putting their pyjamas on over their clothes. The man used that as an excuse to order the embarrassed girls out of bed. Then he humiliated them by demanding they strip in front of him. On other occasions, the man strolled into the girls' shower-room and gawked at the naked teenagers, excusing his voyeurism by saying he had daughters their age at home. The first time it happened, Joyce wrote it off as an accident. The second time, she reported the man's behaviour to other school officials, who accused her of lying. When it was obvious she couldn't be silenced, they expelled her from the school. That was fine with Joyce, who wasn't interested in waiting around to become the man's next victim.

When Joyce returned to Sioux Valley, she soon realized there were few opportunities there for a teenager with ambition. She moved away from the community and spent the next years working at a variety of jobs. With the money she saved, she took a hairdressing course, and then worked in several hair-styling shops before buying her own business in a rural village. During those years, she also began an on-and-off relationship with a man from Sioux Valley, whom she eventually married and with whom she had three children. In the late 1970s, Joyce sold her hair-styling shop and attended Brandon University until she ran out of money. Then the family moved to Winnipeg in 1981, where they ran their own business, a boarding-house for medical patients from rural areas. By this time, although she often visited her family at Sioux Valley, she felt more at home in Winnipeg. But in 1985, the chief of Sioux Valley called her husband, urging him to help his home community by accepting a job as band administrator. Joyce was adamantly opposed to uprooting the family. After much debate, her husband decided to take the job, while Joyce kept their business afloat and commuted to the reserve on weekends. But the strain of the divided household was too much, and by January 1987 she reluctantly moved back to Sioux Valley. Within two weeks of her arrival, a drunken woman banged on her door, demanding to see her husband, and tried to force her way into the house. Joyce managed to push the intruder out. But their homecoming was off to a bad start.

A year later, Joyce applied for a job as a child-protection worker with Dakota Ojibway Child and Family Services. The job interview left her excited at the prospect of working for an agency with such admirable goals. She'd been told that DOCFS was dedicated to saving Aboriginal children from the suffering they'd endured in the mainstream child-welfare system. The agency was rooted in traditional values and tried to offer culturally appropriate services to children and their familes. Joyce felt honoured when she was offered the chance to join the agency's staff in October 1988. Despite having no formal training in social work, she eagerly took on the task of doing child-protection work at Sioux Valley and four other reserves.

But her enthusiasm for the job was soon tempered by a backlash she had not expected. About a month into her work, she investigated a report of physical abuse involving a girl from the Birdtail Sioux reserve. She interviewed the girl, realized from the child's bruised body that she'd been beaten, and removed her from her home. The girl's parents were so hostile that she enlisted the help of an officer from the Dakota Ojibway Tribal Council police to retrieve the child's clothes. When the officer returned to the house, he was dragged from the police cruiser and assaulted by angry relatives. Removing the child had triggered a reaction "like a whole keg of dynamite had blown."

But Joyce refused to be intimidated, and she followed the case through the courts for months until the abuser was convicted. When other abuse victims saw what had happened, her phone began to ring.

Many of the calls were from sexual-abuse victims, both children and adults. Their stories haunted Joyce, revealing a side of the community she hadn't seen. Often children disclosed disturbing details about their abuse when she was driving them to an off-reserve appointment. "Once it starts coming out, there's no stopping it. They'd keep talking and talking. Sometimes they'd throw up. And I've always had a very weak stomach. So I threw up a lot too. They'd be hanging out one door [of the car] and I'd be hanging out the other. Or at times I'd get emotional. I'm a very emotional person. Sometimes they'd start crying and I'd start crying."

Becoming aware of the depth of suffering endured by many women and children strengthened Joyce's resolve to help. Many abused women phoned simply to talk, too ashamed to pursue legal action. Often they turned to alcohol to cope with their pain, and some lost custody of their children as a result. When Joyce listened to their stories, she realized most had lost touch with their roots after being sent to residential school or removed from home by mainstream child-welfare agencies.

However, the more abuse cases Joyce investigated, the more isolated she became in the community. She discovered that her tenacious approach to child abuse had not been shared by some of her predecessors with DOCFS, who had bowed to pressure from relatives and band council officials to drop abuse investigations. People didn't want to be seen talking to her in case they'd be suspected of passing on information. No matter how young or severely abused a child was, relatives often sided with the suspected offender. Joyce interpreted their reactions as deep-rooted denial. But that didn't make it any easier to live through heartbreaking days in court with an abused child whose family appeared in support of the accused. "I'm related to a lot of these people that are convicted too. But when something like that happens, it's wrong and it needs to be stopped."

Joyce also detected serious flaws in the way the justice system handled abuse cases. She noticed a subtle racist bias among legal professionals, who seemed to take a less aggressive approach to abuse cases involving Aboriginal children. She was appalled when offenders received a "slap on the wrist" and were sent back to the community without mandatory counselling. In one of the worst incest cases she investigated, charges against the mother were dropped, and the father received three years' probation. The parents had subjected all of their children to extreme sexual abuse for years. To make matters worse, she wasn't notified that the trial had been cancelled because of the plea bargain. By then, the children had suffered six weeks of nightmares and upset stomachs awaiting a trial that never took place.

Sometimes band members' resentment of Joyce escalated beyond social ostracism. One hot summer night in July 1989, she was home with her two daughters when they heard someone trying to break in. Frightened, Joyce called the DOTC police. As she waited for help to arrive, the intruders banged on the sides of the house and tried to pry the windows open. Forty-five minutes later, two unarmed female officers arrived and chased about a dozen youth from the back of the house. When the officers realized they were outnumbered, they left, promising to return with back-up. But the intruders returned, and Joyce and her daughters huddled for hours in the dark, clutching baseball bats. The DOTC police officers eventually caught one of the suspects, who admitted that he and his friends had attacked the house because they'd heard a rumour—which turned out to be false—that Joyce had sent one of their friends to a foster home on another reserve.

On other occasions, her daughter was threatened with rape, and her son was beaten up and had his motorcycle destroyed. When the harassment showed no signs of abating, Joyce and her family finally fled the reserve in late March 1990 and moved back to Winnipeg. Although Joyce was determined to continue her child-protection work with DOCFS, she could no longer expose her own children to the community's hostility. What she didn't realize at the time was that her relentless pursuit of child-abuse cases would eventually cost her her job with DOCFS as well. That story would come out at the inquest.

By the time Joyce was subpoenaed to testify at the inquest into Lester's death, she'd been unemployed for more than a year. It would be another year until she was hired as an advocate for Aboriginal defendants in the provincial courts, the job she still held in the winter of 1994. But looking back, Joyce said she wouldn't hesitate to take the same stand again, despite the personal toll it had taken. "I don't know why it is, but sometimes when I see something wrong I persist in trying to correct that problem and sometimes that gets me into a lot of trouble."

As charter members of the staff of Dakota Ojibway Child and Family Services, Ella McKay and Bev Flett never dreamed the day would come when they'd publicly challenge the agency to which they'd been committed for more than a decade. On a sub-zero winter night in 1994, the pair arrived together for an interview at a Brandon motel. Both single parents in their early forties, they'd known each other since residential school. Ella, a short, jovial woman, displayed an exuberance that often overshadowed Bev. Anxious at first, Bev spoke in a soft voice that was barely audible, her straight, black hair brushing her slender shoulders. But Ella's teasing humour soon put her at ease. Over steaming cups of coffee, they chatted about the unlikely chain of events which led them to put their jobs on the line during their testimony at the inquest into Lester's death.

Both were quick to credit their devotion to working with children to their grandparents' influence. Growing up in a family of twelve children on the Sioux Valley reserve, Ella often turned to her grandparents for guidance. Known for their compassion and generosity, her grandparents opened their home to the "rejects" of the community. Teenagers returning from residential school in the summer who had nowhere to stay counted on her grandparents to take them in. To Ella, they epitomized the traditional values of caring, sharing, and respect for others. Watching them reach out to the community, she vowed she'd do the same some day.

Born into the Ojibwa reserve of Keeseekoowenin, Bev and her younger sister were raised by their grandmother. A woman of strong principles, Bev's grandmother shielded them from the havoc wreaked by alcohol in the southwestern Manitoba community, located just south of Riding Mountain National Park. Her grandmother's tireless service to those less fortunate impressed the young Bev, who dreamed of having a career helping others some day. But her life changed dramatically when she turned sixteen and her grandmother sent her to a church-run residential school in Portage la Prairie. Away from home for the first time, the teenager found the allure of forbidden cigarettes, alcohol, and boys too strong. As Bev said, she "went wild." After a year and a half, her worried grandmother insisted she come home. But soon after Bev's return, her grandmother died. Within a year, Bev left the reserve to move in with her boyfriend in Winnipeg and became pregnant. Her first child, a daughter, was born in 1971, when Bev was twenty years old. During the next turbulent years, her relationship with the father of her child deteriorated, and she finally left him. Determined to support herself and her child, she took community-college courses in social services and worked at a Winnipeg alcohol-treatment centre. When the fledgling DOCFS agency opened in 1982, Bev eagerly applied for a job and was hired to work on the Long Plain reserve south of Portage la Prairie.

At the urging of her grandfather, who saw education as the key to a successful future, Ella had enrolled in a social-services program at Assiniboine College in the early 1970s. After graduation, she worked for the Children's Aid Society in Brandon for a few years before becoming pregnant and giving birth to her daughter. When DOCFS hired its first employees in 1981, Ella joined the team of the new agency. Both Ella and Bev remember the heady excitement of those early days as they worked together to break new ground. Everyone was committed to providing the best services possible to children and their families.

Bev's only recollection of Lester was meeting him during one of his placements at the Brandon Mental Health Centre. Although she had supervised the DOCFS workers at Sandy Bay, she was on maternity leave during part of Lester's last year. After hearing stories from other staff about the boy's escapades, she'd expected to meet a wild-eyed teenager. Instead, she found a boy who seemed so small and helpless that her heart went out to him. Ella, who was away on a leave of absence during the last year of Lester's life, never met him. Consequently, neither expected to be subpoenaed to testify at the boy's inquest. But as the inquest began to probe all aspects of the agency's operations, stretching into weeks, and then months, the two women grew perplexed at DOCFS officials' stubborn denial of problems such as political interference in child-abuse cases.

About the same time, they ran into conflict with their bosses over a personal-development progam offered by the agency called "Flying on

Your Own." They were asked to participate in a staff training for the program, which used both traditional Indian rituals and psychological techniques to help participants gain insight into their problems. But as members of a Pentecostal church, both Ella and Bev expressed discomfort at being forced to take part in certain ceremonies. Speaking up wasn't easy for Bev, whose natural tendency was to avoid confrontation. She was a recent convert to Christianity, after failing to find solace in traditional Indian spirituality. On the other hand, Ella had long been sceptical about the revival of traditional Indian religions and the promises of self-proclaimed medicine men. She felt they played on the vulnerabilities of people searching for lost identities rather than helping people cope with present realities. Besides, she was suspicious of some medicine men who went out of their way to broadcast their talents. Her mother had told her that, in the old days, true medicine people lived in seclusion and had to be sought out by those who needed help.

The complaints from Ella and Bev about the "Flying on Your Own" program did not sit well with agency officials. In the end, Ella and Bev negotiated a compromise—they attended the seminar but opted out of some ceremonies. In retrospect, Ella realized that breaking rank with their co-workers over a religious issue prepared them for an even tougher task a few months later—testifying at the inquest into Lester's death. What Ella and Bev didn't expect was the backlash they faced after they took the stand and spoke bluntly about their concerns. Nevertheless, the two women, both grandmothers now, said they've relied on each other and their religious faith to make it through some tough moments since they testified in June 1992. "Several times we've sat down and thought about it and laughed about it," Ella says with a smile. "Like, did we actually do that? ... But then, everybody went out on a limb."

Among the collage of stickers on Vice-principal Angela Eastman's office door is one with the slogan "I do it with Love and Logic." Dozens of grinning, green glass and plastic frogs of every shape and size are perched on a shelf to the left of her desk. A bulletin-board on the opposite wall is plastered with school photos of smiling children. Stacks of files and books are piled high in the cramped room. The phone rings constantly, and school staff interrupt with a steady stream of requests for help.

In the midst of the clutter, Angela, a big-boned, handsome woman of forty-nine, presides with a good-natured calm. Always well-dressed, she is wearing a batik vest of purple, blue, and black over a satiny white shirt and long black crinkle skirt. Her hair is pulled back with a white barrette, and she wears a heavy turquoise bracelet. She insists that she can be quite strict when necessary. But this friendly office at Sandy Bay school is not a place unruly children would fear to tread. Rather, it has become a haven for students needing extra time and attention. It was to this office that Lester fled so many times during the last years of his life. The bond that grew between the troubled boy and Angela in this office would eventually prompt her to speak out at the inquest into his death.

Becoming a teacher had been Angela's dream since she was a small child growing up at Sandy Bay. As the eldest of the thirteen Roulette children, her thirst for knowledge was nurtured by her father, a man with only a limited education from the Roman Catholic residential school. Although there was no money for books, her father taught her to read English out of catalogues and magazines before she went to school at age seven. Angela, in turn, practised her future profession by teaching her younger siblings to read.

Her family may have been poor, but Angela was blissfully unaware of that. Her mother made sure her children were well fed. She canned vegetables and fruits, and filled their cellar with enough potatoes from her huge garden to last the winter. Angela's father worked for the city of Brandon in the summers and, later, as a night watchman at the residential school. To bring in extra cash, her mother toiled as a seamstress at the residential school, earning $15 a week. At home, she sewed dresses and winter coats and other clothes for her brood. As Angela says, "There wasn't a day we went hungry. There wasn't a day we didn't have decent clothes to wear ... And there was no welfare in those days."

Her childhood revolved around their extended family. During the long, hot summers, she'd spend time with her grandparents, who raised cows and chickens and horses. Some days, the children would walk the horses to a watering-hole in the marsh along the edge of Lake Manitoba. Other times, they'd join their grandfather on trips to the lake to fill water barrels with his horse-drawn wagon. While he worked, the children would frolic in the waves until the afternoon waned. Life seemed rich and full to young Angela.

She attended as a day student at the residential school until she graduated in Grade 7. During those years, the nuns tried their best to keep students from speaking Saulteaux. By then, more brutal tactics—like clamping clothespins to children's tongues—had been replaced by psychological coercion. The nuns handed out cardboard tokens to students at the beginning of each week, and then reclaimed a token each time they erred by speaking Saulteaux. Students with the most tokens at the end of each week—usually the French or Metis children—would win a prize. As Angela says, "I never had a chance after the first few hours. So I'd just get rid of my tokens and go my merry way!"

When her mother became ill, she was forced to live at the school for a few months. Older girls at the school were assigned to help the younger ones with tasks like bathing and dressing. But some had a nasty habit of tormenting their young charges, including Angela. They scrubbed her skin raw with floor brushes in the chilly shower-room until she finally complained to her father. He put a stop to the abuse. Worst of all to Angela was being cooped up day and night at the school within sight of her home.

One spring evening, Angela heard the throbbing of the drums from the point where the annual sun-dance was about to begin. Every year, her father, a strong believer in traditional Indian ways, pitched a tent, and the family took part in the ceremonies. It was a joyful time, when the children ran free, as adults celebrated the ancient rituals. But as a resident of the school, she was banned from taking part. When the nuns heard the drums, they shut all the windows to distract the restless children. Then, Angela and the others were ordered to recite the rosary to try to drown out the insistent call of the drums. But the nuns weren't able to block out the piercing drumbeats.

Both of Angela's parents lived at residential schools as children. The difference between them was that her father clung fiercely to his traditional Indian beliefs whereas her mother became a devoted Catholic. Her father often teased his wife about her strong attachment to the nuns. But she had her reasons. When she was about four years old, her father was killed in a logging accident, leaving her mother with no way to support her three daughters. The Indian agent arranged for the two oldest girls, who lived in western Manitoba at the time, to be sent to residential school. A priest arrived and took them to a Winnipeg convent, and then to a residential school on a reserve at Fort Alexander in eastern Manitoba.

In the meantime, the priest died without telling their mother where he'd sent her daughters or informing nuns at the school about the children's origins. The nuns, assuming the girls were orphans, went out of their way to lavish love and attention on the two waifs. Almost ten years later, as a teenager, Angela's mother began searching for her mother and was reunited through a strange coincidence. She remembered that her mother, who worked for a Ukrainian farmer, had had a baby girl with blue eyes shortly before they were sent away. Through the grapevine, she heard that a blue-eyed girl was attending residential school at Sandy Bay. With the help of the priest at Fort Alexander, she eventually discovered that girl was her half-sister. Eventually, Angela's mother was also reunited with her mother, who had remarried. After that, she and her sisters attended school at Sandy Bay and went home for summers.

Nuns at Sandy Bay had also played a role in arranging the marriage of Angela's parents. When her mother reached a marriageable age, the nuns told her to put on her Sunday dress and wait with her girlfriend on the hard wooden benches in the school's parlour. Two young men, hand-picked by the nuns, arrived to meet the anxious girls. From then on, the courtship of Angela's parents consisted of prim chats in the parlour while the nuns paced outside the door, sticking their noses in at the slightest sound. By the time her parents married, the nuns had trained her mother to sew and crochet and knit and cook. But she knew nothing about becoming a wife or having children.

Two divergent histories were merged with the marriage of Angela's parents. Her mother had no ties to the Sandy Bay band, having been born in Crooked Lake, Saskatchewan. On the other hand, Angela's paternal relatives could be traced back to the earliest settlements at Totogan, and eventually Sandy Bay. Her father's relatives were of mixed blood, with French and Scottish ancestry intermingling with Ojibwa.

By the time Angela graduated from Grade 7 at the day school, she was one of only two students left in the class. Determined to get an education, she left the community for the first time at age twelve to attend a Catholic residential high school in Winnipeg. There she was overcome with loneliness, as were many of the younger students. At night, she heard homesick children crying in the dorm. When summer finally came, she was always glad to go home. Although her father was strict, she was allowed to attend dances if an adult accompanied her. Her grandmother, who loved to watch the dancing, often went with her. Nobody drank alcohol or did drugs at the socials. The worst offence any of the teenagers committed was to sneak cigarettes.

When Angela finished high school in 1963, she drifted for a while, travelling across the country and dabbling in the youthful idealism of the mid-1960s. At nineteen, she also married a young man named Clifford Eastman, originally from Crane River on the northern shore of Lake Manitoba, who she'd known for about six years. Her parents were opposed to the marriage. Her father considered him to be "a failure" because he'd dropped out of high school. But Angela had a mind of her own and went ahead with the marriage. When she decided to pursue her goal of becoming a teacher and enrolled at the University of Manitoba, Clifford was her staunch supporter, even though it meant he'd be left behind at Sandy Bay while she attended classes. After only two months, she dropped out, overwhelmed by the large, impersonal campus and sea of white faces. As Angela says, "Indians are a very social people. You can't just put them out there by themselves. Like, even now, with my kids grown up and just me and my husband at home, I'll call somebody up and say, come on over and visit—I'm lonely!"

With her husband's encouragement, she decided to give university a second try and enrolled at Brandon University. On the smaller campus, she felt more at home and met other Aboriginal students. There she helped found the Brandon University Native Students group and was influential in developing an Aboriginal-studies program that still flourishes today. She graduated in 1970 and was hired immediately to teach kindergarten at the Sandy Bay residential school. "I was glad that my father lived to see me be a teacher in this community," she says.

When she moved back home, she was one of the first band members with a university degree. But she was careful not to flaunt her hard-won education, resuming old friendships as if she'd never left.

Not everyone understood her drive for a career, especially since it flew in the face of traditional women's roles. Angela just ignored the wisecracks some made about her aspirations. Over the years, she has served as a role model for ambitious girls from the community who have gone on to university and professional careers.

Her pursuit of an education meant putting off having children. Then her biological clock "ran out" and she and her husband decided to adopt two sons, first a three-year-old boy, Edward, and later a seven-year-old boy from Pukatawagan, Oliver. Angela now carries photos in her wallet of her two young grandchildren, Edward's son and daughter, and proudly shows them off.

Over the last two decades, Angela has taught many different grades and watched a couple of generations of kids grow into adulthood. Since becoming vice-principal of the elementary school more than six years ago, she's tried to pay special attention to troubled children who end up in her office. When she first got to know Lester, her heart went out to the boy, who seemed starved for attention. He grew to trust Angela, and often sought her out just to talk. Sometimes he'd share his secrets, because he could tell nothing shocked her. When Lester took his own life, Angela was devastated, feeling—like so many who knew him—that she'd failed him somehow.

Taking the stand to testify at the inquest into Lester's death was traumatic for Angela, who was by then an elder at Sandy Bay. Deeply loyal to her community, she dreaded the prospect of answering questions that could create bad publicity. But for Lester's sake, she spoke honestly. Her testimony, which was widely reported in the media, won her no friends back home, especially among the Desjarlais clan. For two years after she testified, she was reluctant to be interviewed about the inquest because of the backlash she'd suffered. In the end, she spoke carefully, but candidly, about the fall-out from Lester's death—a painful period that nevertheless sparked change for the community.

CHAPTER SIX

POINTING THE FINGER

"I was with that agency and supervisor at Sandy Bay for
not even a year, you know, so how can the finger be pointed at
me with—with Marion Glover being the person who
has everything to hide?"

—Marion Glover

After Lester's death, tensions that had been festering among staff at
Dakota Ojibway Child and Family Services worsened. At the centre of
the conflict was Marion Glover, the woman who had been Lester's
worker in the months before his suicide and who would play a major
role in the events triggered by his death. Several staff members had
complained about Marion to agency director Esther Seidl, as well as
the agency's assistant director, Morris Merrick. The four Sandy Bay
child-care workers supervised by Marion said she talked down to them,
embarrassed them in front of clients, undermined their decisions, and
left them to pick up the pieces. On the other hand, Marion believed
that the workers weren't used to taking directions, especially when it
came to aggressively pursuing difficult child-abuse cases. What fuelled

the friction between them was at least in part the result of a culture gap. With Marion's blunt approach to child welfare, she had unknowingly breached the underlying social ethic of non-interference common in Native communities.

Aboriginal social norms have longed been aimed at preserving harmony between people, as the commissioners of the Aboriginal Justice Inquiry explained in their report. In the past, group cohesiveness was crucial for survival. Today, the ethic of non-interference means respect for others' privacy and a great reluctance to intervene in another's personal affairs. The popular mainstream tactic of confronting conflict head-on is an anathema to many Aboriginal people. Instead, dissatisfaction or conflicts are expressed indirectly, perhaps through an intermediary. Shaming or teasing is also a common way of showing disapproval or bringing someone's behaviour back in line with community expectations. Working within such social mores while following the legal mandate to protect abused children is a complex task requiring cultural sensitivity. That does not mean looking the other way while children are abused. Children who are at risk may still have to be apprehended from their homes. But how it is done can lessen the trauma of everyone involved. Marion's bull-in-a-china-shop approach, even though prompted by a genuine concern for children, created a gulf between herself and other staff at Sandy Bay.

At Sandy Bay, band leaders were increasingly uneasy about what they saw as Marion's overzealous approach to child-abuse cases. The week before Lester's death, Marion was barred from the Sandy Bay school after ordering the apprehension of a young girl who teachers suspected was a victim of sexual abuse. After the incident, Cecil Desjarlais, a band councillor and chairman of the local child-welfare committee, wrote to Marion, chastising her for failing to notify the girl's guardians before taking the child from school and placing her in a foster home on the reserve. Any future apprehensions would have to be discussed with members of the band's local child-welfare committee before action was taken, he said. The child's irate grandparents, who were related to Cecil, had arrived at the foster home within an hour of the apprehension and demanded her return. After a shouting match, an Amaranth RCMP officer convinced the grandparents to leave. But by evening, the child was back home. Marion believed it was no coincidence that the suspected abusers of the girl were male relatives of both Cecil and the grandparents.

By May, the turmoil at Sandy Bay was causing concern among agency officials at the head office in Brandon. Marion had complained to the provincial child-abuse coordinator, John Chudzik, and other officials about her difficulties investigating child-abuse cases on the reserve. During one meeting, DOCFS officials Esther Seidl and Morris Merrick, along with Ernie Daniels, who'd been appointed director of the Dakota Ojibway Tribal Council the previous month, anxiously discussed whether the complaints might spark an investigation by the province or attract bad publicity.

That same week, John Chudzik drove out from Winnipeg to review Lester's file in preparation for a routine death report to the Family Services minister. He thought it odd when the agency's child-abuse coordinator, Elaine Scott, asked to meet away from the agency's headquarters. Tensions were running high in the office, she explained, and it would be better to rendezvous at another location. When they met at the provincial building, Elaine seemed nervous and was reluctant to show him Lester's file. At one point he convinced her to let him glance briefly at it, but she soon took it back. She said she feared a reproof because staff weren't supposed to remove files from the office.

Over the next two months, Marion called John Chudzik several more times to say she felt increasingly intimidated by band leaders at Sandy Bay. John also spoke to Esther, who reported that the atmosphere both at Sandy Bay and within the agency was highly politicized. Esther and Marion, who were both white, believed some officials, such as Morris and Ernie, were trying to force them out of the agency to make room for Aboriginal staff. They also felt they'd become scapegoats for opposing band leaders who tried to meddle in child-abuse investigations.

At Sandy Bay, one of Cecil's uncles, Harry Desjarlais, was chief, giving the Desjarlais clan considerable clout in the community. Several other factors in the web of family ties had also heightened the strain between the Desjarlais clan and Marion. Cecil had a close connection to Lester because of his previous marriage to the boy's mother, Joyce. During that marriage he'd fathered her first four children. Lester was born after they split up and wasn't Cecil's child. But it was Cecil's younger brother Joe whom Lester had named as his abuser. Marion believed Cecil was determined to do everything he could to protect Joe.

In late June, an investigator from the chief medical examiner's office, Hedi Epp, phoned the agency and scheduled a visit for July 6. Under a new law, her office was now required to review the cases of every child who died in the care of a provincial agency. A report outlining the circumstances of each death and any recommendations had to be submitted to the Family Services minister. The day before Hedi was to arrive, Marion called to say she couldn't find Lester's main file at head office. But she offered to look for both the master and the field files when she went to Sandy Bay. Hedi suggested Marion send the files to Winnipeg with the agency's lawyer as soon as possible. When the files didn't arrive, Hedi, an efficient, experienced investigator, became increasingly annoyed and called the agency several more times. She had already run into resistance from other agencies reluctant to share confidential child-welfare files and wasn't about to let DOCFS off the hook. Finally, on July 12, Marion phoned back with unsettling news: all of Lester's agency files had vanished without a trace.

The next day, after consulting with agency officials, DOCFS director Esther Seidl contacted the Brandon Police Department to report the theft of the files containing vital information about Lester's case. The Amaranth RCMP were also notified, because of the possibility the field file had been stolen from the Sandy Bay office. Agency officials also suspended Marion with pay that week, suspecting she was to blame for the missing files and suggesting she had mismanaged child-abuse cases. Agency officials eventually expanded their accusations of her to include general incompetence, insubordination, and submitting fraudulent travel claims. At an acrimonious meeting in late July, DOTC director Ernie Daniels told Marion the suspension was permanent, this time without pay, and ordered her to turn in her office keys. An irate Marion vowed to challenge her suspension and warned that she'd go to the media, if necessary, with her concerns about child-abuse cover-ups at Sandy Bay. She'd already visited the province's director of child and family support the previous week to register her complaints. Ernie, equally furious, responded by warning he'd kick her "white fucking ass all over the place" if she caused trouble. But if he had hoped to intimidate her, he failed miserably. When backed into a corner, Marion had long ago learned to fight back.

Born in July 1954 in Portage la Prairie, Marion was the second of four siblings. When she was three years old, her parents separated, and her mother became involved with the man who would become her stepfather. For the next couple of years, her parents battled over who would gain custody of their children. First Marion's father kidnapped her and her siblings from their mother. When she was about four years old, her mother and stepfather snatched Marion and her younger sister back. The dispute culminated in family court in Brandon, where a judge asked the frightened children who they wanted to live with. "I remember that state of frozen panic," Marion says. "My father had his arms out to us. My mother had her arms out to us." In the end, the judge made the unusual decision to split up the children: Marion and her sister remained with their mother; her oldest sister and younger brother went to their father. It would be eight years until Marion saw her sister and brother again.

As Marion begins to tell her story, she hesitates, lights a cigarette, and opens the sliding glass door on her apartment balcony to let the wintry air filter in. Dressed in a sweatshirt, jeans, and moccasins, she sinks again into one of the worn beige couches in her simply furnished living-room. On the coffee-table in front of her, a glass plate holds a white and rose candle, sage, smooth stones, and a shell. Aboriginal art prints adorn the walls, and a large dream-catcher with an eagle feather hangs over her computer in the corner. A black-and-white poster of Albert Einstein declares: "Peace cannot be kept by force. It can only be kept by understanding."

Marion is wary about revealing details about her past. Despite being thrust into the public spotlight for several years by the events which followed Lester's death, she has disclosed surprisingly little about her background. Some have interpreted her reticence as arrogance, dismissing her as an "attention-seeking crusader." But when she finally opens up during an interview in November 1995, it becomes apparent that her dogged pursuit of answers after Lester's death went deeper.

According to Marion, the sexual abuse began when she was in

kindergarten. A terrified Marion was afraid to tell anyone, even her mother, about what was going on. As she got older, there were times when she also suffered physical abuse, being beaten black and blue with a dog chain. After one of the beatings, Marion has a vivid memory of running and sitting forlornly on the curb outside. She spied a piece of glass on the street and, before she knew it, had calmly sliced open her finger to watch the blood flow. "I needed some kind of validation that I was human," Marion says, pointing to the thin white scar on her hand. "I thought over and over, it isn't me, it isn't my fault."

At nine years old, Marion began to run away from home at every opportunity. "I was a very angry kid," she says. "I did anything to get attention." When social workers tried to lock her up, she escaped, even slipping out of a cell in the Brandon courthouse. "I was the child who would be any social worker's nightmare," Marion says. Those who knew her family were perplexed: why would a child from a good, middle-class home, with well-educated parents and "the best of everything," be so rebellious? A police officer who picked her up on one of her runs lectured Marion for causing her parents so much grief. He said she was "just bad." By the time she was eleven, Marion was often depressed, and dwelled on thoughts of suicide. She was so withdrawn that her parents decided she must be doing drugs.

Her twelfth birthday marked a turning-point: for the first time, she realized that her life was not normal and that no one else seemed to care. Twice, she tried to kill herself, once with an overdose of pills and once by attempting to drown herself. All she could think about was escaping to "The Big Sleep." After one brutal beating when she was thirteen, she ended up in hospital. The RCMP tried to get her to press charges, but she refused. Instead, arrangements were made for her to live at a boarding-house in town after her release from hospital. She earned her keep by working part-time in a motel after school and never went home to live again.

Her teen years were about a different kind of survival. She dropped out of high school in Grade 9 and moved to Winnipeg, where she lived a hand-to-mouth existence on the streets and staying with friends. She put herself through hairdressing school and then returned to south-western Manitoba to marry a former boyfriend when she was eighteen.

She was tired of eking out a living by herself. Over the next nine years, she raised three sons and an adopted daughter while working at a variety of jobs. She also audited university courses but avoided enrolling for credit: her fear of failure was too great. While working in a group home with troubled kids, she discovered she had a knack for such work and applied for a job with the Children's Aid Society in Brandon. In that work she thrived, feeling like she was finally able to use her tumultuous childhood to help others. She sat on a child-abuse committee and helped organize a group for sexual-abuse victims. Then the world caved in again, when her employer fired her after finding out she'd lied on her job application: Marion, a high-school drop-out, had passed herself off as a university graduate.

It was while working with abused kids that Marion realized she was ready to face the fact that she too had been abused. She confronted one of her abusers who refused to acknowledge what had happened. She went to talk to her mother, who eventually admitted she'd ignored the warning signs. "She said she too had been abused and couldn't deal with hers and couldn't deal with mine," Marion says. For Marion, facing that her mother had failed to protect her was an "unspeakable loss, an emotional death." She sank into depression for a while. But as difficult as the truth was, Marion knew she had to stare it down. "I confronted my own abuse to save my own children."

Looking back over her troubled childhood, Marion thinks of two people who offered her a glimpse of the love she so badly craved: a long-time family friend, Lorraine Mathers, who showed a special interest in the defiant little girl, and a high-school principal who invited Marion to his home for visits with his children and taught her to ride horses, showing her a level of patience she'd rarely experienced. Anyone who treated her kindly left a big impression on the lonely teenager.

When her marriage broke down in 1981, she remarried on the rebound, and soon separated again. By the time DOCFS offered her a job, she was a single parent, struggling to make ends meet. This time, she was honest with her employer about her lack of academic credentials and about being fired from the Children's Aid. The job with DOCFS seemed like the perfect opportunity to pursue the kind of work she enjoyed. Then, in less than a year, everything began to unravel again, with Lester's death, the disappearance of his child-welfare files, and her suspension from the agency.

The mystery of Lester's missing files continued to baffle officials long after they had finished their routine investigation into his suicide. Unable to complete her report about the teenager's suicide without the files, Hedi Epp, the investigator with the chief medical examiner's office, called police repeatedly for updates in the autumn of 1988. From the beginning, both the Amaranth RCMP and Brandon police investigations into the suspected theft of the files pointed to only one suspect: Marion Glover.

On the Brandon end of the investigation, Constable Carol Fisher had suspected Marion from the beginning. Marion had said that she last saw Lester's files in mid-April, when she wrote a report about his death to the province. But Fisher noted in a letter to the RCMP in November 1988 that Marion had also "played up" the political significance of the missing files. Both Marion and DOCFS director Esther Seidl had suggested to police that the files were stolen to cover up evidence of abuse at Sandy Bay. The missing files had also offered a convenient excuse to get rid of Marion and might cost Seidl her job as well. The agency was bent on replacing white staff with Aboriginal employees, one way or the other, Seidl told Fisher. Nevertheless, Fisher concluded that only Marion would have had the motive and opportunity to steal the files. In her November letter to the RCMP, she wrote:

> It would certainly not look good for Glover if the inquest proved she mishandled this client. Keeping this in mind, Glover may have had good reason for the file to go missing ... The coincidence of this particular file being lost, just as an inquest was to begin, indicates to me that there was a specific problem with this particular file, as opposed to a major problem on the reserve. Glover could certainly be considered a good suspect.

In Amaranth, RCMP Constable Don Bechtel, who had arrived at the detachment just days before the files were reported missing, had been annoyed by Marion from their first meeting. On his first day of work on July 7, 1988, Marion had reported fifteen sexual-assault complaints to him. His impression was that she was a "crusader against sexual abuse" who believed every child with a problem at Sandy Bay had been sexually abused. Interviews with DOCFS workers at Sandy Bay only reinforced his opinion of her. Child-welfare worker Ron Mousseau told Bechtel he didn't believe Lester had been sexually abused, even though Marion always "pestered" the boy about it. Mousseau also made it clear he resented Marion for removing Lester from his caseload when she became supervisor at Sandy Bay. The worker who took over the boy's case, Bill Richard, complained to police that Marion had soon taken charge of Lester herself. Richard said she insisted that he had a conflict of interest because he was related to Joyce's partner. In his statement to the RCMP, Richard blamed Marion for undermining his efforts to keep Lester at Sandy Bay: "I found Lester to be a bit mischievous but I believe that was normal for a boy of his age," Richard told police. "One day Lester could be happy and talkative and the next day he could change and be very sullen ... I could never figure out what made Lester tick, but I believed getting him home was part of the solution."

When Bechtel spoke to Lester's mother, Joyce, she implicated Marion as well. In a statement to RCMP less than a month before she died, Joyce was bitter about Marion:

> Lester was a normal kid. He got into trouble by hanging around with his older friends. He didn't do anything but they blamed him. He got upset when the RCMP came to talk to him. He drank and sniffed gas a couple of times ...
>
> In January 1988, Marion Glover didn't want Lester to come home. Bill Richard originally had our case but Marion took over. Bill Richard told me he thought Lester should come home but Marion didn't want him to. Lester didn't like that nor did I ...
>
> In [September] 1987 I went to visit Lester at the Brandon Mental Hospital. When Marion found out I was there she came as well. While there, Lester told Marion that he would

kill himself if she kept putting him in foster homes. Lester didn't like Marion because she used to swear at him. When he was in Winnipeg with me, she swore at him and I should have thrown her out. Whenever Lester talked to Marion he would say he was going to kill himself.

Joyce also told the RCMP that Marion had had one of Lester's files when they met on June 23.

By the winter of 1989, Bechtel was convinced Marion had stolen the files to cover up mistreatment of Lester. The suspicions of the RCMP and Brandon Police intensified when they had trouble locating her for several months. Police also wanted to talk to her in connection with criminal charges filed by DOCFS related to five allegedly fraudulent travel claims—charges which were eventually stayed. When finally Marion appeared at the Brandon Police Department to discuss those charges, they asked her to take a lie-detector test to clear herself in the theft of the files. Although Marion initially agreed, within a month her lawyer had advised her not to comply. Without any new leads and only circumstantial evidence, the RCMP closed their investigation of the stolen files in May 1989. They concluded they simply didn't have enough evidence to charge Marion. At the same time, there seemed to be no need to pursue the matter further because the chief medical examiner's office had decided not to hold an inquest into Lester's death. But no sooner was the RCMP file closed than the inquest review committee of the chief medical examiner's office issued a letter in August 1989 ordering that an inquest be held. The committee had concluded that the events leading to Lester's suicide deserved a closer look in light of the suspected theft of his child-welfare files.

In the meantime, Marion had filed a wrongful-dismissal suit against DOCFS with Labour Canada, which had still not been resolved. She first filed the legal action after DOCFS officials stubbornly refused to give her a severance slip after her suspension, leaving her ineligible for either unemployment insurance or welfare. For months, Marion had to rely on friends' help to support herself and her children while she searched for another job. Labour Canada officials eventually ordered DOCFS to issue the slip. But Marion still wanted compensation from

her former employer for being fired. When a round of preliminary negotiations did not resolve matters, an arbitration hearing was scheduled
for October 1990. Later, Marion would say that the only reason she
pursued her claim—especially considering she had only four months remaining in her contract with the agency—was her hope that a formal
hearing would draw attention to her broader concerns about the im-
proper handling of child-abuse cases at Sandy Bay.

During seven days of arbitration hearings between October 1990
and March 1991, DOCFS officials explained they'd fired her on the
grounds of dishonesty, including theft of Lester's files and submitting
fraudulent travel claims; incompetence; and insubordination. In the
end, the adjudicator concluded that too many people had had access to
Lester's files to blame Marion for their disappearance. She also noted
the agency was plagued by confused lines of authority, both between
workers and with local child-welfare committees and band politicians.
On the other hand, she dismissed Marion's claim that band leaders had
deliberately tried to cover up child-abuse cases. Instead, she ruled the
agency had been justified in firing Marion for falsifying travel claims to-
talling less than $200. At the same time, the adjudicator refused to
award costs to the agency because of its unreasonable delay in issuing a
severance slip. Still, before the adjudicator's written ruling was even released, it was obvious the hearing had only fuelled the antagonism
DOCFS and DOTC officials felt towards Marion. In May 1991, two
months before the adjudicator made her ruling, DOCFS and DOTC officials met with the Brandon Police Department in an attempt to revive
a criminal investigation into the fraudulent travel claims against Marion.

The task of handling the inquest into Lester's suicide landed on
the desk of Brandon Crown attorney Lawrence McInnes in the autumn
of 1989. When he first received the assignment, McInnes wasn't certain why the inquest had been called. The boy had committed suicide,
which was unfortunate but, sadly, not unusual. Perplexed, McInnes
called Manitoba's chief medical examiner, Dr. Peter Markesteyn, who
told him that questions about the missing files had led to the decision.
Without Lester's files, McInnes had a hard time preparing for the hearing. But by the time the one-day inquest was slated to begin in August
1990, he had ferreted out a few disturbing pieces of information.

Lester's records from the Brandon Mental Health Centre showed he'd been removed against medical advice twice during the year before his death. McInnes had also interviewed Marion, who'd raised concerns about how reports of sexual abuse were being investigated at Sandy Bay. Considering she was the prime suspect in the theft of the files, McInnes was sceptical about anything she said. But he had begun to wonder about how the agency had dealt with Lester, and asked that the inquest be delayed to allow more time for his investigation.

A short, round man with a frank, jovial manner, McInnes was a seasoned Crown attorney by the time he took on the inquest into Lester's death. Despite dreams of becoming another Perry Mason, McInnes had moved to Brandon after attending law school at the University of Manitoba. He first moved there to accept an articling job with the Crown attorney's office in 1974 and never left. A quintessential prairie boy, he'd lived in only two houses in his entire life: first, his boyhood home, until his marriage in 1974; then, the home in Brandon that he and his new wife had bought after moving from Winnipeg and in which they were now raising their children. After almost two decades of prosecuting crimes involving every kind of human cruelty, McInnes had learned to leave his work at the office. But this time would be different. The inquest into Lester's death would haunt him like few other cases ever had.

A chronic shortage of courtroom space in Brandon meant that the inquest, scheduled for four days in October 1991, was booked into an auditorium in the basement of the Agricultural Extension Centre. The room had the aura of a bingo hall, with high ceilings and row upon row of wood-and-metal stacking tables. As provincial court judge Brian Giesbrecht convened the hearing on the morning of October 7, the only person in the audience was a *Brandon Sun* reporter. No one appeared on behalf of DOCFS or Lester's family.

Thirteen witnesses took the stand in quick succession on the opening day, explaining the circumstances surrounding Lester's suicide and his missing child-welfare files. One of the first witnesses was Angus Starr, the boy's foster father in Brandon at the time of his death. A stocky man of medium height with slicked-back black hair, Starr had moved back to Sandy Bay after Lester's death and been elected chief for the second time. When he took the witness stand, Starr described what he knew of Lester's last day. Under questioning by McInnes, Starr also disclosed a disturbing conversation he'd had with Lester: "He made an attempt once to talk to me about an incident that happened in Sandy Bay with a gentleman by the name of Joe Desjarlais," Starr told the court. "He said, 'He tied me to a tree and then he raped me,' but he didn't elaborate exactly. He didn't go into details and then he broke down and he cried." Rather than reporting Lester's allegation, Starr decided not to press the issue out of concern that Lester might resent him for prying.

The next witness to take the stand was Joe Desjarlais, the man Lester had accused of raping him. After reminding him his testimony was protected under the Canada Evidence Act, McInnes confronted Joe, a big-boned, tall man with rounded shoulders, a spreading middle, and oily black hair.

"We've heard some suggestion that Lester alleged that you had sexually assaulted him," McInnes said to Joe.

"No, I never did," Joe replied.

"You never did?" McInnes said.

"No," Joe said.

"Okay," McInnes said.

"What happened at that time what you're talking about is I—I—was intending on starting—starting—a foster home for boys at my place with Lester," Joe explained. "Everything wasn't processed to get that house open for, like, a foster home, and the DOTC police, Al Miller, made up a story like I committed buggery on [another boy] and that's what buggered up the whole thing."

Before finishing his brief testimony, Joe also denied seeing Lester's child-welfare files or asking his older brother Cecil Desjarlais to obtain them. Cecil, tall, and bespectacled, took the stand next and said that, as a former band councillor in charge of child welfare, he'd once seen Lester's files at a meeting at Sandy Bay before the boy's death. But Cecil denied playing any part in the theft of the files from either the Brandon or the Sandy Bay child-welfare offices.

Morris Merrick, executive director of DOCFS, was the tenth witness of the day. A large man with a brusque manner, Merrick made it clear Marion had been a source of strife within the agency. Merrick, who had been assistant director during Marion's tenure, said she'd repeatedly changed Lester's treatment plans and refused to listen to advice from other workers and the community. On the stand, Merrick also took the opportunity to expound upon the agency's goal of returning children to their parents or extended family wherever possible. Reclaiming control over children's futures also meant respecting the wishes of local communities, he said. But Marion had ignored that commitment, acting like a "knight on a white horse" intent on saving the Indian people, he said. Complaints from co-workers and others about Marion had gone nowhere because then DOCFS director Esther Seidl had protected Marion. In the long run, Merrick did acknowledge that Lester had likely been revictimized by the internal conflicts between workers. As for the missing files, Merrick said they suspected Marion, but had no proof. Her dismissal had nothing to do with the missing files, he insisted. Instead, she'd been dismissed because of fraudulent travel claims and her poor job performance. When asked if he had stolen the files, Merrick said no.

Before adjourning at the end of the first day, McInnes asked Judge Giesbrecht to issue a warrant for the arrest of a witness who had evaded the police's attempts to serve her with a subpoena. Police had left messages on Esther Seidl's answering-machine, knocked on her door, and contacted her employer, to no avail. A former landlord told police that Seidl, who was working part-time for a tribal council at The Pas and enrolled in a graduate social-work program at the University of Manitoba, had no intention of appearing. The judge reluctantly issued the warrant, but asked police to give her one day's grace before making an arrest. Within hours, Seidl had agreed to appear at the inquest.

Day two of the inquest began with testimony from John Chudzik, the provincial child-abuse coordinator, who had often had phone calls from Marion complaining about her difficulties investigating child-abuse cases at Sandy Bay. Chudzik said he was aware that there had been cases of the chief and council interfering when their relatives became the target of child-abuse investigations. Band officials had also insisted children not be removed from the community, limiting the resources available to child-welfare workers, he said. He said he had no doubt that workers who ignored such edicts at Sandy Bay or any other reserve put their jobs on the line because band officials had the power to hire or fire.

That tension had been a chronic problem since the earliest days of the Native child-welfare agencies, he told the court. Although governed by provincial legislation—the Child and Family Services Act—local communities had deliberately been given a voice in the operation of the agencies through reserve-based child-welfare committees. In some communities, the committees, which often included an elected band councillor, functioned well, acting as an invaluable source of information about children and their families. In other places, heated conflicts developed among committee members, the chief and council, and child-welfare workers. Chudzik said he was fully aware that workers sometimes gave in to pressure not to pursue abuse investigations for fear of reprisals.

At Sandy Bay, Marion had stirred up controversy by jumping on child-abuse cases too quickly, without adequate local consultation, he said. Chudzik also believed Marion and Seidl, as non-Natives, were under extra pressure because of the agency's push to have Aboriginal staff. After Marion's firing, her complaints to provincial officials had been one of the factors which had prompted then Family Services Minister Charlotte Oleson to order an internal review of DOCFS in the autumn of 1988. Although Chudzik had been one of two officials assigned to the review, he was vague about what they had found after examining files of Sandy Bay cases and meeting with agency officials and workers to discuss problems. He said provincial officials had avoided trying to impose any solutions out of respect for the chiefs who comprised the board of DOCFS. The chiefs were the ones who had to decide what to do. When asked for a report about the review's findings, Chudzik said it wasn't available because it was never completed. Months later, the unfinished report containing damning evidence about the government's handling of the matter would surface at the inquest.

One of the other witnesses who testified on day two also raised serious concerns about the Aboriginal child-welfare system. Hedi Epp, the chief medical examiner's investigator who had worked on Lester's case, said the agencies didn't have enough staff or money to cope with burgeoning caseloads. As a result, workers often lurched from crisis to crisis, sometimes leaving children at risk in unsafe homes. On the other hand, children who were apprehended were often shuttled between a string of foster homes because placements broke down. The outspoken Epp, who had worked as a nurse on reserves in the past, said she'd seen situations where political interference from a chief or councillor had made it difficult for workers to protect a child. So, when Marion called and recounted her frustrations with the political meddling she'd faced at Sandy Bay, Epp wasn't surprised. Before she stepped down from the witness stand, McInnes asked Epp if she had any final observations based on her investigations of thirty-six children who had died in the care of Aboriginal and white child-welfare agencies over the previous four years. In her usual blunt way, Epp replied: "Do you have a week off the record?"

On the morning of the third day, the elusive Seidl, a petite, blue-eyed blonde, took the stand and asked for protection from prosecution under the Canada Evidence Act. Seidl had been the director of DOCFS for four years, ending in December 1988. As McInnes questioned her, she volunteered little information. Seidl said she'd hired Marion with full knowledge that she'd been fired from the Children's Aid for falsifying educational credentials. DOCFS had urgently needed to fill the contract position, and all of Marion's other references had checked out. As friction increased between Marion and other staff, Seidl asked her to attend a workshop on Indian culture to sensitize her to cross-cultural differences. As time passed, other problems, like Marion's personal financial woes, left Seidl wondering about whether she could be trusted. Yet Seidl made it clear she'd opposed firing Marion and had clashed with Ernie Daniels, director of the Dakota Ojibway Tribal Council, over his decision. When asked if she'd stolen the files, Seidl said no.

On the issue of political interference by band officials in child-abuse cases, Seidl's testimony seemed evasive, especially considering her decade of experience in Aboriginal child welfare. When asked whether a chief accused of abuse could squelch an investigation, Seidl said, "Not to my knowledge." She denied that, as an administrator at DOCFS, she had had problems with chiefs trying to exert undue influence. Occasionally a chief would raise a concern on behalf of a band member with a DOCFS supervisor or the local child-welfare committee, she said. And she did remember one child's case at Sandy Bay in

which band officials tried to intervene directly. But after several meetings, they'd agreed to let the agency handle the matter. When Seidl
stepped down from the witness stand, her testimony had shed little
new light on either Lester's death or the theft of his files.

Up to this point, the inquest had unfolded as McInnes had expected. He'd deliberately waited until the end to call the witness who'd
been the target of so much animosity. Now it was time to have Marion
answer the accusations against her, from criticism of her handling of
Lester's case to the theft of the files. As McInnes called his twentieth
witness, he believed he was about to wrap up the inquest. McInnes had
little doubt Marion was responsible for both the missing files and the
sloppy handling of Lester's case. But almost as soon as he launched
into his carefully plotted list of questions, Marion's testimony began to
veer off course. Like a tap that had suddenly been turned on full,
Marion poured out her story. From the beginning, she said, she had
been warned by both Esther Seidl and Morris Merrick that becoming a
DOCFS supervisor at Sandy Bay wouldn't be easy because of the politically charged atmosphere. They told her she'd been chosen for the job
because she wouldn't be easily intimidated. She described how Lester
had been on the run from the Sioux Valley group home for weeks
when she arrived at Sandy Bay. She'd had the boy picked up and sent
to the Brandon Mental Health Centre after a teacher reported the boy
was burning himself with cigarettes and slashing his wrist. But, against
her wishes, the chief and council had insisted Lester be removed from
the BMHC against medical advice and returned to the reserve. As
Marion talked, McInnes glanced over his shoulder several times and
noticed three Aboriginal women seated around a table at the back of
the huge room. Each time Marion commented about the problems
child-welfare workers faced, the women nodded in agreement.

Towards the end of her first hour on the stand, Marion faltered.
Her eyes suddenly filled with tears and she struggled to keep her composure. She apologized, tried to go on, saying she hadn't realized how
hard it would be to talk about Lester. The judge ordered a five-minute
break. Marion pulled herself together, and continued. As the hours
went by, McInnes realized, to his surprise, that Marion's recounting of
events seemed credible and was often well documented. He'd also been

gauging the reactions of the trio at the back of the room, whom he'd met during one of the breaks. "As I'm questioning her, I'm looking over my shoulder and these ladies are kind of like a jury and are nodding their heads in agreement about what she was saying about the agency," McInnes recalled. "I knew they were associated with the agency. And so afterwards, I went and talked to them and said, 'What do you think of what she was saying?' And they said, 'Well, it's right on. That's the way it is. It's a disgrace.' And so at that point I became convinced there was a lot more to this than what we had so far found out."

A central theme in Marion's testimony was her frustration with trying to investigate sexual-abuse cases at Sandy Bay. She not only said she had felt unsupported by the agency when the going got rough, but accused certain band leaders of interference on behalf of alleged offenders who were relatives or friends. Over a period of four months, Marion had reported about thirty cases of sexual abuse, triggering plenty of tension and anger in the small community. As she told the inquest: "There was always political interference. The offenders in most of these cases—a lot of them were very tightly tied to the chief and council at that particular time. And in particular, Cecil Desjarlais, and Isaac Beaulieu, who was the chairperson of the local child-welfare committee, appeared to have a much greater stake in protecting the adults in the community than they did protecting the children. They provided no support whatsoever for me. The [DOCFS] workers were always stuck between a rock and a hard place. If you do it as Marion says you should ... the chief's going to come down on you or Cecil's going to come down even harder and you won't have a job and that's exactly how it was."

As evidence, Marion referred to the controversial case of the young girl whom teachers suspected was being sexually abused. She described how Cecil Desjarlais had prevented her from apprehending the child, whose alleged abusers were related to him. Four years after that incident, Marion firmly believed the child was still at risk. As a result of the concerns raised by her testimony, McInnes asked the judge to order that the girl's file be subpoenaed for the inquest. A series of witnesses would ultimately reveal troubling questions about the agency's handling of the child's case.

On the fourth day of the inquest, Marion was recalled to finish her testimony. By now the strain of the hearing had begun to show. Initial media reports had painted Marion as the villain. She told the court she had begun to wonder if she was a witness or a defendant. She passionately denied stealing Lester's files, saying she had gone to great lengths instead to ensure someone would investigate his death. Instead, she pointed the finger back at Morris Merrick and Cecil Desjarlais as the most likely suspects in the theft of the files. Merrick had been out to get her, she said, and had taken the files, knowing she'd be blamed. The only other reason anyone would steal the files would be to cover up the agency's neglect of Lester over a six-year period and the allegations of abuse involving Joe, she said. As Marion told the court: "I was with that agency and supervisor at Sandy Bay for not even a year, you know, so how can the finger be pointed at me with—with Marion Glover being the person who has everything to hide? The agency in this case has a tremendous amount to hide and so does Cecil Desjarlais."

Nevertheless several unexplained inconsistencies arose during her testimony. Marion insisted she had no recollection of being interviewed by Brandon Police Constable Carol Fisher about the theft of the files. She also contradicted police statements that she had refused to take a lie-detector test and didn't remember being visited by an RCMP officer about the matter. She flatly denied that she had once dropped Lester off in Portage la Prairie and told him to hitchhike the rest of the way back to Sandy Bay, as one DOCFS worker had testified.

Before the day was over, Judge Giesbrecht ordered that a long list of additional documents be submitted to the inquest, including Lester's school files and Marion's wrongful-dismissal arbitration ruling. During Marion's first day on the witness stand, both McInnes and Giesbrecht had suddenly realized that the issues unravelling before them went far beyond one boy's suicide. Giesbrecht recalled the pivotal conversation during which McInnes suggested extending the inquest. "It was at that point that I really had to make the decision— should I limit this or should I let it get bigger," Giesbrecht says. "Although I really had no idea yet how big the issues were, it was fairly clear that if I let it get bigger, then I was going to have to let it get a lot bigger. That was the biggest decision I had to make in that case." He adjourned the inquest and gave McInnes the go-ahead to pursue those larger questions. The hearings would not resume until almost six months later.

Presiding over the inquest had been a random assignment for Giesbrecht. When the inquest was rescheduled after being delayed from August 1990, the original judge was unavailable. The trial coordinator passed the matter on to Giesbrecht, a judge with more than a dozen years' experience in family and juvenile court. He'd been the youngest person appointed to the bench in 1976, at age twenty-seven, just four years after graduation from the University of Manitoba. Working in the family court in Brandon had exposed him almost daily to the mainstream and Aboriginal child-welfare systems. With Native families comprising over 50 per cent of the child-protection cases he handled, Giesbrecht knew that Native-run child welfare agencies like DOCFS were essential. Now he faced the daunting task of criticizing an agency he essentially believed in.

Raised in a white, middle-class family in the West Kildonan neighbourhood of Winnipeg, Giesbrecht was well aware of the social and economic gulf between his own background and that of the children whose lives were under scrutiny at the inquest. Although he still had a lot to learn about Aboriginal culture, Giesbrecht had been fortunate to have parents who valued racial diversity. His mother's keen interest in teaching English to new Canadians had widened their family's horizons as she turned their home into a haven for her students. His parents had left behind their roots in a small southern Manitoba Mennonite community before Giesbrecht was born. They'd also left the Mennonite Church after his father defied that denomination's pacifist tradition and served in the Canadian army during the Second World War. The family settled in Winnipeg, where his father taught school. Needless to say, educational achievement was prized in the household. When the teenage Giesbrecht's obsession for playing guitar in a rock 'n' roll band almost turned him into a high-school drop-out, his parents were exasperated. But to their relief, Giesbrecht's intellectual side finally blossomed in university. During law school, he married, but the relationship broke down after three years. After moving to Brandon and becoming a provincial judge, Giesbrecht remarried in 1979, and bought an acreage south of Brandon. He often thought about his own four children when making difficult decisions on the bench about how best to help other young people.

After the inquest was adjourned in October 1991, Marion contacted the Winnipeg media, seeking publicity for her concerns. The only media outlet to cover the initial four days of hearings had been the *Brandon Sun*. In response to Marion's pleas, both the tabloid *Winnipeg Sun* and CBC's national *Sunday Morning* radio program carried feature stories about the inquest in late December. The stories raised concerns about DOCFS's handling of both Lester's case and that of the Sandy Bay girl whom Marion had described at the inquest. Marion's accusations about DOCFS prompted an angry response from Morris Merrick. He was quoted in the *Winnipeg Sun* as saying she had "a bone to pick with Indians" because they'd fired her. Merrick also downplayed abuse allegations against Joe Desjarlais, suggesting the man had become an unfair target. A few weeks later, Merrick and other DOCFS officials also went on the offensive against Marion, holding a news conference to say they'd investigated the abuse allegations involving the Sandy Bay girl in 1988 and found no evidence to substantiate them. They accused Marion of being a "pathological liar" and gave reporters copies of the Labour Canada arbitration ruling, which said the agency was justified in firing her. DOCFS also demanded an apology from the Winnipeg media for "besmirching" their reputation.

Marion also used the media to aim harsh criticism at the provincial Family Services department for its reluctance to intervene on the girl's behalf. She lambasted Family Services Minister Harold Gilleshammer for asking the same bureaucrats to review the girl's case who had earlier deemed she was not at risk. By now, a grass-roots group, the Aboriginal Women's Unity Coalition, had also joined Marion in demanding safeguards to prevent political interference by band officials in child-abuse cases. Three months earlier, the same coalition had supported a mother's hunger strike to protest alleged political interference from a chief, her ex-husband, in an abuse investigation involving their children. Now the coalition was lobbying to have chiefs banned from the boards of child-welfare agencies, and an independent child advocate appointed by the province to mediate complaints. They'd also asked the Assembly of Manitoba Chiefs to set up a task force to scrutinize the quality of care being offered by Aboriginal child-welfare agencies. They repeated their demands a month later, when a controversial series of stories in the *Winnipeg Free Press* in January 1992 suggested political interference had been a problem in several suspicious child-death investigations.

Just before the inquest into Lester's death was about to resume in mid-February 1992, McInnes asked for another delay after his wife suffered a severe heart attack. The intervening months had been chaotic for McInnes, as he struggled to keep up his regular caseload and prepare for the upcoming hearings. Widespread publicity about the inquest had prompted a wave of calls to McInnes from people eager to pass on information about DOCFS. The pile of additional child-welfare files subpoenaed by McInnes had also provided a string of new leads, and the list of potential witnesses was growing longer. Although the RCMP assigned an officer to assist McInnes, his workload burgeoned. When his wife became seriously ill, the combined stress at home and work was overwhelming. But McInnes was determined to see the inquest through to its conclusion. Judge Giesbrecht agreed to reschedule the hearings for early April with the hope of finishing within a month. Neither Giesbrecht nor McInnes realized that the inquest had gained a momentum of its own.

CHAPTER SEVEN

FORTY DAYS AND FORTY NIGHTS

"Lester didn't kill himself. The system killed him."

—Angela Eastman

Publicity about the inquest had generated so much interest that reporters from the major Winnipeg media arrived early to make sure they got seats when hearings resumed in April 1992. The stuffy basement room in the old, red-brick Brandon courthouse filled with reporters and onlookers as Crown attorney Lawrence McInnes thumbed through files in preparation for calling the first of forty more witnesses. Soon, a lawyer and an official from DOCFS lugged in briefcases and began unpacking documents at a wooden table on the left side of the makeshift courtroom. When Marion arrived, she carried a stack of papers as well, heightening curiosity about what her role would be in the second phase of the inquest.

As the inquest got under way, Doug Paterson, a tall, reedy lawyer hired by DOCFS, asked for legal standing in order to cross-examine witnesses. Judge Giesbrecht quickly granted his request. Then, to everyone's surprise, Marion rose from her seat in the front row and asked the judge for the same status. She argued that her credibility was under attack by DOCFS. Since she couldn't afford a lawyer, she wanted to represent herself at the inquest. Caught by surprise, Paterson immediately objected. Allowing her to question witnesses would bog down the proceedings, he insisted. After listening to their arguments, Giesbrecht ruled that the credibility of both Marion and DOCFS would indeed be major issues throughout the hearings. To the dismay of DOCFS, the judge granted Marion legal standing alongside the agency, a decision that would dramatically alter the course of the inquest. She quickly stepped forward and took her place between Paterson and McInnes at the table.

The rest of the day was consumed with testimony from former DOCFS social worker Danta Kunzman, whom the agency had flown in from Texas to testify. Kunzman, a middle-aged woman wearing a black suit and a dour expression, didn't try to hide her hostility towards Marion. She made it clear that she blamed Marion for the confusion surrounding Lester's case. Marion had a way of keeping everyone off-balance and stirring up conflict, she testified. They'd clashed over everything, from Kunzman's plans to reunite Lester and his sister Annette with their mother, to Marion's insistence that the boy had been sexually abused. Kunzman defended her belief in Joyce's claims of sobriety but admitted she'd never seen the family's file. Joyce had deserved another chance with Lester, in keeping with the agency's policy of returning children to their families, she insisted. As for the abuse allegations involving the boy, Kunzman said she had dismissed them because Marion offered only vague information. Instead, she concluded Marion was projecting her own unresolved problems onto Lester. During questioning by Paterson, Kunzman went further, divulging that Marion had made no secret of the fact that she'd been sexually abused as a child. Kunzman believed that was why Marion saw abuse everywhere she looked. When Marion rose to cross-examine Kunzman, they quickly became embroiled in a heated battle. By the time the afternoon ended, the animosity between them had completely overshadowed the substance of Kunzman's testimony.

The next morning, Angela Eastman, vice-principal of Sandy Bay elementary school, took the witness stand and revealed a startling new twist to the mystery of Lester's missing DOCFS files. Eastman calmly described how school officials had searched for Lester's school files after Giesbrecht subpoenaed them five months earlier. To their astonishment, Lester's main academic file, another confidential file, and Eastman's personal file on Lester had all vanished, despite being kept under lock and key. Only school staff, DOCFS workers, and band officials could peruse the files, and no one was allowed to remove them. Eastman, an elder with the Sandy Bay band and twenty-year teacher, said she couldn't recall another instance of a student's entire file disappearing. She also said the possiblity that Marion could have stolen these files was "extremely remote." Marion wouldn't have been able to gain access to all of the files and remove them from the school without being noticed. When asked by Marion whether Cecil Desjarlais had such access, Eastman hesitated and seemed reluctant to respond. Then she replied, that as chairman of the education board, Cecil would have had the right to look at any school files. His wife also worked at the school. For the first time, Eastman's testimony about the missing school files cast serious doubt on whether Marion had been responsible for masterminding the disappearance of Lester's child-welfare files as well.

Eastman, who had been Lester's confidante, also testified how the boy had told her about being sexually assaulted by Joe. She had no doubt Lester had told the truth. "He's [Joe] the bogeyman of Sandy Bay," Eastman earnestly told the court. "All the children are afraid of him. All the mothers caution their children." When Eastman finished her testimony, she slipped outside into the chilly spring morning to smoke a cigarette on the worn stone steps of the courthouse. Reporters followed her outside to do interviews. Obviously relieved at finishing her testimony, she told them she had decided to speak her mind for Lester's sake, even if it meant a backlash back home. Then she made a comment which would eventually sum up the sentiments of many who appeared at the inquest. "Lester didn't kill himself," Eastman said bluntly. "The system killed him."

The controversy surrounding the six-year-old Sandy Bay girl whom teachers had suspected was a victim of sexual abuse in the winter of

1988 soon became the focus of several witnesses' testimony. McInnes was obviously trying to draw parallels between her case and that of Lester. The girl's former Grade 1 teacher, Trudy Muirhead Yu, testified that the child had often disrupted the class with her bizarre, aggressive behaviour. One day the girl stripped in class, and Yu noticed a heart with an arrow drawn on her stomach in ballpoint pen, accompanied by the words "Joe and [name of girl], best lovers in Sandy Bay." Realizing that the child could barely print her own name, let alone write a sentence like that, Yu reported the incident to the principal. She said another teacher also wrote to the principal, complaining that the girl often said she "hated" a certain relative. When asked to draw a picture of her family, the girl had drawn a man with a large, protruding penis and said that "all boys were bad." Such reports from teachers had eventually led Marion to order the child's apprehension. That sparked a confrontation with the girl's guardians and Cecil, who intervened on their behalf. In the end, DOCFS failed in its attempt to remove the girl from her home. After the incident, Yu said one of the girl's relatives showed up at the school and threatened her. The principal warned the anxious Yu not to stay alone at the school.

The next day, Ellen Cook took the stand, wearing a bright pink t-shirt with the slogan "World's Greatest Grandma." Cook began by telling the judge that a separate public inquiry into political interference in child welfare on reserves was needed. She felt an inquest into a child's suicide wasn't the right forum to investigate the problem. Then she pulled out a picture of Lester, explaining that she carried his photo as a reminder to treat each child as an individual. "I always hear our leaders saying children are a resource and our future," Cook told the court. "At the same time I see these children are not being protected as they should be. Does that mean we have no future?"

While teaching music at the Sandy Bay school, Cook too had noticed the young girl's strange behaviour and seen the drawing on her stomach. For two or three weeks, the child had tried to strip almost daily in her music class. Cook said she talked to Yu and urged her, as home room teacher, to report their suspicions. Yu was afraid of a backlash. But Cook said she'd back her and go to the teachers' union if there were job repercussions. In the end, little was done to help the child, Cook said. When McInnes questioned her about Cecil's role in the community, she said many people feared him because they believed he used "bad medicine"—calling upon evil spirits to bring harm to others. Cecil's father had been known to put curses on people, she said.

Fear of reprisals from relatives for reporting child abuse was a widespread problem for both teachers and child-welfare workers on reserves, Cook testified. She described the reaction she got from a worker with the Awasis Agency of Northern Manitoba after reporting incest involving one of her young students at the school where she now taught in Birch River, a small town in western Manitoba. The Awasis child-welfare worker told Cook she "might as well kiss her job goodbye" if she proceeded with the case, because the girl's family was in power on the reserve. "To me, it all boils down to politics," Cook said. "If you step on that person's toes and that person has umpteen family members on the reserve, you aren't going to get in in the next election."

To go one step farther, Cook said, for many Aboriginal women, such problems have fuelled fears about self-government. Handing over more power to male leaders who have not protected the rights of women and children will only lead to further victimization, she said. Power is already concentrated in too few hands under the Indian Act–style of governing imposed by the federal government. In order that the power be wielded responsibly, widespread healing from the devastation of colonization must take place. She said the first step is for men to face the way they've taken out their pain and anger on those closest to them. "They seem to definitely have their heads in the sand," she told the court. "It's a denial."

Realizing the impact Cook's testimony was having, Paterson tried to discredit her during his cross-examination. He asked her in a condescending tone whether her views came from a "feminist slant." Cook replied: "I would not say feminist. I would say a protector of children." Next, Paterson tried to throw her off balance by asking whether she'd been an abused wife in the past. Without hesitating, Cook fired back, "Yes I have, but not for long." Their verbal sparring continued, with Paterson losing each round. He finally retreated in frustration.

Clearly impressed by Cook's candid testimony, Giesbrecht leaned forward, to pose questions of his own, and asked if she had any final comments. Cook responded that at the heart of many parents' apparent neglect of their children are their own unmet needs. But, she added, as psychologist Abraham Maslow outlined in his hierarchy of needs, until basic physical requirements for shelter and food are met, people have no energy left for self-actualization. With so many Aboriginal people struggling to survive, it's no wonder they have little left to give their children, she said. "Most parents are stuck in neutral at the bottom of that hierarchy," she said. "It's not until their basic needs are met that they will be able to meet their children's needs." Cook said that the biggest challenge for Aboriginal leaders is to find a way to free their people from the crushing burden of poverty.

Although Cook's testimony had consumed most of the day, a final witness was called late that afternoon. Dennis Roulette, a Sandy Bay resident who had worked for DOCFS until 1987, said he'd been fired from his job for refusing to send files on seventeen local child-abuse cases to the agency's head office in Brandon. Roulette, a bearded man wearing a white nylon jacket emblazoned with the Sandy Bay band logo, said he'd withheld the files on orders from the chief, Harry Desjarlais, and the chief's nephew Cecil Desjarlais, who was a band councillor at the time. They, along with other council members, were locked in a dispute with DOCFS over their lack of local control. The chief and council were threatening to set up their own child-welfare agency at Sandy Bay. After being fired, Roulette said, he'd kept the files, which he pointed out were really his own notes on cases, at home. Around the time Lester died, Cecil had come to him and asked if he still had his notes. When Roulette said yes, Cecil ordered him to burn them. Roulette explained: "He didn't want the information going out of Sandy Bay about our own people. He said, 'These are our own people. We have to protect our own people.'"

At first, Roulette refused to speculate on Cecil's motivation for the destruction of the files. But when Marion rose to cross-examine him, he acknowledged that Cecil's brother Joe had been named as a suspected abuser in some of the case notes he'd burned. Marion asked if Roulette believed Cecil was trying to protect Joe. Roulette replied, "He always did." Then Marion posed this question: "If I said Cecil didn't take the files, what would you say?" Roulette said such a denial "would be questionable." Cecil, as the band councillor with both the child-welfare and policing portfolios at the time, had had access to both the missing child-welfare and the school files.

Roulette's own disillusionment with DOCFS was obvious. The agency had strayed far from its original mandate of community-based child-welfare services, said Roulette, who was vice-chairman of Sandy Bay's education board. The agency had become too centralized, with officials more preoccupied with paper-pushing and policies than serving children's needs. Child-welfare workers feared losing their jobs if they apprehended children of influential families. That meant youth like Lester were being abandoned. "Kids are being dropped," he told the court. "They're being thrown away."

One of the final witnesses called that week was a member of the Dakota Ojibway Tribal Council Police. Corporal Al Miller, a muscular man in a grey DOTC police uniform, testified that Joe had a reputation in the community for violence, and had had a number of confrontations with police. At the same time, Joe repeatedly asked the local child-welfare committee for approval to open a group for troubled boys on the reserve. When McInnes questioned Miller about the number of child sexual assaults in the community, Miller said they'd averaged two or three complaints each week during the time he'd worked there, from late 1985 to May 1988. The allegations were always referred to the Amaranth RCMP for investigation. He said an RCMP officer had told him recently that the number of complaints had not diminished since then. Miller also said DOCFS workers were reluctant at times to apprehend children of leaders at Sandy Bay. In one case where a band councillor was suspected of abusing his children, child-welfare workers told Miller they didn't want to apprehend the children. "You just don't do that," Miller said they told him. "You just don't apprehend a councillor's family."

By the end of the first week, a pattern was emerging in both the witnesses' testimony and the dynamics in the courtroom among McInnes, Paterson, and Marion. The inquest was rapidly expanding far beyond the circumstances surrounding Lester's death into questions about whether DOCFS, and even other Aboriginal child-welfare agencies, were fulfilling their legal mandate to protect children. Paterson, a lawyer with a thriving Brandon law practice across the street from the courthouse, had done his best to try to narrow that focus, rising often to object to questions posed by both Marion and McInnes. But, frustrated by Giesbrecht's leniency in both the scope and the style of questions, Paterson soon gave up his offensive. During that week, Isaac Beaulieu, vice-chairman of the DOCFS board and a member of the elders' council at Sandy Bay, also began attending the hearings full-time to monitor events and field questions from the media. Beaulieu, a short, stout balding man with a long, grey ponytail, defended the agency at every turn.

Meanwhile, Marion was displaying a surprising knack for drawing information from witnesses. In part, she had the advantage of inside knowledge, having been a participant in many of the events under scrutiny. But she also had the ability to detect cracks in a witness's defences and to keep up a barrage of questions until they were answered clearly. McInnes had watched in amazement, for example, as Marion extracted key details from Roulette about the burnt files that he, a seasoned Crown attorney, had been unable to obtain.

When the inquest resumed the following week, Giesbrecht announced that Joe Desjarlais had breached court procedure by seeking to influence the judge with a letter. Giesbrecht submitted the letter as an exhibit and urged Paterson to instruct Joe not to do it again. In response, Paterson rose with a list of complaints stored up from the previous week. The negative publicity from the inquest was causing problems for the entire Desjarlais family, he said. Joe had been fired from his job as janitor at the Sandy Bay school, and a couple who had applied for a foster-care licence—and happened to have the name Desjarlais—had been told they might not get it. Paterson demanded that Giesbrecht limit any further testimony related to Aboriginal self-government, referring to Cook's speech the previous week. Giesbrecht responded by saying he had no intention of delving into self-government issues during the inquest, but would allow plenty of leeway in the questioning of witnesses. As for media coverage and the resulting fall-out for members of the Desjarlais clan, Giesbrecht said there was nothing he could do—the press had a right to report the facts.

Joe's rambling, four-page, hand-printed letter provided one of the few glimpses the inquest would get into how his mind worked. In the letter, he complained that he had lost his job because of publicity which had turned him into a "boogie man child molester" and violated his rights. He went on to explain that he had been labelled a "boogie man" at Sandy Bay because of his work as a security guard at community events:

> Traditionally at gatherings for a celebration or spiritual cere-monies, several young men were selected by the elders to be a "boogie man" [windigokanak]. It was a great honour and such men took days of preparation, designing and making their outfits. These were the people that provided security and enforced the rules of the event and the moral guidelines of the tribe (while camping on the ground, where the event took place) such as during the annual sundance. Subsequently, often when children were misbehaving, the parents would threaten to call on the windigos. An acquaintance of mine from Whitefish Bay, Ontario, known as "LaLa," shares this kind of image. He is a good security person at their pow-wows. In fact while camping there, I overheard a mother telling her child "go to sleep, LaLa is coming." Otherwise, LaLa is a respected family man in the community.
>
> You may never have experienced the feeling of utter frus-tration when you have no recourse to being attacked, being judged and publicly humiliated as if you were less than an an-imal. I have feelings, hurts, love, friends and relatives. I once had a mother and father and I am sure they loved me while they were alive. I survived as an orphan. I wonder how you (courts, media, lawyers etc.) would feel if you were put in such a helpless position. Have you ever been so publicly and hurtfully humiliated and have no way to defend yourself. Perhaps I am not attractive or able to cross my legs to expose my thighs for the pleasure of those around me. No. On the contrary, I have been referred to in various degrading ways not the least being "child molester" ogre or boogie man.

He went on to accuse Native politicians and "white self-proclaimed crusaders" of blaming him for the mistakes made in Lester's case. He said he had made an offering to the spirits of Joyce and Lester, asking them to forgive the people involved in the inquest for bad-mouthing the dead. He criticized school administrators for firing him while ignoring sexual-assault charges against another band member who worked at the school. He also lashed out at the justice system, saying Aboriginal people needed a separate system whereby individual rights would be protected:

> The present governing system at Sandy Bay or other native communities is plagued with systems subject to abuse and neglect by its leaders. At this time there needs to be a great deal of consideration given to the establishment of fair and honourable codes based on moral and spiritual standards. Writing to you is probably out of line, but I could not find any other alternative. If I am charged for this action, please make it clear it is NOT for a sexual offence. In reading this letter, I hope you realize that I am not the same figment the media created.

> Thank you
> Joe (Pee-Ance) Desjarlais

During a break in the hearing, Beaulieu tried to defend Joe, saying that he was a conscientious employee and had worked at the school only after students were gone, from 4:00 P.M. until midnight. But Beaulieu also admitted complaints from concerned parents had prompted the decision to fire Joe.

The first witness to take the stand during the second week of the second phase of the inquest was Elaine Scott, who had worked on and off for DOCFS since 1987. Scott, a slender, reticent woman, cited now-familiar complaints about Marion—that she had created confusion between workers and with Sandy Bay leaders, treated them in a condescending manner, and been disorganized in her handling of cases. Obviously unhappy about being called to testify, Scott responded to many of Marion's questions with one-word answers and glared at her with open hostility. Like previous DOCFS witnesses, she admitted the power struggles within the agency during Marion's tenure had interfered with providing the best care for children. But she steadfastly insisted that Marion was the source of those conflicts.

Part way through her day-long testimony, McInnes began to question Scott about the controversial case of the six-year-old girl whom Marion had tried to apprehend after teachers reported suspicions that the child was being abused. McInnes had just received the girl's child-welfare and school files, which the judge had ordered. Referring to the girl's child-welfare file, McInnes pointed out that DOCFS had closed her case in August 1989. The closing summary on her file indicated that an RCMP investigation and assessment by a psychologist found no evidence of sexual assault. But McInnes noted that the girl's school file contained several urgent referrals to DOCFS from worried teachers in the months after her file was closed. Scott acknowledged the referrals from the teachers should have been in the girl's file but couldn't explain what had happened, because by then she'd left the agency.

That day reporters noticed that McInnes had placed a braid of sweetgrass and a brown leather medicine pouch on the table in front of him. At the time he would say only that the traditional Indian objects had been lent to him for protection of the court because of concerns about "bad medicine." Each day for the rest of the inquest, McInnes laid the sweetgrass and medicine bag on the table beside his wooden lectern. Long after the hearings were completed, he explained that he'd been warned that his role in the inquest would make him vulnerable to "bad medicine." The two objects had come from a woman who had a vision in which a young boy, who looked like Lester, appeared and told her what to put in the medicine pouch. McInnes respected the potential power of the sacred objects to counter the fear of "bad medicine" that troubled many witnesses.

On the second day of testimony that week, McInnes called a surprise witness. The hearings had been moved to a high-ceilinged, second-floor courtroom so spacious that reporters had to sit in the jury box to hear witnesses' testimony. Before the man took the stand, McInnes asked the judge to ban publication of the witness's name or place of employment, except that he was now a police officer in another province. Then the witness, a man with a brush of salt-and-pepper hair, broad shoulders, and gentle black eyes, haltingly began to tell a story which dated back over thirty years. He was about thirteen at the time, and living at the residential school at Sandy Bay run by the Roman Catholic Church. Late one evening, he'd gone outside to the outhouse. That's when it happened.

Tears welled up in the big man's eyes and trickled down his face as the memory flooded back. He stopped talking, hung his head, and struggled to regain his composure. Someone offered a box of tissues and, after a long pause, he continued.

He said that when he stepped into the outhouse on that long-ago night, a teenager who was a year older, and much bigger, was already there. The teenager said he wanted to have sex, but he refused. Then the older boy forced himself on him and raped him. "I told him no a few times, but it was as if he didn't hear," the man testified, his voice cracking. "It was very painful."

McInnes asked the identity of his attacker. The witness responded with the name of a prominent man who, years later, had been involved in Lester's care. The witness said he'd decided to come forward after publicity about Lester's suicide mentioned the man's role in the case. "I had to come here and tell people what kind of person he was," the man said. "When I was a teenager, I constantly drank and blamed myself. I didn't know if it was my fault ... I feel as if my life's been taken away from me." About the same time as that assault happened, one of the lay brothers at the school also began sexually abusing him and two other boys. After years of misery, he ran away from the school and the reserve, and has been back only briefly for family visits since then. But recovering from the devastating impact of the abuse had been tough. He became a loner, had trouble trusting anyone. Finally, he'd sought treatment less than two years earlier at the urging of a police psychologist. Testifying at the inquest was the first time he'd spoken publicly about his abuse.

The man's testimony stunned everyone in the courtroom. Not only had his raw pain shaken those listening, but it had raised the troubling question of whether Lester also had been victimized by the same abuser. Reporters' eyes filled with tears, while the lawyers sat in silence. Marion rose, stumbled through a few questions, and gave up. Paterson did the same. Before the man left, Giesbrecht gently praised him for having the courage to come forward. Then, without a break, McInnes called the next witness, the man who had just been accused of rape. McInnes wasted no time in confronting him with the allegation. Taken aback, the man vehemently denied the accusation. He also denied knowing about any sexual abuse at the residential school. Then he stepped down from the witness stand and the judge ordered a brief recess.

After consulting with Paterson during the break, the man returned to the courtroom to answer more questions. He testified that he had hardly seen his accuser over the years, and that the man had likely confused him with another band member with the same name and of a similiar age. He also suggested the victim might have made up the story to get back at his namesake, who had had an affair with the man's wife. Faced with an accusation of mistaken identity, Giesbrecht ordered that the police officer be recalled to the stand. But he'd already left the city by car, so the RCMP's highway patrol were notified to track him down.

Within an hour, the police officer had been located and once again took the stand. Obviously taken aback at the suggestion he might have mistaken the identity of his abuser, he said he had absolutely no doubt who had assaulted him. As for his wife's affair, he said that had been dealt with between himself and his partner and had nothing to do with the inquest. "I don't feel any revenge for anybody," he told the court in a steady voice. "The only reason I'm testifying is so that the courts might decide what transpired with this boy that committed suicide."

On a frigid November evening more than two years later, the man sat in a Winnipeg restaurant, his wife at his side, and recalled how frightened he'd been at the inquest. The night before his testimony, he'd tossed and turned for hours in his motel room. When he walked into the courtroom the next morning, he'd been intimidated at the sight of DOCFS board chairman Isaac Beaulieu, whom he knew would treat his testimony with disdain. "I got very, very scared," he says. Somehow, he pulled himself together and told his story to the judge. But by the time he finished, he was stunned. The two-hour drive east to Winnipeg and the stop he made to call his wife are a blur. On the phone, he broke down in tears.

His decision to come forward had not been easy, but he could not live with his secret any longer. He had to testify for both Lester and himself. "When I made the decision to go, it was like a weight lifted," he says. His wife was behind him all the way. Originally from another reserve, she'd also attended the Sandy Bay residential school as a child. She too suffered abuse at the school, as well as within her family while growing up. Together, they'd worked to overcome those scars during their more than twenty years of marriage. "We're healing together," his wife says. An outspoken woman with an inviting countenance, she has clearly made remarkable strides in surmounting a torturous childhood. Between age three and her early twenties, she was sexually assaulted by fifty men, including an attack that triggered a miscarriage. But working with a medicine woman has helped her face her grief and pain. She knew her husband had to find his own way of doing the same. They both hoped testifying at the inquest would help. Little did they know at the time the backlash that awaited him.

Over the next couple of weeks, more evidence of political interference in everything from child welfare to police and school matters surfaced at the inquest. Brandon Police Constable Ed Riglin, a former DOTC police officer at Sandy Bay, testified that band officials twice threatened to "BCR" him—that is, pass a band council resolution banning him from the community—when he tried to arrest relatives. By 1989, he'd asked for a transfer to another reserve because of the political pressure, he said. An RCMP officer and several former staff members from the Sandy Bay school also testified about interference from the chief and band council in the case of the six-year-old girl whom teachers suspected was abused. Former school principal Bill Hamilton also described how Chief Harry Desjarlais threatened to fire him for suspending the chief's son from school. Pressures like that contributed to the high turnover of teachers at the school, with at least a dozen quitting every year, he said.

Two psychologists, who had each been asked in 1988 to assess whether the six-year-old girl was being abused, offered conflicting testimony when they took the stand. Dr. Art Blue, a psychologist with a private practice in Carberry, said the child was emotionally disturbed when he saw her in April of that year. But he downplayed the possibility of sexual abuse. He testified that her inappropriate behaviour could have been caused by her having seen adults having sex or by having access to porn movies because of the crowded living conditions. Her explicit drawing of the stick man with a protruding penis was more likely a man urinating, he said. Blue, a balding man with wire-rimmed glasses, said he had wanted to pursue neurological testing and explore whether her bizarre behaviour was linked to foetal alcohol syndrome. But the child's guardians had refused to give permission for further tests. During questioning by Paterson, Blue said his own ancestry, a mixture of Indian, French, and English, contributed to his understanding of the Aboriginal culture's reluctance to remove children from their homes. Earlier hunting-and-gathering societies had depended on the family system for survival. Traditionally, an abuser would be pressured to change his behaviour or risk being isolated from that crucial network, he said.

But when Dr. Ron Richert testified about two weeks later, a different picture emerged. Richert, a psychologist with a private practice in Brandon, said a worried teacher had referred the girl to him while he was doing counselling at the school in October 1988. After talking to the girl, Richert contacted DOCFS to report that her behaviour was consistent with that of a child who had been abused. In fact, she showed "classic symptoms" of sexual abuse—from an extreme preoccupation with sex to bizarre behaviour, like showing men her underpants and drawing the stick man with a large penis. Attributing her behaviour to crowded living conditions was not realistic, he said. The girl needed intensive treatment or she would be at great risk for drug abuse, promiscuity, or suicide as she reached adolescence.

The testimony of a former DOCFS worker that same week raised more concerns about the agency's handling of another child, who was related to Lester. Georgina Houle, a Sandy Bay resident who had worked for DOCFS from August 1989 to October 1991, described how this eleven-year-old girl was shuttled among at least eleven foster homes in just over a year. The child had to be moved off-reserve for her own protection after she reported to the RCMP that she'd been gang-raped by two of her uncles at a pow-wow. Her furious relatives had done everything they could to force her to recant her allegations, from threatening her verbally to slapping and punching her. Soon after, the girl attempted suicide by overdosing on pills. The soft-spoken Houle said she'd felt discouraged, in this case and others, with the lack of resources at Sandy Bay for helping children. "I had a lot of sympathy and empathy for these kids," she told the court. "A lot of times, when I worked with these kids I broke down and cried for the pain they were in." With the additional frustrations of interference from band leaders and the local child-welfare committee, Houle said she eventually burnt out and quit.

When McInnes showed Houle the eleven-year-old girl's DOCFS file, Houle noticed that it was missing a lot of information which had been there before. She also testified that more than half of the DOCFS file on Lester's mother, Joyce, had vanished. That confirmed earlier testimony from other DOCFS workers who had said files from both the Desjarlais family and several other cases under scrutiny at the inquest were obviously incomplete.

Before leaving the stand, Houle shared some poignant drawings and notes that Lester's sister Sherry had sent with her to the inquest. The notes had been written by Lester to his mother. One note said, "Dear mom, Wherever you are I will always love you. Please phone me tomorrow." It was signed with a sketch of a sad little round face with tears and the word "mom" coming from his mouth. One of Lester's notes which had gone missing after his death had really struck Houle and she'd written down as much as she could remember from it: "Dear mom, How are you feeling? ... They promised I could go home to see you. Another broken promise. Another broken promise." Again, the note was signed with the sad face.

Giesbrecht, who had listened intently, as always, during Houle's testimony, responded immediately. Saying he had grave concerns about the agency's handling of the eleven-year-old girl's case, Giesbrecht ordered her file sent to the provincial director of child and family support for a complete review. "Her problems appear to be very severe and there doesn't seem to be any particular plan for her," the judge said. "Her history is horrendous ... I can't ignore the frightening similiarities to Lester Desjarlais' case." As the hearing adjourned, McInnes told a reporter he had felt sick at heart when reading through the child's file.

By mid-May, the inquest had been under way for a month, with no end in sight. Nerves were becoming frayed among the lawyers and reporters attending the hearings. Long days spent listening to disturbing, often emotional testimony, were followed by late evenings for reporters filing news stories. McInnes, Paterson, and Marion spent their nights preparing for the next day's questions. The daily onslaught of negative publicity about DOCFS was also putting a strain on both Paterson and Beaulieu as they tried to salvage the agency's beleaguered reputation. During breaks, even the usually jocund Beaulieu had become more subdued, and Paterson rarely spoke to anyone.

On May 11, Joyce Wasicuna's testimony once again broadened the focus of the inquest beyond Sandy Bay, pointing to similiar problems in other communities. The former DOCFS worker told how she had been harassed and threatened for apprehending abused children on the Sioux Valley reserve. But she also aimed some harsh criticism at DOCFS official Morris Merrick. She said her first disillusionment with Merrick came when she discovered he'd failed to report a child-abuse case a few years earlier. The case involved two young children on the Long Plain reserve who had been diagnosed and treated for gonorrhoea. But there was no record of a sexual-abuse investigation or of any counselling being offered the children, whose mother was living with one of Merrick's relatives. Wasicuna was shocked by her discovery, and mentioned the matter during a meeting with John Chudzik, the provincial child-abuse coordinator. But although she made Chudzik aware of this and other problems she'd encountered in trying to protect children, she said she received little support from provincial officials. "I saw it as a fear," she told the court. "A fear of having fingers pointed at them as racists [if they intervened]." She said she noticed the same reluctance from lawyers and child-welfare workers from mainstream agencies. But Wasicuna said that treating Aboriginal children differently was nothing but a form of reverse racism.

Wasicuna testified that her relationship with Merrick deteriorated rapidly after she reported him to Chudzik. At about the same time, in the winter of 1990, a letter was circulating among DOCFS staff containing complaints about Merrick's managerial style. Somehow the letter got into Merrick's hands. Staff were called to a meeting to ferret out who was to blame for the letter, and Merrick immediately put Wasicuna on the spot. He asked her point-blank why she was scared to speak up. Wasicuna responded that she was afraid of Merrick because of his violent outbursts. At that, Merrick slammed his notes down on the table, shoved his chair with a bang into the wall, and stormed out of the room, threatening to resign. But it was not Merrick but Wasicuna who was pressured to resign three months later. Agency officials had warned she could not keep her job if she tried to commute from Winnipeg, where her family had fled because of the harassment at Sioux Valley. But Wasicuna believed she had been forced out for doing what was right. In an emotional moment, Wasicuna summed up her feelings: "Nobody is thinking about the children any more. It's either politics or kinship. And that's wrong ... This agency isn't operating in a traditional way. If they were, they'd be protecting women and children."

When Paterson rose to cross-examine Wasicuna, he took a tough approach, barraging her with questions in an attempt to rattle her. He demanded to know why she didn't endorse the traditional Indian way of keeping abused children in the community and isolating the offenders. But Wasicuna shot back that such an ideal had little to do with reality. "That would be nice if that were the way it happened," she said. "I've seen communities supporting offenders more than victims, and that's not traditional." At one point, when Paterson openly sneered at one of Wasicuna's answers, Giesbrecht was so annoyed that he reprimanded him, saying his behaviour was offensive. After a few more rounds with Wasicuna, Paterson sat down. He had finally realized that her candidness was only digging him in deeper.

The next day, Cecil Desjarlais was recalled to testify. Refusing an invitation to be seated, the tall man held an eagle feather in his hand and stood defiantly beside the witness chair at the front of the courtroom. The first thing Cecil did was to make clear that Lester was not his son. He also denied, for the second time, that he'd stolen Lester's missing files. When asked about his intervention in child-welfare cases, he said that, as an elected band councillor, he had every right to act on residents' behalf. But he insisted that he had not interfered. Then Cecil announced he was going to share some thoughts, pulled notes from his briefcase, and launched into a lengthy speech in defence of DOCFS and his community. He said the agency had been created after Indian children were "kidnapped" and taken to other countries. Those children had been deprived of their culture and lost their language. Despite limited resources, the agency had done its best to help children since then. Rather than calling it political interference, Cecil said that he and other leaders advocated politically for children. At forty-seven years of age, Cecil said he was proud to be the product of the "glory years" of the residential school at Sandy Bay, an institution he had enjoyed attending. He insisted he was a "God-loving" person who embraced both Catholicism and traditional spirituality, rather than the "notorious man" the inquest had portrayed. As he told the court: "Ladies and gentlemen, I, as that notorious band councillor who had served my people, this is what I get: I get dragged the deeper the better."

After about thirty minutes, it was obvious Cecil was just getting going with what turned into a rambling, ninety-minute filibuster. The longer he talked, the angrier he became as he lashed out at the inquest for dragging his family name into disrepute. He said he was tired of media reports full of allegations about his relatives. His rights had been violated by all of this. He also chastised Giesbrecht for allowing the hearings to expand beyond the immediate circumstances of Lester's death. For that matter, he said, even talking about the dead in such a way was disrespectful. He said he resented the "monstrous picture" that had been painted of his chief and council. Calling himself a "humble man," he said that, before coming to testify, he'd prayed that justice would prevail. "That's why I'm taking this opportunity—so you will know who Cecil Desjarlais is," he boomed. "A monster? A person with horns? I'm a damned good person." When Cecil's tirade showed no sign of letting up, Giesbrecht gently intervened, saying he had allowed him to speak freely out of respect for his culture. But the judge warned that, when Cecil returned another day to finish his testimony, he would be required to answer questions. As Cecil left, a member of the audience turned to a reporter and summed up the essence of what had just happened: "He's just told the inquest to go fuck itself."

Internal documents revealing how the province had handled complaints about DOCFS were quietly entered as an exhibit at the inquest the week before two Family Services officials were scheduled to testify. Discussion of the documents was delayed until the officials would appear. But before they could take the witness stand, a front-page story in the *Winnipeg Free Press* divulged that the documents suggested political considerations had influenced the Conservative Filmon government's response to those complaints. Senior child-welfare officials had ruled out a public review of the agency in 1988 for fear it might spark a confrontation with Aboriginal leaders during an election year. "Any external review might be viewed as political inteference into the operation of an Indian child and family service agency," the documents said. The province had opted for an internal review by Family Services officials instead in 1988–89, which focused primarily on the agency's complaints about Marion. Yet the review also contained evidence about many of the complaints of political interference which were now coming to light at the inquest. A second internal government review had been done in January 1992 in response to Marion's public complaints that DOCFS had failed to investigate properly the case of the sexually abused girl from Sandy Bay. Predictably, the hastily done review had cleared the agency of any wrongdoing. Liberal leader Sharon Carstairs responded to the *Free Press* article by accusing the Filmon government of putting politics before child protection. The article hit a sore spot with Premier Gary Filmon himself, who took the unusual step of personally phoning the newspaper to complain that the documents had been taken out of context.

After the wave of bad publicity, the Family Services department sent its own lawyer, Isaac Frost, to join the growing number of intervenors at the inquest. The next witness to take the stand was Evelyn Mathers, the department's provincial coordinator for children in care. She was the one who had been sent out to Sandy Bay five months earlier to find out if Marion's concerns about the possible sexual abuse of the girl under discussion at the inquest had any validity. During her one-day visit, Mathers interviewed three teachers and a public health nurse who knew the child. But the girl's guardians, who had not been warned about Mathers's visit, refused to see her or to let Mathers talk to the child. Without pursuing the matter further, Mathers reported that the girl was not at risk. However, McInnes grilled Mathers about how she'd reached that conclusion without meeting the girl, or her guardians, or talking to any of the people who had reported signs of abuse over the previous four years. Mathers insisted over and over that she was just "following orders" to review only the girl's current situation.

At one point during Mathers's testimony, Frost asked Giesbrecht to ban publication of evidence about the girl, saying the publicity was not in her best interest. Paterson rose to support Frost's request, saying the media coverage had exacerbated the child's problems. The girl had not been in school for over four months because the publicity had made her a target of harassment from other children, he said. But both McInnes and Marion argued against the ban on the pivotal case, saying the public had a right to know how the agency had treated her. "I would question whether it is in the best interest of the child not to have this evidence published, or the best interest of the province," Marion said sarcastically. In the end, Giesbrecht expressed concern about the backlash against the girl, but refused to grant the publication ban.

The most senior provincial official to take the stand was called the next day. Jim Bakken, an assistant deputy minister of Family Services for the previous two years, was the official Marion had gone to with her complaints after being fired by DOCFS. Bakken, a middle-aged man with the smooth style of a seasoned bureaucrat, spent the rest of the day engaged in a gruelling game of cat-and-mouse with McInnes. No matter how McInnes posed his questions, Bakken refused to concede that his department, or DOCFS, had made any mistakes in their handling of child-welfare cases at Sandy Bay or elsewhere. When backed into a corner by McInnes, Bakken peered out from behind wire-rimmed glasses and calmly recited departmental policies that justified a particular action. Occasionally his hand would linger at his throat, the only sign of strain in his otherwise cool demeanour. What about political interference? McInnes asked. After countless rounds, Bakken finally admitted band officials should probably not get involved directly in individual child-abuse cases. But at the same time, he said, First Nations agencies had the right to run things the way they wanted to, including having band officials involved in local child-welfare committees. What about the political decision to avoid confrontations with Aboriginal leaders during an election year? Bakken said that was just a passing reference in a report that was not intended for public consumption. What about the safety of the Sandy Bay girl who teachers suspected was abused? She's fine, everything's fine, trust us, he said. The department is monitoring her situation. But wasn't it a conflict of interest for the department to review its own actions in that case? Of course not, he insisted.

After hours of hammering away at Bakken, McInnes suddenly cut off his questioning in mid-afternoon, asked for a recess, and rushed out of the room. Later, he told a reporter he'd been on the verge of losing control. As McInnes put it, "I had to do it before I wrung his neck." He wasn't the only one who had found the bureaucrat's testimony maddening. In an interview two years later, Giesbrecht cited Bakken's testimony as a personal low point of the entire inquest. To Giesbrecht, it was a bitter revelation to hear the senior government official breezily dismissing the problem of political interference rather than expressing concern about the agency's integrity. "I was extremely disappointed in what that person [Bakken] did and did not say," Giesbrecht said. "That was my reaction. Extreme disappointment, and I was almost embarrassed of our system of child welfare at that point ... That was very distressing."

On doctor's orders, McInnes, who was suffering from high blood pressure, had begun carrying a blood-pressure cuff to the hearings to monitor himself. The first time he'd appeared with it, reporters had jokingly asked whether he was going to survive the inquest. But in truth, the hearings were weighing heavily on McInnes. He had become, in his words, "obsessed" with the tragic story unfolding before him. The inquest now seemed driven by some external force. His days were spent in the courtroom pulling often painful testimony from witnesses, while evenings were spent poring over files filled with graphic details of children's suffering. His phone never stopped ringing with people wanting to tell their stories or pass on tips. At the same time, he was caring for his sick wife and two children. Still, when he looked at his son and daughter, who were about the same age as Lester was when he died, he knew he was doing the right thing.

The counterpoint to Bakken's "everything's fine" testimony soon appeared in the form of Dr. Charlie Ferguson, the director of Winnipeg's Child Protection Centre. An outspoken advocate for children's rights, Ferguson bluntly described a child-welfare system that puts politics before child protection. During his day-long testimony, the pediatrician, a tall man with a shock of white hair, spoke passionately on behalf of the abused children he treated. He aimed harsh criticism at both provincial officials and the Aboriginal child-welfare agencies for failing them. "Many children, and particularly Aboriginal children, are suffering horribly ... in families which are dangerous and where nothing is being done for them," Ferguson told the court. Aboriginal child-welfare agencies were overwhelmed by the growing number of abuse disclosures and limited resources. But rather than accept help from white professionals and institutions, some agencies "hid the kids away," choosing to leave abused children in risky situations rather than undermine their philosophy of keeping families together. "Leaving the home was looked upon as anathema," he testified. Many of the problems emerging at the inquest, including the epidemic of sexual abuse on reserves, had been identified as far back as 1987 in a report done by the Child Protection Centre called *A New Justice for Indian Children*. To Ferguson's dismay, Aboriginal leaders had branded the report "racist" for linking the problem of sexual abuse to their communities. At the same time, provincial and federal politicians ignored the report's long list of recommendations, including the desperate need for multidisciplinary teams to diagnose and treat victims of sexual abuse in rural areas. In the end, those who authored the ground-breaking report were seen to be opponents of Aboriginal child welfare. "It was one of the most difficult issues I've ever dealt with," Ferguson told the court. "It was like walking on hot coals." While Ferguson strongly supported Native-run child-welfare agencies, he believed they were repeating the same mistakes as the mainstream system.

But Ferguson also lambasted Family Services officials for abdicating their responsibility to children. He labelled bureaucrats' refusal to intervene in cases for fear of a confrontation with Aboriginal leaders as nothing short of "pathological benevolence." That "hands-off" approach left front-line workers with no one to turn to when band officials interfered. Provincial officials tried to excuse their lack of action by saying it was based on respect for Aboriginal self-government. But Ferguson viewed it as outright neglect. His testimony clearly pointed beyond one agency to an entire system that he believed was "grinding up children" while claiming to help them.

In late May, Cecil Desjarlais was recalled to the stand. This time, hearings were being held in a classroom at the Agricultural Extension Centre. During a day of heated exchanges, Cecil defended his intervention in two child-abuse cases in 1988, saying he'd been acting on orders of chief and council. When he claimed not to have known details of the cases, including that the suspected abusers in one of them were his relatives, McInnes confronted him. "I'm going to suggest to you that it was totally irresponsible of you ... to put the child back into the home where she was allegedly abused when you didn't have the facts of the case," McInnes said. Cecil replied that he'd done it on orders of the chief, who was his uncle. They were upset because Marion had failed to consult them and was "out of control" with apprehending children. He also brushed aside the complaints of at least eight previous witnesses that he had tried to intimidate everyone, from police to teachers and child-welfare workers.

When Glover began cross-examining him, their mutual animosity crackled like static electricity between them. Marion accused Cecil of intervening in one case to protect his brother Joe. Cecil, in a condescending tone, replied that she seemed to believe he knew far more than he did. Marion shot back, "Then perhaps you shouldn't have interfered." Cecil answered some of her questions and ignored others. He lectured her, insulted her, and blamed her at every opportunity. Marion accused Cecil of lying, which only infuriated him more. At one point, Giesbrecht had to step in and referee the verbal brawl. Before Cecil left that day, McInnes stood up and challenged him one more time: "What you did was take the adults' rights ... and intervene to the detriment of the children," McInnes told him. Cecil refused to back down: "I always acted for the children of Sandy Bay," he declared.

The testimony of Ernie Daniels, former director of the Dakota Ojibway Tribal Council, also escalated into a showdown the next week. After taking the stand in the cavernous courtroom on the second floor of the courthouse, Daniels angrily blamed Marion for the conflicts that plagued DOCFS during her tenure. Her aggressive style stirred up people's worst memories of the white child-welfare system, he said. He'd fired her to protect the agency. But Daniels did apologize for threatening to kick her "white fucking ass" during the acrimonious meeting after her firing in 1988. He said he'd been angry after Marion vowed to report the agency to the media. As for political interference, Daniels denied it was a problem at Sandy Bay. But he did concede the chief-and-council system of government, imposed on First Nations through the Indian Act, left the door open for such problems. Political leaders weren't always sure where advocacy ended and interference began when it came to child welfare, he said.

Before Daniels left the stand, McInnes acknowledged Daniels's anger at the historic injustices inflicted on Aboriginal people. Then he began to recite, one by one, the cases of children who had suffered while in the care of DOCFS over the previous decade, piling each file in front of Daniels as he went. When the stack of paper had grown to almost a foot, McInnes turned to Daniels.

"Does that make you angry?" McInnes asked.

"Any human being with a sane mind, sure they're angry," Daniels replied.

"And these kids—it doesn't matter a tinker's damn to them whether their cases have been mishandled by a white agency or a Native agency. They're still in the same situation," McInnes said.

"Yes," Daniels said.

"And we have a right to be angry, don't we?" McInnes asked.

"Right," Daniels said.

"Right," McInnes agreed.

The bulk of the next week's testimony alternated between Marion and Isaac Beaulieu, who each spent days offering diametrically opposed views of DOCFS and its work. Beaulieu, a man with several university degrees and three decades of experience working for national and provincial Native organizations, had the unenviable task of answering the exhaustive list of complaints levelled at the agency. As chairman of the DOCFS board for most of its existence, Beaulieu provided a detailed history of the agency's development and achievements since 1981. Agency officials had worked long and hard to find and repatriate children snatched from their communities during the Sixties Scoop, he said. They had started providing child-welfare services on eight reserves where no help existed before. As the first Native-run mandated child-welfare agency in Canada, DOCFS had attracted a lot of attention from academics, government officials, and Aboriginal leaders across the country. The agency had been subjected to about half a dozen reviews during its first years of operation to assess its strengths and weaknesses, he said. In the mid-1980s the independent board of the agency was disbanded by the chiefs, putting it more directly under the control of DOTC. DOTC also controlled the agency's budget, which had given it less autonomy.

As for Lester, Beaulieu admitted he'd become a victim of the conflicts between DOCFS workers and the local community. What should have been a "routine case" became a disaster when Marion and other child-welfare workers insisted upon sending him out of the community to institutions like Seven Oaks Centre for Youth and the Brandon Mental Health Centre, he said. The stigma of being sent to the mental hospital would have embarrassed Lester with his peers. Instead, Marion and other workers should have left Lester within his "circle of love," he said, pointing to a family tree of the boy's relatives. The diagram had been drawn in a circle showing the interrelatedness of Joyce's family and that of Cecil and her common-law partners. Before he left the stand, McInnes would question Beaulieu on his characterization of Lester's family tree as a "circle of love," pointing out that many of those people had neglected and abused the boy.

Beaulieu steadfastly refuted that political interference had occurred in child-abuse cases at Sandy Bay. Any intervention by band officials was done in good faith, he said. When Beaulieu talked about child abuse in general, he readily acknowledged it was a serious problem. But when questioned on the specifics of certain cases, Beaulieu revealed a perplexing intransigence. Right to the end of the inquest, he maintained there was no proof Lester had been sexually abused. He also insisted there was no evidence the six-year-old girl had been abused. During one of his last days on the stand, McInnes showed Beaulieu the girl's drawing of a man with an erect penis. To the amazement of many in the courtroom, Beaulieu turned the drawing on its side and said, in all seriousness, that it was just as likely a picture of a sailboat as of an erect penis. Exasperated, McInnes spun around, held the picture up to reporters, and walked away in silence.

When backed into a corner during his testimony, Beaulieu used what reporters eventually dubbed the "keep-talking defence." By contrast, Marion's style while testifying was jokingly labelled "the confusion theory." She would throw out so much information that, before long, no one could remember what the question was, let alone whether she'd answered it. At any rate, both Beaulieu and Marion had a remarkable talent for outlasting their questioners. Beaulieu delighted in painting the broad picture, but expertly dodged specifics. Marion launched into lengthy sermons given the slightest opportunity. Like a weary parishioner, McInnes, on the edge of physical exhaustion, dozed off several times during Marion's days on the stand, his pen dropping from his hand with a loud clatter.

Since Marion couldn't cross-examine herself, she hired a lawyer to fill her shoes when she took the stand. On her first day of testimony, she wore a bright yellow sweatshirt with a boa coiled around it, a curious choice in light of the snake's legendary association with deception. Marion told the court that, when she was hired on a temporary contract at DOCFS, it was her first job with an Aboriginal agency. When she became supervisor at Sandy Bay, she found herself in charge of poorly trained workers with little grasp of child abuse, she said. They were used to a low-key, non-interventionist approach, and resisted following policies and procedures or providing detailed file notes. Often, they were "caught between a rock and a hard place" when she ordered them to apprehend children of influential families. To her surprise, she discovered that few of the foster homes in the community were licensed. On top of that, she'd been warned when she went to Sandy Bay that tackling child abuse in the highly politicized atmosphere of that community would be "opening up a can of worms." She had no idea how true that prediction would be. The more child-abuse cases she reported, the more problems she encountered. People began to accuse her of seeing sexual abuse where it didn't exist because of her own history of childhood abuse. But Marion said she'd dealt with her own abuse in therapy. Rather than hindering her work, she insisted, her own past had heightened her sensitivity to both victims and offenders. Marion had developed a nose for sniffing out abuse, and Sandy Bay was a minefield.

When she began working with Lester, she said she was surprised that the boy had been offered so little help by DOCFS over the previous six years. She said she did her best to find him a stable foster home but was constantly blocked by interference from Beaulieu, Cecil, and other DOCFS staff. She was especially upset when another child-welfare worker sent Lester to the Seven Oaks Centre for Youth—which she called a "holding pen for kids"—after he stole the rifle and fired shots on the reserve. When she looked back, she believed that was the beginning of the end for Lester. But at the time, she did not believe he was actively suicidal. No one was more shocked than she was when he killed himself.

After Lester's death, the tension at Sandy Bay escalated. She said Joe Desjarlais began "stalking" her, and once cornered her in an empty room at the band office. After blocking her exit, he threatened her by reminding her that he was the gravedigger in the community. On another occasion, Marion said she ended up on the wrong end of a rifle after she tried to talk to one of the guardians of the sexually abused six-year-old girl who had been at the centre of controversy.

She finished her opening testimony—which had taken two days—by passionately denying once again that she had any reason to steal Lester's files. Instead, she pointed the finger at Morris Merrick, saying he had been out to get her. She believed she had become "the perfect scapegoat" for the agency's multitude of problems, even though she'd only worked there just over a year. She lashed out at Beaulieu for describing an unrealistic picture of the agency and portrayed herself as one of the only stable people in Lester's life. Unaware of how arrogant she sounded, she concluded: "Perhaps Sandy Bay wasn't ready for someone like me." And then she unwittingly launched into a speech that would undermine her credibility more effectively than anything the agency had lobbed at her. Angry and hurt by the weeks of accusations, Marion tried to bolster her image by recounting how she had been given the name "warrior woman" during a ceremony at an Aboriginal centre a few weeks earlier. Her flare for the dramatic got the better of her as she pulled out a number of traditional Indian objects given her as protection from "bad medicine." One by one, she described them: sweetgrass, a medicine pouch, a crystal, a red ribbon, a basket of sage, an eagle feather. As she talked, reporters squirmed in their seats. By publicly flaunting sacred objects given as gifts, she had displayed a bewildering insensitivity to Aboriginal culture.

During cross-examination, Paterson confronted her with some of her own flaws. He asked her about her personal financial problems and her past criminal charges for passing bad cheques. Marion replied she was "one of those people who shouldn't have a chequebook." She admitted she had trouble handling money, but said she'd received a conditional discharge on the bad-cheque offences. Then Paterson tried to call another of Marion's former employers as a witness. He hoped he would be able to further discredit her by introducing testimony about how she had mishandled the Interlake arts group's finances. But Giesbrecht overruled his request, instead suggesting that affidavits be submitted. As Paterson attacked Marion from various angles, vehement arguments erupted between them, prompting Giesbrecht to intervene. In the end, Paterson gained little ground. If anything, Marion's stamina and feistiness under relentless attack won her grudging admiration from courtroom observers. What Paterson didn't seem to realize was that trying to destroy Marion's credibility was no longer enough. The issues under scrutiny no longer revolved around one woman's character.

In the broader political arena, the inquest had prompted a deluge of bad publicity for Family Services Minister Harold Gilleshammer. Opposition politicians like Liberal leader Sharon Carstairs and NDP Family Services critic Becky Barrett hammered away at Gilleshammer for his refusal to acknowledge the problems at DOCFS and his own department's failure to adequately monitor the agency. Gilleshammer suffered another blow when a scathing letter addressed to him from the provincial ombudsman was released in mid-June at the inquest. In the letter, the ombudsman, Gordon Earle, whose office had been monitoring testimony at the inquest, chastised Family Services officials for their sloppy investigation of sexual-abuse allegations involving the Sandy Bay girl. Earle wrote that the province's review six months earlier had ignored past concerns about the child and left him with serious concerns, including the following: the agency had failed to review the girl's file; the investigator didn't interview the child or her guardians; the investigator failed to interview professionals who had reported suspicions of sexual abuse; the child had not been attending school; the child's guardians had refused to give consent for a psychological assessment of the girl. Earle's letter appeared to be the last straw for the besieged Gilleshammer. Jim Bakken, assistant deputy minister of Family Services, suddenly backtracked and announced his department had reopened their investigation of the girl's case. At the same time, the province revealed plans to launch yet another internal review of DOCFS as soon as the inquest was over.

The final few days of the inquest raised the stakes for both DOCFS and the province as a new round of incriminating evidence emerged. To everyone's surprise, McInnes called two veteran DOCFS employees to testify: Bev Flett, the agency's assistant director, and supervisor Ella McKay. Looking back, McKay recalled the morning she and Flett realized they would have to testify. They were sitting in Flett's office, talking about the inquest, when McKay joked that maybe they should call the judge and have a chat with him. Both women felt DOCFS officials had erred by digging in their heels and refusing to take responsibility for their mistakes in Lester's case and those of other children. Suddenly, there was a knock at their door, and an RCMP officer appeared. He handed both of them subpoenas to testify at the inquest. The two women just looked at each other and smiled. "I said, well, I guess this is our chance to speak to the judge," McKay recalled, laughing at the strange synchronicity of events.

By the time she took the witness stand, Flett was a nervous wreck. Her soft voice was barely audible as she began answering questions on a June afternoon in the makeshift second-floor courtroom at the Agricultural Extension Centre. Flett told the judge she believed there was a possibility her testimony would cost her her job. Earlier that day, she'd had a confrontation with Morris Merrick, who had also been subpoenaed to reappear later in the week. He'd warned her the agency might not exist by Friday because "certain individuals were out to get him." Having borne the brunt of Merrick's hostility in the past, Flett said she had no illusions what speaking up at the inquest might mean.

She explained that the agency was in turmoil, with a lack of direction for workers, and constant confusion. There was no room for differences of opinion between staff. Referring back to her own years as supervisor at Sandy Bay, she said it had been a struggle to work in the community because she'd been intimidated by those in power. Since band councillors ran local child-welfare committees in most communities, political interference was common, she said. Child-welfare workers felt they had nowhere to turn when their decisions were overruled by band leaders. Flett had begun testifying late in the afternoon, and it was obvious she would have to return the next day to finish her testimony. In the meantime, Giesbrecht ordered Merrick and other DOCFS officials not to have any contact with her or McKay. The judge also made it clear that he would not tolerate any reprisals against the women for testifying.

The next day, McKay also took the witness stand. She testified that politicians had control over every level of the agency, from the chiefs who made board policies to individual leaders' interference in individual cases. McKay cited a case where she'd decided to apprehend a girl who had been sexually abused by a band leader. She'd wanted to send the child to a foster home on another reserve to prevent her relatives from pressuring her to recant. But the local child-welfare committee overruled McKay, insisting the child remain in the community. Police had to be called to help apprehend the girl, who—to no one's surprise—soon withdrew her complaints in the face of reprisals from her family. "This particular community is in total denial of abuse," McKay said. "It's not an isolated case."

When Paterson rose to cross-examine McKay, he suggested that being a "born-again Christian" had hindered her ability to provide culturally appropriate Aboriginal services. He also accused her of undermining the concept of the local child-welfare committee. McKay replied that the concept was fine, and would work even better without political interference. As Paterson leaned harder on McKay, Giesbrecht finally stepped in and reprimanded him for his personal attacks on her.

But McKay's strongest words were yet to come. Before she finished her testimony, Giesbrecht leaned forward and gently asked what had led her to risk being so candid. Tears streamed down McKay's cheeks as she replied. What had started as the agency's noble vision to help children had somehow become blurred over the last decade, she said. Faced with overwhelming problems in many communities, the agency had failed to take a strong stand against child abuse to avoid angering band leaders. "I think we're in a political mess where the grassroots people are not getting the services they need," McKay said. "You either protect children or you don't ... To me it's clear." When both McKay and Flett had finished testifying, Beaulieu quickly dismissed their emotional pleas, telling reporters they were the words of "disgruntled employees" who should have aired their complaints with the agency's board.

The next day, Marion rose to tell Giesbrecht about a startling discovery. She'd found out that DOCFS had withheld a file containing crucial information about the sexually abused girl at Sandy Bay. Wrinkling his brow with annoyance, Giesbrecht sternly ordered the agency to produce the file he'd asked for the previous October. Then, on the second-last day of the inquest, Flett was recalled to explain what she knew of the controversial file. She said she'd attended a meeting about the child's case with other agency officials in January, after Marion stirred up trouble by going to the media. At the meeting, Flett realized that an additional file had suddenly surfaced containing not only the sexual-abuse allegations DOCFS had claimed it never received, but new ones as well. However, during a meeting with Family Services Minister Harold Gilleshammer about the same time, no mention was made of the file. Instead, she recalled that the meeting was entirely focused on bad-mouthing Marion rather than worrying about the well-being of the child. Concerned about the contents of the file, Flett said she approached Merrick and also asked a local Sandy Bay child-welfare worker to follow up on the allegations. But Merrick overruled her, telling the worker he'd handle the situation himself. As the inquest unfolded, Flett said she eventually realized provincial officials had never seen the file. She notified official John Chudzik about the missing file on June 2, and confronted Merrick about it, saying she wasn't prepared to cover up any longer. On June 5, the file was delivered to the province. Surprisingly, more than a week later, on June 16, Bakken, assistant deputy minister of Family Services, had testified at the inquest and said nothing about the file's appearance. Flett's revelations about the withheld file were astonishing in the context of all that had gone before at the inquest. Endless hours had been spent questioning witnesses about the agency's perplexing decision to close the girl's file in August 1989 despite further referrals from teachers concerned about the child. Now there was evidence the agency had known about the allegations all along, and little had been done to protect the girl.

After lunch, Merrick arrived to take the witness stand, his own personal lawyer in tow. A tall man, he was clad in a grey sport jacket, heavy belt, and cowboy boots. Tense and angry, Merrick denied withholding the girl's file, saying he thought it had been turned over to the province and to the inquest in January. Lashing out at the inquest, he said he felt like the proceedings had put him on trial. He insisted agency officials had done their best to cooperate with the inquest and had not tried to hide the file: it had been accidentally misplaced because of a clerical error and had not resurfaced until January.

But Giesbrecht wasn't buying Merrick's explanation, and didn't try to hide his anger at having key evidence withheld. The girl's file contained information crucial to the inquest, the province's review of her case, and the ombudsman's investigation. "This is no clerical error," Giesbrecht told the court. "This is a gravely serious matter." He ordered McInnes to investigate further, including finding out why Assistant Deputy Minister Jim Bakken had failed to give the file to the inquest. When McInnes asked whether the matter should be referred for a police investigation, Giesbrecht replied: "You're going to have to consider the possibility of criminal charges ... You may take whatever action you see fit."

McInnes then proceeded to question Merrick, who had listened nervously to the judge. During examination by McInnes, Merrick disputed the earlier accusation by Wasicuna that he had failed to report a child-abuse case involving a relative. McInness probed further, after apologizing for raising personal issues. He asked Merrick about his reputation for volatile outbursts. Merrick denied trying to intimidate DOCFS staff, although he admitted he sometimes raised his voice. He also acknowledged that he'd pled guilty to an assault charge after an argument with a girlfriend nine years earlier. Just as Marion began to cross-examine Merrick, the judge adjourned the proceedings for the day. Merrick would have to return the next morning to complete his testimony.

Tuesday, June 23, the final day of the inquest, dawned hot and muggy. By then there had been forty days of hearings held in makeshift courtrooms all over Brandon, and even as far afield as Minnedosa, about forty kilometres away. Now the inquest was about to end in the location it had begun the previous October—the Agricultural Extension Centre in Brandon. The second-floor classroom that served as a courtroom was located at the top of two flights of wide wooden steps. As the hearing began that morning, Giesbrecht was seated at a table at the front of the crowded room. A couple of metres away was the empty chair where the witnesses would sit. A bank of lawyers, surrounded by stacks of documents, sat at a table in the middle of the room, while reporters from both the local and the national media lined another table at the back. An air of weary anticipation filled the room as the last hours of testimony began.

Looking strained, Merrick was recalled to the stand, and Marion resumed her cross-examination. Accusations were soon flying, as each labelled the other a liar. Then Marion confronted Merrick with complaints made by other witnesses who had said he was abusive towards women. Merrick angrily refused to answer, saying he didn't care if he was held in contempt of court. Marion asked the question several more times, as Merrick's lawyer repeatedly objected. But Giesbrecht overruled the objections, telling the lawyer that more leeway was being allowed than in a criminal trial. Merrick nervously reached for a glass of water as he continued to spar with Marion. With fifty-three employees under his direction at DOCFS, he said, he sometimes had to raise his voice to get his point across or to discipline someone. If workers were afraid of him, that was their problem, he said defiantly.

Then Marion shifted gears again and suddenly suggested Merrick himself had been the victim of an abusive background. His lawyer, Richard Literovich, jumped up.

"This just can't possibly be relevant, and I object," Literovich said.

Giesbrecht acknowledged Marion's question went far beyond what would be allowed in a criminal proceeding.

"But the abuse part of it, the denial part of it, has all been raised [before]," Giesbrecht said. "I will allow the question."

"Isn't that true, Morris?" Marion repeated.

"In a residential school, when I was thirteen years old, I was sexually abused by a supervisor," Merrick began bitterly. "That supervisor is dead now. He died a few years ago. I have dealt with that in my own way. I have healed myself. I have left that far behind me where it belongs." Merrick raised his voice until he was almost shouting.

"I've dealt with my abuse ... and the belief that I have and the ways of my people ... Today I am not self-righteous like some people I see here before me today. But I can say honestly that I have dealt with it."

Suddenly, his voice cracked, his defiant gaze crumpled, and his shoulders slumped. In a second, the big man's aggressive façade dissolved as he broke down weeping. In the face of such raw emotion, people looked away or bowed their heads. Tears streamed down the cheeks of a reporter in the back row. In one agonizing moment, the proud man had been stripped of his defences; the line between abuser and abused had blurred. Giesbrecht abruptly ordered a recess. As Merrick stood up to leave the room, he borrowed a braid of sweetgrass from McInnes, then disappeared.

When he returned to the witness stand, Merrick carried an eagle feather lent to him by Marion. As the hearing resumed, Giesbrecht gently explained to Merrick that Marion, too, had been subjected to tough questioning about her past. "Mr. Merrick, I recognize personal pain when I see it, and I regret this was necessary," Giesbrecht apologized. Merrick, who had regained some of his composure, said again that, in order to move on, he'd dealt with his own pain. He'd left behind his hard-drinking and abusive past five years ago. But he pointed to deeper roots of the problems he and many others suffered from. Many people have not yet healed from losing their children through forced adoptions or residential schools, he said. His mother had been forced to attend residential school, and he himself had run away three times from such institutions. However, his people no longer wanted to be "spectators" but in charge of their destiny. Yet DOCFS was now being blamed for trying to do just that. The agency had been put under a microscope at the inquest and unfairly subjected to harsh criticism. "We're not perfect," he told the court. "We're only ten years old. And I think we've done a helluva job with what we've had to work with." About the time Marion joined the agency, they'd just begun to realize the extent of abuse in communities. He acknowledged they had made some mistakes, and even admitted that having politicians on the DOCFS board might be a mistake. But he also emphasized how much the agency had done with its annual budget of $2.2 million in 1992: serving 302 children in care; working with an additional 268 cases; providing 108 foster homes. When Merrick finished his passionate defence of DOCFS, Giesbrecht tried to reassure him by saying that he fully supported Native-controlled child-welfare agencies. A few minutes later, his testimony finally completed, Merrick rushed out of the room and down the stairs, refusing to speak to reporters as he left.

During the noon-hour break, Marion munched on a tuna sandwich at a Brandon restaurant and discussed the morning's events with a reporter and her aunt Lorraine Mathers. Marion had been taken aback by Merrick's revelation on the stand. With only rumours to go on, she'd debated with herself about whether to raise the matter in court. When Merrick suddenly admitted having been sexually abused as a child, Marion said she'd felt like "Jack the Ripper" for forcing the public confession from her adversary.

She was exhausted by the roller-coaster ride of the last months of the inquest. Without the support of her aunt who had faithfully appeared day after day in the courtroom, she wasn't sure how she would have made it this far. "That's what got me through," Marion said. "Having one person who believed what I was saying." There had been weeks of commuting from Winnipeg, leaving her two teenage sons to fend for themselves for days on end. Defending her own credibility while cross-examining often hostile witnesses had also been a huge strain for someone with no legal training. While she said she didn't regret her role at the inquest, in the end she felt she too had become a victim. Although she didn't realize it that day, it would take many months, and the help of a counsellor, to put the experience behind her.

McInnes too felt bone-weary and deeply shaken as the hearings wound down. Dubbing it only half-jokingly the "inquest from hell," McInnes was cynical about whether anything would change as a result.

The toughest part for McInnes had been chipping away, day after day, at child-welfare officials and others who seemed unable or unwilling to see that children were suffering. He wasn't at all sure where the impetus was going to come from for the necessary changes. Instead, he saw a child-welfare system that too easily became the pawn of provincial and band politicians alike.

In his gruelling triple role as DOCFS spokesman, adviser to their lawyer, and witness, Beaulieu, too, was eager to put the inquest behind him and return home to his wife and youngest daughter. He'd been shuttling back and forth between Brandon and Sandy Bay for months. Friends and family considered his mission an unpleasant one and gingerly inquired about him, as if he were in hospital. And there had been plenty of restless nights, when he'd dreamed about walking into the inquest and handing over Lester's missing files to the judge.

The final witness at the inquest was Sherry McIvor, Lester's oldest sister. Looking frightened and overwhelmed, Sherry, wearing a black dress and dangling gold earrings, softly answered questions, usually with one-word responses. Haltingly, she said she had mixed feelings about the inquest. She said the hearings had reopened the emotional wound of losing Lester, while at the same time giving his death more meaning. Sherry ended her brief testimony by repeating her mother's fears that Lester had died by someone else's hand. Then the young woman left as quietly as she'd come. Much later, Sherry would reveal that she'd been terrified someone would ask her about Joe that day. She wasn't yet ready to tell her own story.

After a round of thank-yous to lawyers and reporters who had weathered the months of hearings together, Giesbrecht promised to complete his report on the proceedings by fall, and adjourned the inquest on the afternoon of Tuesday, June 23, 1992. More than sixty witnesses had testified during forty days of hearings, stretched over eight months. One hundred and fourteen exhibits had been submitted, filling several cardboard boxes, and, as McInnes said, weighing more than Lester ever had. What had begun as a one-day probe into the boy's suicide had mushroomed into the longest inquest in Manitoba history, raising disturbing questions about every aspect of the system that failed Lester.

CHAPTER EIGHT

REVELATIONS

"He was my bogeyman as a child."

—Nancy McIvor

For the people of Sandy Bay, the inquest resurrected old hurts. Residents felt that the barrage of publicity about child abuse had painted an unfair picture of their community. Insensitive comments from outsiders—remarks like "Sandy Bay is starting up again"—didn't help. Many band members simply stopped listening to the troubling daily news coverage of the inquest. There were tearful, late-night phone calls to community leaders from people who had been harassed after relatives testified at the hearings. Mervin Houle, the community's coordinator of youth programs, summed up the inquest's impact a few days after the hearings concluded: "Wounds, wounds, wounds—that's what I call it," he said. "These people are hurting."

Chief Angus Starr went further. He accused the media of "mercilessly crucifying" both the community and individuals like himself. In an interview just after the inquest ended, Starr acknowledged that DOCFS officials had made mistakes. But Starr said that was part of any learning process. If anyone was to blame, it was the province for failing to provide enough help for the fledgling child-welfare agency. Instead, bureaucrats had preferred to watch those running the agency "fall flat on our faces," he said. At the same time, Starr said the inquest had forced the community to pull together in the face of adversity. It was similiar to what the residents of Martensville, Saskatchewan, another small rural community targeted by sensational media reports of widespread child abuse, were dealing with, he said. Martensville had rocketed into the national news in 1992 after police charged nine suspects with more than 100 physical abuse and sex-related charges involving children at a day-care in the town located about ten miles north of Saskatoon. In the end, only one man was convicted on sex-related charges, but the town's reputation suffered. "I can understand what Martensville is going through," Starr said. Ironically, his comparing Sandy Bay with Martensville would soon be even more apt than anyone expected.

Still, the public airing of Lester's story had shaken loose deeper concerns than the tainting of the community's image. For some at Sandy Bay, especially Lester's sisters, the inquest had become the catalyst they needed to break their silence about their own abuse. Lester's sister Nancy McIvor, by then the mother of four children, had not been able to attend the hearings. But she'd closely followed media reports about the proceedings. Before the second half of the inquest began in February 1992, Nancy's older sister, Sherry, dropped in to visit her one day at her home at Sandy Bay. Sherry had fled to the women's shelter in Portage la Prairie from Sandy Bay with her three children the previous summer because of conflicts with her partner and his relatives.

That evening, Nancy and Sherry put their children to bed and sat up late, slipping into a sombre mood as they reminisced about their childhood. They rarely touched on those memories with each other, preferring to let the turbulent years fade away. But as they talked, Sherry suddenly blurted out that she wished a "certain person" was dead. The sound in her voice, the way she said it—Nancy looked across at her sister and instinctively knew whom Sherry meant. For the first time, Nancy began to talk to her sister about what that person had done to her. As tears filled her eyes, Nancy revealed that she'd been molested as a child by their uncle Joe Desjarlais. Sherry listened in silence. Then she stunned

Nancy by revealing her secret: Joe had done the same thing to her as a child. Tears streamed down their faces as they thought of how they'd suffered alone for so many years, each believing she was the only one.

By the time the inquest ended a few months later, Nancy was determined to speak up about the abuse she'd suffered as a child. She knew Sherry felt the same way. It was too late to wipe out what had happened. But Nancy had to do something with her rage towards Joe Desjarlais, the uncle who had sexually assaulted not only herself and her sister, but her little brother Lester. She'd tried hard as a child to tell the adults around her about the abuse she was enduring at the hands of Joe and other relatives. Yet despite her efforts, the abuse had continued. She told herself, over and over, that it wasn't her fault, she was just a little girl. So why was she still haunted by guilt and shame? She couldn't shake the feeling that, somehow, she could have done more to protect Lester from Joe. She also worried about the safety of her own kids, even though she was now living off-reserve. And what about the other children who lived within Joe's reach at Sandy Bay? Her anxiety weighed heavily on her. "I was just tiny, like in a tiny, small little ball," Nancy says. "That's how I felt. Like I was so small and so afraid of everything."

Somehow, Nancy swallowed her fear and did the only thing that made any sense to her—she began to talk about the abuse. She poured out everything to a DOCFS worker at Sandy Bay, who reported her allegations to the Amaranth RCMP. In mid-July 1992, Amaranth RCMP Constable Marc Dureau, who had joined the force three years earlier, was handed a piece of paper with a long list of names of possible abusers and victims. An affable, conscientious officer, Dureau had switched careers after a dozen years as a mechanic in the Canadian Armed Forces because he wanted to work more closely with people. Amaranth was the first posting for the moustached francophone who had arrived two years earlier with his wife. When Dureau first phoned to arrange an interview with Nancy, who had recently moved to Portage la Prairie to live with Sherry, he had no idea how consuming the case would become.

As Nancy recalls what she told Dureau that day, the pain seems to run through her body like a live current. Slumped in a black imitation-velvet easy-chair in the living-room of her low-income townhouse in Portage, the young woman in the pink t-shirt and powder-blue pants talks in a soft, almost childlike voice. The floor around her chair is strewn with children's shoes, and a yellow truck and other toys. On the stereo is a school photo of her oldest son, a handsome seven-year-old with a big smile, while the wall above is adorned with three large pictures of a white-suited Elvis Presley.

As Nancy talks, it is easy to imagine her as a little girl in a pink-and-white flowered dress. When the abuse began, she and her older sister and brother were living with their Desjarlais grandparents after the break-up of their parents' marriage. One morning, as Nancy waited for the bus to pick her up for nursery school, her uncle Joe, who was eighteen, called her over to the old green couch by the living-room window. The older children had already left for school, and her grandmother was asleep in a curtained-off area at the far end of the room. She can still see Joe, lying on the couch, calling her "his little girl" as he molested, then raped her. And she'll never forget, she says, the smell—the nauseating scent of the slimy stuff he left on her. The ordeal ended when the school bus pulled up and she ran out.

Next, Joe began assaulting her on an old bed beside a shack in the yard. He'd bring a tape-recorder and ask her questions as he molested her. She can't remember how many times this happened. But, day after day, she'd go to school feeling "dirty" and wondering if the teacher could smell his sickening odour. She began having nightmares, and messed herself during the night because she was afraid she'd meet Joe on the way to the bathroom. To punish Nancy for these night accidents, her relatives would throw her into icy water near the house, or humiliate her by forcing her to sleep in a bag at night. "He was my bogeyman as a child," Nancy says. "I tried telling them, like, bogeyman's going to hurt me again. And they told me to shut up ... So I just shut up about it. All these years I shut up about it." Nancy finally escaped Joe's abuse after her grandmother Desjarlais suddenly sent her and her siblings to live with their McIvor grandparents. She didn't find out until many years later that the move came after her sister Sherry tried to tell Grandmother Desjarlais about the abuse. Furious, the old woman had ordered them out of the house. But even after they no longer shared a roof with Joe, Nancy's terror didn't abate. As a child, she never stopped fearing he would come after her again.

When the floodgates opened, Nancy not only told Dureau about Joe's assaults, but also reported being sexually abused as a child by three teenage male relatives and two of her mother's boyfriends. When Nancy and her siblings moved in with her McIvor grandparents, the sexual abuse started all over again, with new tormentors. When she moved out to live with her mother, two of Joyce's boyfriends sexually assaulted Nancy. It's no wonder, as a child, she felt the abuse would never end. By the time Nancy grew into womanhood, she felt "used up." "I suffered with all of this," she says. "All the shame. All the guilt. The smell—the smell of the semen. I just wanted to die. I always figured the world was hard on us."

Nancy also disclosed to Dureau the names of others she believed had been assaulted, including her sister Sherry. Sherry agreed to meet with Dureau and give a statement as well. Although torn about whether to tell police about her uncle's abuse, Sherry decided it was a once-in-a-lifetime opportunity: she would not be in it alone. Had Joe abused only her, she knew she likely would not have gone to court. After all, Joe had stopped assaulting her after their family moved out of his house. She'd seen other sides of him and believed he wasn't all bad. But when she added up the toll he'd taken on the lives of other children, including Lester and several other siblings, Sherry knew she had to do something. "All those years, he never stopped," Sherry says. "I was concerned about my own kids' safety and all the other kids' safety."

The abuse began when she was seven years old and living with her Desjarlais grandparents. Her uncle Joe offered to give her a ride on his horse. Joe led the horse into the bushes and lifted her down from her perch. Before she knew what was happening, he pulled down her pants and raped her. Another time, she was playing with other kids when Joe cornered her in the run-down shack behind the house. Frightened, she tried to hide from him behind an old stove as her playmates ran away. She was barefoot and couldn't escape across the nails and broken glass. But Joe found her, forced her screaming onto the ground, put his hand over her mouth, and assaulted her. Over the two years they lived at Joe's house, Sherry lost count of how many times he forced her into his bedroom and raped her behind closed doors. Too ashamed to tell anyone, she suffered in silence. At night, she tried to protect herself by sleeping between two of her siblings on the floor. But there were many sleepless nights when she lay awake, wondering when Joe would come after her again. One time, she even mustered the courage to try to tell her grandmother Desjarlais what was going on. "She didn't believe me," Sherry says. "She was very mad. I can still see how her face went. She called me that stupid girl, that crazy girl."

Like Nancy, Sherry dreaded going to school. She felt "dirty," and sensed a huge gulf between herself and others her age. When kids teased her about being overweight, or wearing dishevelled clothes, she felt humiliated. Even worse were taunts about her smell, because she feared other kids might have guessed her agonizing secret.

Although Joe's abuse ended when she moved out of his house, the memories haunted her. A couple of years later, when she was about eleven years old and living with her McIvor grandparents, the pain bottled up inside her exploded. Sherry was sitting on the couch in the living-room, brooding about the past. All of a sudden the normally quiet girl began to yell hysterically. She screamed and screamed, and then collapsed in a heap on the floor. Something was terribly wrong. "I felt like I was going crazy," Sherry says. "And I was all alone."

Then there was the time, while living with her McIvor grandparents, that her grandpa tried to take her to Joe's place for a visit. Frightened, Sherry baulked at seeing him. For the first time, she told Joyce and her boyfriend about Joe's abuse, as well as about the times her grandfather Desjarlais had molested her. They were startled by her disclosures but said nothing, and never mentioned the abuse again. Sherry felt more ashamed than ever. "I hated living," Sherry says. "I hated life. I used to sit alone all the time, just being quiet, sitting on the couch. My grandma told me I was the quiet one."

Besides disclosing Joe's abuse, Sherry also told Dureau she'd been assaulted by the same male teenage relative who had abused Nancy. Unaware that police would act upon all her disclosures, not just those concerning Joe, Sherry also named another adult relative who had molested her.

When Dureau returned to Amaranth, he tracked down one of Nancy and Sherry's younger sisters, Annette, who was living at Sandy Bay. By now, Annette, a young woman with bright, almond-shaped brown eyes, was the mother of a two-year-old son. She reluctantly reported being sexually assaulted repeatedly by Joe when she was fourteen years old. Annette also named three male teenagers, at least one of them a relative, who she claimed had sexually abused her. Looking back, Annette said she was pressured by her sister Nancy to cooperate with police, even though she didn't feel ready. She felt she could barely cope with her own life and had been abusing drugs on and off. But in the end, she decided to speak to Dureau because of what Joe had done to Lester. Joe had "hurt Lester's pride" by assaulting him, she said, explaining that it was much worse for a boy to suffer sexual abuse. Annette also worried her uncle might someday hurt her own young son. By reporting Joe to the RCMP, Annette hoped it would help Lester's spirit "be at rest."

Reflecting back on those initial interviews with Lester's sisters, Dureau recalled how the painful disclosures unleashed a torrent of feelings in the young women. He felt as if he was watching an emotional chain-reaction as they relived the abuse, fluctuating between sadness and anger over what they'd been through. Dureau listened patiently to their stories, through tears and long, painful silences. One of his tougher tasks was pinning down specific dates and places when the abuse took place, some of the incidents dating back over a decade. And by the time he completed interviews with the three sisters, he had a long list of others whom the women believed had been assaulted by Joe. Joe was arrested in July 1992 on sex-related charges involving the three sisters and was jailed pending his trial. Over the next weeks, Dureau contacted almost twenty other people, most of whom refused to talk to him. As he went from one suspected victim to the next, he found that most insisted nothing had happened. One man, who was related to Joe, accused the sisters and the police of fabricating the allegations. In the end, only two of those named agreed to speak to Dureau—both young men in their twenties. As Dureau later explained, Joe was "feared" by many in the community, in part because of his rumoured link to "bad medicine."

By the time Dureau showed up on David's doorstep in Portage la Prairie in August 1992, the young man was expecting him. With the intense publicity surrounding both Lester's inquest and the ensuing sexual-abuse investigation, David, assumed police would eventually stumble across a statement he'd made about Joe to the Amaranth RCMP in 1987. That's when David, which is not his real name, had first reported that Joe had assaulted him. He'd come forward after Joe was charged with raping his younger cousin at knife-point in the spring of 1987. Joe claimed the sixteen-year-old teenager had agreed to sex. In order to bolster his cousin's case, David agreed to testify about what Joe had done to him. He'd been wracked by guilt over what happened to his cousin, tormenting himself for not reporting Joe sooner.

But the case never made it past the preliminary hearing. There were problems with the testimony of the victim, a teenager with brain damage likely caused by foetal alcohol syndrome. The victim also spoke little English. On the witness stand, the youth became confused about the exact date of the offence, prompting Judge Bruce McDonald to dismiss the charges. What stuck in David's mind the most was an off-hand comment made by McDonald before the hearing began. As McDonald walked by Joe, the judge, who recognized the accused from previous court appearances, flippantly remarked, "I hear you've been a bad boy." David's heart sank when he heard that: "I just turned and walked away. And I went to the witness room. I thought we'd lost, if Judge McDonald would say that." Six years later, McDonald would resign from the bench in the wake of widespread complaints about his insensitive handling of abuse cases.

No one is sure why the RCMP did not lay charges against Joe in 1987 for the assaults David had reported. Now, five years later, David was once again being interviewed by the RCMP about the abuse he'd suffered as a child. According to David, the first incident happened when he was only four years old. It was winter, and he and his older brother were skating on the ice in the ditch. As dusk fell, Joe, who was twelve years old at the time, came by with a sled and offered to give David a ride home. They took off their skates, and his brother ran ahead home. David climbed onto the sled, and Joe pulled him along a road that curved through the bush. Suddenly, Joe stopped, took off his coat, and laid it on the snow in front of the sled. Then he pulled down the little boy's pants, forced him face-down onto the coat, and raped him.

In the pain and terror of that moment, the little boy experienced for the first time the sensation of falling out of his body. He was floating above his body, where it was all quiet, no pain, nothing. He watched Joe assaulting the small body. And then he was suddenly back at his house, dishevelled, with blood on his pants, telling his brother that he was late because a bear had chased him on the way home.

Over the next ten years, David told the RCMP that he lost count of how many times Joe assaulted him. His parents were often drunk, and, according to David, that's when Joe would come by the house and assault him. Terrified of Joe, David felt trapped by the abuse, believing there was nothing anybody could do to help him. The last time Joe raped him was in the summer of 1979, when David was fourteen years old. On that occasion, David hoed the garden outside his home before joining his brother and niece at the lake to swim. To get to the lake, he had to walk past Joe's house, which always made him nervous. As he got closer, Joe came out of the deep ditch next to the road, grabbed David, pulled him into the ditch, and assaulted him. After it was over, Joe abruptly informed him that this was the last time.

One of the youngest in a large family, David said that he kept silent about the abuse he was suffering. The one time he tried to tell his dad about Joe's assaults, his father beat him. Both of David's parents drank heavily, and physical abuse wasn't unusual. David isn't sure when his family's problems began. His parents both attended the Roman Catholic residential school on the reserve as children. But his mother, a devout Catholic, told only glowing stories about her life there. Besides, she firmly believed that people should accept whatever fate God bestowed.

A bright student, David got good grades in most subjects during high school. But the strain of holding himself together emotionally was often excruciating. He couldn't figure out what was wrong. But he knew he was different from everyone else. There were memory gaps, times when someone else took over his body and then left again. In Grade 10, some other part of him attended school, winning academic awards at the end of the year. At the award ceremony, David was paralysed with anxiety because he was no longer in contact with the part of him that had won the awards. He was sure someone would find out he was a fraud.

By the last year of high school, David was drinking heavily and sinking into despair. He was biding his time until he could escape from the community. When his English teacher tried to encourage students to be proud of their roots by introducing books about Indian culture, David could hardly bear to read them. He wanted nothing to do with being Indian. The only book he enjoyed that year was *Catcher in the Rye* by J.D. Salinger, about a young boy's coming-of-age. As soon as he graduated, he moved away from the reserve in an effort to escape the bad memories.

When he was twenty-one, David's inner turmoil drove him to try to kill "his body." Since he couldn't get his hands on a gun, he went to the bank and withdrew a lot of money. Then he bought hard liquor, which he rarely drank. He took the bottles to a nearby railway track and drank until he passed out, hoping a train would run over him. Instead, the police found him and he ended up in the Brandon Mental Health Centre. While there, he disclosed that he'd been abused by Joe. Five years earlier, he'd told a social worker with the Children's Aid Society in Gladstone as well. No one took it seriously either time.

After leaving Sandy Bay, David wrote a test for university entrance and discovered the quality of his education had been dismal. To his dismay, he tested at a Grade 8 level in most subjects, despite having graduated from Grade 12. It was a real blow to his self-esteem to find out his academic achievements didn't count for much in the outside world. Determined to upgrade himself, he took correspondence courses until he obtained his general education diploma and was accepted into Brandon University. But after a few months in the university dormitory, David started to fall apart. The trigger was the drinking parties in the dorm. "Every time they drank, I was sure Joseph was going to show up," David says. "I started having nightmares. I started not going to classes. I locked myself in. I was afraid to go out ... When people started to drink on the reserve, Joseph would always show up." Unable to cope with his growing panic, he ended up at the Brandon Mental Health Centre.

During one of his stays at the BMHC, David spotted a familiar face and realized it was Lester. Looking back, he distinctly remembered it was the spring of 1987. The date stuck in his mind because he was despondent at being in the hospital rather than at home watching the spring bulbs he'd planted in his garden burst into bloom. When he met Lester, David was relieved to meet someone whom he could chat with in the comfortable lilt of his own language. Although David and Lester didn't talk about why each of them was at the BMHC, they spent hours shooting pool together.

A few months later, David ran into Lester on a downtown Winnipeg street. Lester was with David's cousin, the boy who had reported being sexually assaulted by Joe a few months earlier. When the charges against Joe were dropped, the boy and his family had been forced to move to Winnipeg for a while to escape the cloud of shame. To David, it was obvious that the victim, not the perpetrator, suffered when the truth came out. Watching Lester and his cousin together, David suspected that Lester had been one of Joe's victims. As well, David had another eerie feeling: that Lester likely wouldn't survive the black cloud of despair engulfing him. "And then I knew he was going to be dead soon," David says. "He didn't say anything about killing himself. It's sort of like, I tried it when I was young. There's this abuse and then you live on, and then all of a sudden you try to kill yourself. Then, if you make it through that, you live on. But I thought he was now approaching that time when you try to kill yourself. And I thought he was going to succeed."

A major turning-point for David came in March 1988, when the complex, frightening inner world was finally given a name. A psychologist referred him to a Winnipeg doctor who was an expert in multiple personality disorder (MPD). Dr. Colin Ross diagnosed David as having MPD, a dissociative disorder commonly linked to child sexual abuse. In order to cope with the trauma of extreme abuse, David had unknowingly learnt to block out what was happening and escape into another part of himself. Over time, the splits between different parts of himself had grown more fixed. That led to a feeling of having no control over his life. There were memory gaps when one part of himself would be in charge and then suddenly retreat, taking the memories along. He had grown used to making excuses to cover his lapses. Making friends was almost impossible, because he couldn't count on the same part of himself being present at their next meeting. He was plagued by what he called "missing time," when he could not connect with the moment but would be lost in blackness. And there was "wrong time," when he'd look at people and see fuzzy images because another part of himself was trying to use his eyes at the same time. "When you don't know you have MPD it's hell," David says. "It's so terrible. It's awful. It's frightening also. It's almost like you're constantly afraid. You hear stories about people being abducted by aliens—and you feel that way too." Naming his inner turmoil would be the first step towards understanding and healing his splintered identity.

After David gave his statement to the RCMP in the summer of 1992, he decided to prepare his family for the possibility he'd go to trial. When he told his mother, she suggested that he hide his identity by wearing a balaclava if he had to testify. As far as she was concerned, her son would be better off if he forgave Joe and forgot about the long-ago incidents. David realized that admitting the abuse publicly would make his family vulnerable to harassment and humiliation on the reserve. Growing up, he had often heard others make fun of boys who were rumoured to have been assaulted by another male. The reason, according to David, was that male victims involuntarily violated an unspoken code of masculinity: a male is supposed to be on top, no matter what.

To make matters worse, testifying against Joe in court would break another unwritten rule: protecting the family and community took precedence over airing problems in the outside world. The last thing Sandy Bay residents wanted was more damaging publicity. Everyone at Sandy Bay already knew what Joe was like. Parents used stories about "the bogeyman" to scare their children into obedience and warned their offspring to avoid Joe. Forcing the truth into the open by going to court would not win any kudos for the victims. "They all knew," David says. "People knew Joseph did that. So it wasn't really a freeing thing. It was known inside the reserve but not outside the reserve. So there wasn't really that feeling of, oh, thank God it's out in the open."

During the investigation into the allegations about Joe, the RCMP also contacted the boy who had reported being assaulted in 1987. Now twenty-one, slow-witted, and suffering from a serious drinking problem, the young man gave another statement to Dureau. By the time the investigation concluded, Dureau had charged Joe with sixteen sex-related offences involving the twenty-one-year-old man, David, and Lester's three sisters. Joe had been in jail since he was arrested on the first charge in July 1992. His bail application had been denied because of his criminal history. Sexual-assault charges were also laid against eight other men and youth in connection with allegations made by Lester's sisters. Most of those charged were relatives from both sides of their family.

As the investigation triggered by Lester's sisters unfolded, the RCMP was simultaneously unravelling another complex case involving a separate set of sexual-abuse disclosures at Sandy Bay. That investigation was launched after a seventeen-year-old boy from Sandy Bay revealed some startling information to his therapist in Brandon. Just as the inquest into Lester's death was ending, the boy, who had already been charged with sexually assaulting his younger cousin, disclosed he had also abused a long list of other children, and was himself a victim of sexual abuse. At about the same time, the boy's father was jailed for sexually abusing a daughter.

By the time news of the two sexual-abuse investigations became public in late July 1992, Amaranth RCMP had interviewed dozens of adults and children, including some as young as four years old. "We're swamped," Amaranth RCMP Sergeant Bob McAfee, who was in charge of the detachment, told a reporter that summer. "When we went to talk to other kids, it just started snowballing." A brusque, middle-aged officer, McAfee left no doubt this was a massive task. Two officers, one of them Dureau, had worked on unravelling the seventeen-year-old boy's allegations on a full-time basis for the first month until Dureau had to be reassigned to the other investigation. Before this probe was concluded, at least thirty-four suspects would be identified in connection with a total of more than 200 sex-related incidents involving dozens of victims. At least fifteen of those charged were youths under age eighteen, both boys and girls. Most of those charges were eventually stayed or dismissed, although four youths were put on probation. Several adults, both men and women, were also charged. Two of the men received prison terms of less than three years. About 100 other offences were dealt with by alternative measures, like counselling, because the suspects were under twelve years old, and therefore too young to charge under the Criminal Code. In other cases, the victims were too young to provide detailed testimony. Almost every major family grouping in the community was touched by the investigation, which included several cases of intergenerational sexual abuse that went back three generations. As well, a generation of young offenders had been identified, pointing to a desperate need for intervention.

When both sexual-abuse investigations landed on Brandon Crown attorney Krys Tarwid's desk in September 1992, she was already well aware of the cases. She had speculated with colleagues about who would end up handling them. No one was eager to volunteer because of the huge time commitment the complex cases would demand during a period in which everyone felt stretched to the limit. When Tarwid's boss assigned her to the cases, she asked why she'd been chosen. "And I thought, well, he's going to say, you've done terrific work, or because of your reputation," Tarwid says with characteristic self-deprecating humour. "And instead he said, 'Because you're the right gender.'"

The legal profession was a second career for the tall, slender woman with wheat-coloured hair and round, blue-framed glasses. An experienced Crown attorney, with 15 years' experience under her belt, she'd started out as a social worker. After graduating from university with a social-work degree, she'd gone north to Thompson in the mid-1970s to work for Indian Affairs for two years. In those days Aboriginal child-welfare agencies didn't exist, and services to families living on reserves were provided only in life-and-death situations. When emergencies arose, officials simply flew to a reserve, snatched the children in the name of protection, and shipped them to institutions or group homes in southern Manitoba. As Tarwid said, "In essence, we were kidnapping kids."

One case in particular stuck in her mind. On one of her visits to the remote, fly-in reserve of Shamattawa, a mother approached her, pleading for help finding her son, who had been taken away four years earlier. Since then, the mother had not heard a word about him. Tarwid promised to do what she could. After an extensive search for information about the boy's whereabouts, she discovered he'd been sent to an institution for the mentally disabled in Portage because he'd been caught sniffing gasoline. But when she asked her boss for permission to charter a plane to fly the mother from Shamattawa to Portage for a visit, he insisted it would be cheaper to send the boy's father. A translator would have to be hired to accompany the mother, who didn't speak English. But Tarwid, who knew the father had no desire to go, ignored the edict and booked the flight. When the day of the trip arrived, bad weather forced the cancellation of the flight. After several more delays, it seemed like the reunion would never take place.

One bitterly cold winter's day, after the trip had been delayed again, a twelve-year-old boy showed up in Tarwid's office in Thompson. As soon as he said his name, she realized he was the son of the Shamattawa woman. Frustrated by his long wait to see his mother, the boy had escaped from the institution and made the 700-kilometre journey north to Thompson. Tarwid called the institution and was annoyed to discover they hadn't even noticed he was missing. Nevertheless, they demanded his return. Realizing the boy was anything but mentally handicapped, Tarwid refused, and instead booked his flight home. "He was leaving to grab a taxi when he turned and walked back and said, 'Thank you,'" Tarwid says, her brusque tone softening. "He was my one and only 'thank you' in three years of social work. And I said, 'You're welcome.'" Soon after that, she ditched social work and enrolled in law school.

With her no-nonsense style, Tarwid was not in the habit of getting emotionally involved with victims while preparing cases for court. Keeping some distance was important to objectivity, she felt. But, from the beginning, the case involving Lester's sisters was different. With no other support, the young women turned to her for reassurance. They'd call in a panic, insisting they couldn't go through with testifying. Charging Joe Desjarlais and other relatives had turned them into outcasts at Sandy Bay, creating a relentless emotional strain. David also phoned several times to say he'd changed his mind about going to court. Knowing she couldn't force them to testify, Tarwid would acknowledge their fears, offer encouragement, and urge them to reconsider. "They all wanted to see a resolution, but they didn't know if they were capable of it," she says. "So you saw this agony going through these individuals all the time. It was just horrible."

Annette was especially anxious, calling to vent personal problems or to ask for a five-dollar loan when she ended up at the BMHC at one point. Lending money for toiletries and lengthy phone counselling sessions were not routine parts of a Crown attorney's job. Normally, after the first interview with a witness, she had no contact until the preliminary hearing. But Tarwid knew that if she didn't go beyond the call of duty this time, the case would fall apart. "You couldn't say, please don't call me, click, see you in court," Tarwid says. "You'd lose them. They were obviously in need." At times though, the extra emotional demands combined with the long hours she was logging seemed overwhelming. Although Tarwid had been told she'd be freed from other duties while working as special prosecutor on the two Sandy Bay investigations, that had not happened. Her schedule became an exhausting blur of daily return-trips to Amaranth—over two hours one way from her home in Brandon—or to Portage to interview witnesses and consult with police. Fortunately, a victim-services worker, Theresa Raines, and Dureau also teamed up to offer support to the women during the fifteen months they waited to go to trial. Raines, who usually worked with child witnesses, did everything from referring the young women to counsellors, when necessary, to finding emergency housing. Dureau's gentle, patient manner with the sisters was also invaluable. As Tarwid wryly observed later, Dureau became a "taxi service," providing countless rides to appointments and court dates because none of the sisters owned a car. During the long drives, it wasn't unusual for them to pour out their troubles to him. "I had to also be their friend, care for them," Dureau says. "They would call me any hour of the day, night, at work. Just to talk."

Of the three, Annette leaned the most on him, until he felt he'd become almost a father figure to her. The down side of her attachment was that she sometimes vented her anger and frustration at him as well. When he told her he was being transferred to northern Manitoba in June 1993, just four months before the trial, Annette lashed out at Dureau. At first, he was perplexed and put off by her outburst. What had he done to deserve this? he wondered. But as he pondered her fury, he realized she felt abandoned by his impending departure. The only reassurance he could offer was the promise that he'd return for the trial.

On another occasion, he drove to Portage to pick Annette up for a court date. But when he arrived, she refused to leave the house because she didn't have shoes that matched her white dress. To end the crisis, the ever-patient Dureau drove to another sister's house, borrowed a more stylish pair of shoes, and brought them back to Annette, who then agreed to go to court. Like Tarwid, Dureau didn't usually become so emotionally entangled in an investigation. But this time was different. "I did all that because I knew what they went through," Dureau says. "And once they'd get on the stand, I knew it would happen again. They were going to have to go through the whole emotions again. It was hard for them." Child-abuse cases had begun to touch Dureau deeply for another reason as well: the birth of his first child, a son. When he went home and gazed at his own lively, innocent toddler, and recalled what Lester's sisters had suffered, he'd ask himself: "God, how?"

As David and Lester's sisters waited to go to trial, malicious rumours were circulated about them, including gossip that they'd been paid to testify against Joe. David and Sherry had a good laugh about that, saying they only wished it were true. There was also the unspoken pressure of knowing leaders back home weren't happy about the publicity their disclosures had brought. David felt that Chief Angus Starr was especially annoyed. "They were so afraid that more terrible things would be said about the reserve," says David. "He was afraid that if more things were said about the reserve, it would crush whatever spirit there was left."

The allegations against Joe, as well as the other complex sexual-abuse investigation involving a long list of children and adults, had once again put Sandy Bay in the news for the wrong reasons, causing a nasty backlash for some. Teenagers refused to wear jackets bearing the Sandy Bay logo outside of the community, complaining it made them a target for cruel taunts. In February 1993, Brandy Strong, a vivacious sixteen-year-old with dreams of becoming a model, told a newspaper reporter she was tired of the barbed remarks from other teenagers when she went to off-reserve parties. "It makes you feel bad about where you grew up," she said. "This [abuse] happens in white society too. It's not only here."

The principal at the Sandy Bay school compared the fallout from the sexual-abuse investigation to the aftermath of a major bus accident. Ron Brown said residents were struggling with hurt, anger, and denial

over what had happened. Mostly people avoided talking about the allegations which had torn apart the community. But sometimes reality hit
them in the face. One of the most painful incidents had happened six
months earlier, when the community was preparing to welcome eight
Ontario high-school exchange students. Local women had planned a
feast and stitched traditional star blankets as gifts. A pow-wow was
planned in their honour. But a week before the guests were to arrive,
an Ontario school official abruptly cancelled the visit, offering a vague
excuse about inadequate supervision. Letters from the Ontario students, who had already hosted a group from Sandy Bay, soon revealed
the real reason. Their parents had refused to let them go, after hearing
about the sexual-abuse investigation. "It was a real kick in the guts for
a lot of people," Brown said.

The allegations had also created rifts between people within the
community. In February 1993, band councillor Andrew Beaulieu told
a newspaper reporter that long-time neighbours were looking over
their shoulders at each other now, wondering if the person they'd
known for so long was an abuser. "There's not one criminal in my family," Beaulieu said. "But now I'm afraid to go to Portage. How would
you feel if people said because your neighbour is a sex offender, then
you must be one too?"

Band leaders used the publicity to demand a meeting with then
Indian Affairs Minister Tom Siddon in the winter of 1993. They sent a
letter to Siddon, linking the sexual-abuse allegations to deplorable living
conditions in the community. Overcrowded homes and alcoholism left
children at risk for abuse, they told Siddon. A housing shortage forced
about one-third of the families to live in dwellings with as many as fifteen people, usually with no running water. With 275 families waiting
to get new homes, there was no easy solution on the horizon. At the
same time, there wasn't any money to provide treatment to either sexual-
abuse victims or offenders in the community. The most damaged children were being shuttled two hours away to Brandon every week for
counselling appointments. Teachers and child-welfare workers tried to
cope with the rest. The appeal to Siddon for help seemed to bring some
temporary relief to the community's crisis. A month later, the band se-
cured new funding for housing, hired an on-reserve psychologist, and

obtained a grant to renovate a building that would become a counselling centre.

For Nancy, living off-reserve, in Portage, was the buffer she needed against the backlash sparked by her disclosures. Back home, she'd been ostracized, and feared for the safety of herself and her children in the face of simmering resentments. She simply didn't have the energy to cope with relatives' anger and her own inner tumult. Through the women's shelter in Portage, she found a counsellor and began the long, slow process of healing. "If I hadn't left that reserve, I would have suicided myself," Nancy says. "Because I needed help. I was never getting help up there. When I graduated [from high school] that was my one goal—to leave the reserve."

Sherry, too, was living in Portage with her three children when she made her statement to the RCMP. She had urged Nancy to seek help at the women's shelter, which had become "like a second home" to Sherry. There, she had begun to open up to counsellors about the abuse that still haunted her. The day after Sherry told her story to Dureau, Joe Desjarlais startled her by suddenly appearing at her door. He'd just returned from a trip and had no idea what was about to happen. But Sherry couldn't bear to face him and escaped to a neighbour's house. There, she phoned the police, and then watched as they arrested her furious uncle and led him away in handcuffs. Confused and drained by the confrontation, Sherry needed to talk about what had happened. Turning to her sisters wasn't an option, because police had advised them not to discuss the case to avoid tainting their testimony. She couldn't lean on her partner, because he was in jail for impaired driving. If it weren't for her kids, she would have lain down in front of a train. Instead, she hired a taxi to drive her to Sandy Bay, with the hope of finding a sympathetic ear with her mother-in-law. But when she arrived, kids in tow, her mother-in-law was in no mood to listen and chased the desperate young woman out of the house before she could explain about Joe. Sherry trudged away, overcome with despair.

As the date of the preliminary hearing in November 1992 approached, Tarwid got a stream of anxious phone calls from Lester's sisters. "They'd say, I don't want to go ahead, the family hates us, they're not seeing us through this, we're outcasts," Tarwid says.

"That was the big thing—we're outcasts. And I had no doubt they were ... Nobody ever came and held their hand and gave them sympathy—not one friggin' relative." A cousin of Joyce's from Sandy Bay dropped in to visit Sherry in Portage around the same time. Arlene Levasseur hadn't seen Sherry for a long time and wondered why she hadn't been up to the reserve. She had heard people bad-mouthing Sherry and her sisters for taking Joe to court. "And she began crying, and I said, don't worry, not everyone hates you for what you're doing," Levasseur recalls.

On the day of the preliminary hearing in Amaranth, none of David's family showed up. That was fine with him, because he didn't want them to hear the graphic details of his abuse. Sherry asked her mother-in-law to attend the hearing, which she did. But to the dismay of Lester's sisters, another group of their relatives showed up to support Joe. Before the hearing began in the rectangular white community hall which served as a makeshift courtroom, Sherry told Crown attorney Krys Tarwid that she was going to smudge the room with burning cedar, a traditional symbol of purification and protection from evil. Having never been faced with such a request before, and unsure of how the judge would react, Tarwid suggested she do it before he arrived. "So the judge comes in and the first thing he says is, what's that smell?" Tarwid recalls with a chuckle. "I said, I don't know, because I wasn't watching when she did it. I made a point of not watching!"

Shortly after that, in her eagerness to show respect for Ojibwa culture, Tarwid blundered. Noticing a whitish substance covering Sherry's arms, she jumped to what seemed like an obvious conclusion. This too must be part of some spiritual ritual Sherry had not yet explained, perhaps providing some sort of protection from evil, Tarwid mused. When she got a chance, the curious Tarwid queried Sherry about its significance. Perplexed, Sherry stared at her for a moment before answering. "It's hand cream," she said, in a what's-wrong-with-these-white-folks tone.

All five young people who had made statements about Joe's abuse were scheduled to testify at the preliminary. When Joe arrived, Tarwid pulled from her briefcase some special objects she'd borrowed from Lawrence McInnes, the Crown who'd handled Lester's inquest. In front of her on the table, she laid out the medicine pouch and sweet-grass braid McInnes had carried to most of the hearings into Lester's death. When she'd begun prosecuting the case against Joe, people had warned her to beware of the "bad medicine" he might put on her. Sensing the significance of the spiritual to everyone involved, Tarwid believed the medicine pouch and sweetgrass would serve as a kind of "moral support," a symbol of good in the face of evil—like the cross, or garlic braid, of her own Polish Catholic background. When she glanced across the courtroom, she saw Joe gazing in horror at the items. "He just freaked out," Tarwid recalled. "He kept gawking at it the whole time. It really bothered him. Of course, then I knew I was on the right track. I took it to every court appearance with him."

Testifying in front of friends and relatives from Sandy Bay about their abuse was agonizing for all of the witnesses. Sherry could not keep back her tears as she answered the necessary, but painfully intrusive questions in front of relatives whom she knew were there in support of Joe. "I was crying, that's how much I wanted to be believed," she says. When David took the stand, he could not bring himself to look at Joe or say his name. Tears welled up, choking his words, and the judge ordered a brief adjournment to give him a chance to regain his composure.

When the two-day preliminary ended, a series of charges involving Joe's abuse of four of the five young people were sent to trial. The charges involving Joe's assault on David's cousin did not proceed. The slow-witted, shy young man, who easily became muddled about dates, could barely describe the assault and had been unable to provide adequate testimony. Tarwid couldn't help wondering if the suggestible young man had been pressured into once again testifying to the wrong date of the assault.

During the winter of 1993, the anxiety of waiting to go to trial took its toll on David. Shortly before the trial was slated to begin in April, Joe injured himself, and the hearing was rescheduled for October. That was the last straw for David, who could not face another gruelling six-month wait. He felt like a "pawn" in a system which paid little attention to the damage the process was inflicting on him. His old symptoms—like "lost time"—had begun to recur. At times, he was so angry he considered telling police he'd lied about Joe's abuse. Fearful of losing all of the hard-won ground he'd gained in therapy, he hired a lawyer to pressure the Crown into moving up the trial date. When Tarwid realized David was on the brink of refusing to testify, she moved the trial date up to June.

The trial began on June 28, 1993, in the old, two-storey beige-brick courthouse in Portage la Prairie, just a block off Saskatchewan Street, behind the Tim Horton's Donut Shop. Ivy crawled over the front of the once-stately building, and the stone front steps were worn smooth from thousands of anxious footsteps. Inside, two flights of carpeted wooden steps led to the spacious second-floor courtoom. There, Court of Queen's Bench Justice Peter Morse spent the entire first day of the trial listening to testimony from the Crown's expert witness, Dr. Lynn Ryane. Tarwid had called Ryane, a Winnipeg psychologist who specialized in treating multiple personality disorders, to help the judge understand David's testimony. Without that background, Tarwid feared the judge would be put off by David's strange behaviour when he switched into one of his alter egos. The one complication with using Ryane was that she had never counselled, or even met, David. It was a detail that would come back to haunt Tarwid.

When she began preparing the case, Tarwid had sought permission from her superiors to subpoena the psychologist who had originally diagnosed David's MPD five years earlier. But the former Winnipeg psychologist, Dr. Colin Ross, also an expert in MPD, had since moved to Dallas, Texas. Ross wanted about $3,000 U.S. per day to testify. To Tarwid's dismay, her boss told her the fee was too high. She would have to find someone in Manitoba to provide expert testimony, even though Ross was the only one who could verify David's original diagnosis.

On the stand, Dr. Ryane explained that MPD is a mental disorder resulting from severe childhood trauma, like sexual or physical abuse. Recognized as a diagnosis by the psychiatric community, it was recently renamed "dissociative identity disorder." As that name suggests, MPD is simply an extreme form of dissociation on a continuum which includes everything from daydreaming to depersonalization, to amnesia. A normal personality has many different facets, comprising the differing roles each person plays. People who develop MPD split off parts of their personality to contain the pain they've suffered at certain ages. The separation is so complete that they aren't aware that they have "vacuum-packed" parts of themselves in order to avoid that pain. One of the peak periods for dissociation is around the age of five, when children are at an "egocentric" developmental stage in which they believe they have caused everything that happens to them. If they're abused at that age, they often believe they've somehow caused it to happen and easily dissociate to cope with the trauma. By the time such victims are adults, they may develop MPD, defined as two or more distinct personalities, each with its own way of perceiving, relating, and thinking. Symptoms of MPD include being unable to remember chunks of the past, black-outs not related to alcohol, hearing voices, self-mutilation or suicide attempts that later can't be recalled, being easily hypnotized and easily startled, and unexplained avoidance of certain situations. Once a person seeks therapy, reintegrating the personalities, or learning how to live with them, is a long-term process that can take six to ten years.

The day after Ryane testified, David took the stand and haltingly began to answer Tarwid's questions. Joe's lawyer, Tim Killeen, jumped up several times during the first hour to complain he couldn't hear David, whose voice sometimes trailed into a whisper. Soon, David's other personalities began to emerge and talk to each other, prompting more objections from the uneasy Killeen. But, speaking in short phrases, David managed to provide a detailed, emotionally raw account of Joe's assaults, which began when he was four years old and continued for a decade. As he testified, a current of pain ran through the young man. When Tarwid asked him to identify Joe, he froze at the prospect of looking directly at his tormenter. After a pause, David pointed in the general direction of Joe, without turning his head.

When Killeen began his cross-examination, David's anxiety escalated. Killeen questioned him repeatedly about his other personalities, suggesting that David's testimony could not be credible if various parts of him disagreed about what answers to give. David tried to explain that he had to consult each personality because each of them had access to only certain memories: "One person might have a memory this long, while another person's memory may start here and continue on," David told Killeen. "And if to answer your questions we needed all this memory, it is best that we used all of everybody to answer it properly."

As David became more rattled, another personality, who he identified as "R.E.," interrupted by whispering: "I think that's what happened. Why did you say that? Oh, God." Killeen pounced on the sign
of inner conflict, pointing out that the personalities must not have
reached consensus about what had happened after all. David responded
by saying R.E. was not supposed to talk because he had no firsthand
memories of the assaults. As Killeen hammered away, picking out inconsistencies in David's testimony, the young man didn't waver on the
matter of Joe's assaults. But he felt increasing panic about whether he
was being believed. At one point, the perceptive young man, realizing
how his testimony was coming across, said despairingly: "If you were
sitting here, and I was sitting there, and I was listening to you, I
wouldn't believe you."

When his testimony ended, David stormed out of the courtroom
and into the waiting-room for witnesses. He was sure he'd lost the case
and that Joe was about to go free. Tarwid tried to reassure him, saying
he'd told the truth and done his best. RCMP Constable Marc Dureau
also attempted to cheer him up, saying he'd done just fine. But David
wouldn't listen and told Dureau: "Don't talk to me, don't ever talk to
me again ... I was so angry. I felt that someone who had destroyed my
life had just won."

He didn't return the next morning to hear closing arguments or
the judge's decision. Later that day, when he got home, he saw the
message light on his answering-machine blinking. When he turned it
on he heard Tarwid's excited voice: "You won! He got five years! See
you later." The judge had not only believed David, but given Joe a stiff
sentence. David couldn't believe the good news and phoned Sherry to
help him celebrate.

During the trial, Joe had chosen not to testify in his own defence.
When the judge handed down his verdict, the stunned man lost his composure and began to shout across the courtroom at Tarwid. The object of
his fury was the medicine pouch lying on the table in front of her.

"What's in there?" Joe yelled from the prisoner's box. "What's in
the pouch?"

As he was being led away, Tarwid got her chance to respond:
"Well, you can ask Lester," she told Joe. "Lester did that."

Although incredibly relieved by the verdict, the only family member David shared his news with was his mother. He had no desire to tell anyone else at Sandy Bay, believing they wouldn't understand. Eventually, as word spread about Joe's sentence, David's prediction proved accurate: he heard band members joking that the well-known trouble-maker had finally been jailed—and for raping a boy, no less. The closest David's family came to acknowledging the trial was to make more barbed remarks about the Desjarlais clan.

The outcome of David's case offered the encouragement Lester's sisters needed, despite the backlash they faced from relatives as they awaited Joe's next trial. On October 21, 1993, the three sisters arrived to testify against Joe in the same Portage la Prairie courtroom in which David's trial had taken place. David also came to offer his support by sitting with them in the witness room as they waited to testify. Determined to see Joe convicted on these other charges as well, David was shadowing his former abuser through the court process.

Tarwid put Annette, who was pregnant with her second child, on the witness stand first. The Crown attorney was worried about how the young woman's testimony would hold up. Tarwid had already noted inconsistencies between Annette's statements to police and her testimony at the preliminary hearing. That's where Tarwid got her first inkling that Annette had a hard time sticking to one version of events. Her tendency to embellish the facts plagued her testimony again at the trial. By the end of the day, Annette had contradicted herself often enough that Tarwid knew this part of the case had fallen apart. Court of Queen's Bench Justice Scott Wright dismissed the charges against Joe related to Annette but agreed to proceed separately with the complaints involving the other two sisters. Although Tarwid had no doubt Annette had suffered at Joe's hands, the young woman's recollections were too scattered to withstand legal scrutiny.

The next day, both Sherry and Nancy were scheduled to testify. The problems with Annette's testimony left Tarwid all the more anxious. She had no idea what to expect when she put her next two witnesses on the stand. Sherry and Nancy were still vacillating about whether they could go through with it. To make matters worse, their relatives had shown up at the trial in support of Joe. In a silent show of intimidation, members of the Desjarlais clan sat in the audience, whispering and passing notes to Joe, until Tarwid demanded the sheriff intervene. Even the women's father, Cecil, appeared at the courthouse, stopping to speak to Joe but ignoring his daughters. At one point, Sherry came to Tarwid and said, "My heart is heavy. I don't think I can go ahead. I can't remember." Exasperated, yet acutely aware of the pressure Sherry was under, Tarwid replied, "Well work on it!" She knew they all wanted a conviction but were tormented with doubts about testifying. "You saw this agony going through these individuals all the time," Tarwid says. "It was just horrible."

Until then, Sherry had been standoffish with Tarwid, avoiding discussion of the details of Joe's abuse. But when Sherry testified, her reticence vanished. As she began, she seemed to be standing at the edge of a precipice, hesitating about whether to step over the edge. And then the shy young woman dropped her guard and became the terrified little girl who had been hunted down by the Joe.

"When I seen the kids running there, then I was starting—trying to run," Sherry told the court. "I seen Pee-Ance coming."

"He was coming?" Tarwid asked.

"Yes," Sherry said.

"And who is he?" Tarwid said.

"Joe," she said.

"Joe, yes. And what do you remember?" Tarwid said.

"I didn't—I was at—well, I hid somewhere in the—" Sherry began.

"You hid somewhere?" Tarwid said.

"Yeah," Sherry said.

"And then what do you recall?" Tarwid prodded gently.

"I hid by that—behind that old stove," Sherry said.

"Behind the old stove?" Tarwid repeated.

"Yeah," Sherry said.

"All right. And then what do you remember happening?" Tarwid said.

"He found me," she said, her voice barely a whisper.

"He followed you?" Tarwid said.

"He found me," Sherry repeated.

Slowly, she described the ugly details of Joe's abuse—the shame, fear, sleepless nights, and terrible loneliness of knowing she wasn't like other children.

"I was even scared of the children to play with them," Sherry said.

"Why was that?" Tarwid asked.

"'Cause I was 'way different," Sherry said.

"How were you different?" Tarwid said.

"Because they were all playing and I never played. I was just hiding, always hiding," Sherry replied. "Or just standing. Where the school—school grounds was."

When the abuse ended, she said, she tried to put it behind her, "like it never happened." And despite her suffering, she didn't hate Joe, she said.

By the time Sherry left the witness stand that afternoon, Tarwid was overwhelmed, her usual professional detachment shattered: "I could disconnect myself until the day of the trial," Tarwid says. "It was, like, awful. You're thinking how devastated their lives are—how totally wrecked. And I could put my own kid in that position and I'm going, I don't think I could live with this—this is horrible. And then it sort of all became real ... The emotion was just awful. It was overwhelming."

Then it was Nancy's turn to testify. Although she was unsure until the last minute if she could go through with it, once on the witness stand her memories poured out.

"He used to play with us a lot, but the touching and all that was—I knew it was wrong," Nancy told the court. "I know I was just a child. But I knew it was wrong already because he hurted me."

During cross-examination, defence lawyer Tim Killeen tried to get Nancy to admit she'd enjoyed Joe's attention. He suggested that, because of her young age, she might have been mistaken about what had taken place.

"Okay. At the time you just said it seemed like it was just funny, more like playing a game; right?" Killeen asked.

"Yeah. But I'm older now and I know what he did," Nancy replied.

"Okay. Years later, after these things had happened, that's when you learned that what he did was have sex with you?" Killeen said.

"Yes," Nancy said.

"Okay. And years later you came to realize him doing this to you was something that you thought was wrong; right?" Killeen said.

"Yes, because I'm carrying his scar. I'll probably carry it all my life," Nancy shot back.

At the end of the gruelling day, the hearing was adjourned for the weekend, and Sherry and Nancy were left to wait for the judge's verdict. During dinner that evening at a Chinese restaurant, Sherry snapped open her fortune cookie to find a good omen. The words on the slip of paper said: "Today, the hard part is done. You can live happy and go on with your life!"

Only Nancy returned to the courtroom the following Monday to hear the judge convict Joe on both counts of sexual assault. Before the sentencing, Tarwid made a statement to the court, calling Joe the "bogeyman of Sandy Bay," a label Nancy had used during her testimony. The nickname infuriated Joe, who yelled from the prisoner's box.

"The Crown calls me a bogeyman and they say I practise bad medicine. But what about the Crown? What's she got there behind her desk?" Joe shouted, referring to the ever-present medicine pouch lying behind Tarwid's lectern. "I want to know what's in there!"

The judge, who had no idea what Joe meant, called for order in the court while Tarwid turned to respond.

"Ask Lester," she said, again.

When Sherry and Annette arrived at the courthouse, the sentencing had already finished. Anxious about the outcome, they walked into the clerk's office on the main floor to ask about the verdicts. The clerk announced the good news: Joe had been sentenced to four years in prison on each charge, to be served consecutively. The verdicts left the sisters feeling a mix of relief, anger, and sadness tinged with guilt. His consecutive four-year sentences—added to the five years Joe was already serving for abusing David—didn't satisfy Nancy, whose anger was close to the surface. "They should have given him life," Nancy says. "He's destroyed a lot of people's lives. He should have died instead of my brother. It's for the sake of the children. The more he is in there, the safer those kids will be. He's dangerous to society."

For Sherry, the anger was buried deeper. She, too, felt that taking Joe to court was the only way to stop him. "We felt we protected a lot

of children," she says. But when the trial ended she just wanted to forgive and forget. She had moved back to Sandy Bay about three weeks
before the trial began. Now she returned home, glad she could finally
put it all behind her. It would be months until she allowed herself to
feel the anger still simmering inside.

Both Nancy and Sherry blamed themselves for being unable to
protect Lester and their other siblings from Joe. They each agonized
privately over why they hadn't spoken up sooner about their abuse,
forgetting that they had tried as children to seek help. Annette's reaction was different. As a reluctant witness from the beginning, she was
simply relieved to put the trial behind her. Being ostracized by the
Desjarlais clan had been hard for her to bear, with her closer ties to
that family.

But the feelings of relief for Sherry, Nancy, and David were short-
lived. To their dismay, they soon discovered that Joe's lawyer had filed
notices to appeal all three convictions. Joe's relatives had rallied behind
him, vowing he'd been treated unfairly. Back at Sandy Bay, people for
the most part avoided talking about the case. But Sherry was acutely
aware of the silent disapproval from relatives and others who couldn't
understand why she'd taken her uncle to court. She tried not to let it
show, but the cutting remarks hurt. Former friends avoided her, saying
"Who knows who she's going to charge next?" Pregnant with her
fourth child and experiencing a rocky time in her relationship with
Norbert, Sherry felt more alone than ever that winter. What she
wanted most was to forget the trial had ever happened.

Nancy, on the other hand, was eager to talk about her abuse after
too many years of silence. By the winter of 1994, she was living in the
two-storey townhouse in Portage with her four children and partner.
She attended weekly counselling sessions and enrolled in adult literacy
classes, after discovering she had tested at only a Grade 7 level despite
having graduated from the Sandy Bay school. Trying to get by on a
$774-a-month welfare cheque that never stretched far enough was a
constant strain. But she was determined to give her kids more of a
sense of stability and family than she had had. At Christmas, she deco-
rated her front window and put up an artificial Christmas tree with
cheery red and gold metallic garlands in her living-room. Somehow,

she also scraped together the money to buy presents for her children. She knew it was the little things that mattered to kids, after the countless birthdays and holidays that passed without celebration in her childhood. When her children fought, she talked to them, and tried to help sort out their conflicts, instead of yelling. She was struggling to be the kind of parent she'd never had.

At the same time, daily life was often chaotic in Nancy's household. Conflicts with her partner prompted her to flee with her children to the town's battered-women's shelter several times that winter. Some months, she ran out of food and had to rely on loans from friends who were just as financially strapped. Health problems, including being diagnosed with diabetes, drained her energy. There were days when she felt that, no matter how hard she tried, nothing would ever change—days when the dishes piled up in the sink, and even her toddler's bright-eyed antics couldn't lift her spirits; days when she couldn't keep the past at bay; days when she felt she was drowning in grief over her lost childhood.

Ever-present in her life were the spirits of Lester and her mother. She often offered a prayer to them and the gift of a small dish of food. Or she broke open a cigarette as an offering. Sometimes she even wrote letters to her brother and mother. The rituals brought her loved ones close and kept disturbing dreams away. She believed that, if their spirits wanted something, they'd come to you in dreams. When the sadness of missing them overwhelmed her, she put music on the stereo and cried until she had no more tears. Each night before she fell asleep, she prayed again.

In mid-March, word came that the Manitoba Court of Appeal had turned down Joe's appeal of his convictions on the charges related to Nancy and Sherry. Nancy was elated, feeling she could finally get on with healing. Sherry, seven months pregnant by now, was also relieved that the ordeal was over. For David, who was waiting for the appeal of his case to be heard the following month, the news was encouraging. He'd been on an emotional roller-coaster all winter, worrying about how the appeal would end. Surely the court would uphold that conviction as well.

David had planned to show up for the hearing on April 19 in Winnipeg. But when the day arrived, his trepidation was too great. He could not face seeing Joe again. But Cecil Desjarlais and four other relatives of Joe's arrived early at the high-ceilinged courtroom in the downtown courthouse. A sheriff escorted Joe from the remand centre across the street. A large man with a broad face and shoulder-length, greasy straight black hair, Joe was clad in drab, grey prison garb, the shackles just above his sneakered feet jangling as he shuffled by. He slumped into a wooden chair on the left side of the courtroom, the sheriff at his side, and waited for the hearing to begin. With his weak, almost double, chin and poor posture, he seemed to have an air of defeat about him. But when he turned, his gaze was cold and arrogant.

As soon as the three black-robed judges settled into their ornate wooden chairs on the elevated platform, they made it clear Joe's appeal had a good chance of succeeding. Calling the case "troubling," they said the trial judge's verdict was in question because David's diagnosis of MPD might not have been properly established in evidence. They questioned Crown attorney Greg Lawlor, who soon acknowledged that the doctor who had first diagnosed David—Dr. Colin Ross—should have been called to testify. Instead, the judge had accepted a written diagnosis by Ross that was five years old. But Lawlor also stated the Crown had no intention of calling Ross should a new trial be ordered, hinting that the decision was cost-related. Mr. Justice Kerr Twaddle then told Lawlor: "Maybe the Crown will have to pay the consequences of that decision." A few minutes later, Lawlor readily agreed that the Crown didn't deserve another "kick at the can" when it had erred the first time. Lawlor also provided no reason why a new trial should be ordered. In the end, Joe's defence lawyer had no reason even to rise from the chair.

Without establishing David's MPD diagnosis, his testimony became problematic, the judges decided. The expert testimony about MPD provided by Winnipeg psychologist Dr. Lynn Ryane was irrelevant because she had not met the victim. The judges also revealed their lack of understanding about MPD, mislabelling the mental disorder a "fairly eccentric disease." Another suggested David might have confused Joe with others who abused him or been influenced by therapists' suggestions. Before the trio even began their deliberations, the outcome was obvious. With the scent of victory in the air, Joe's relatives flouted the court's rule forbidding contact with the prisoner and chatted loudly in Saulteaux with him. After a couple of half-hearted attempts to intervene, the sheriff looked the other way as Joe pulled a newspaper clipping from a manila envelope and passed it to Cecil. Ironically, the *Winnipeg Free Press* article of a few days earlier described a proposal from the DOCFS agency for an Aboriginal healing centre for abuse victims.

When the judges filed back into the courtroom, they quashed Joe's five-year sentence, saying that, without the MPD diagnosis, David's testimony "did not have the qualities of detail and continuity that would justify a conviction." Considering the Crown's position against calling Dr. Ross, a new trial did not seem to be warranted, they said. They also stated that, even with Ross's testimony, they had not been convinced the case would succeed. Finally, the judges expressed concern about the "stress and trauma" a new trial might impose on the victim. Joe revealed no emotion as the judges handed back five years of his life.

Meanwhile, David was waiting nervously at home in Portage for the verdict. About 6:00 P.M., he braced himself, picked up the phone and made a call. The unexpected bad news left him stunned. He listened in silence as the judges' decision was read to him. Trying to hide his disbelief, he at first expressed relief that he wouldn't have to endure another trial. But there was a tremor in his voice.

The next day, David awoke at 6:00 A.M. after a restless night. The knot of pain inside him was swelling, threatening to engulf him. He felt like vomiting. Or rushing out and committing a crime so he'd be locked up with Joe and could seek revenge. Was it too late to change the judges' minds? he wondered. He would much rather testify again than endure this emotional torment. Wasn't it up to him to decide if he wanted to repeat his testimony? How could the judges be so patronizing? What right did they have to put him through this? Why didn't they believe him? He felt powerless, worse than in a long time. Why wouldn't the Crown spend the money to do the trial right? After paying thousands of dollars for the inquest into Lester's death, why wouldn't they make every effort to lock up the man who had hurt not only Lester and David, but so many other children? Was this justice? He decided to call Tarwid and find out if there were any legal options left.

Tarwid, too, agonized over the outcome of the case, vacillating between anger and guilt åt her inability to secure a solid conviction. Most of all, she ached at David's revictimization by the justice system. But this was the end of the road legally. The Crown had no intention of appealing the latest decision.

However, the final round was yet to come. Two weeks later, David's case was front-page news in the *Winnipeg Free Press*. The May 3 article focused on the way the Justice department's penny-pinching had ultimately contributed to the unravelling of the case against the notorious pedophile. Senior Crown officials denied that cost was a factor and went so far as to accuse David of refusing to be seen by Dr. Lynn Ryane, the Winnipeg psychologist. The truth was that David had never been asked to see Ryane. In the article, Tarwid took the unusual step of contradicting her superiors, confirming that cost had indeed been a key factor in the decision not to call Ross. When questioned about her department's handling of the matter, Justice Minister Rosemary Vodrey repeated the points made by her senior officials. She too hinted that perhaps David himself had been to blame. The case was closed.

By now, Sherry had emerged from the emotional cocoon she'd retreated into with her pregnancy. She gave birth to her fourth child, a son, in late April. With the passing of winter, her buried anger towards Joe had begun to thaw. Joe's acquittal on the charges involving David seemed incredible. When she first heard the bad news, her anger and frustration made her head feel like it was going to explode. A couple of weeks later, Sherry decided she was ready to speak out.

Sherry was dressed in a morning-glory purple sweatshirt and stretch pants, and her hair fell almost to her waist as she slid into the back booth of the Amaranth café. Outside the window, a heavy spring rain washed the dust off the trees' tender green. She'd hitched a ride into the village adjacent to Sandy Bay for the noon-hour interview because it was too risky to meet on the reserve. Chief Angus Starr had done everything he could to discourage further publicity about Lester's case, including warning Sherry and others not to give interviews. But Sherry was no longer intimidated by Starr. Instead, she wondered why he was so threatened by their family.

When the waitress stopped at the table, Sherry ordered the buffet lunch and a cream soda. As she ate, she expressed annoyance at what she perceived to be Joe's recent attempts to threaten her indirectly. He'd phoned her friends and relatives and hinted he'd go after Sherry and her sisters when he got out. Unless he contacted her directly, there wasn't much she could do legally about the harassment.

Like Nancy, Sherry had sometimes wished as a child that she knew how to get rid of Joe. The rest of the time she had brooded about taking her own life. Convinced she was to blame for the sexual abuse, for her, death seemed like a release. But what pulled her back from the brink as a child were the religious taboos of both the Catholic Church and traditional spirituality. Suicide doomed you to a Christian Hell of fire and brimstone overseen by the Devil. And traditional Ojibwa beliefs warned that dying by your own hand meant you'd wander aimlessly in a black cloud, tormented by the cries of your loved ones, until your predestined time of death. When she got older, her love for her children kept her from giving up on life. "I didn't want anyone to hurt them the way I was hurt," she says. "At least I'd be here for them." Instead, when the pain got too bad, Sherry turned to the bottle. Drinking was a solace, a way to forget. Booze offered a lifeline when she needed it most. "That's how I managed to live so long," she recalls. "Sometimes I wonder, why do I drink? I used to think about that. Yeah, you get sick after you drink. But at least you get to go around and have parties and laugh for a while." Three years earlier, she'd been forced to spend a month in an alcohol treatment program at Sagkeeng First Nation. DOCFS had apprehended her children, and the only way to regain custody was to comply.

Even as a child she'd turned to prayer for comfort. She wasn't sure exactly how it was supposed to be done. Anxious about being teased, she'd often lie awake until everyone was asleep. Then, in the privacy of darkness, she'd make the sign of the cross, quieting her fears with a ritual she'd learned at Mass but didn't completely understand. As a young girl, she'd been baptized in the Roman Catholic church that both her maternal grandmother and her great-grandmother attended. What struck Sherry most about Catholicism were all the rules, including the strict taboo against birth control that previous generations of women had faithfully followed.

Visits to the community's medicine man were also a source of strength. Sherry was reticent to talk about his traditionally reclusive role. But she has turned to him to bestow sacred Indian names on each of her children after birth and sought help discerning the meaning of troubling dreams. After Lester's death, her brother came to her in dreams. To appease his spirit, she was instructed to take a gift of food to his grave. To this day, she brings an offering of tobacco when she visits the graves of Lester and her mother. And when she tucks her children into bed at the end of a day, she also says goodnight to the spirits of her loved ones.

Chapter Nine

FULL CIRCLE

"Lester deserved something better."

—Judge Brian Giesbrecht

A brilliant red-and-yellow sailboat glides through the water in the framed print above Judge Brian Giesbrecht's desk in the Brandon court-house. On the opposite wall of his second-floor office hangs a large sketch of a man whose midriff bulges over shorts while he brandishes a squash racquet. Giesbrecht, an avid tennis and squash player, explains that the drawing was done by a friend. "That's how I'll look someday," he jokes.

But his mood turns sombre when I ask about the photo on the end-table next to the couch. A little girl wearing a headscarf, and a dress with a white peter-pan collar, grins sweetly back from the photo. It's his eight-year-old daughter, Karen, who died of brain cancer three years earlier, in March 1991. She'd been ill for four years. The loss of his daughter was always in his thoughts as he presided over the inquest into Lester's suicide just six months later. "I became a more serious person," Giesbrecht says. "You just assume your children are going to grow up, and grow up healthy and all of those things. Well, as a parent of a sick child, we found that's just not the case. Just the idea that children are so precious and have to be protected—I think that feeling grew." Children's rights would be a prominent theme in his massive 292-page report on the inquest into Lester's death.

The summer after the inquest ended, Giesbrecht devoted all his time to writing his report. Although he'd started outlining the document during the final months of hearings, witnesses' testimony had shifted direction too many times to make much progress. In July and August 1992, he booked off several weeks for a holiday and travelled with his wife, to their favourite corner of Nopiming Provincial Park on the Manitoba–Ontario border. Along with their canoe and supplies, they also lugged stacks of notes from the inquest. While canoeing his favourite lake in the wilderness region, Giesbrecht wrote his report. Each morning he'd rise early, perch on a sunny rock, swat mosquitoes, and write. Then he'd mull over his next chapter as he paddled during the middle of the day. He agonized over the uncomfortable task of writing a highly critical report about DOCFS. From his years in family court, he knew many of the same problems existed in the non-Aboriginal child-welfare system. Singling out DOCFS would inevitably offend some people. But the bottom line he returned to again and again was that children who were taken into care deserved nurturance and protection. Giving them anything less could not be ignored. As the summer went by, he periodically drove back to Brandon to turn in his latest drafts for typing. By the end of August, the document was completed and ready for release.

Giesbrecht knew his report would provoke criticism from both Aboriginal leaders and the provincial government. Rather than trying not to offend the powers that be—both Native and non-Native—Giesbrecht had chosen to be blunt. "I didn't know any other way of doing it," he says. "Either the witnesses were listened to and the report was written in a direct style or else you get into what I would call a manufactured political study where everything is done from a sympathetic view and great attempts are made to try not to offend anybody. What you end up with then is a bunch of porridge."

Giesbrecht's strongly worded report was released on Friday,

September 4, 1992. The judge made it clear he believed the protection of children like Lester had been sacrificed to the political agendas of both Aboriginal leaders and the provincial government. "What is clear to me is that Lester Desjarlais had the right to expect more," he wrote. "His family let him down; his community let him down; his leaders let him down; then the very agency that was mandated to protect him let him down and the government chose not to notice. Lester deserved something better." He went on to make more than two dozen recommendations. These included everything from more training for Aboriginal child-welfare workers to reiterating the earlier recommendation of the Child Advocacy Project that interdisciplinary teams of specialists be set up to respond to child sexual abuse in rural areas.

Among his more controversial recommendations were those addressing political interference in child welfare. Giesbrecht leaned hard on Aboriginal leaders, proposing that the province draft legislation banning chiefs and band councillors from the boards of child-welfare agencies and local child-welfare committees. "It is my conclusion that DOCFS and other Aboriginal child care agencies are in great danger from political interference," he wrote. "An Indian leadership that cannot discipline itself is not worthy of governing." On the other hand, he also harshly criticized provincial child-welfare officials like Jim Bakken, assistant deputy minister of Family Services, saying they were more concerned about "political fallout" from Aboriginal leaders than protecting children. The province's "hands-off" approach to Aboriginal child welfare must be reformed, he said. Giesbrecht also recommended that, if necessary, the province wield its power to withdraw the legal mandate of agencies like DOCFS if they didn't resolve internal problems. In the end, the judge's report took aim at both Aboriginal and non-Aboriginal politicians and bureaucrats, laying the blame for children's suffering at their feet. The final line in his report summed up his concerns: "Children must come first."

Aboriginal leaders reacted swiftly to Giesbrecht's report. Assembly of Manitoba Chiefs leader Phil Fontaine declared that Giesbrecht had gone too far. Fontaine was especially offended by recommendations that might encourage the province to intervene in child welfare without the approval of Aboriginal leaders. "Those days of having governments impose their will on First Nations are over," Fontaine told reporters at a press conference on the day the report was released. Fontaine insisted such drastic measures as banning chiefs from the boards of child-welfare agencies weren't necessary. Instead, he suggested that strict conflict-of-interest guidelines could prevent undue interference. "We recognize there are some serious problems and we're willing to take corrective action," Fontaine said. "That's a recommendation from just one person."

What offended Aboriginal leaders and child-welfare officials was the sharp tone of Giesbrecht's report. Some suggested that an inquest presided over by a white judge and a white Crown attorney was incapable of producing relevant suggestions. The Sandy Bay band council faxed a defiant press release. "We want it clearly understood that Judge Giesbrecht is wrong when he says the community knew and looked the other way or accepted that abuse of children was and is a way of life here," the council wrote. At the same time, they said they were considering withdrawing from DOCFS out of concern for the quality of care the agency was providing. "We were a nation of strict moral upbringing and many of us still are and we will not succumb to the views and accusations of one person, even if that person has more knowledge than the police, clinical psychologist and all the social workers and doctors that appeared before him," the statement said. "We will survive and overcome this crisis as we have done before. We have survived smallpox, infested blankets and we will survive yet another attempt to destroy our nation."

Provincial politicians bided their time in responding to Giesbrecht's report. Family Services Minister Harold Gilleshammer at first refused comment, except to say he didn't plan to fire any of his officials involved in mishandling the case. Over the summer, senior Justice department officials had quietly decided not to pursue a criminal investigation against Jim Bakken, assistant deputy minister of Family Services, or DOCFS officials, for failing to provide evidence to the inquest about the case of the Sandy Bay girl. Liberal leader Sharon Carstairs lost no time in suggesting that decision was motivated by a desire to avoid an embarrassing probe of senior government officials. In the end, not a single government or DOCFS official would face disciplinary action for the mishandling of child-abuse cases at Sandy Bay.

Privately, some Aboriginal child-welfare professionals breathed sighs of relief when Giesbrecht's report dragged the problem of political interference into the open. Previously, they had been forced to choose between their jobs or deferring when band leaders meddled in child-abuse cases. Giesbrecht's remarks also hit a nerve among Aboriginal child-welfare workers in other provinces, who flooded the court with requests for copies of his report. Manitoba's Native-run agencies, and especially DOCFS, had been a model for child-welfare programs across Canada. Aboriginal leaders in other parts of the country were eager to learn from the agency's mistakes as they sought greater control of their own child-welfare services. The concerns raised by the inquest into Lester's death were carefully studied in many communities.

Beyond the controversial topic of political interference, professionals in the Aboriginal child-welfare system were also glad that Giesbrecht pointed to chronic problems like insufficient training, lack of treatment in First Nations, and inadequate support from provincial officials. But while many appreciated Giesbrecht's emphasis on children's rights, they also felt he had verged on paternalism with some of his recommendations, especially those urging greater provincial government intervention. After all, provincial child-welfare bureaucrats who had been of little help so far could hardly be expected to save the day at this late date. They worried that Giesbrecht's criticisms had played into the hands of the Filmon government's reluctance to support Aboriginal self-government. They also said Giesbrecht's analysis had failed to touch on several key problems: the lack of adequate funding, and the unresolved jurisdictional issues among the province, the federal government, and First Nations over who would control child welfare. The tripartite agreements among the three levels of government, which had originally established agencies like DOCFS a decade earlier, had long since expired. Efforts to reopen negotiations had been stalled for years by the federal and provincial governments.

Two weeks after the release of Giesbrecht's report, Gilleshammer and Fontaine called a joint press conference to announce that they, along with the federal government, were setting up a First Nations Child and Family Services task force. The task force was to be co-chaired by Wally Fox-Decent, who had previously led the provincial task force on the Meech Lake Accord, and Dr. Marlyn Cox, a Cree physician from Grand Rapids. Gilleshammer and Fontaine promised the task force would address concerns raised by Giesbrecht's report. Hearings would be held in Aboriginal communities across Manitoba over the following year. Four additional members were also appointed to the task force, with each level of government choosing two representatives. Fontaine also announced that a separate Service Appeal Panel would be set up on an interim basis to handle complaints about political interference in child-welfare matters or poor service. Anyone, from foster parents to social workers, could contact the appeal panel for help in resolving disputes. The total price-tag for the task force and appeal panel: more than $500,000.

But rather than alleviating public concern sparked by Giesbrecht's report, the new task force was eyed sceptically by Aboriginal women's groups, children's advocates, and child-welfare officials. They were furious that governments would spend a half million dollars to study the problem one more time, yet could not find more funds for staff training or treatment for abused children. The director of one First Nations child-welfare agency suggested the money would have been better spent training staff so they'd be more able to resist political interference. As far as this director was concerned, the task force was about politics, not improving services to children and families: "You have two politicians, Fontaine and Gilleshammer, trying to get the heat off their asses," the director said. Others criticized the political nature of the appointments to the task force, predicting they would produce a status quo report that tried to satisfy everyone. Also, while four of the six members of the task force were Aboriginal, only two had any background in child welfare. The task force was off to a bad start, tainted by political baggage that would hinder its work. One of its greatest difficulties would be getting community members, other than band and child-welfare officials, to attend the hearings. In some First Nations, residents asked for private hearings, for fear of a backlash from local leaders. Members of the task force didn't help matters when several indicated publicly that political interference was a "non-issue" to them, leaving the impression that they had already sided with the status quo.

Still, many thoughtful presentations were made reiterating issues which have often been brought to the attention of politicians. During a presentation in June 1993, Chief Harvey Nepinak, chairman of the board of the Dauphin-based West Region Child and Family Services, offered a long list of recommendations, from setting up a First Nations Child and Family Services Commission to taking over regulation of agencies from the province, to establishing a comprehensive staff-training program. He pointed out that more federal funding for everything from family-violence programs to healing centres was urgently needed. Similiar concerns were echoed by other child-welfare officials, including Chief Frank Abraham, chairman of the board of Southeast Child and Family Services. Abraham also addressed the issue of political interference, noting that Southeast had already removed chiefs and band councillors from their board. He urged chiefs to lobby at the political level on behalf of child welfare rather than intervening in individual cases.

Towards the end of the hearings, in June 1993, the task force travelled to Brandon, where its members came face to face with the author of the report several had criticized—Judge Brian Giesbrecht. Despite the judiciary's traditional reluctance to appear at public forums, Giesbrecht agreed to meet with the task force. During a tense, ninety-minute session, members of the task force grilled the judge about his recommendations. They made little effort to hide their disdain for some of his conclusions, especially those suggesting the province improve its monitoring of Aboriginal child-welfare agencies. Giesbrecht calmly defended his viewpoint, explaining that he had deliberately used strong language to grab people's attention and avoid the pitfall of being "incredibly sympathetic to the point of being meaningless." "One of the things I was saying was that in the process of dealing with these political questions [self-government], don't let child welfare be a pawn," he told the task force. "If a child is being abused in a community, whether Aboriginal or non-Aboriginal, that child is entitled to protection." As a family court judge, Giesbrecht said he'd been concerned for years that Aboriginal kids weren't getting a "fair shake" from the child-welfare system. But task force co-chairman Wally Fox-Decent dismissed Giesbrecht's perspective. "I suspect that had you been on the voyage of discovery we have been on, your report would have been much different," Fox-Decent told the judge.

Fifteen months and almost twenty hearings later, the First Nations task force scheduled release of its report for mid-December 1993. Two weeks before the final printing of the 161-page report, a copy of it was leaked to the *Winnipeg Free Press*. A front-page story appeared outlining its contents. The document was entitled "Children First," ironically echoing the last sentence of Giesbrecht's report. Among its major recommendations, the task force urged that full control of child welfare be handed over to First Nations within five years. While deliberately downplaying the problem of political interference, the report did warn that more safeguards were needed to ensure children no longer became "pawns" in a politicized system. Suggested precautions included strict conflict-of-interest guidelines and a dispute-settlement mechanism for complaints that couldn't be resolved at the local level. One of the key recommendations was that the province immediately set up a First Nations Directorate to assume full authority over the seven mandated Aboriginal child-welfare agencies which provided services to more than 37,000 Status Indian children both on and off reserves. The report also recommended that each of Manitoba's sixty-one bands be allowed to set up its own child-welfare agency. This massive decentralization of services should be accompanied by national First Nations child-welfare legislation outlining standards of care.

It was no surprise that many of the task force's recommendations flew in the face of Giesbrecht's report. Giesbrecht had urged reining in the power of the agencies until problems like political interference, poorly trained staff, and mismanagement could be ironed out. The task force took the opposite tack, saying that fast-tracking Aboriginal control over child welfare would resolve those problems. Yet some of its recommendations seemed contradictory. For example, the task force emphasized the need for better-educated staff, while insisting that an Aboriginal heritage was more important than any formal education. Like the Giesbrecht report, the task force recommendations avoided the critical issue of the funding crunch which had hindered the development of community-based treatment. The task force report naïvely dealt with the lack of funding by saying the redistribution of existing resources would solve the problem, without providing any supporting data.

Like many observers, Wayne Govereau, Manitoba's children's advocate, had little positive to say about the task force report during a June

1994 interview. Govereau, a rotund man with a round face and neatly trimmed moustache, was casually dressed in blue jeans and a black-and-white short-sleeved cotton shirt as he talked in his downtown Winnipeg office. A Metis with fifteen years' professional experience working in child welfare, Govereau had been appointed Manitoba's first children's advocate the previous year. Sipping coffee from a cup with the motto "Thanks" splashed in bright red letters, he spoke disdainfully about a task force member who had complained about not having enough time to adequately study the issue. "I said, come on, we've been studied to death," he said. "We know what the problems are. What we need are the balls to address the issue!" In his opinion, the task force had restated the obvious, serving as a delaying tactic for all three levels of government.

On the other hand, Govereau's assessment of the Giesbrecht report was more generous. He dismissed accusations that the report was racist or overly harsh in its judgements. Instead, Govereau respected the judge for tackling the touchy problem of political interference. The close ties between service delivery and political structures had become a liability for child-welfare agencies. "He fortunately had the courage to speak out," Govereau said. "Children and families have been political footballs for years." At the same time, Govereau believed provincial politicians and bureaucrats had gotten off easy during the inquest: too much blame had been directed at DOCFS and too little at the province. Govereau should know. He worked alongside Assistant Deputy Minister Jim Bakken and other senior bureaucrats in the province's child-welfare directorate for six years beginning in 1986. He didn't mince words as he described the "political ass-covering" that was commonplace during several different administrations. Officials' number-one priority had been avoiding confrontations with Aboriginal leaders that might embarrass the minister of the day.

What Govereau remembered most from his job as Native services coordinator were the patronizing attitudes his colleagues displayed towards Aboriginal agencies. They seemed to expect the agencies to fail and couldn't be bothered to intervene when the going got rough. "When I look back in hindsight, I don't think anybody gave two bits about kids," he said. "This hands-off approach, which was well articulated in the inquest, was, well, it's Natives, let them do it, they wanted the responsibility." At the same time, some directors of Aboriginal child-welfare agencies were so hostile that it left little room to move. "Every time we raised concerns, we were criticized by the Native agencies. I was called an apple, too paternalistic, because I was on the other side of the fence."

Govereau predicted that the key to strengthening the Aboriginal child-welfare system was a process of self-examination and healing. "I think we've gone past the point where you can blame everybody else," he said. "The communities have to take a look at themselves in terms of what they want, what lifestyles they want, what family values they want, and how agencies can support them." When the Aboriginal agencies first began, they kick-started that process. But the agencies also uncovered "hornets' nests" in some places, like Sandy Bay, without putting the resources in place to cope. Most of all, Govereau believes more sensitivity to the needs of children and families caught in the system is essential. "If Lester's spirit is out there, I think he'd want his story told. I think it's that story we need to hear ... There are hundreds of Lesters out there."

When Judge Giesbrecht looks back over the inquest, he has few regrets about his role or the tough report he authored. But, like many who were drawn into Lester's story, he paid a price for his uncompromising stand. Aboriginal leaders and provincial politicians weren't the only ones to criticize his report. Fellow judges also let him know they disagreed with his outspokenness. They told him judges weren't meant to be social engineers. Some believed his first mistake had been letting the inquest expand beyond Lester's case into a probe of the entire DOCFS agency.

When the job of chief provincial judge came open in 1993, Giesbrecht, who was filling the role in an acting capacity, was considered to be a strong candidate. But the job is a political appointment made by the provincial Justice minister. In December of that year, Justice Minister Rosemary Vodrey chose someone with far less experience for the position. Although Giesbrecht would not talk about the matter, others in the legal community wondered whether his blunt criticism of the Filmon government during the inquest had contributed to his being passed over for promotion.

In the end, Giesbrecht believes the inquest, however painful, was worth it if some of his recommendations eventually lead to better services for children. "I'd like the legacy of Lester's death to be that an Aboriginal kid is entitled to the same things that a non-Aboriginal kid is," Giesbrecht said. "Simply saying it's someone else's responsibility and sort of hoping children will get the care they deserve is I think abrogating responsibility."

For others, the inquest also had a cost. A month after the inquest ended, Crown attorney Lawrence McInnes took a medical leave to recuperate from the physical and emotional toll it had taken. During an interview two years later, he was asked whether he suffered any professional backlash because of his role. McInnes paused for a long time before answering: "I don't think my star is in ascendancy," he said finally. "I haven't been asked to sit on any commissions." Yet he has no regrets about his single-minded pursuit of the story behind Lester's death. He realized some would resent the inquest for exposing flaws in the system and prying into people's lives. But he "didn't really give a damn." "Do you know the expression 'murder will out'?" he asked. "It was like this story was going to be told, regardless. And in some ways I was just a conduit for it to happen." In the long run, he hopes the inquest will make a difference for children at Sandy Bay and elsewhere. "Anytime you do something, in my experience, it has a ripple effect and you never know how it's going to affect somebody's life or something in the future. There are kids on that reserve who will not be abused by certain people because Lester Desjarlais died ... There are people working to solve the problem that weren't doing it before."

The months after the inquest were difficult for Marion as well. Emotionally and physically drained, and financially strapped, she sank into a depression. Her chances of finding a job seemed remote after her controversial role in the hearings. Eventually, she sought counselling to make sense of what had happened. In many ways, she felt her worth as a person had been on trial during the hearings. "There were times when [the inquest] ignited pieces of my life that were extremely torturous," she said. "I looked at Lester, and sometimes it was like looking in the mirror and seeing me." At some level, she'd not only been battling for Lester and other abused kids but for the neglected, wounded child within herself. Still, Marion doesn't see herself as a "crusader": "To me it was about what was the right thing to do ... Part of my survival was to take those things I learned and to turn [them] around." Ever resourceful, she set up her own consulting business in Winnipeg in 1994 to organize services like suicide-prevention workshops and home studies for child-welfare agencies.

In the months after they testified at the inquest, DOCFS workers Ella McKay and Bev Flett were shunned by other agency staff. Then both Ella and Bev were reassigned to other jobs without being consulted. Bev, who had been assistant director at the time of the inquest, became training coordinator, a demotion in the agency's structure. Ella was relocated from Long Plain First Nation to Birdtail First Nation. "We weren't given a choice," Ella said. "The choice was either take this position or be terminated." But despite the ostracism, both women said they believed they'd done the right thing by speaking their minds at the inquest. As Bev said, "I think I had a very deep need to be honest. And to say, 'I don't recall' wasn't an honest answer. I need to be honest for my own self or well-being." Ella believes their testimony helped open the judge's eyes to the ways children were being left at risk. "Somebody had to take that stand," she said. "Just because the majority is taking one position, we don't have to go along with it." In 1995, Morris Merrick resigned as director of DOCFS and left the agency after more than a decade on staff. That year, Bev also regained her position as assistant director of the agency, and has since become director.

Both women have been gratified by some of the positive changes sparked by the inquest. Agencies, including DOCFS, worked together to develop conflict-of-interest guidelines to lessen political interference in child-abuse cases. Ella also noticed that band leaders in the communities where she worked were more careful about intervening in child-welfare cases, preferring to let workers resolve matters. She also sensed a new willingness in some communities to acknowledge and confront problems like child abuse. "I see hope for our communities," Ella said. "Lester wouldn't want another kid to go through what he did."

In her own way, Ellen Cook has made sure Lester's story is not forgotten. She talks about him with her Grade 6 students at Niji

Mahkwa Elementary School, many of whom remind her of Lester. By sharing what happened to him, she helps them open up about their own struggles with alcohol, drugs, and despair. Most of all, her caring for her students and her buoyant love of life give them the best role model they could have.

To Ellen, child welfare took "two steps forward" with the inquest into Lester's death, which highlighted the lack of protection for abused children, as well as the thorny problem of political interference. But the task force turned out to be "twenty steps backward," according to Ellen. "They said everything's cosy and we're looking for self-government so give it to us," she said. "It was all about power, more power ... There was the potential that something positive could come out of it and then they turned around and denied there was political interference." Yet as frustrated as she often feels with those in power, she believes Aboriginal women will continue to push for the changes needed to create healthy communities.

Like Ellen, Joyce Wasicuna also believes in the power of Aboriginal women reclaiming traditional values of love and caring for their families and the community. She has gradually reconnected with her home of Sioux Valley First Nation after feeling ostracized for several years. In the spring of 1994, she ran as a candidate in the band election. Although she didn't win, she made a good showing and won support from those she least expected to back her. "If we want our communities to be healthy, time is of the essence," she said. "We have to do things now. Not tomorrow after some report comes out or tomorrow after we get a certain amount of funding. If we're being traditional, we have to do things now and use our own resources within our own communities." When she looks back on the inquest, Joyce doesn't regret speaking up, despite the backlash she faced. "I wasn't really afraid to testify if it was going to help at least one child somewhere," she said. "Because I knew there were a lot of potential Lesters out there. I knew that if my testimony could help one of those kids from taking his life, I would do it."

The months after the inquest were especially stressful for the anonymous police officer who testified about his childhood abuse at the Sandy Bay residential school. No sooner did he return home, than the man he'd named as his abuser launched a defamation lawsuit against him, demanding a public apology. The angry man claimed the police officer had ruined his reputation and violated the law by repeating the abuse allegations to reporters outside the courtroom after testifying. Because the police officer was no longer on the witness stand when he made those remarks, he had opened himself to legal action. The alleged abuser also notified several media outlets that he intended to sue for naming him in news reports. As a result of the man's threats, the police officer was forced to hire a lawyer in the summer of 1992 and use precious vacation time to travel to Winnipeg for consultations. "I had to fight because I told the truth," he said. After his lawyer tracked down several other men, all former residents of Sandy Bay, who also said they'd testify that they were sexually abused by the litigant, the man quietly dropped the lawsuit. Despite the tremendous anxiety caused by the unexpected legal battle, the police officer isn't sorry he appeared at the inquest. "I knew that little boy didn't kill himself for no reason," he says passionately. "The image of what had happened to Lester came into my mind. I'm sure [sexual abuse] was why he hung himself. I'm sure of it. I guess I saw myself in him." As for the web of sexual-assault cases which came to light at Sandy Bay in the months after Lester's inquest, his wife said she'd seen that coming for years. "I've said before, one of these times this community is going to erupt," she recalls. "I guess a little boy had to die for it to happpen." What she hopes for most of all now is that this has opened the door to healing.

At Sandy Bay, the inquest is still a sore spot for some, although the community as a whole seems to have moved on. Some of those who were the most angry and vocal about the damage done by the inquest—like former chief Angus Starr—are no longer in power. As a result, others have felt freer to express their views. Angela Eastman believes that the inquest, and the decision by Lester's sisters and David to take Joe Desjarlais to court, went a long way towards raising the community's awareness about child sexual abuse. Child-protection services at Sandy Bay have improved, and more support is available for troubled families, although it still isn't enough. Healing circles have been held for victims of abuse. What many outsiders do not understand, Angela says, is that the desire to forgive offenders and offer them another chance—even someone like Joe—is at least as strong for most members of the community as the urge to punish them. That's why many were troubled when the inquest became what they perceived to be a "witch hunt" against certain people. Angela recalled being questioned by a reporter after Joe was jailed for abusing Lester's sisters. The reporter asked if she was glad Joe had been locked up. Perplexed, Angela responded: "How can you be happy with someone else's suffering? What kind of suffering did he go through as a little boy to do the things he did? You can't be happy. It's sad."

She firmly believes that the roots of some of the sexual abuse which has devastated families in the community is an insidious legacy of the residential school. Angela knew of at least one Catholic brother who molested boys at the school during the 1960s. A school supervisor is also known to have sexually abused boys, and there may have been other offenders on staff as well. Still, Angela's compassion for those who became abusers as a result of being victimized doesn't lessen her conviction that it is time for accountability. She supports those who, like Lester's sisters and David, have taken their offenders to court. More than anything, Angela hopes the legacy of Lester's death, and the inquest, is this: "I like to think it was positive for the kids in this community. Like, it'll be safer for them. And I hope people never forget that, the would-be abusers, anyways. That somehow, someday, it'll get back to them."

Some in the community still blame Joyce Desjarlais for her son's death. That bothers Violet Roulette, a middle-aged woman who considered Joyce to be a close friend. As she sipped coffee in the living-room of her tidy ranch-style bungalow on a warm August afternoon in 1994, Violet defended her friend. She said it wasn't fair to judge Joyce, who did her best for her children while struggling with her own heavy burdens. As Violet talked, a washing-machine swished in the background. Her walls are adorned with an intriguing mix of family photos, a religious print of Jesus with his disciples, and a variety of Aboriginal artwork. Violet's soft, raspy voice was barely audible as she talked about how she herself suffered sexual abuse in the past. She only recently began to deal with that pain. So she felt proud when Lester's sisters took their uncle to court. "It opened up a lot of things, what they did," she says. "It was pretty good." She remembered her mother telling her that sexual abuse had been happening for a long time at Sandy Bay. And Violet believes the sexual abuse of children has exacerbated many of the community's other social problems, from alcoholism to gas sniffing. "People just want to forget—that's why they drink. To forget what happened to them when they were young." She's cynical about band leaders' commitment to ending the cycle of abuse. Perhaps the solution might be having a woman run for chief in the next election, she suggests with a smile. Somehow, the abuse of children must continue to be a priority. "It's a healing time now," she says.

One September afternoon in 1994, Arlene Levasseur, Joyce's cousin, reflected about what life is like for the youth of Sandy Bay. A stout, friendly woman with a round face, Arlene smoked Player's Light cigarettes at her kitchen table as she talked. The year before Lester's death, her seventeen-year-old brother Harry had killed himself. Lester had been deeply troubled by Harry's death, and often mentioned him in the months leading up to his own suicide. Arlene's family were devastated by Harry's suicide. When Lester, and then Joyce, died the next year, the grief was overwhelming. Arlene is constantly reminded of the loved ones she's lost when she gazes from the eastern window of her home across the fields to the graveyard where they are all buried.

Like Violet, Arlene suspects that child abuse is the root cause of problems like drugs, sniffing, and alcoholism at Sandy Bay. "I think this sexual abuse has been going on for ages," she says. "People just want to block it out. And they won't say anything because nobody will listen." She too is frustrated about the lack of services available to children and families. A major reason why residents are reluctant to use the services that do exist, she says, is the lack of confidentiality for someone seeking help in the close-knit community. There aren't any professionals she'd trust enough to confide in. As well, established community resources such as Alcoholics Anonymous have often become more of a means to an end—like a way to win back a driver's licence—than providing a true catalyst for change.

Who's to blame for these problems? As in any community, politicians bear the brunt of residents' dissatisfaction at Sandy Bay. Arlene said band leaders haven't made counselling for children and families a priority, let alone providing for basic needs such as decent housing. Her family has been forced to use an outhouse and have water delivered each week as they wait for a new house. If adequate housing is so scarce, what hope is there for better social services? she wonders.

For Lester's siblings, the actual inquest had only a peripheral impact on their lives. Yet at the same time, that event provided the catalyst for Nancy and Sherry and Annette to pursue charges against their uncle Joe. Since he went to prison, they have all struggled in their own way to move on.

For Sherry, her four lively young children are the hub of her life. They hovered about her during visits to her home at Sandy Bay in the autumn of 1994. Six-year-old Norbert, her oldest, was the clown. With an impish grin, he stood on the porch of the modest, cinnamon-brown bungalow, calling out for "Cindy," a pregnant neighbourhood mutt. In his hand, he clutched a frying pan, eager to share its greasy contents with the dog. When Cindy didn't appear, Norbert trudged back into the kitchen, flashed a smile, and casually reached for raw sausages, intent on trying again, until Sherry intervened.

The police scanner on top of the refrigerator buzzed away in the background. Five-year-old Jocelyn, bright-eyed and inquisitive, begged to join the grown-ups drinking tea sweetened with evaporated milk at the kitchen table. A sumptuous still-life print of french bread, fruit, and a violin hung on the wall, suggesting luxuries rare to this home. Nearby, Michael, a slight, quiet four-year-old, pressed his face close to baby Dylan, who responded with a cooing smile. Sherry's fondest hope is that she can give her kids the childhood she—and Lester—never had.

But that has been an uphill battle, with a welfare cheque that never goes far enough, a sparsely furnished house in serious disrepair, and the ever-increasing needs of growing children. Sherry has supplemented their meagre income by mail-order sales, seasonal vegetable picking, or whatever odd jobs come her way. But her frustration was obvious when two band welfare workers dropped by to inspect the premises. Before they left, the workers promised to come up with much-needed beds and chairs after next week's band election. They didn't seem to notice the broken window in the kitchen or the gaping, toaster-sized hole in the bathroom floor through which the basement can be seen. Sherry could only hope their promises were more than a thinly veiled election ploy.

Ever-present are memories of her mother and Lester. Prominently displayed on Sherry's living-room wall were two pictures of Lester, each in a burnt-wood frame. He smiled sweetly from his school picture taken a couple of years before his death. In the other, Lester wore a colourful square-dance sash around his waist as he posed proudly with two men, one a fiddler. On the wall opposite Lester's pictures, was a three-dimensional crucifixion scene which, from another angle, became the ascension, with Jesus rising into the air while the disciples watched from the ground.

Relationships with some of her Desjarlais relatives have been strained since Joe's conviction. But one of Sherry's cousins did apologize to her for his failure to support her when she testified against her uncle. To her surprise, her cousin said he'd had no doubt Sherry was telling the truth because he too had been sexually abused at age sixteen by Joe. Still, he didn't plan to pursue charges. He just wanted to forget about the assault. "He told all our cousins what happened to him," she said. "That's why they've come around. Now they talk to us."

In the autumn of 1994, Annette was living at Sandy Bay with her two young children, sharing a small white-frame bungalow with the father of her son. To her relief, she reconciled with the Desjarlais clan after a couple of years of painful ostracism. "Since 1992 I felt lost," she said. "They wouldn't talk to me after Pee-Ance [Joe] got charged. Now they all talk to me, they call me sister." Having been raised by her father's relatives, Annette had felt the shunning more keenly than her other siblings. She has never shaken the feeling of being an outsider when it comes to her sisters and brothers. As her ten-month-old daughter slept peacefully at her side on the couch, Annette said that when she looked back she felt she wasn't ready to go to trial against Joe. At the time, she had been abusing drugs, and wasn't emotionally prepared to cope with the backlash she faced. Besides, she preferred to forgive and forget.

The walls of her living-room were adorned with family photos, a picture of the Pope, and another of Elvis Presley. The house had a freshly scrubbed scent lingering in the air. When her daughter is a few years older, Annette said, she hoped to go back to school for college upgrading. The burden of caring alone for two young children weighed on her at times. Always changeable in her moods, she seemed restless, unsure of her future, and talked of moving to Winnipeg.

In October 1994, Nancy separated from her partner for six months and moved from her townhouse to another rental in Portage la Prairie. That winter, she continued to see her counsellor at the women's shelter but gave up trying to take academic upgrading as well. "I had too much other stuff to deal with," Nancy said. "My counsellor really helped me. Some day I'd like to thank her." The following summer, her youngest son was riding his bike in the alley when a drunk driver backed into him and almost ran over the little boy. The near-tragedy prompted her to move back to Sandy Bay with her children in July 1995. There she found another counsellor, so she could continue the process of healing. "I've found out a lot about myself through talking—how strong I am to have lived through all of this," she said. "And what a better parent I have become."

On a brilliant September afternoon, Sherry suggests a visit to the Sandy Bay graveyard just off Lake Road on the eastern edge of the community. A wire fence defines the boundaries of the burial ground. A soft wind rustles through the tall golden grasses beyond, dragonflies dip and flit, while a seagull soars against the dazzling azure sky. But as Sherry approaches Lester's grave, she's disturbed to find the weathered plain wooden cross marking it has been snapped in half. Silently, she leans down and picks up the top crosspiece carved with the words "Lester Norman Desjarlais, R.I.P." She gently props the marker at the west end of the mound of earth covered with grasses. Two years ago, bright pink plastic roses stuck in a styrofoam ring adorned the wooden cross. Now those flowers are gone. So are the white and red plastic roses which were strewn over the length of his grave. Sherry turns to the north, lights a cigarette, and lays it carefully at the head of her mother's grave as a gift to her spirit. A tiny plume of smoke curls skyward. At the base of the wooden cross marking Joyce's grave, someone has placed a little brown teddy bear with sunglasses and a bouquet of pink plastic roses encased in a globe of glass.

Standing at the head of Lester's grave looking east, the flat grasslands and marsh stretch to the sparkling waters of Lake Manitoba on the horizon. There, huge white pelicans wander in search of fish near the strip of sand lining the shore. The hot sun beats down, glancing off crimson reeds and casting a golden hue. In the stillness, Lester's words to Angela Eastman come back: "When I die, will you buy me flowers?" And she replied: "Don't be silly Lester, you're too young to die."

FOR THE SAKE OF THE CHILDREN

"We can create a safe place for our children."

—Charlene Belleau, Canim Lake Family Violence Programs

Aboriginal communities across the country have struggled with how to respond to disclosures of abuse for the last decade and a half. When Native-run child-welfare agencies began to offer services in the 1980s in Manitoba and other provinces, public awareness about abuse gradually increased. Many communities began to realize they had what would eventually be described as an "epidemic of abuse" on their hands.

One of the earliest attempts to gauge the extent of child sexual abuse on reserves in Manitoba was a little-known study done by staff at Winnipeg's Child Protection Centre, a program of Children's Hospital. In 1983, they noticed that a disproportionately high number of their patients—one-third—were Aboriginal children. With a grant from the federal Justice and Solicitor General's departments, staff set up the Child Advocacy Project to examine whether the system was failing to protect Aboriginal children. The researchers surveyed the cases of 149 children, both Aboriginal and non-Aboriginal, who were seen at the centre during a six-month period in 1983–84. They then zeroed in on 45 of the cases involving children of Status Indian or Metis descent. Within that sample, they found that the 34 children who lived in Winnipeg had received about the same services as non-Aboriginal sexual-abuse victims. But an examination of the 11 cases from reserves indicated that those children were less likely to get the medical, legal, and social services they needed. In fact, an investigation of 8 of the sexual-abuse cases from reserves revealed a series of other offences involving a total of 33 child victims and 23 different offenders.

One of these cases involved a seven-year-old girl from a southern Manitoba reserve who was seen at the Children's Hospital. The report cited what happened to her as a "typical situation and a typical outcome" for a victim of child sexual abuse at that time. The child told medical personnel that she'd been sexually assaulted on more than one occasion by a group of five teenage boys who attacked her on the playground. The child had been seen at the hospital only two months earlier after being sexually assaulted by two other teenagers. At that time, she'd also disclosed that her grandfather, who was her guardian, had sexually abused her for several years. The girl's four aunts had all alleged chronic sexual abuse as well from their father; one of them had had two children as a result of the abuse. A family history also revealed that both the girl's parents and grandparents were alcoholics and that family members were chronic gas sniffers. The girl and her siblings had all been removed from their mother's care, except for one infant who showed signs of foetal alcohol syndrome. There were also suspicions that the girl's father had abused her. The girl received medical treatment and was placed with her aunt in Winnipeg. In violation of bail conditions banning contact with the child, her grandfather visited regularly. Other family members also pressured the girl to recant her allegations. When the case finally went to trial the following year, the judge decided the girl was too young to give sworn testimony, even though she'd provided a clear account of the abuse while on the witness stand. The judge acquitted the grandfather. The grandfather's charges related to his assaults on the girl's aunts were dismissed because the victims failed to appear at the hearing. No charges were laid against the teenagers who had allegedly assaulted the girl, or against the child's father.

In their final report, "A New Justice for Indian Children," released in 1987, project staff identified a host of reasons why abused children weren't getting help. Their report acknowledged that the "razing of Indian societies" had caused the disintegration of cultural norms that once prevented abusive behaviour: "Social constraints and solutions have been rendered impotent in the face of conflicting cultures and the massive social disorganization stemming from Indian poverty," the report said. That lack of cohesiveness also made it difficult to mobilize communities to protect children. Geographical isolation limited the resources available to victims, and left them more vulnerable to offenders. Also, the small size of reserves meant that those who disclosed abuse faced social ostracism or were pressured to recant by relatives or others.

The project also pointed the finger at those who were supposed to intervene, including social workers, police, Crown attorneys, and medical professionals. Often, professionals didn't work together on complex child-abuse cases, leaving victims in the lurch. As well, everyone, from police to social workers, lacked training in child sexual abuse. Child-welfare agencies suffered from high turnover rates as poorly trained staff buckled under heavy caseloads. Without enough foster homes, workers frequently had to move children off-reserve, traumatizing the young victims all over again. The other option was to place them with extended family, where they were sometimes further abused or pressured to recant. This was especially true in families where a pattern of sexual abuse extended back through three or four generations. To make matters worse, little or no treatment was available in communities.

The report said many rural physicians lacked the training to recognize symptoms of sexual abuse and weren't knowledgeable about mandatory reporting procedures. When cases did go to court, long delays caused needless anxiety for victims and left them vulnerable to intimidation by offenders. Cases were sometimes shuffled between Crown attorneys, resulting in child witnesses who were not properly prepared to testify. Finally, the project found that most offenders were never charged, and even fewer were convicted. Those who did go to jail received no treatment before being sent back home.

Project staff made nine recommendations to address what they believed to be a crisis for Aboriginal children. Their suggestions included in-depth training in child sexual abuse for medical personnel, RCMP, tribal police, and Crown attorneys; establishing reserve-based multi-disciplinary teams made up of both community members and outside professionals to oversee abuse investigations; providing funding for culturally relevant treatment facilities on every reserve; and developing more foster homes for children on reserves and better scrutiny of existing placements. Their report concluded with these disturbing words:

> The need for bold action is apparent. Children are suffering from trauma, physical injury, and psychological devastation that results from sexual abuse. The injuries to self-esteem, trust, and emotional functioning last a lifetime. The incidence of sniffing, alcohol abuse, eating disorders, suicide, depression, and sexual acting out among Indian children suggest that the problem of child sexual abuse has reached epidemic proportions.
>
> The social cost of child sexual abuse is higher than we can imagine. These child victims continue to be victimized throughout their lives. The burden of this victimization is preventing many Indian children from becoming the healthy, functioning adults they might otherwise be. The failure of the social, medical, and legal systems to provide a safe environment for the normal development of these children perpetuates the existence of future generations of victims. It is time to break the cycle of victimization. It is time to break the longstanding pattern of non-action on reserve-based child sexual abuse. Quite simply, it is time for a new justice for Indian children.

Their report was submitted to the federal Justice and Solicitor General's departments and the provincial government in November 1987. But to the disappointment of its authors, the report gathered dust on government shelves. Mainstream politicians ignored the report for fear of a backlash from Aboriginal leaders, some of whom viewed its findings as an attempt to discredit their community. As Dr. Sally Longstaffe, co-author of the report, said several years later: "It was an extremely disillusioning experience. There was a great deal of fear and apprehension that this was, as one official said, 'too hot to handle.'" With the shelving of the report, Longstaffe felt an important opportunity to help victims of child sexual abuse had been lost. "This was a watershed time when a lot of Native people went out on a limb to talk to us because they wanted to make things better," she said.

Politicians weren't the only ones who ignored the problem. Many communities were simply not ready to take the first steps towards healing. Tony Marten's 1988 book on child sexual abuse, *The Spirit Weeps: Characteristics and Dynamics of Incest and Child Sexual Abuse*, provides an insightful analysis of why abuse is so tough to confront. Brenda Daily and Maggie Hodgson, staff at the Native-run Nechi Institute in Edmonton, each contributed a chapter focusing on the special dynamics of abuse within Aboriginal communities. Whenever sexual abuse occurs, family members suffer from low self-esteem, guilt, depression, and alienation. But, as Daily says, those problems are compounded in Aboriginal families already weakened by residential schools, foster care, and the prison system. For example, a woman who grew up being shuffled between foster homes isn't likely to have a positive self-image or healthy role models for raising children. If she was abused, she may feel powerless to prevent the same thing from happening to her children. She marries a man who has become an abuser as a result of being molested while in jail, and the cycle is set to repeat itself.

The high incidence of substance abuse in Aboriginal communities means that many families are what Daily calls "dually affected" by both alcoholism or drug abuse, and child abuse. Since most Aboriginal people have been affected by substance abuse—either by direct involvement or by a family member's addiction—understanding the links between substance abuse and child abuse is crucial. While substance abuse does not cause sexual abuse, Daily describes how it lowers inhibitions and provides an excuse for the abusive behaviour. An offender who drinks will often use the same "defence mechanisms" to justify his abusive actions. He may minimize his drinking by saying "I only had one or two," while excusing his abusive actions with "I only touched her once or twice." He'll blame his alcoholism on his boss, and his abuse on his wife's refusal to have sex. He'll rationalize his need for a few drinks "to calm me down," and his abuse of his daughter by saying he "needs to teach her about sex." For victims, substance abuse is a way to escape the bad memories, guilt, and pain. They use the same defence mechanisms—minimizing, blaming, rationalizing—to excuse their self-destructive behaviour. Before sexual abuse can be dealt with, the substance abuse must end.

While sobriety doesn't automatically stop abusive or self-destructive behaviour, it is an important first step for offenders, non-offending parents, and victims. A useful image for explaining the healing process is offered in the book *Let the Healing Begin: Breaking the Cycle of Child Sexual Abuse in Our Communities* by Maureen McEvoy. She compares this process to peeling the layers of an onion. On the surface are the obvious problems caused by drinking, like fights, black-outs, and job losses. The next layer is made up of all the ways alcohol-related problems are minimized. Beneath that are the feelings of guilt, shame, hurt, and fear related to drinking. Then come several layers linked to sexual abuse: denial or repression of the abuse; then the shame, guilt, and anger; and, below that, the actual memories of the abuse. At the centre of the onion is the true self. In order to heal, a victim, or offender, must work through each painful layer camouflaged by the alcohol or drugs.

Denial of abuse, within both the family and the community, is the biggest barrier to recovery. As Hodgson says, "For years, to our great disadvantage, we have accepted three rules of denial: don't talk, don't feel, don't trust. Using these, we have tried to close up and hide the sexual-abuse issue: we have tried to envelop the problem. Now we must choose the opposite road: to open it up, and develop treatment approaches." Alcoholism is one way to avoid the truth, and alcoholic families are experts at denying what is going on. But Daily says denial also happens for a host of other reasons in close-knit Aboriginal communities, where everyone is related by blood or marriage. Loyalty to the family and community may prevent victims, or those aware of the abuse, from reporting it to outside authorities such as the RCMP. Even talking to a social worker may be too threatening because of their reputation as "baby stealers." Anxiety about the lack of confidentiality in a small community also prevents disclosures. Victims fear being gossiped about or being pressured to recant by angry relatives. In families where the abuse is intergenerational, some members may have unconsciously come to accept incest as the norm. Sometimes even spiritual beliefs can be linked to denial, as in the case where a child's unusual behaviour was attributed to "bad medicine" rather than to abuse. Finally, an offender's status in the community can deter victims from reporting assaults. There are cases where elders molested children during sweat-lodge ceremonies. Although some people found out, they were too afraid to confront a respected spiritual leader.

Denial can also fuel a backlash against anyone who tries to break the cycle of abuse. As McEvoy says, "They'll hit you as strong as their denial is." Abuse workers are often treated with suspicion or accused of trying to be "better than us." Sometimes those lobbying for change are socially ostracized or plagued by vicious rumours. They're labelled "angry women picking on men." They can even lose their jobs. Meanwhile, chief and band councillors may offer little support because they're uninformed about abuse, are trying to protect relatives who are offenders, or are attempting to hide their own abusive behaviour. Band leaders can make life miserable by denying funding or refusing to let the band office be used for workshops. The only antidote is to lay the groundwork for change by educating the community and political leaders before setting up abuse programs: "If a flood of disclosures occurs before the community is ready to deal with sexual abuse, people will try to shove everything back under the carpet," McEvoy says. The reality is that dividing a small community into "good guys" and "bad guys" based on those who are abuse victims and those who are offenders does not promote healing. And, often it's not that clear, because some offenders are also victims.

In Aboriginal communities, the extended family has long been a source of great strength. Putting the interests of the family before the individual has been a basic value. But the greatest strengths can also become weaknesses. When it comes to sexual abuse, the pressure to keep family secrets is often intense. McEvoy compares sexual abuse to a "ticking time bomb" which everyone is afraid to defuse for fear of destroying the family: "Unchecked, the cycle of abuse continues in the family and community," she says. "Secrets keep everyone locked in silence and shame."

Today, many communities are determined to break that cycle. The Alkali Lake band, located southwest of Williams Lake, B.C., pioneered the Aboriginal sobriety movement in the 1970s. By the end of that decade, most of the 400 members of the Shuswap community had quit drinking, and bands from across Canada visited Alkali to learn how to achieve the same success. But once the scourge of alcoholism ended, Alkali band members began to disclose the sexual abuse they'd suffered. Since then, the community has been grappling with an even more painful recovery.

Hollow Water First Nation in Manitoba, an Ojibwa community of about 600 located a couple of hours' drive northeast of Winnipeg, also achieved hard-won sobriety only to discover that many residents had suffered abuse. In the early 1980s, about 80 per cent of the community abused alcohol. Then, in 1984, members of the community organized a program to tackle substance abuse. As a result, the alcoholism rate declined dramatically, to about 20 per cent. But once alcohol no longer dulled the pain, disclosures of sexual abuse began. Local surveys discovered that a staggering two-thirds of residents were sexual-abuse victims, and one-third had been abusers. Once more, community members looked to their traditions for wisdom. Instead of sending abusers to jail, they won permission from the court system in 1986 to set up an alternative program for sex offenders who admitted their guilt. Under the agreement, offenders were sentenced to probation by a provincial judge on the condition that they take part in community healing circles. Spiritual ceremonies were an integral part of the program, including sweat lodges; prayers; and the burning of sweetgrass, sage, and cedar. Abusers were also required to take anger-management courses and perform a certain number of hours of community service.

Although RCMP and court officials were initially sceptical about the diversion program, time has proven it to be more effective than anything the mainstream system has to offer. Abusers have been more willing to come forward, admit their guilt, and take responsibility for their crimes if they know they won't be jailed. In fact, by early 1995, 52 offenders had taken part in the program. Only 2 had reoffended, both of whom were sent to prison. A total of 94 victims and more than 260 relatives of offenders and victims have also participated in the healing program, which is a model for other communities in Manitoba and across the country.

In December 1993, the community also took another step towards a more traditional justice system by participating in the sentencing of two band members who had pleaded guilty to incest. After a sunrise ceremony, during which offerings of tobacco were made as prayers for guidance, court was convened in the community's bingo hall by Judge Murray Sinclair. Sinclair is an Ojibwa and was co-commissioner of the Aboriginal Justice Inquiry. As the sentencing began, two circles were formed. In the inner circle sat about 40 people, including victims, offenders, and court officials. They were surrounded by an outer circle of about 200 relatives, friends, and members of the community. During the sentencing circle, an eagle feather was passed to each person as he or she spoke. Participants talked about why they were there, offered support to the victims, described how the crimes had affected them, and spoke to the offenders. After twelve wrenching hours, the community decided that the couple should be sentenced to three-year terms of supervised probation and take part in the healing program. That sentence was in sharp contrast to the minimum five-year prison term they would have faced in the mainstream courts. But being accountable to their family and community for their crimes is no easy task. Reaching beyond punishment to reconciliation and healing creates the possibility that the cycle of abuse will be broken.

Many in mainstream society are perplexed by the theme of forgiveness which underlies such programs. What about punishment? outsiders ask. What about justice? The answers lie in a deeper understanding of both those concepts. A 1992 Indian Child and Family Services (ICFS) standards report published by the First Nations Congress in Vancouver explained that the compassion shown by Aboriginal communities towards both victim and offender is linked to their history of economic and social oppression. There is a reluctance to condemn abusers, who are seen as "victims of forces over which they have little control." That doesn't mean abusive behaviour is accepted. But most would opt for rehabilitation rather than punishment. "There was a sense that, regardless of what a person did, they still remain a part of the community and that the community has some responsibility to assist in their rehabilitation," the ICFS standards report said. In most communities, all residents are acquainted, and many are related, making it difficult to "depersonalize" offenders or avoid contact with them. "As a result, the process of criminalizing an offender's behaviour and putting that person in jail is a solution (if incarceration is a 'solution') that is not readily acceptable to many Aboriginal people," the report said. At the same time, communities want safeguards to protect children from known offenders.

Canim Lake First Nation set up an innovative sexual-abuse treatment program in 1994 which integrates the need both for healing and for community safety. Canim Lake is a Shuswap band of almost 500 people in the central interior of British Columbia, near Williams Lake. Here too, widespread alcoholism had camouflaged memories of child sexual abuse. After band leaders led a successful fight for sobriety more than a decade ago, the abuse began to surface. Many had suffered abuse at the St. Joseph's residential school, run by the Oblate Fathers, near Williams Lake. Others had been assaulted by family or friends. As the community assessed the impact of the residential-school system, a survey of band members uncovered some alarming statistics. "It became really clear to us that 75 to 80 per cent of our people had been sexually abused," Charlene Belleau, a band member and director of Canim Lake's Family Violence Programs, said during an interview in January 1996. "It was really high."

Given the band's history of seeking progressive solutions to social problems—from setting up a community-based university program to designing services for children with foetal alcohol syndrome—its leaders were determined to develop a holistic response. They believed mainstream society's method of dealing with sex offenders—prison terms and/or counselling related to a specific offence—was inadequate for the scope of the problems confronting them. After drawing on the expertise of outside professionals, Canim Lake developed a community-based program to foster healing for both victims and offenders. To ensure the community's support, project leaders first held public meetings, circulated a questionnaire, and went door to door to solicit everyone's views on the proposal. Workshops were organized to educate residents about sexual abuse, and to outline the legal rights of victims and offenders. Lengthy consultations with the RCMP, Crown attorneys, judges, and others were held to win approval for the project.

The most controversial aspect of Canim's program, which is funded by an array of provincial and federal departments, is its strategy for treating sex offenders. Abusers who voluntarily disclose all sex offences and enrol in the eighteen-month program are eligible for "deferred reporting" of any charges. That means the Crown agrees not to proceed with charges pending the outcome of their treatment. The credibility of their disclosures, and their compliance in the program, is monitored by lie-detector tests administered every few months by the RCMP. Sophisticated techniques like sexual-arousal testing are also used in treating offenders. Those who violate conditions of the program, or who reoffend, still face the possibility of criminal charges. Victims also retain the right to pursue charges at any time.

The program offers victims five months of intensive group and individual counselling, including traditional healing methods such as sweat lodges. Victims are also expected to disclose their entire history of abuse to aid in their healing. In cases where abusers are considered ready to return to their families, a gradual reconciliation process is available. Compared to the mainstream justice system, where offenders often escape punishment, or receive lenient sentences and little treatment, Canim's program is geared to greater accountability. Although some worry that keeping offenders in the community could put children at risk, most believe that providing treatment close to home will offer more safeguards in the long run. An "oversight committee" has been set up so that band members can report concerns about offenders' behaviour. "Not one person can do something without everyone else knowing," Belleau said. "Really, the community is providing the policing." A couple of victims have also pursued criminal charges. One of those victims faced further trauma when the Crown attorney decided not to lay charges. But with the support of the family-violence program, she was at least able to have the satisfaction of confronting her abuser.

So far, forty victims and seven offenders have enrolled in Canim Lake's program. At some point, the community will put a time limit on abusers' eligibility for deferred reporting to encourage more offenders to come forward. But Belleau said they are proceeding slowly to give everyone, from children to elders, the chance to prepare for what lies ahead. "Eventually, our whole community will be in treatment," Belleau said. Her belief that abuse has affected the entire community comes from her experience so far working with victims and offenders. The pattern of disclosures has been typical of sexual abuse elsewhere, with victims reporting assaults by as many as forty offenders, or offenders admitting to abusing up to fifty victims. The sheer scope of what has happened means the program could never cope if all victims and abusers came forward at once. Since governments consider it to be an experiment, the program is also constrained by a $250,000 annual budget, which can treat only a limited number of residents at once.

While the majority of band members support the project, there have been pockets of resistance. "There's a lot of fear," Belleau said. "The majority of people that rejected the idea of even treating victims and offenders were men, because for the most part the high percentage of the offenders are men." At the same time, many male leaders have strongly supported the project, even though they, too, will have to face the consequences of any past misdeeds.

What keeps Belleau and others committed to the program is the hope for a better future for the next generation. "We've been through a very traumatic time in our lives through residential school and, having suffered physical, emotional, mental, spiritual abuse, are handing that down to our children," Belleau said. "But really, that can stop with us—making that conscientious decision to do that so our children don't have to suffer through what we did." To Belleau, the best indicator that the program is already making inroads is that young people are refusing to tolerate assaultive behaviour.

The catalyst for tackling child abuse among the fourteen Nuu-Chah-Nulth communities on the west coast of Vancouver Island was the tribal council's takeover of mandated child-welfare services in 1985. They named the new agency Usma–Nuu-Chah-Nulth Child and Family Services Program ("Usma" meaning most precious ones). After

Usma opened, disclosures of physical and sexual abuse began to multiply. Debra Foxcroft, who has directed the Port Alberni–based program since its inception, said people began seeking help because they no longer feared "losing" their children to the white child-welfare system. As in other First Nations, the disclosures of sexual abuse came after a vigorous campaign against alcohol and drug abuse led by tribal leaders in the 1970s and early 1980s. Foxcroft called it the "second wave" in the healing process. "I don't think we realized the impact of sexual abuse in our communities," she said. "We were just new at coping with it." From the beginning, the agency's seven staff have worked closely with child-protection committees in each community, as well as an elders' advisory council, to develop culturally relevant responses to child abuse. When a child needs protection, social workers hold a family meeting to discuss the problem. Sometimes as many as twenty relatives attend. Genealogy research is done on children who are apprehended to help identify extended family members and provide a family history. The majority of children in care—forty-seven of a total of fifty-seven in 1995—are placed in "extended family homes."

Despite their many successes, protecting children hasn't been easy for the staff of Usma, which was absorbed into the Nuu-Chah-Nulth Community and Human Services program in 1993. "The major issue for us over the years has been denial, anger, threats," Foxcroft said. "There was a lot of resistance at the political level." When abused children were apprehended, their relatives complained bitterly to chiefs who would then put pressure on Usma staff. "We were always seen as the bad guys because we were apprehending to protect children," she said. "The real issue was there was a lot of fear." Allegations of sexual abuse against elders or other prominent leaders also caused tremendous friction at times. Agency staff stood their ground and investigated every complaint, but the resulting backlash was difficult. "We had all the power [when it came to abuse investigations], and we were women," she says. "They saw it as a women's issue—that we were out to get all the men. Because men were the ones going to jail."

Over the years, there have been many lonely moments for Foxcroft, a member of the Tseshaht band in Port Alberni—times when she wasn't sure Usma would survive the political turmoil. Dealing with child abuse day in and day out, especially when cases involved her own relatives, has been painful. In 1991, she left the agency for a year and a half to rejuvenate her sagging spirits. When she returned, the agency was restructured to become part of a larger organization that Foxcroft now directs. The new agency provides a range of health and social services, including child welfare. But more than Usma's structure has changed. After a decade of focusing on family violence, Foxcroft has begun to see the seeds of change she planted take root. Now women from various communities have joined her in demanding action. At a tribal council meeting in November 1995, a woman who had been physically abused by a prominent leader spoke up about family violence and appealed for more help for victims. About a hundred other women from different villages also attended the meeting to offer their support. As a result, the tribal council pledged $100,000 to deal with the problem more effectively. "When I saw that, I knew my job was done," Foxcroft said. "People aren't going to put up with this anymore. They are more and more empowered. I believe the Usma program was the voice for women and children to speak out."

Not all communities have been able to rally the resources needed to tackle the overwhelming social problems they face. The residents of Shamattawa First Nation, an isolated community of about 700 located 750 kilometres by air northeast of Winnipeg, are still grappling with devastating rates of alcoholism, sniffing, and physical and sexual abuse. Until the late 1960s, the fly-in community maintained a stable traditional lifestyle based on trapping and hunting. But as soon as liquor became widely available, village life began to disintegrate. By the mid-1970s, Shamattawa made national headlines when fifty children had to be air-lifted out of the community to be treated for gas sniffing. Some of the addicts were as young as four years old. Two decades later, little has changed. Even though the community is a "dry" reserve, meaning that alcohol and solvents have been banned by the band council, about 90 per cent of its residents are substance abusers. It's not unusual for fifteen or twenty people to live crowded together in one plywood shack, with only a wood stove for heat and no running water. Unemployment is an overwhelming 95 per cent. In 1992, 160 children, or almost half the community's young people, had to be apprehended by the Aboriginal-run Awasis child-welfare agency because of rampant neglect, physical and sexual abuse, and sniffing. With little or no treatment available on-reserve, the children had to be sent far away for foster care and counselling.

In the face of such despair, there are courageous individuals who are trying to break the cycle of violence. "No matter how hard it is ... no matter how hurt you are, you have to change yourself," Maggie Miles, the community's home-school coordinator, told a visiting provincial task force on child welfare in March 1993. "There's a lot of garbage in Shamattawa. There is sexual abuse, there's incest and a lot of the junk has to come out." But the first step is getting sober. For several years, a "gas patrol" has roamed the community at night, picking up kids who are sniffing and taking them home. Various band leaders have tried to crack down on the illegal import of alcohol and solvents, as well as joining other communities in lobbying for a solvent treatment centre for northern Manitoba. In May 1995, the federal government finally announced that it would fund a centre to be built on the Nelson River, midway between Norway House and Cross Lake First Nations. When the twenty-bed treatment centre is completed, it will offer a six-month, inpatient program for children aged eight to seventeen. At the time of that announcement, fifty young people from Shamattawa were attending solvent treatment centres outside of Manitoba.

For some victims of child abuse, the pain is too much to handle. There is little doubt that the emotional devastation caused by abuse has contributed to the high incidence of youth suicide in some Aboriginal communities. After all, suicide is simply an extreme form of self-abuse. A recent report authored by Montreal psychiatrist Laurence Kirmayer for the Royal Commission on Aboriginal Peoples cited federal government statistics showing that, between the ages of ten and twenty-nine, Aboriginal youth on reserves have a suicide rate five or six times higher than that for the same age group in the general population. Suicide rates are climbing steadily among young teenagers, especially younger males, in both Aboriginal and non-Aboriginal populations. What Kirmayer calls the "collision of two cultures," and the resulting "acculturation stress" on the community, family, and individual, is certainly the backdrop to this problem in Aboriginal communities. But he also notes that a significant risk factor for suicide is a history of childhood separations, losses, trauma, and abuse. Suffering physical or sexual abuse shatters children's self-esteem and trust, leaving them at a greater risk of attempted or actual suicide. "Owing to their isolation and complex web of family relations, there may be intense taboos within some [Native] communities against exposing and confronting family violence and abuse," Kirmayer says. "Lack of opportunity and support to confront the problem leaves victims to struggle alone with their pain and so may contribute substantially to the risk of suicide."

In its special report on suicide, released in 1995, the Royal Commission on Aboriginal Peoples also pointed to the link between child abuse and youth suicide. It cited a study which had found that adolescents who were physically abused in childhood were 4.7 times more likely to attempt suicide than their peers who were not abused. The same study found that sexual abuse made suicide attempts 5.1 times more likely, while both physical and sexual abuse increased the risk to 9.2 times more likely. The commission's report went on to say that this link is only beginning to be understood: "Research evidence is emerging of critical links between early experience and the development of coping skills. These findings support the commonsense view that children who have love and security in early childhood cope better with stress and challenge later in life. Those who are abused or deprived have fewer inner resources. This research suggests strongly that although suicide is an act most often attempted by those aged 15 to 29, the protective—or corrosive—groundwork is laid much earlier."

What happened at Wunnumin Lake First Nation, a remote community of 400 located 500 kilometres northwest of Thunder Bay, Ontario, is a tragic example of how abuse ruins young lives. In July 1994, a former Anglican minister and boy-scout leader who had worked at Wunnumin between 1975 and 1982 was sentenced for sexually abusing sixteen young boys from the village. At an emotional court hearing in the school gymnasium, Ralph Rowe, fifty-three, pleaded guilty to twenty-eight sex-related charges involving boys as young as six. Rowe, a pilot as well as a priest in the church's Keewatin diocese, had flown in and out of isolated communities like Wunnumin throughout northwestern Ontario and northern Manitoba during the 1970s and 1980s. A charismatic, highly respected church leader, Rowe had easily convinced parents to let their sons join him in camping trips or sleep-overs at his home. Once they were entrusted to his care, he molested the boys, sometimes while they slept. Like most children who are abused, they retreated into frightened silence. More than a decade later, one of Rowe's victims summoned the courage to disclose his terrible secret to the Ontario Provincial Police. Police charged Rowe after an intensive, two-year investigation. When they finally caught up with him, police discovered he'd already served time in jail in Manitoba on nine sex-related charges involving boys.

Wunnumin chief Simon Winnepetonga was one of several hundred community members who attended Rowe's sentencing. Before reading an impassioned statement to the judge, Winnepetonga referred to the devasting loss of his teenage son to suicide a few years earlier. Winnepetonga was haunted by the knowledge that his son, like most boys in the community, had likely been abused while spending many hours with the once-beloved Rowe. "Today we as parents suffer from a burden of guilt, that we were unable to protect our children," Winnepetonga said, as Rowe sat with bowed head, guarded by two OPP officers wearing bullet-proof vests. "The parents have searched inside themselves, blaming themselves for their children's self-destructive behaviour. The mothers cry in desperation trying to keep their children from committing suicide ... He betrayed the trust of innocent children, some who are not here with us today. Our children have been robbed of their childhood."

After the sentencing, one young man talked privately about the abuse he'd suffered at the hands of a man he'd once idolized. A chilly summer rain pattered on the roof of a pick-up truck as he spoke softly into the darkness. He was just seven when Rowe molested him during a sleep-over at the mission house, the first in a series of assaults. "I didn't even know what was happening to me," he said. He was too scared to tell anyone, blaming himself for the abuse. "I used to be suicidal a lot," he said. "For twelve years I carried that pain inside me. I felt like a time bomb." He sniffed gasoline and drank to block out the memories. But even that couldn't halt the frightful nightmares of someone choking him in the dark. Finally, police came to ask him if he had been abused by Rowe and he divulged his secret.

Another of Rowe's victims also talked about being plagued by nightmares. He was eleven years old when the assaults began. Around that time, he began having trouble sleeping because of a recurring dream in which a hand reached out in the dark for him. He developed insomnia, a problem he still has, and could sleep only with the light on. To dull his anxiety, he began sniffing gas and spray paint. Talking about what had happened was impossible, especially to his parents, who were staunch members of the Anglican Church. Finally, when he could no longer stand the pain, he tried to hang himself at fourteen. His brother discovered him in time and revived him. After being hospitalized in Sioux Lookout, he returned to Wunnumin in a state of emotional numbness. By the time he was twenty, he got off alcohol and drugs. But the frightening flashbacks returned once he was sober. Over and over, he dreamt of a dark, monstrous figure who would change into Rowe and assault him. Between his moodiness and his anger, he continually worries that he'll lose control and lash out at his wife and children some day.

The depth of Rowe's betrayal was almost unimaginable for many in the picturesque community nestled on the sandy southern shore of Wunnumin Lake. Unlike many isolated First Nations, Wunnumin has not endured extreme poverty, widespread alcoholism, and social disorganization. Until the late 1980s, the Oji-Cree community prospered through the fur trade, and still has about 70 per cent seasonal employment. It has been blessed with strong, progressive band leaders who have worked hard to provide adequate housing, running water and a sewage system, and community-based health care and education. Many younger adults grew up working the traplines, went to university, and have returned home to apply their skills. Between the long-standing presence of the Anglican Church and a revival of traditional spirituality, there has been a strong religious base. No one dreamed that one of the institutional bastions of the community, the church, harboured such a threat.

Looking back, parents recalled urging their sons to take part in church and cub-scout activities with Rowe, all the while puzzling over changes in the behaviour of their previously well-behaved children.

Unsuspecting, they missed the warning signs: emotional withdrawal, nightmares, disobedience, drug and alcohol abuse, academic problems, depression, suicide attempts. When two teenage boys, one of them Winnepetonga's son, killed themselves between 1988 and 1989, parents were frantic. Four more suicides in 1993 prompted community leaders to seek outside help. The band council set up a suicide-prevention team to respond to the immediate crisis, as well as to develop long-term strategies for healing. Two outside social workers worked with band leaders and community-based social workers for seven months. Workshops were held for both the crisis team and the community on everything from suicide prevention to sexual abuse. Residents were asked to share their views on what had prompted the crisis. Community members believed to be at risk of suicide were offered counselling. A self-help group for suicide survivors was started.

The team found that childhood sexual abuse, while not the only issue, was a major contributing factor to the suicide problem for residents of all ages. Certainly Rowe wasn't the only perpetrator of abuse. Some adults had been assaulted decades earlier at residential school, while others had suffered at the hands of family members. Sexually provocative behaviour by very young children indicated that the abuse was continuing in some families. Suicide attempts were common among the community's youth. Some children carried ropes "in case they decided to kill themselves," or threatened suicide regularly. Many parents were understandably overwhelmed and intimidated by such behaviour.

Although Wunnumin's band council solidly supported the team's work, some in the community did not. The team knew the backlash was triggered by denial and anger, predictable reactions when dealing with deep-rooted pain. "There is hope in the experiences of communities in worse crisis than Wunnumin Lake," the team's final report to the band council said. "Similar reactions to the exposition of pain have occurred in other Aboriginal communities in Canada. In Grand Lac Victoria in northern Quebec for example, a Grand Chief initiated exposure of a suspected 90 per cent incidence of sexual abuse. He lost his job and even experienced threats against his life. With patience and meticulous documentation, he facilitated the disclosures. He is now

Director of Social Services and is leading his community through its healing journey."

Sadly, it was not only the children of Wunnumin who were preyed upon by Rowe. Because he travelled on church business to many other isolated communities in the region, he left a trail of damaged lives throughout northwestern Ontario and northern Manitoba. The clinical director at Nodin Counselling Service in Sioux Lookout, Arnold Devlin, said counsellors from his agency listened to dozens of Rowe's victims pour out their pain—young men whose self-esteem and ability to love were badly damaged. While Rowe's abuse is only one factor in the region's suicide epidemic, Devlin said the impact of one such pedophile can't be underestimated. Jim Morris, leader of the Nishnawbe-Aski Nation, a group of more than forty bands in the Hudson Bay watershed, also said Rowe's prolific molestation of young boys has contributed to the suicide epidemic which plagues the twenty-eight communities in the Sioux Lookout region. "I know some of his victims have killed themselves," Morris said. "The problem is that you can't talk to dead people." There were 5 suicides in 1994 in the region and more than 200 known suicide attempts. The previous year, 24 young people killed themselves, and there were 212 suicide attempts. With the region having one of the highest suicide rates in the world, Morris and his organization are using every possible means to try to save lives. They have organized crisis teams, lobbied for more funding for mental-health programs, and organized a youth commission that held community hearings to search for solutions.

Ultimately, the search for healing is inseparable from the First Nations' journey back to self-government. In 1994, Manitoba's sixty-one First Nations signed an agreement with the federal government which began the complex process of dismantling the Department of Indian Affairs. Child welfare is scheduled to be among the first services to be fully taken over by individual bands. Some communities will run their own child-welfare agencies, while others may opt to continue supporting regionally based services. In the interim, negotiations are under way to set up Aboriginal child-welfare directorates to gradually take over the monitoring of agencies from the provincial Family Services department. One of the major concerns throughout this process is that Ottawa and the province will off-load responsibility without providing the funds needed to set up alternatives. Such fears are well founded in light of the overwhelming needs facing most Aboriginal communities and the scarcity of treatment programs available. A decade and a half after agencies such as DOCFS began, the vision of providing holistic, preventative services to children and families is still hobbled by inadequate, unstable funding.

One of those watching the dismantling process with mixed emotions is Margaret McCartan, former director of Anishinaabe Child and Family Services, which serves Manitoba's Interlake region. McCartan, a member of the Lake Manitoba First Nation, directed the agency from 1991 until the end of 1995, and has worked in the Aboriginal child-welfare system for almost a decade. The daughter of a chief, McCartan also grew up in a family shattered by her father's violence. To escape the abuse, she ran away at age sixteen, but was eventually sent home because of her father's political clout. When she sought help as a young adult for her family, both the Aboriginal and white child-welfare agencies failed to intervene. "Nobody listened," McCartan, now thirty-four, said. When two of her brothers committed suicide, an inquest pointed to their father's abuse as a contributing factor in their deaths.

Today, she has no illusions about the difficulties that lie ahead for communities trying to eradicate family violence. While she was running Anishinaabe, the biggest barrier McCartan said she faced was constant interference from chiefs who control the agency's board. "A lot of it has to do with the politics, because you are blocked from going in and doing things like healing circles," McCartan said during an interview in the winter of 1996. "I believe some of our leaders haven't dealt with their issues and because of that they don't want to see those kinds of things happen in their communities." The chiefs on the board fought with each other about the division of agency funds, doled out jobs to unqualified relatives, tried to meddle in abuse cases, and diverted family violence grants to other uses. Agency staff were often too intimidated by the chiefs to remove children from abusive families, so McCartan would have to step in. "I felt my job was on the line all the time," McCartan said. Pleas to provincial officials for assistance were largely ignored by bureaucrats who preferred to avoid such messy situations. As

McCartan struggled to keep the agency on track, she wasn't surprised to hear witnesses during the inquest into Lester's death describe similiar problems at DOCFS. When the balance of power on the Anishinaabe board shifted after the election of a new chief, McCartan was fired in December 1995. "A lot of them don't seem to care for the kids any more, especially the politicians," she said. "They're more interested in other things than protecting kids ... The same thing goes for the white system, just on a larger scale."

In light of her discouraging experience at Anishinaabe, McCartan is sceptical about whether self-government will guarantee a brighter future. Yet she also pointed to small but significant changes that give her reason to hope. Some of the chiefs who were most adamant about controlling the boards of child-welfare agencies have recently done an about-face. Several Native-run child-welfare agencies in Manitoba have already removed chiefs from their boards, developed conflict-of-interest guidelines, and are providing more in-depth staff training and treatment programs. "It's going to be a long hard road, but I guess I've come to realize that you have to take one step at a time," McCartan said. "I'm going to do what I can in the political forum and just be very vocal and open about things I've seen and continue to see."

Women like McCartan and Foxcroft and Belleau are the ones making sure that the link between healing and self-government is forged. Their voices are a constant reminder to politicians that abuse must be confronted to ensure a healthy future. "What we're dealing with at Canim Lake, every First Nations community in the province and across the country is going to have to go through," Belleau said. Too often, in the rush for political control, she has watched communities set up institutions, like child-welfare agencies, that are no better than those in mainstream society. Plagued by a lack of accountability, such agencies tragically repeat the same mistakes as their predecessors. "The result is that a young person ends up dying," Belleau said. Being accountable means getting the necessary training to handle complex child-abuse and -neglect cases, acknowledging and learning from mistakes, and setting aside other allegiances. "You have to be willing to hold people accountable, even if its your own uncle or grandpa, to set aside those barriers that could prevent you from making sure a child is safe," she said. But to meet that challenge, individuals must face their own past traumas and begin to believe in themselves. Only then will they be able to become the lawyers, doctors, teachers, social workers, and leaders needed to carry out the vision of self-government. "That cycle of abuse can stop with us," Belleau said. "We can create a safe place for our children."

EPILOGUE

The first serious March thaw has turned Sandy Bay's pitted roads into treacherous rivers of mud and ice. Unaware of the hazard, I drive up from Winnipeg to meet with three of Lester's sisters about the book. As I turn onto one of the reserve's side-roads, my low-slung Honda jolts, slides, and shudders through ruts flowing with icy run-off. Towering snowbanks line the road. By the time I've gone a kilometre, I'm white-knuckled. But it's too late to retreat—trying to turn around would put me in the ditch. I grip the steering wheel even tighter and focus on navigating the next gaping pothole.

When I pull up in front of Nancy's home, she looks at me like I'm crazy. She'd phoned earlier to warn me that the roads were almost impassable, but I'd already left. Nancy chides me gently for failing to check with her, and she's right. If I'd known how difficult the driving would be, I never would have made the trip. So much about this book has been like that.

It's been over a year since I visited Sandy Bay. My unexpected pregnancy and the demands of new motherhood had almost derailed the book. My son was three months old when my publisher called about my long-overdue manuscript. Considering that I hadn't had a good night's sleep since my baby was born, the challenge of writing even one coherent sentence seemed insurmountable. I had nowhere to turn for child care. Nevertheless, I decided to make a last-ditch attempt to finish the draft. Whenever my son napped, I stumbled to my computer and tapped away. My husband, supportive as always, took occasional days off to give me more time to work. Somehow, the words began to flow again. But my vision for the book didn't reignite until an autumn afternoon in 1995, when I met with David, one of those who had charged Joe Desjarlais with sexual assault, to discuss the manuscript. As we sipped coffee in a downtown restaurant, he said he'd heard rumours that I'd given up on the book. I looked across the table at him and thought about all he'd suffered, about how he and others had opened up their lives to me. At that moment, I knew I had to finish, come hell or high water.

Nancy invites me into her house while she phones her sisters to tell them the foolhardy writer has arrived. Then we venture back out onto the roads to pick them up. The next stretch is even worse, with slick muddy trenches that send us slipping towards the oozing shoulders. Nancy watches for oncoming vehicles as I pick my way through the channels. The next few kilometres seem endless. When we finally ease onto a marginally better main road, we both heave sighs of relief. Our first stop is to pick up Sherry. Annette isn't home, so we drive to the café in Amaranth, where she's waiting. As we pore over the manuscript, Nancy jokes that she'll have to move to a desert island when the book comes out. Her sisters laugh, bantering back and forth. Then Nancy reiterates what she has told me before—that she has "nothing to hide." She believes the book will help others who have suffered abuse as children. But the reality is that some will also resent the sisters' honesty. Already, Joe Desjarlais has sent harassing letters from prison, declaring his innocence. Sharing their stories has been, and continues to be, an act of courage for Lester's sisters.

Life is still not easy for any of them. All three have chronic health problems, the legacy of poverty and neglect. Money is scarce, and jobs hard to come by. Nancy is pumping gas on a casual basis at the band's station, while Sherry has a part-time babysitting job. Sherry tells me she'll soon be leaving for a month-long Native-run alcohol treatment program at Pritchard House in Winnipeg. They are struggling against great odds to give their children a better future. When they sometimes see old patterns repeating, it is all the more discouraging. On those days, the past haunts them. But each of their children's small successes also brings great joy.

During my visit that day, I hear about a twelve-year-old girl from the community who is pregnant. She is the daughter of a mother who was just twelve when she was born. Two generations earlier, Lester's mother, Joyce, was only thirteen when she gave birth to her first baby. The cycle goes on. Now that I, too, am a mother, the grinding poverty I see in communities like Sandy Bay makes me angrier than ever. Children deserve to grow up in decent housing, with enough to eat and parents who have the financial and emotional resources to nurture them. Until they do, all of us are to blame. Answers to these dilemmas are coming from within Aboriginal communities. The people I've met, especially the women, leave no doubt that the spirit and the strength to make changes exist. The rest of us simply need to learn to listen.

By the time I say my goodbyes and leave for Winnipeg, I'm exhausted and eager to get home to my little one. As a nursing mother, I've never been separated from him this long, although my impending return to work will soon change that. To stay awake, I turn the cold-air vent on my face and crank up the radio. I drive south through gathering storm clouds and think about the advice writers are commonly given—to write about what you know. On the surface, this book seems to fly in the face of that. Yet, looking back now, I see the familiar thread more clearly: I came to this book as someone well acquainted with loss—my mother, grandmother, uncle, aunt, cousins, close friends. That knowledge became the common ground between myself and the many fine people whom I met along the way.

I started this book, and finish it, as an outsider who was privileged to share briefly in a circle of lives linked by a little boy I will never meet. But in the process, I have learned much more about what it means to transform grief into a force for change.

SOURCES

This book is based upon hundreds of interviews conducted over a four-year period. I have also relied upon a wide variety of other sources, including testimony at Lester's inquest, the 114 inquest exhibits, Judge Brian Giesbrecht's inquest report, trial transcripts, newspaper interviews and clippings, major child-welfare reports and books. The following is a list of some of the key print sources consulted for each chapter.

CHAPTER ONE

Transcript of inquest testimony; inquest exhibits (including autopsy/ medical examiner's report on Lester, RCMP report, Dakota Ojibway Child and Family Services [DOCFS] documents); suicide statistics from *Five-Year Review of Youth Suicide in Manitoba* by Dr. Eric Sigurdson (unpublished report: 1991); information about Norman Anderson from autopsy report and newspaper clippings in *Winnipeg Free Press* and *Winnipeg Sun*.

CHAPTER TWO

Historical information from several books, including Helen Buckley, *From Wooden Ploughs to Welfare* (Montreal and Kingston: McGill–Queen's University Press: 1992); Olive Dickason, *Canada's First Nations* (Toronto: McClelland & Stewart, 1992); Alexander Morris, *The Treaties of Canada with the Indians of Manitoba and the North-West Territories* (originally published Toronto: Belfords, Clarke, 1800; facsimile edition published Saskatoon: Fifth House, 1991); Geoffrey York, *The Dispossessed* (Toronto: Little, Brown [Canada], 1992); Norma Sluman and Jean Goodwill, *John Tootoosis* (Ottawa: Golden Dog Press, 1982); Celia Haig-Brown, *Resistance and Renewal: Surviving the Indian Residential School* (Vancouver: Tillacum Library, 1988); Pauline Comeau and Aldo Santin, *The First Canadians* (Toronto: James Lorimer, 1990); Patrick Johnston, *Native Children and the Child Welfare System* (Ottawa: Canadian Council on Social Development, 1983).

Published and unpublished reports used include N.F. Davin, "Report on Industrial Schools for Indians and Halfbreeds" (1879; Ottawa; Public Archives); Edwin C. Kimelman, *No Quiet Place: Review Committee on Indian and Metis Adoptions and Placements* (Winnipeg: Manitoba Department of Community Services, 1985); A.C. Hamilton and C.M. Sinclair, *Report of the Aboriginal Justice Inquiry of Manitoba* (Winnipeg: Province of Manitoba, 1991); Assembly of First Nations, *Breaking the Silence: An Interpretive Study of Residential School Impact and Healing as Illustrated by the Stories of First Nations Individuals* (Ottawa: Assembly of First Nations, 1994); Pete Hudson and Brad McKenzie, "Evaluation of Dakota Ojibway Child and Family Services Final Report," June 1984.

Information on Sandy Bay residential school from Archdiocese of Winnipeg fact sheet in files of Department of Indian Affairs, Winnipeg office.

CHAPTER THREE

Inquest testimony and exhibits, especially DOCFS files on Lester and his family, Sandy Bay school files, RCMP files, files from Child Protection Centre in Winnipeg; information about big rabbit or "trickster" of Ojibwa legend from Jennifer S.H. Brown and Robert Brightman, *The Orders of the Dreamed* (Winnipeg: University of Manitoba Press, 1988).

CHAPTER FOUR

Inquest testimony and exhibits, especially Lester's file from Seven Oaks Centre for Youth in Winnipeg, Brandon Mental Health Centre files, DOCFS files.

CHAPTER FIVE

Aboriginal Justice Inquiry report; information about Aboriginal women's groups from articles in *Winnipeg Free Press* between September 1991 and April 1992.

CHAPTER SIX

Aboriginal Justice Inquiry report; inquest testimony and exhibits, especially DOCFS files, Brandon police files, RCMP files, files from Marion's Labour Canada arbitration hearing; *Winnipeg Sun* article, December 22, 1991; *Winnipeg Free Press* articles, January 1992.

CHAPTER SEVEN

Inquest testimony; Giesbrecht report; articles from *Winnipeg Free Press* between April 1992 and June 1992.

CHAPTER EIGHT

Trial transcripts (June and October 1993); RCMP documents;

Winnipeg Free Press articles from July and August 1992, February 1993, May 1994.

CHAPTER NINE

Winnipeg Free Press articles from September 1992, June and December 1993; Giesbrecht report; "Children First" report of the First Nations Child and Family Task Force, November 1993.

CHAPTER TEN

Published and unpublished reports used include Rix Rogers, *An Overview of Issues and Concerns Related to the Sexual Abuse of Children in Canada* (Ottawa: Department of Health and Welfare, October 1988); Rix Rogers, *Reaching for Solutions* (Ottawa: Department of Health and Welfare, June 1990); Report of the Aboriginal Committee of the Community Panel on Family and Children's Services Legislation Review in B.C. entitled *Liberating Our Children, Liberating Our Nations* (Victoria: October 1992); Laurence Kirmayer, "Suicide in Canadian Aboriginal Populations: Emerging Trends in Research and Interventions," a report prepared for the Royal Commission on Aboriginal Peoples, Division of Social and Transcultural Psychiatry, Department of Psychiatry, McGill University, Montreal, April 1993; Royal Commission on Aboriginal Peoples, *Choosing Life: Special Report on Suicide among Aboriginal People* (Ottawa: Ministry of Supply and Services Canada, 1995); "A New Justice for Indian Children," final report of the Child Advocacy Project, Child Protection Centre, Children's Hospital, Winnipeg, October 1987; Indian Child and Family Services Standards Project, Final Report, July 1992, First Nations Congress, Vancouver.

Books used include Tony Marten's *The Spirit Weeps: Characteristics and Dynamics of Incest and Child Sexual Abuse* (Edmonton: Nechi Institute, 1988), especially chapters by Brenda Daily and Maggie Hodgson; Maureen McEvoy, *Let the Healing Begin: Breaking the Cycle of Child Sexual Abuse in Our Communities* (Merritt: Nicola Valley

Institute of Technology, 1990); Judy Steed, *Our Little Secret: Confronting Child Sexual Abuse in Canada* (Toronto: Random House of Canada, 1994); Geoffrey York, *The Dispossessed* (Toronto: Little, Brown [Canada], 1990).

Newspaper articles on child sexual abuse include *Globe and Mail* articles on Hollow Water, April 1995, and Canim Lake, January 1994; and *Winnipeg Free Press* articles on Hollow Water, December 1993; on Shamattawa, September and October 1992, March 1993, and May 1995; and on Wunnumin Lake, July 1994.